COURTNEY KRISTEL

Beautifully Shattered

Lea,
You're always helping me, making me laugh when my day is going to shit. Thanks for all the wonderful memories! We need more with wine!

♡ Courtney Kristel

Happy Reading

Courtney Kristel

DEDICATION

This book is dedicated to all of the readers that want to hide away, cry, or scream at the top of their lungs. It may not always be easy, but it does get better. Keep holding on. Life is beautiful, including the shattered pieces.

ACKNOWLEDGMENTS

A special thanks to my very first reader, my sister Heather. Thank you for believing in me and pushing me to follow my dreams. Words can never describe how grateful I am for you being here for every step of the way, every word I typed, and every thought I had. Because of you, this story came to life. I love you.

Thank you Dad for helping me make my dream a reality. You have always helped me with reaching every goal of mine. You are the best dad a girl could ever ask for. I love you Daddy.

Monica, you are as much to thank for this story being finished as anyone else. Your love for the characters was the push I needed to finish. Thank you for all of your nagging and staying up until 4am reading the first draft. Now it's your turn to see what I put Heather through. Love you big sis.

Twinsy, thank you for being you. I am so grateful that you would always listen to my ranting even though you had no idea what I was talking about. Thank you for stepping in when I needed you the most. You will forever be the first person to ever know my dream to write.

My wonderful editor, Stacy Juba, THANK YOU! Your insight has helped me tremendously. Without you, I would have ripped my hair out. You've made this whole process so much easier. Thank you for all of the wonderful feedback, emails, and comments about the plot twist.

The fantastic cover couldn't have been done without the amazing designer, Danielle Hurps. Thank you for the numerous cover designs, and all of the other artwork. You're incredibly talented.

PROLOGUE

Connor nods to the left, indicating that Jax is striding our way. Stubbornly I stare straight ahead, refusing to face the man who has destroyed me. I wave my hand at my family, conveying that now is not the time for me to confront Jax.

"You're here to celebrate my last meet of the year, not to force me to talk to him," I mutter to Connor.

Connor doesn't say anything as he walks the short distance to my family. Connor bends to whisper something in Hadley's ear. Her thirteen-year-old self jumps up and down, giddy to do Connor's bidding.

His footsteps become louder the closer he gets. I breathe deeply, enjoying my last breath of fresh air until he leaves. The Thai aroma almost brings a smile to my lips. I really wanted greased-filled pizza, the kind that is so delicious you know it's blocking your major arteries, but because he's here I wanted to make him suffer. So of course I chose the one food he hates. I even gave him a vindictive sneer when he searched the menu for something he would be able to stomach. Once he's near, his scent will invade my senses like it always does; everything will disappear leaving only Jax. I can't let that happen, not anymore. Because of what he did, I can never forgive him. I have to forget the love I still feel for him.

My brother says something to Dad, but I don't catch it. I'm too focused on listening to the way Jax's steps sound on the concrete. He's almost near me. I go for indifference as my Mom studies my reaction. I fear she's aware of why I'm suddenly anti-Jax, but she has yet to voice her suspicions. I used to stay up late at night wishing that Jax would change, crying into my mom's lap while she ran her fingers through my hair, consoling me for something I can't be honest about. My wishes never came true. I should have known that Jaxon Chandler would ruin me.

I slide on my sunglasses even though it's cloudy. The rare Southern California storm has arrived. Hopefully it's gone by tomorrow, or the barbecue my parents have planned for my seventeenth birthday won't happen. Not that I'm in the mood to celebrate. Every spring, for the past eight years, I've looked forward to my birthday for one reason. Jax. He always sneaks in and gives my present to me in private. Our tradition is now broken, like us.

I check whether anyone is watching us. They're not, their attention glued to my little sister showing off some ballet move. Without turning to see if he's following me, I stalk behind the Thai restaurant. His footsteps thud against the pavement.

He starts in as soon as we're deep enough in the alley that my parents won't hear me shouting. "Ads—"

I whirl around, eyes blazing. "No! You lost the chance to call me that when you stepped onto the plane." I stab my finger into his hard chest. "You lost the chance to ask ANY questions! You have no right to speak to me!"

His arms hover over me, as if he wants to touch me. He's fighting the same battle I am. If he pulls me into his arms, I'll melt into him. His pretty words will wash over me; everything will disappear. Jax isn't the sun, he's the darkness, preventing me from shining. I can't let him in again.

Decision made, I step away. His arms fall to his sides. "Why are you here?" I demand.

"Please give me the chance to explain. You stopped taking my calls, you've locked your window. You leave when I come by."

I laugh. "So you thought ambushing me earlier, at my swim meet and in front of my family, was the right choice? You thought if I laid eyes on your handsome face, all would be forgiven? I HATE YOU, JAXON! Nothing you can say will ever make me forgive you."

He drops to his knees in front of me. His hands dig into my hips as he looks up at me. I wipe my angry tears away. I won't cry because of him. Jaxon Chandler has been the reason for too many of my tears. No more.

"I'm here. Doesn't that count?" he says against my stomach.

We're standing in front of the dumpster. The stench should be overwhelming, but all I smell is Jax. I torture myself with the woodsy scent, hating that I'm enjoying his close proximity.

It takes a second too long for my legs to carry me away from his touch. "It's too late. You should have stayed in New York."

"Ads—"

I shake my head as I back up. "I never want to see you again. I'll be fine without you." I grab my iPod from my pocket.

"I want to—" His words die as I insert my earbuds and leave the alley.

Coldplay blast in my ears, blocking out Jax. I lean against the brick wall of the restaurant and watch my family in the parking lot. My heart stops when I feel him behind me. He makes no move to touch me. He leans over until his breath pours over my bare shoulder.

His nearness still has the same effect it always has on me. I shouldn't have given him such power over me. He makes me feel helpless. I can't be the lovesick teenager anymore. I have responsibilities now. I allow myself to breathe him in before pushing off the wall and wandering back to my family.

Each step takes me further from the man I love.

As much as I hate him, I can never regret us.

"There you are, Adalynn. Where have you been?" my mom asks as I reach the car.

My spine stiffens. I know we're going to fight. That's all we do now. I hate fighting with my parents, but I can't tell them the truth. I promised myself if he got on the plane then we would be over. All he is now to me is Logan's best friend, a guy I have to avoid at all cost. He has no right to be more.

I never meant to fall in love with my brother's best friend, but twelve years ago I fell for his charming smile. As the years went by, little by little I allowed him into my heart. I thought he was my knight in shining armor. I was wrong. As I settle into the backseat of my dad's Range Rover, I have only one thought.

Jaxon Chandler will be the death of me.

CHAPTER ONE

Six years later . . .

Every Tuesday is the same for me. I work at the bakery in the mornings, go to my therapy appointment in the late afternoon, and finally I have dinner with the guys. The only thing that changes is the location. I live a simple life, well, as simple as I can manage after causing my parents' and sister's death six years ago on my seventeenth birthday.

My body automatically tenses. I stare at the blank eggshell walls in my penthouse and shove those memories in the back of my mind before they can haunt me. I tell myself to relax, but no matter how many times I try to get comfortable on my suede couch, I can't seem to unwind. Ed Sheeran plays in the background, but the solace I usually feel listening to the calming music is missing. My hands itch to do the one thing that will bring a peaceful calm over me. I visualize using the sharp blade I keep taped underneath my sink, feeling the cold of the steel as it nips my skin. I can practically see the blood dripping down my thigh. I slap those images away, too. I'm not that girl anymore.

As soon as I woke up today, I immediately knew something was off. I can't put it into words; it's something that I can feel all the way to my bones. I haven't been able to shake off this sensation all day. I try concentrating on anything but today's date. It's almost as if my mind is in a war with my heart. My soul won't let me forget and my mind attempts to push me past it, to move on. Something changed between the time I closed my eyes last night and when I opened them this morning.

I've been in and out of therapy ever since the accident. My brother, Logan, insists that I continue to see Olivia White since I have made "noticeable progress" with her over the other therapists that I have seen since the accident. If he has to go out of town for work he leaves either Connor or Jax, his two best friends since childhood, to babysit me. In other words I'm not to be left to my own devices.

Within these last six years, Logan has become less of a brother and more of a parent. He moved me from California to Manhattan, sent me to college for a business degree, and bought me a penthouse in walking distance from his place. I refused to move in with him after graduation so he made sure that he didn't have to wait in New York traffic to visit me. He feels better knowing that I'm close, so I don't fight him on it.

Before the accident I wouldn't have stood for Logan treating me like I'm made out of porcelain. After? I allowed it because I didn't care about anything. Now I'm starting to crave the independence I gave up to my brother without a fight.

He takes protectiveness to a whole new level. It wouldn't surprise me if he had one of my doctors insert a GPS tracker in me. I can't really blame him, though. I'm the reason that we have no family and he's almost lost me twice. He won't allow there to be a third time.

It's my night to host this week's dinner. The boys had to leave for an emergency at the office, but promised to bring dinner. I already laid out the white plates that Logan bought me when he purchased the penthouse. Everything in here is white, just the way I like it. The only color comes from a painting, mounted above my couch, that the interior designer snuck in. It's a shadow of a girl holding a bright yellow umbrella while the storm rages on, falling from the dark, unforgiving night sky. I allow it to stay because I can't care about pointless decorations when all my energy goes into not giving up.

I'm antsy, counting the minutes since the guys left. Once they return, they'll distract me. They'll buy Thai food to please me, even though Jax hates it, they'll paint smiles on their faces, and not voice what's on everyone's mind. Today, May 21, six years ago, my life was consumed by darkness, stealing my every promise of a happy future.

I grab my phone to see if any of the guys have texted. Nope. I've been sitting here for almost an hour staring into space. Fantastic. I can't wait here and do nothing. I become lost in my thoughts and that's *never* good. I force myself off the couch and change into workout clothes. Hopefully a few miles on the treadmill will chase this unnerving feeling out of my gut. I send Logan a quick text while I press the L button in the elevator.

Me: Gonna hit the gym. Bringing my phone. Call when you guys are leaving the office. Love you.

I don't bother to put away my phone. No matter what he is doing, Logan will always respond to me. Always. Best brother award goes to him.

Logan: No problem. You might get a full hour in. This is taking longer than I expected or I would have waited until tomorrow to handle it. Love you too baby girl.

Logan: Oh and don't forget to do weights too not just cardio.

I roll my eyes. Of course my meathead brother would remind me to do weights. He is such a body builder.

Me: I understand your need to take over the world so take your time. Just give me a heads up so I can shower.

I tiptoe through the lobby, hating how my footsteps echo on the marble floor. I look down and avoid anyone I pass. I don't have the energy to smile and nod. Not today. Opening the glass doors to the gym, I ignore the Olympic size pool I can see from the entrance. It's impossible to miss with the glass walls on one side. The pillars have vines wrapped around them, giving it the appearance of a magical place. I've never stepped in there even though it beckons me. From here, I know I'll secretly love the decor, though, because it reminds me of the Greek Gods. Of him.

I head straight to the treadmill to clear my mind. I still don't understand the point of continuing this stupid, futile charade of seeing Olivia White every other Tuesday afternoon. I think the whole idea is crazy. Nothing is going to change. I don't want it to change. I don't want to move on. I can't. I need to remember what I did, who we lost.

I deserve to suffer unbelievable pain because of my actions. I am barely able to live now and what Liv wants seems impossible. That little voice in the back of my head thinks differently, though. *I can do it. I can learn how to live again. I can have more. I want—*

Nope, I shove that thought in the furthest part of my mind along with all the useless ones.

After a quick warm-up on the treadmill, I increase the speed. I focus on the sound of my feet hitting the belt with each step. I control my breathing the way my brother hammered into me at a young age when I got serious about working out. I wanted to strengthen my muscles for swimming. I spent hours upon hours training daily, never obtaining enough sleep. A small trail of sweat drips off my forehead and lands on the belt. My surroundings start to disappear as I replay today's therapy session in my head.

"Adalynn, what do you think?"

I glance up from my hands and see Liv staring at me. I can tell from her disturbed expression this isn't the first time she's attempted to jostle me out of my thoughts.

"What's the question? Sorry, Liv, I either stopped paying attention the moment I walked in, or the moment you brought up my dead parents and dead sister."

I gawk at Liv, mortified. I can't believe I actually said that out loud. I swear under my breath. "Sorry, Liv, I'm just distracted today."

"Addie, you and I both know that I am used to your . . ." She pauses and I decide to help her out.

"Unique sense of humor?" I joke as I collect my long brown hair into a messy bun.

I wish that I took the time to gather my waves into a nice updo like she has done with her honey hair. She always looks so regal, something that I aspire to be. Even in a simple pair of black jeans, I carry myself as if I don't have a care in the world. I refuse to let anyone see me as the broken twenty-four year old that I am.

"Let's go with that. I'm used to your unique sense of humor by now. You can't offend me. I want you to speak your mind. If you need sarcasm to do that, then by all means, just don't shut me out, especially today of all days."

Liv is my favorite therapist out of all of them. She always talks to me like I'm a human being, not just someone she has to focus on for an hour to get paid. I respect her as a person, but I still hate that she's trying to encourage me to talk about them today. Although I was expecting it; after all it is the anniversary of their deaths. May 21, my birthday.

"Okay, I'm paying attention now. What was the question?"

I know the second the words leave my mouth I'm going to regret it. I should have just continued to tune her out until our session ended. My leg bounces up and down, a nervous habit of mine, when I notice the look she's giving me. It's the one that tells me I'm not going to take it well, but she's going to say it anyways.

"I know discussing your family is extremely difficult, especially today. You can talk about them here, to me." She pauses. "You think you don't want to be here." I manage to give a light nod. She is right after all. I don't want to be here.

My gaze wanders to the panoramic window behind her like it usually does whenever she exposes my past. I can never seem to hold her gaze. Her thoughtful eyes are more knowing then I would like. I watch the outside world as she studies me. I know she's waiting until she has my undivided attention before she speaks. I sigh loudly before turning my unwilling violet eyes back to her hazel ones.

"You're wrong. You want to be here as much as your brother wants you here. There's a point to this. I want to help you. We can sit here silently the entire time or we can talk. It's up to you, Adalynn."

I know I shouldn't ask, but the words fall out of my mouth before I can stop them. "How are you so sure I want to be here, Liv?"

"You still come, don't you? You can walk out at any second, but you don't. You continue to show up for every appointment. Even though you fight with yourself, you still stay until the session is over. You don't stay because of your brother. You stay because deep down you want to overcome your past, and that scares you."

Olivia sees the wheels turning in my head. She waits for me to patiently digest what she's saying. I study my hands again. There's no point in arguing with her. As much as I hate to admit it, she's right. It is scary. I don't think I can move forward, I don't think I deserve it. What if I fail and let everyone down again?

"Some people feel anger towards their family members because they're furious that they left. It's okay to be angry with them, Addie. Whatever you feel is okay. You need to let it out or it will consume you. If you don't feel like you can talk to me, then talk to anyone you feel comfortable with.

Little by little, you need to open up or you will never be able to move forward with your life."

I bite my lip so hard it bleeds. I focus on that pain then the emptiness inside of me. The little bite isn't enough so I dig my nails into my palms. Noticing the blood, I slowly relax my hand. I interlace my fingers together so that Liv doesn't see. I stare at the tiny trail of blood that barely shows. It doesn't take away the emptiness. I need more.

"I am angry. They died and I didn't. I'm angry that my world stopped that night and nobody noticed. All night I thought someone would see us, that someone would help us, but nobody stopped. Everyone kept driving. So, yes, I am angry, Liv. My world sank into the darkness and everyone else went on with their lives while the most important people in my life were dying beside me. I was helpless, unable to do anything but . . ."

Words leave me. I can't finish that thought. It's too much. Too painful.

The session drags on. Liv continues to demonstrate patience. Towards the end of it, Liv straightens her shoulders as if preparing for battle.

"I need you to start living your life. Go out. Meet new people, even take a vacation. Just live without thinking about the past and how you shouldn't be having fun because they're gone, as you put it earlier. The past is just that, the past. You can't change it; no matter how much you wish you could."

My thoughts are anywhere but in this gym while I run on the treadmill. I play everything that Liv said on a continuous wheel in my head. It still seems surreal that she thinks I can go a month without seeing her, that I am ready to progress.

I have my doubts. My mind is going in circles. Suddenly I realize that I am sprinting and coming up on my ninth mile. I try to focus on the panel, but my vision has blurred. While chugging my water, I press the down button to slow my pace. As soon as I set my water down in the cup holder and reach for my towel, I'm seeing spots. The world tilts. Blindly I grope for the string to pull the emergency stop. Everything goes black before I hit the still moving track.

When I come to, I'm laying on the floor next to an unbelievably attractive man who's leaning over to get a clear view of my face. His lips are moving, but all I hear is a loud ringing noise. My head hurts. I try to process what other body parts hurt, but all I can focus on is that it seems like someone took a sledgehammer to my head. I attempt to move and pain shoots up my ankle.

I breathe through the pain. Strong hands squeeze my shoulders. The hot guy is still talking. I can't understand what he's saying, or why he's bending over me. He looks so edible, I end up staring into his dark blue eyes. They remind me of the ocean and a peaceful calm takes over me, but it's short-lived when the pain comes back with a vengeance. Once the pain subsides to a more manageable level, I can focus on his words.

"Can you hear me? What's your name? Do you know where you are?" Concern is evident in his voice.

He's speaking slowly for my benefit. I struggle to sit up, but he presses his strong hands on my shoulders. Mr. Edible smirks at me.

"No you don't, sweetie. Stay still until I know you're okay. Can you tell me your name? Do you know where you are?"

The sudden desert that has taken residence in my throat makes speaking impossible. Mr. Edible lifts my head and tilts a cold water bottle to my dry lips. When he starts to pull it away, I grab it and gulp half of the water down.

"You should take sips right now."

Wiping my mouth with the back of my hand, I roll my eyes. "Oh yeah, why's that?"

"If you have a concussion, you could throw up," he says.

Today is just not my day. Of course I would be the one to hurt myself on a treadmill and attract a cocky Good Samaritan.

"Adalynn," I say in a calm voice, answering his question from earlier.

He raises an eyebrow expectantly. Right . . . he asked two questions. He couldn't just walk away and leave me here. I find it hard to believe that he would be able to turn his back on someone needing help. There's something about him that screams Mr. Good-Guy.

The light bulb goes off.

"At the gym." Who has the smug smile now, Mr. Edible?

Gazing into his eyes, I'm aware I'm not fooling him with my casual act. I also know from previous experiences that I need to stay calm so I can talk him down from doing something rash like calling 911. I need to extinguish this situation so I can make it back to my apartment before the guys return. I'll pretend like everything is fine and go to the doctor tomorrow. Ha, who am I kidding! I'm not going to the doctor tomorrow. I can't remember the last time I voluntarily went for a check up.

"How are you feeling?" he ask as he interrupts my thinking process. "You were out for a couple of minutes. Your forehead's still bleeding, not as bad though." Pausing, he moves so he can examine my leg. As he touches my ankle, I wince. "You may have a sprain. You'll need an X-ray to be sure."

Ah, it's my ankle, not my entire leg, that's a little more comforting. That will be easier to hide from the guys. I need a mirror to know how bad my face looks. From the throbbing pain on my forehead, my guess would be anywhere from horrible or death. My guess is on the latter.

"Fuuuccckkkk!" I draw that one syllable into about twenty, give or take, when he starts twisting my ankle.

"I'm sorry," he says once I'm done screaming. "I'm just checking for breaks. Do you have a boyfriend that I can call before we head to the hospital?"

That one word causes me to go into full blown panic. I sit up way too quickly, making him drop my ankle on the floor. I'm surprised my earsplitting scream doesn't break the glass doors. Once the pain subsides, I try to stand only to fail. Graciously, he helps me to my feet and leads me to a nearby bench.

"I really don't need to go to the hospital," I tell him when he pulls his cell phone out of his basketball shorts. I wave him off, hoping to convey that this isn't as bad as it seems. "Honestly this is no big deal, just a scratch." I shrug, eyes glued to the silver device that will seal my fate.

"Adalynn—"

I hold up my hand, silencing him. "No, really, I'm fine. I just need to go back up to my place. I'm a little lightheaded, but we don't need to make an unnecessary scene. You don't need to call anyone. Once the bleeding—"

He cuts me off with a glare that clearly says "don't mess with him." The Good Samaritan that I'm somehow stuck with isn't going to give up.

"Listen, Adalynn, you need stitches. This is too deep for just a Band-Aid." He stares at my forehead. "You also might've suffered a concussion, not to mention you need to have your ankle checked out and be possibly fitted for crutches.

I give him my most pleading look. "Please, just help me to my apartment. I have crutches somewhere in one of my closets from the last time I decided to do a gravity check. The bleeding has stopped. I'll go to the hospital if I need to. I know all the signs of a concussion. This isn't my first accident." And it won't be my last, I'm sure. Clumsiness doesn't even begin to describe my *unique* quality of walking skills.

He shakes his head. "Give me your boyfriend's number so he can meet you at the hospital."

Okay, now, I'm mad. Who does he think he is? Good Samaritan or not, he doesn't get to boss me around. Since standing isn't an option, I sit up straight, attempting to appear taller. "Look, buddy, I already told you I'm not going to the hospital. So either help me back to my apartment or move out of my way."

Rubbing his face, he says in a forced calm voice, "Fine Adalynn, you win. But I need to grab my emergency bag from my apartment. You *will* call me if there are any signs you need to go to the hospital. Take it or leave it."

Without waiting for a response, he stands and gathers towels to support my ankle. Once he's satisfied that I'm not going anywhere, he glances down at me with a question in his eyes.

"Fine. Hurry up."

"I'll be right back. I don't need to ask you to stay put because with that ankle you're not going anywhere." He gives me one last smirk before walking away. At the door he turns and asks, "And what about your boyfriend, do you need to borrow my phone to call him?" He holds up the phone in question.

"Nope, no boyfriend so nobody to call."

He shoots me a knowing grin before leaving. Why didn't I ask for his name? I'm about to have a random, hot, controlling guy escort me to my apartment, and I didn't even ask for his name. Smart. What was that nonsense about him retrieving his bag? Deciding I don't really care, I rest my eyes.

They spring open when something cold presses on my ankle. It's hard to focus at first, but when my I adjust to the bright lights in the gym I see my sexy stranger wielding a bag of ice.

I ask the most basic question that I should have asked from the beginning. "Does my knight in shining armor come with a name? Or should I just pick one from my favorite fairy tales? I have to warn you, though, my fairy tales are different from Disney."

"Oh?"

"Instead of reading to me, my Dad made up his own fairy tales."

He chuckles. "Do I remind you of the knights in shining armor?"

I shrug. "There weren't really any knights in shining armor. The princess always saved the day. She didn't need anyone to rescue her."

I'm surprised that I just told that information to a stranger. I never open up. Never. There's something about him that makes me want to bare my soul. Which means I need to shut up. This can only be heading somewhere dangerous.

He rummages into his bag and pulls out a pair of gloves and a white bottle with a spray cap before answering. "Kohen Daniels. Now hold still. This may hurt a little."

Before waiting for me to catch on, he sprays the liquid on a cotton ball and then gently cleans my forehead. I scream a string of profanity that would make any sailor proud.

"Well, lucky for you I was wrong," Kohen says after cleaning the wound.

"Oh?" I ask through my teeth. The sting is still fresh in my mind.

"You won't need stitches. I have butterfly stitches that will keep this closed and it'll heal nicely."

He finishes cleaning the wound and applies the final bandage. Lightly he brushes his fingertips over my cheek and down my jaw. As he stares into my eyes, I feel a pull that I have only felt with one other person. Right when I think he is going to lean in, he quickly averts his attention to my ankle.

"I need to wrap your ankle and then I can help you back to your apartment."

Not trusting my voice, I nod. What just happened? I must have hit my head a lot harder than I thought.

He wraps my ankle with practiced ease. Without asking, I know immediately that he's a great doctor. Women must fall at his feet with those dark blue eyes and sandy blond hair that can't seem to stay in place. I know without a doubt that he has an incredible body to match his handsome face. There's no hiding it, even with a black sweatshirt on. When he's satisfied with his work, he stands and holds out his hand for me. Smiling, I take it and wobble to his side.

"Thanks."

Kohen must have collected my things when I was resting because now he is slinging the strap of my gym bag over his shoulder along with his medical bag. We're standing so close that all I have to do is look up and our lips will meet. My hands fidget at my sides because I can't make myself kiss him. The attraction I feel for him is foreign. My heart forever belongs to another.

Slowly, his hands trail from my shoulder to my wrists and back up again. By the second time his hands glide down my arms, goosebumps cover my whole body. As much as I don't want to look up, I tilt my head back. My violet eyes connect with his azure ones. His hand caresses my face as he leans into me. Logic kicks in at the same time the gym doors bang open.

Kohen manages to angle his body in front of mine and yet he's still supporting my weight. He watches me as Jax comes running around the corner in a desperate search for something, for me.

"Ads!" he shouts with relief.

I'm ogling him without shame, Kohen forgotten. My gaze is drawn to his brown hair that is styled in it's usual messy fohawk, his forest green eyes, and his sinfully kissable lips. Everything is the complete package and I haven't even taken in his body yet. I barely try to fight the pull I always feel when he's around. He's wearing a simple maroon dress shirt, first two buttons undone, with the sleeves rolled up displaying his tattooed arms. Once there was a time where I was able to study every picture, every black detail on his tanned arms. I would spend hours tracing every curve of his body.

Suddenly Jax comes to an abrupt halt when he sees the blood on my shirt, the bandage on my forehead, and me balancing on one leg. From the expression on his face, I can tell that his relief is short-lived. Sighing, I pinch the bridge of my nose and helplessly try not to make it obvious that I wished things were different between us, but they're not. I'm just Logan's little sister to him now.

"Please don't start. I'm fine. I was on my way back to my place when you came storming in here." Taking a deep breath to stall, I silently beg him to not make a big deal of this. I know there's no use, he's just as bad as my brother. "Please . . . just don't, Jax."

The only way this could be any worse is if Logan found me. At least with Jax I have a small window where he might be reasonable. With my brother I have no chance. It's always take charge first, ask questions later. I know I only have a minute, maybe two if I'm lucky, to convince Jax not to make a scene. Suddenly I remember Kohen next to me. It's amazing how just Jax's presence can command a room.

I hate it.

"Seriously, Jax, I'm fine. Kohen," I add pointing to the man still holding me upright, "is a doctor and he's already looked me over. Gave me a clean bill of heath and everything. I just need to stay off the ankle and we both know I have crutches somewhere in my apartment."

I'm wearing a huge grin knowing that I've talked my way out of this until the traitor opens his big fat mouth. "Actually I've been trying to convince her to go to the hospital for an X-ray. I don't think anything is broken, but it wouldn't hurt to have her examined. There's a good chance she has a concussion."

Kill me now.

My grin is now a scowl. I can't believe Kohen ratted me out. Great, hospital here I come. Jax doesn't say anything. He smiles that crooked smile I secretly love, the one that says he knows exactly what I'm thinking. Reaching into his black slacks, he grabs his vibrating phone.

"Yeah, man, found her. No idea, I haven't asked yet. No, you're going to need to meet us in the lobby. We need to make a quick run to the emergency room. Calm down, she's fine. Yeah, tell Connor to bring the car around. Oh, I'm sure, I didn't ask that either." Pulling the phone away from his ear, he curses quietly so that my brother can't hear. "Calm down, Logan. She's fine. Yeah, I know. See you in a second."

When Jax hangs up, he opens his mouth to speak. I hold up my hand. "No, Jax. Just don't. Save it, okay? Let's go before Logan loses his mind."

I rub the side of my temple, hating that there's a stranger witnessing the bubble that I live in. Wisely, Jax nods without saying anything. Turning slightly to face Kohen, I give him a weak smile that I don't feel. "Thanks again for everything."

Because I can't help myself and I want to see Jax suffer, I rise up on my good foot and kiss his cheek. I hear a growl and have to bite my lip to keep from beaming.

Kohen smiles down at me, ignoring a steaming Jax. "You're welcome . . . let's try to be more careful next time?"

"I'll see what I can do."

Momentarily forgetting about my ankle, I stumble towards Jax, which makes both Jax and Kohen reach for me. There's one on each side of me, helping me from face-planting.

"Jesus, Ads, stop trying to kill yourself." I don't have time to respond before Jax sweeps me up into his arms and cradles me to his chest. Jax grins down at me when I glare at him.

"Thanks for helping her," he tells Kohen, his green eyes fixed on mine.

Then Jax strolls out of the gym without waiting for a reply. I bury my head into his chest from embarrassment. God, could he act anymore like a caveman? When we reach the door I take a quick look over Jax's shoulder. Kohen hurls his medical equipment back into his bag.

"You don't need to carry me," I tell Jax.

"No, but I want to. Besides if your brother sees me letting you limp your way to the car, I'll be dead."

My brain has short-circuited. Jaxon Chandler wants to carry me. He wants me in his arms. I know I'm making a bigger deal out of this then I need to, but I can't help it. This is Jax. The man that I've been in love with for as long as I can remember.

"Besides, most women would love to be in my arms."

Ignoring the pain in my chest, I smirk at him. "Don't flatter yourself, Jax, those women only want your money. The rest of us don't want to hurt your feelings. You're not as good-looking as you think." We both know I'm lying. He is the very definition of beautiful.

"Great," I mumble under my breath when we reach the lobby.

Connor leans against the wall idly typing on his phone while Logan paces. Logan rushes to my side. He tries to grab me from Jax, whose hold on me tightens.

"No, I got her. She doesn't need to move more than necessary with her ankle."

Logan nods while sliding off his suit jacket from his buff shoulders to lay it over me. "Thanks, man. You okay, Addie?"

"Of course. I'm a little tired, though, so maybe we should go back up to my place and watch a movie?"

His light blue eyes that are the exact replica of our father's plead with me not to fight with him. I give him a tight nod. There's so much of our father in him; his build, his tone of voice, even his brown hair. I have that, too. We both have our mother's smile. Thanks to our mom I was blessed with her rare shade of violet eyes.

Logan kisses the top of my head. "Not a chance, baby girl," he says using Dad's nickname for me. To Jax he says, "Let's go."

Putting away his phone, Connor hurries over to the door to hold it open for us. The chill in the spring night air washes over me. I burry myself closer into Jax's warm chest, secretly loving his potent cologne. I breathe deeply once before watching Connor's 6'6" frame clear out the back seat of his car.

Like my brother, Jax treats me as if I'm a porcelain doll as he maneuvers me in the car. By the time he has the buckle in place I'm covered in goosebumps and it's not from the cold. Jax is so close, but still so many miles away from me.

After making sure that I'm comfortable in the back, Logan surprises me by manning the wheel. He hardly drives since the accident. He utilizes his massive amounts of money and has a full-time driver. I feel his fear resembles mine in a way, even if he wasn't there that dreadful night.

I nearly groan when Jax settles himself next to me and Connor slides into the passenger seat. I was hoping that Connor would sit with me. It would be easier to keep my distance from Jax. When we finally arrive at the hospital, Connor rushes to snag a wheelchair for me while the rest of us wait in the car.

Logan breaks the silence. "You didn't think to call us?"

I turn to face the window. "No, I was a little preoccupied. Besides, I knew you three would make a big deal out of this." I wave my hand down my body.

Luckily, Connor returns with the wheelchair before Logan or Jax can respond.

"All right, Addie, you know the drill," Connor says.

Jax picks me up like I'm a child and sets me in the chair. I breathe my first breath of fresh air since being in his arms. Being so close to him yet so far away is torture.

I sigh dramatically for his benefit. "Oh, well thank you, kind sir. I don't know how I would have made it the whole half a step to the wheelchair without you."

Someone clutches my hand. I look up and smile at Connor. His tall frame bends slightly so that he can continue to hold my hand while Logan steers me towards the automatic doors. I watch Connor as we near the entrance. Not for the first time, I wish that I felt something for him besides friendship. It would be so much easier to be in love with the blond stud squeezing my hand, but of course I consider him a brother. He brushes his long hair behind his ears. It's only then that I realize his wrist is missing the pink hair-tie I gave him earlier. Without saying anything, I give him the extra I keep on my wrist just for him. He smiles appreciatively as he gathers his shoulder-length hair into one of those manly ponytails at the bottom of his head.

My anxiety rises the closer I'm wheeled to the hospital's doors. Ever since the accident, I avoid them. Well, I try to at least; me being accident-prone doesn't help with my fear since the guys always insist on me seeing a doctor. Logan wheels me into the crowded Emergency Room at New York Presbyterian Hospital, oblivious that I'm dying inside.

Jax walks up to the counter like he owns the place. Flashing the receptionist his trademark smile he says, "I need to have someone look at my friend Adalynn Maxwell. She hit her head pretty badly and we're worried she might have a concussion."

He's so charming it should be illegal. The lady doesn't shift her focus from the computer screen; apparently there are women immune to Jax's charm. That's just *too* bad. Really, my heart breaks for him.

"You're going to need to fill this out and wait in the waiting room like everyone else." She hands him a clipboard with the paperwork attached. When Jax doesn't make a move for it, Connor is forced to seize it.

"I didn't introduce myself earlier, my apologies. I'm Jaxon Chandler, as in the owner of Trinity. Which happened to give the largest donation this year at the pediatric fundraising event last week."

He doesn't even wait for the light bulb to go off. I'm surprised how fast she recognizes the name of their company. Understanding dawns on me when I glance around. The new self-help posters have the Trinity logo in the lower left corner. What doesn't their company dabble in these days?

"I would like Miss Maxwell in a private room and to be seen by the best neurologist."

She's already standing and walking around the counter. She might be immune to Jax's charm, but she doesn't want to piss off their biggest paycheck. I doubt their CEO, who I know just went golfing with Logan, would be happy to hear from a fuming Jax. I have to try extremely hard not to laugh at her sudden willingness to help. It's hilarious how name-dropping can change people, even in a hospital, where it shouldn't matter.

"Of course, sir. I can have someone show you to Miss Maxwell's room right away. Unfortunately you will have to see the on-call doctor, as our head of neurology has the night off. I assure you Miss Maxwell will be in good hands."

Connor groans with me. Jax ignores both of us. She couldn't have just kept quiet, could she? No, it's not like she would have known that Jax isn't a man to be deterred. I tremble when he slams his strong hands on the counter. He glares at her as if she just said the most outrageous thing in the history of the world.

"That's unacceptable. I want the best. Make it happen or do I need to call Don?" He reads her name tag. "Mrs. Adams?"

"My apologies, sir. I'll have someone take her for all the tests while you wait for the doctor. It might take awhile longer since this is his only day off this week."

Mrs. Adams calls over a nurse to manage the desk before snatching the wheelchair from Logan. The guys are forced to hurry along after us to catch up. I have to hand it to Mrs. Adams, she doesn't just take it lying on her back. Go her! I pick imaginary lint off my bright orange leggings as Mrs. Adams silently pushes me. I stare straight ahead as we pass through the doors that she has to use a keycard to access. The urge to break the silence is overwhelming.

"I'm sorry about him. He's harmless, by the way," I tell her as she wheels me into a room.

"Yeah, he's like a rabid dog without teeth." I turn just in time to see Jax slap the back of Connor's head. "Ow!"

I can tell from her tight smile that Mrs. Adams wishes she were anywhere else right now. Can't say that I blame her. She starts to help me from the chair, but Jax pushes her out of the way.

"I got her."

My jaw drops. He needs to stop acting this way in front of Logan. I force myself not to react to his closeness as he lifts me up before gently laying me in the bed.

"Your nurse will be right in." Mrs. Adams inches her way closer to the door.

"You're not my nurse?" I ask, surprised.

After a shake of her head, she slips out the door.

"Jax, any doctor would have been fine." I let my annoyance show in my voice. "I'm pretty sure they all went to medical school, but who knows, some might have gone to clown school."

Jax ignores me as he makes a point of walking over to Logan, who's leaning against the far wall across from the bed. I'm still irritated that I'm here when a male nurse knocks on the door. He couldn't have come at a better time. Being here is making my entire body tense. Pretty soon I'm going to snap. Hopefully nobody is here to witness it.

Forty-five minutes later I have my ankle re-wrapped. Just a bad sprain, thank goodness; I just have to wait for the doctor to go over my CT scan. I survey the room for Jax, but he's missing. I want to ask where he's gone, but I don't want to clue in Logan to my feelings for his best friend. Talk about awkward.

"Don't be so hard on them, Addie," Connor says, "You know they're both just worried."

I frown at my best friend, hating that he's right. He's known me my entire life, and he's usually the one who makes those two see reason when it comes to me. He's like another big brother. I love him even if he annoys me 99 percent of the time.

I stare at Logan as he types away on his phone, probably responding to the thousand of emails he receives daily. As I inspect him closer I notice the shadows under his eyes. Without asking, I know he didn't sleep last night. Most likely he was restless like me, remembering everything we lost. But unlike me, he doesn't have the gory, haunting memories I do. I'm glad as my brother doesn't deserve to suffer like me. He's innocent.

"I know, Connor. I'm not mad at them. I just wish Jax didn't make a big deal out of this. Between the two of them, I don't know who's worse."

His twin dimples are prominent. "If you haven't noticed, Jax likes to make a show out of everything when it comes to you." Before I can say anything, he quickly changes the subject. "Have you picked your dress for the Masquerade Ball yet or are you—" He breaks off when there's a soft knock on the door.

We all turn to see a tall, muscular doctor with sandy blond hair that just can't seem to stay in the right place. Tonight is getting better and better.

CHAPTER TWO

"What are you doing here?" I ask even though I know the answer.

He's wearing a white lab coat with his endearing smile. "I got called in for a possible concussion." He shrugs as if it's no big deal. It is.

I stare wide-eyed at Kohen. Then at my confused brother. Logan moves to my side. I know overprotective brother syndrome is emerging, fast.

"Have you two met?" he asks me but his focus is solely on Kohen.

I can tell Kohen interprets Logan's question as innocent. Logan knows everyone in my life. I already know he is itching to place a call to his PI to investigate Kohen. Being the gentleman that he's shown me he is, Kohen steps forward and extends his hand to Logan and then to Connor.

"Yes, we met earlier this evening at the gym. I was the one who bandaged her up and insisted that Adalynn seek medical attention. However, Adalynn is a little stubborn and refused to go until her boyfriend came in and rescued her."

"Boyfriend?" Logan asks, baffled, at the same time Connor says, "Don't we know it."

Luckily Kohen is studying my CT scans so he's not paying much attention to them. I notice that his smile slips for a second. I can feel Logan's gaze on me, but I don't acknowledge him. He shouldn't have to ask about the boyfriend comment; he knows I'm unattached.

"There's no swelling, or anything else to be concerned about, but I would still like to check your balance, reflexes, coordination, vis—"

I interrupt him as I know exactly what he has to do. "Vision, and any possible memory loss."

He doesn't seem surprised that I am familiar with the examination. Maybe he realizes I'm accident-prone. That could be a new thing that shows up on CT scans now.

He pulls out a silver looking pen that I recognize as a flashlight. "Look to the left, good. Now the right, good. Follow the light with your eyes please."

"Well?" Logan ask impatiently once Kohen finishes testing my reflexes.

Kohen turns to my pacing brother. "I need to check her balance next and then I'll be done."

"Is she going to be okay?" Logan asks, ignoring the fact that the examine isn't over. "Yes, she has a slight concussion but she'll be fine." He focuses on me again. "Stand up, please."

I do everything he asks, wishing with each command that we were alone so he wouldn't have to deal with the my brother. He's already had to come in on his day off. I want to make this as easy as possible for him, and him receiving the third degree from my brother isn't easy for anyone in the room.

His back is to the door when Jax swaggers in and Connor decides to make matters worse. I have no idea how I'm even surprised by anything that he says. I should be used to it by now, but not even a lifetime with this guy can prepare me for what comes out of his mouth.

"Oh, look here's the boyfriend now." He tilts his head toward Jax.

"I'll hide your body where nobody will ever find it," I mutter only loud enough for Connor to hear.

"Boyfriend? Ahh Connor I'm touched, but baby you're not my type."

Kohen looks from Connor to Jax, then finally to me. Connor and Logan aren't even trying to hide their grins now while Jax is momentarily surprised to see Kohen again.

"Kohen, meet Jaxon Chandler. He's another childhood friend of my brother's." I try to assure him that he isn't my boyfriend.

Kohen nods in understanding and visibly relaxes. "Well, Adalynn, you're ready to go home once the discharge nurse has you sign the release papers. You'll need someone to check on you a few times throughout the night. Rest that ankle for at least two weeks before you take on any treadmills again."

"Great, thanks again, Kohen. Sorry you were forced to come in so late."

My brother steps forward and shakes his hand. "Yes, thank you for everything."

"You're welcome." He moves towards the door. "The discharge nurse will be in shortly."

Once the door closes, Jax asks, "Do I even want to know about the boyfriend comment?"

Logan shakes his head, but of course Connor decides silence isn't necessary. "The doc is interested in Addie so I thought it would be funny to mess with him and let him think that you're her boyfriend."

Jax's jaw tightens. It's the only sign that he's fighting to stay in control. Good. Maybe now he will notice that I'm not that broken teenager I once was and see me as an adult.

There's a soft knock on the door and a male nurse enters, carrying crutches. After another minute or two, the crutches are in Connor's hands, and the nurse is telling Logan where the pharmacy is to pick up my medication. Jax broods behind me, ready to wheel me out to the car. Connor wiggles his eyebrows at me. I glare at him and silently beg him not to do what I know he's about to do.

He winks as he shouts, "Wait up!" to my brother. He hurriedly runs to catch up with Logan, leaving me in my wheelchair with a stone-faced Jax.

Awkward seconds turn into minutes as Jax wheels me into the waiting room. He sits down with the wheelchair in front of him. As I people-watch, I curse Connor for leaving me here. He could have at least taken me with him. That prick! Out of nowhere I'm spun around so I'm facing Jax. He leans forward and rests his chin in his hands. We're so close, we're breathing each other's air. I don't know how long we're sitting here like this when I hear Connor's laugh bouncing off the walls. He's obnoxious, but I love him.

We're finally able to leave. As the exit comes into view, I exhale in relief. My entire body is strung so tightly, I'm positive that I'll snap if I'm forced to stay a second longer. It's taking everything in me to be appreciative, but a small part of me is still pissed that Logan made me come here, today of all days.

Kohen strolls around the corner with a purpose. Hoping to evade his attention, I inspect my nearly perfect cuticles as he comes closer. When the wheelchair stops moving, I'm forced to lift my head to see Kohen kneeling in front of me.

He hands me a card. "My personal number is on the back. When you feel up for it, I would love to take you out." Without waiting for a response, he kisses my hand and then he's gone.

My face flushes beet red. That was hands-down the most mortifying thing to happen since we arrived at the hospital. I can't believe he just asked me out in front of everyone. I turn slightly to see Jax rubbing his clean-shaven chin in thought. Not the envious reaction I was hoping for. Logan helps me into his suit jacket before we leave the hospital.

When we reach the parking lot, I wrinkle my nose as we pass a couple leaning against the back of their car, smoking. I hate the smell of cigarettes. I turn my head and see Jax glaring at them. Of course he would have a reaction to them and not to Kohen asking me out. *We're nothing to each other anymore. I'm just his best friend's little sister.*

I start to drift off before Logan drives out of the parking lot. I'm vaguely aware of Jax stirring in the middle seat. He leans my head on his shoulder and starts to draw patterns onto my arm. With the rhythmic movements of the car and the calm feeling Jax brings me, I'm asleep within seconds.

I have a momentary panic attack when I feel someone wrap their arms around me, but once the feel of Jax's body against mine sinks in, I relax and snuggle as close to him as possible. All too soon we're in my apartment and Jax carries me into my bedroom. I'm acutely aware of Logan watching us as Jax tucks me in. Once Jax ensures that I'm comfortable, not that he asked me, he promptly exits my room, leaving Logan and me alone.

"I have bad news, Addie." Logan sits on the edge of my bed, careful to avoid my ankle. He runs a hand over his buzzed-cut brown hair. "Connor and I need to take the plane tonight for a meeting in San Francisco."

It always amazes me how well my brother is doing. He and his best friends own Trinity together. And their company has its own plane. Just like Connor's parents, ours would be proud of all three of them. They've dominated the business world, the tech world, and the sports world all at the same time. They combined their strengths and made a lucrative marketing company.

"I have to leave so Jax is going to stay here and watch out for you until I get back in two days."

Ah, now the pieces of the puzzle are all here. I'm being put under house arrest with Jax as my warden. Wonderful. You would think for someone about to turn twenty-eight, Logan would be more lenient towards his younger sister, but you'd be wrong.

Jax decides to enter right as I'm about to protest. Which is good because I know it would be pointless. Logan wouldn't leave me alone, especially after an Emergency Room visit. Turning away from Jax, I give my brother the biggest smile I can manage. I'm vaguely aware of Jax making more noise then he should, but I solely focus my attention on my brother.

"Make sure to say hi to Connor's parents for me." I know that they will get together since Connor's adoptive parents now reside in the bay area. "I'll be fine. Call me when you land."

"Always do."

Our eyes are drawn towards Jax when he lets something drop to the floor next to my bed. I can't even hide my irritation when I see the air-mattress. Jax is just as bad as my brother. The drugs they gave me are kicking in and it's becoming harder to fight off sleep.

For some reason, my witty personality seeps through my hard exterior. I'm usually closed off, barely muttering a "no" when I'm upset. Well, until recently. I've been standing up for myself a lot more.

"Ummm no. There's a perfectly usable bed in the guest-room with your name on it, Jax." I hope he doesn't listen to me. Even though I can't have him, his presence brings me comfort.

In his most mocking voice Jax says, "This is my new bed." He points down at the air mattress. "Oh, and I sleep naked."

I have to look away from Jax as I remember a time when his sweaty, naked body was gliding over mine as he slid inside me. I don't want Logan to suddenly ask questions.

"Leave her alone. I swear if I find out that you slept naked in the same room as my sister, I will cut off the favorite part of your anatomy."

Jax is smart enough not to say anything. A few minutes later, Logan leaves after I promise that I'll call him immediately if I need anything. I'm so exhausted that I don't have the energy to watch Jax walk out of my in-suite bathroom wearing only red boxer briefs.

I wake up, distraught and in a lot of pain. I regret ever opening my eyes this morning. My head feels like I decided to play chicken with a bus and lost, severely. Once my equilibrium returns, I manage to lean against my pillows. I attempt to brush my hair in a somewhat presentable style with my fingers.

I can't help wanting to look good for Jax. I shake my head, knowing that nothing will ever happen between us. That notion floated away a long time ago. Giving up, I attempt to climb out of bed.

When I can finally manage to stagger to my feet, I notice that Jax spread my robe out on the duvet. He was even kind enough to move the blow-up mattress against the far wall so I wouldn't have to maneuver around it with my crutches. That would just be asking for trouble. After I knot the silk sash to my robe in place, I hobble on crutches to the bathroom to freshen up before I go search for him.

Peering into the mirror, I almost don't recognize the person staring back. I'm facing a complete stranger. I have a nasty bruise turning a wonderful shade of purple on my forehead and there aren't enough brushes in the world to calm my hair. But what's different is my eyes. Instead of being vacant, a look that I have grown accustomed to, there is a fire in them for the first time in six years. I look like I'm finally alive again. Just as quickly, the fire is gone.

I can't shake the feeling that it's time for me to move forward. I need to make a decision. I need to either start living, or I need to give up . . . for good. As I leave my bedroom I realize that I don't have a choice to make. I already made it. I made it a year after the accident when I decided to seek help. I want to live . . . I just don't know how.

I make my way to the living room before I call out for Jax. It's hard to ignore the disappointment that immediately follows the silence. I limp my way to the kitchen, hating the crutches. I fight the smile that wants to appear when I see a note from Jax in his neat handwriting.

Had to run out to buy you a new phone since you decided to take your poor, helpless phone down with you. I'll bring home breakfast so don't eat. I already called the bakery and explained why you won't be in for the rest of the weekend so don't bother getting dressed for work. Take the medicine I left out for you with a glass of milk

-Jax

Call Logan.

Rolling my eyes, I do as I'm told. I'm annoyed that he placed all of my medicine on the counter for me, even going as far as grabbing a glass, as if I don't know where I them. Men. Shaking my head, I open the fridge. After I take the medicine, I snag my house phone and wobble to the living room. I collapse onto the couch as gracefully as I can manage with a sprained ankle.

While waiting for him to answer, I wonder if Logan will make Jax stay the entire time he's away. Logan picks up on the third ring, and by his worried greeting, I have my answer to my unasked question. Yes, Jax will be my new shadow until Logan returns. Hey, things could be worse. I could be locked up in a basement with a serial killer. Okay, so it's not that bad, but I would enjoy myself a lot more if Jax would stop playing with my emotions.

"How are you feeling? I know you didn't sleep that good."

"How do you know how I slept? I swear if you put cameras in my room last night I'm going to kill you. That's taking overprotective brother syndrome to a whole new level, even for you."

"HA HA HA, Addie. No, I didn't need to put a camera in. I had the next best thing . . . an actual person to watch over you for me. You kept him up all night."

My brother isn't as funny he thinks he is.

"How could I have possibly kept Jax up all night? I was out in seconds once the pain meds kicked in."

"You were tossing and turning all night while sleep-talking."

And just like that, all of the air leaves me. There are too many horrible possibilities of what I could have said last night. I hope it wasn't anything about my unrequited love. Crap, suddenly I don't want Jax to come home.

"Everything you said was incoherent, but you were talking gibberish all night and kept Jax up. So I would be a lot nicer to him than you're being to me."

"I'm always nice to Jax." Deciding to change the subject I ask, "So when are you going to take over babysitting duty?"

Logan hesitates before answering. Not good.

"We won't be back until Saturday night now. Take it easy and try to listen to Jax." Pausing, he says something to Connor that I can't hear and then I have his full attention again. "I just need to know you're safe."

It's hard to hide my irritation. I think it's time for my brother to treat me like the adult I am. "Fine, I'll play nice since you gave me soooo many options."

"Great, Addie. I knew you would see it my way. Listen, I have to go. I love you."

"Love you too," I say before he hangs up.

I hate that they all treat me like I'm still five and that I can't take care of myself. All three of them need to realize that I'm twenty-four. Jax is the last person that I need to take care of me.

After discarding the phone on the coffee table, I will myself to relax. My mind drifts over last night's events and as much as I want to, I can't dismiss the feeling that I know Kohen. There's something about him that's telling me that I know him from a long time ago. That thought is beyond idiotic since I met him for the first time when he rescued me at the gym. He didn't even know my name until I told him. I chalk it up as seeing him in the building before in passing.

I don't know why I can't stop thinking about him. It's not like we'll end up dating. I never date. My last date was six years ago with Jax. For a moment I wonder what it would be like to date someone in the open, not having to keep everything a secret; every caress, every smile, every kiss. All too quickly, the image evaporates. Kohen seems like a great guy, too good of a guy for someone like me. The guilt of what I've done weighs heavily on my shoulders, crippling me. He deserves someone who isn't haunted by the past.

Even though I keep telling myself that it's pointless to continue thinking about him, I can't help smiling whenever I picture his face. As much as I wish I could just ignore this foreign attraction, that might be hard since we live in the same building. I know I need to think of how to go about the whole Kohen thing, but by the time I come up with a game plan, my medicine has kicked in. My last thought before sleep pulls me under is Jax's strong arms around me.

The aroma of bacon wakes me. Someone's fingers brush my hair out of my face. I open my eyes. After rubbing the sleep out of them, I'm able to focus on the second best sight in the entire world.

Food.

Jax crouches beside me with a platter of food and orange juice on the table. My mouth instantly fills with saliva as I take in all of my favorite breakfast foods in front of me. My stomach growls so loudly I'm sure people in Brooklyn can hear it as clearly as if they were in my living room.

He chuckles as he passes me a glass of orange juice. I give him a small smile when I notice the straw. For some unknown reason I've always hated drinking orange juice without a straw. As much as I want to comment on the fact that Jax is the only person that seems to remember my quirks, I don't. I know it will only cause an awkward silence. Some things are better left unsaid when it comes to us.

He hands me my platter full of food; eggs, hash-browns, bacon, a bowl of freshly cut fruit, and a stack of pancakes, along with my new iPhone.

"Thanks!" I notice that he somehow managed to back up my phone so all my music is already on it.

Nodding, he says sternly, "Eat all of the food."

Before I realize what I'm doing, words spill out of my mouth. "Do you think I should call him?"

His grip on his fork tightens. "Who?"

Well if he wants to play dumb . . . "The hot doctor who rescued me."

He chokes on his food. Miraculously, my next bite of hash-browns taste better than it did a second ago. Must be because Jax isn't as in control of his feelings as he would like to be.

"Maybe we can double?" he asks.

And just like that I lose my appetite. *Don't do it,* I repeat in my head as I eye my bowl of fruit. I snatch a few pieces and throw them at his handsome face.

I shrug. "Whoops."

He stops eating and glares at the fruit scattered on him. When he finally looks back at me, I laugh. He's biting his cheeks to keep from smiling, his emerald eyes sparkle with excitement. Even with fruit in his lap, covering his expensive suit pants, he's still ridiculously hot.

In a movement so fast that I don't even see it coming, Jax has my platter of food on the floor, and in the next second he dumps a glass of water all over my head. That's the exact second I know I will kill Jaxon Chandler.

I wipe my wet hair out of my face angrily. "Ahhhhh I'm going to kill you! I can't believe you just did that!"

The ice cold water drips down my hair and down my back. I'm now freezing and my shirt is practically see-through. Spotting a few ice-cubes on me, I fling one at him but he ducks out of the way. I hate his fast reflexes.

"Relax, Ads it's just a little water, it won't kill you."

Jax has the balls to chuckle then sit back down on the couch and eat like he didn't just dump water on me. WATER! The nerve this man has sometimes! Gah, I want to scratch his eyes out in his sleep.

"A little water, Jax? Are you kidding me? You dumped your ENTIRE glass of water on me!" I scream at the soon to be dead man.

Jax waves his hand at my little outburst. "Calm down, Ads."

I flick my orange juice at him. Wrong move, it splatters all over my suede couch. I groan, thinking how long it's going to take to clean. My gaze wanders to Jax's perfect, orange-juice-free face. Not good. I know that evil twinkle in his eyes, it's an expression that I have gotten very familiar with over the years.

"I swear, Jax, you better not! I'm hurt and I swear if you even think about it, my revenge will b—" I'm not able to finish my rant before he scoops me up and throws me over his shoulder.

Hitting his back I start yelling at him, but does The God even listen to me? Nope. Instead he smacks my backside so hard I'm sure I now have a clear imprint of his hand. My heart-rate picks up the second I realize we're in my bedroom. That intense pull I always feel towards him comes back in a huge wave, as if it's going to devour me. My heart beats so loudly I'm positive that he can hear it.

As Jax walks past my bed, I quickly realize what he has planned. I smack his toned butt as hard as I can manage in this position. Jax lets a growl escape his throat that I'm sure is supposed to be a warning, but all it manages to do is excite me. When he opens my bathroom door, I squeal and try with no avail to get down from his iron-like hold on me. Finally reaching his destination, he turns on the shower. I scream and hit his back harder with each smack, but it doesn't even faze him, he just smacks my now very red butt again.

HARD!

Holy-hotness I might have a bruise, but I don't think that I have ever been so instantly wet before in my life. Oblivious to how turned on I am, Jax just laughs as he steps into the cold shower with me on his shoulder.

He quickly repositions me so that now I am cradled in one of his arms, while his other hand grabs the shower head and drenches me in cold water. This is the moment that I despise playful Jax! The water is freezing!

I start fighting his hold more once the shock wears off. I manage to capture the shower head so that I can soak him, too. After a few seconds Jax laughs in a way that lets me know that my turn is over and he quickly yanks the shower head out of my hands and begins a new war of making me as soaked as he possibly can.

Vindictive jerk!

Just because I laughed at him, he carried me into *my* shower and decided to soak me with *cold* water. He couldn't even turn it to hot. The fact that

I'm injured angers me more because I can't retaliate. We're both dripping and our soggy clothes cling to our bodies, outlining *everything*.

My attire leaves nothing to the imagination. And Jax . . . he looks like the Greek-God that is feeling gracious enough to show his presence to us mere mortals. All of a sudden, he takes in my near-naked appearance as if he just realized the same thing I did. His eyes change from playful to hunger. It's all consuming, he's all consuming. That pull surrounds us, so thick I can almost taste it.

Suddenly I am no longer freezing. I'm shaking, but it's not from the cold. When he sees me shiver, he places the shower head back and turns the water hot. I slowly slide down his body when he unwraps his arms around me. His hands go to my hips to steady me while I stand on one leg. He is so close to me that my breasts press into his hard chest.

Hot water pours over the both of us, as steam fills the air. I hold my breath . . . neither of us makes a move. He watches me, waiting, his eyes locked onto mine. *Devour me, Jax.* With such slowness that he's barely moving, Jax lifts one hand from my hip to my face, and traces my jawline back and forth with his fingertip.

"Ads." Jax uses his nickname for me as if it's the most pleasant name he's ever uttered, but I can still hear the pain laced in his voice.

I notice the abrupt change in the air around us and in him. He's no longer looking at me with such hunger that I can taste his need. He's now the tortured man that always stops us from being together again. I know that this is over.

"Use me to support your weight so you can get out of your clothes and finish your shower while I bring your crutches in. I'll help you out when you're done."

With the moment long gone, he turns his head away from me. As fast as I can manage, I strip out of my clothes and once Jax is sure that I don't need any further assistance, he steps out of the shower and grabs a towel. I don't attempt to stop him as he leaves.

CHAPTER THREE

Glancing around my abundant closet, I finger the hanger holding my work clothes. I shake my head while I think of all the reasons it's a bad idea. Jax will be pissed, he'll tell Logan . . . I can't think of anything else. Two, just two reasons why I shouldn't pull the red shirt that has *Sweet Tooth* embroidered over the right breast off its hanger. Thinking about sitting on the couch next to him, wanting him but knowing he will never give into us again, is too much. I smile wickedly as I drop the towel. I don't need a babysitter. Jax can be mad all he likes.

After getting dressed as quickly as possible, I hobble back to my bed to retrieve my phone only to realize that it's still in the living room. So much for sneaking out of here to decorate cakes. I huff in exasperation. This isn't going to go over well at all.

He seems to have no care in the world as he reads something on his iPad. He hears me, it's impossible not to with my wood floors, but he ignores me. Good. Hopefully I can swipe my phone off the table and leave before he notices. I bite my lip as I try to bend down for my phone. I avoid him entirely as I straighten back up. As I turn around to leave, I exhale.

"You don't think you're going to work do you?" he asks, startling me. "I already called in for you."

I glare over my shoulder at him. "Last time I checked, you're not my father and I'm a big girl. I don't want nor need you calling into work for me."

He shrugs. "Either way, you're not going in."

"Watch me."

I don't even make it a step before he's behind me. He runs his nose through my wet hair and speaks so close to my ear that his lips brush against my skin. "You know I can't let you go."

Right. Because of Logan. "Well, tell my dear brother that I'll be fine doing nothing but decorating." I turn my head so my nose nearly touches his. "My butt will be firmly attached to the stool the entire time."

"No."

The way he says it leaves no room for discussion. This new feisty person I woke up to is steaming. I will not be told no by Jaxon Chandler anymore. I've heard that word from him one too many times.

I open my mouth to tell him exactly that, but he's already sitting on the couch again. What a jerk! He honestly thinks I'm just going to bow down to him. Well, why would he think any differently? All I've been doing for the past six years is rolling over and going along with whatever is demanded of me. Am I ready to put up a fight? Is right here, right now, the time for me to say enough and do what I want? Yes. Because if I'm locked in here with Jax, I won't be held responsible for what comes out of my mouth, or worse, my actions.

I bite down on my lip as I put weight on my sprained ankle. Wow, one night isn't enough time for it to heal. I don't use the crutches, I'm making a point here. When I reach the door, I turn to face him. He's seething. His jaw is so tight I wouldn't be surprised if he snapped it.

"You have two options. Lie to Logan and say I'm here with you, or come with me."

He runs his hand through his fohawk while he grinds his teeth. Okay, so I admit maybe walking on my injured ankle wasn't the best way to prove that I'm ready to be taken seriously.

"I can just keep you here against your will," he bluffs.

I smirk at him while opening the door. "You can, but you won't. Besides, if you come with me I'll make your favorite."

When he sighs in defeat, I know I won. "Carrot cake cupcakes?"

"Even with brown bunny ears as decoration." I almost smile at the memory from when we were younger.

He sits up and slides his feet into his black chucks. It's only then that I realize that he's changed. Obviously he's changed; his suit was dripping wet. He's in a red Flash T-shirt and black jeans. Him and his superheroes. He's always been fascinated by the comics, never realizing that once upon a time he was my hero.

He points at the crutches as he meets me at the door. "You can either use those, or I'll be carrying you. Don't you dare pull a stunt like that again."

I mock salute him. "Yes sir."

The bell chimes as Jax holds open the bakery door for me. Sam glances up from the register and frowns when he sees me. The bakery is almost empty. I knew it would be. There's one couple sitting at the red iron table to the left of the door. After lunch, usually the only customers are the ones putting in an order for a party. It's my favorite time to bake.

"I was told you were on bed rest," Sam says in the fatherly tone he's mastered from being a dad for two months.

I nod in Jax's direction. "Is it okay if my shadow is back there with me?"

Once he finishes up with the last customer, Sam turns his attention back on me. His frown deepens. "Adalynn, as much as I need your help today, I can't have you working like that. Besides, Clark is going to kill me if he finds out."

I give Sam my best puppy dog eyes. It's the same face I gave him two years ago when I applied for the job he wasn't offering. To this day, I believe my winning personality and my superb baking skills are the only reason he took a chance on someone without references or cooking experience. Apparently, baking for your family doesn't cut it in the baking world. Who knew?

He watches me lead Jax behind the counter to the back room. I'm thankful that Jax has chosen for the first time in his life to stay quiet. I search the room for the white apron with my name on it. Sam appears with my missing apron.

"Clark washed it." He grins whenever he mentions his adorable better half. The twins they adopted earlier this year are so lucky to have such caring parents.

I accept it and tie it into place around my waist. "Does this mean I'm working?"

He peers at Jax. "Does this mean you're going to make sure she doesn't break anything else?"

"I won't take my eyes off her."

It seems like Sam mutters, "I bet," under his breath but I'm not sure. "Create something new," he tells me.

I can't help but beam at him. This is my favorite part about working here, creating something new, something different, that will make your taste buds come to life. The very first time I told a customer that I could invent a cake that wasn't on the menu, I thought Sam would have a stroke. Granted, once he took the first bite, he was sold. Now, two years later I have free rein of the kitchen. Sam works the customers, Clark handles the business along with their adjacent restaurant, and I do my magic. It's perfect and I love it. I can't wait for Jax to witness it, too.

I face Jax, who leans against the stainless steel counter tops. Even though he's trying not to show it, I know he's uncomfortable. Jax has never been one to sit idly. He needs a task and I need help.

I point at the white apron hanging on a hook on the far wall. "You'll need to put that on if you're going to be of any use."

"You're putting me to work?" he asks but he struts his way to the apron.

I walk to the fridge to snag the ingredients. "Yes, I'm in need of an assistant."

I feel him behind me but I pretend that I don't. I swallow loudly. "Can you grab the butter and cream cheese?"

He reaches in front of me for the items. I suck in a breath as his hard chest presses against my back. Desperately I want to melt into him, but I can't. I don't deserve happiness. I stole away theirs.

I direct Jax to everything we will need. As he sets the bowls in front of me, his other hand trails down my spine. It takes every ounce of will power to not shiver at the contact. *Happiness is for everyone else but me.* Jax watches the movements of my hands as I pour the first batter into the cupcake tins. Hopefully he's paying attention because he's doing the next batch. As I wipe a paper towel over the extra batter on the tin, I can feel him studying me. I focus on the task at hand.

An hour and a half later, I have Jax —who is covered in flour— pull out the cupcakes. He sets them in the cooling area as I directed. He's the perfect assistant. Perfect as in, drops everything and makes a mess. Weird, since he usually has such steady hands. I won't allow myself to think it has to do with me. As hard as it is to not become lost in the moment with him, I hold myself back.

The frosting is suddenly the most important thing in the world to me right now. I dip in a tasting spoon. Just a little more vanilla and it's perfect. As I drizzle in the vanilla, Jax's long finger swipes at the frosting. I slap his hand away.

"It's not like this is going out there!" He licks the frosting off his finger.

"It was before you did that!" I can't even pretend to be angry with him. Said too soon. My tongue seeks out the frosting that is falling off my nose. "Really, Jax? What are you, three?"

I'm struck speechless as his tongue cleans up the mess on my nose that he created. Jax looks from my eyes to my mouth, causing me to chew my lower lip. He lets out the most erotic growl from the back of his throat that I feel all the way to my toes. I suck in a breath and stay as still as possible. I'm not even breathing while Jax caresses my check with his frosted finger tips. Leaning into his touch, I close my eyes and welcome the sensations he brings me by just this simple act.

I want to pretend that I can be happy for once, that my memories don't haunt me. I want to cherish this moment with him. I want to let go of my past more than anything for this one moment. Deciding that I'm going to allow myself some freedom from my demons, I open my eyes, ready to give myself over to him.

I don't know who leans in first, but suddenly we are as close as possible without melting into each other. Forehead-to-forehead, nose-to-nose, breathing each other's air, we stare into one another eyes. After several seconds without moving, Jax finally makes the next move.

It's as if he can't hold back anymore, either. He kisses me so quickly that I don't even notice he's making a move until his lips are on mine. All too soon, he's gone.

Even though I could feel his urgency in the kiss, it was surprisingly soft. So soft that if I wasn't watching him, I would have never known that he kissed me. I need more, that barely-there kiss isn't good enough. Of course it was perfect, I doubt that Jax can do anything that isn't perfect, but I need more to relieve this tension building inside of me. I lean into him again, but Jax shakes his head, face full of regret.

If I was someone else, someone that wasn't able to shut off their feelings at will, then the ways he's rejecting me now would kill me. Thankfully the second I see the guilt on his face, I shut down. I'm not even surprised that he's feeling guilty, that he doesn't want me. Who would?

I'm broken.

I will never be good enough for Jax.

Jax surprises me again by bestowing that beautiful smile of his and giving me another quick kiss on the lips. Then he seizes his phone from the front pocket of his jeans. I was so caught up in the moment that I didn't even hear it ringing. That's something that always happens when Jax is staring into my eyes. The world disappears whenever he's near, making it nearly impossible to remember why we shouldn't be doing this.

Jax's body goes rigid when he sees who's calling him. I know that whoever it is has ruined our moment. Rubbing his hands across his face, he lets out a deep breath before sliding his finger over the screen.

"Yeah, Logan."

And just like that, an entire bucket of ice is poured over me. Hearing my brother's voice on the other end of the phone certainly puts a stop on anything that was about to happen. Which I'm thankful for as Sam could have walked in here at any second.

"No, she's fine, man. Of course."

I pull the first tray of carrot cake cupcakes towards me. I concentrate on frosting them as Jax talks to my brother. I try to put distance between us, but it's impossible with his hand on my thigh. With him touching me, the white walls seem to be closing in. There's not enough air. Every breath I breathe is full of Jax's woodsy scent. It's torture.

"I don't know, I don't think she has it on her, let me check." He turns to wipes the last dab of frosting off my cheek. "Phone in your room?"

I glance at the phone on the counter in front of us. I'm about to point to it, but then I realize what he's doing. He's covering for me. With all the emotions swirling in my head, I don't trust myself to speak, so I nod.

I ignore the cupcake in my hand and study Jax as he speaks to my brother. I can't believe he's lying to my brother for me. Wow. I'm speechless.

"Yeah, I knew they were going to try to do that. Handle it and have everything sent over to Peter." He bends down and bites the barely frosted cupcake that I'm working on.

My attention is once again brought to the cupcakes. I avoid listening to the rasp in his voice and focus on my next task. Frosting the bunny ears is my favorite part. I used to put them on the cupcakes I made Jax because of *The Velveteen Rabbit*, his favorite book when we were children.

I attempt to reach for the light brown frosting that Jax made, but he beats me to it. He slides the bowl into my waiting hands. As our fingers touch, I think it's an accident until he grips mine for a second, letting me know it was intentional. That simple graze of our fingers sets a fire within me. My mind wanders as I scoop brown frosting from the bowl and into the vinyl decorating bag.

Is it possible for Jax to still view me as more than Logan's little sister? Maybe after all these years, we have a chance. I shake that outrageous idea out of my head. It doesn't matter how he sees me. I won't let anything happen. He deserves so much more than me. He deserves everything.

I lick my upper lip as I concentrate on creating the ears just right. I bite my cheek to keep from smiling. It's just bunny ears, not the Mona Lisa, but I still can't help beaming when Jax gives me his winning grin.

"Of course, man, I'll work from here until you're back. I understand . . . I know. Okay, see you in a few days."

Jax hands his phone over to me. Reluctantly, I press it to my ear.

"Hey." I can't seem to say anything else because I'm watching Jax butcher the next cupcake.

Cupcake-decorating is not a skill he's mastered.

Logan's voice jolts me back from the happiness swelling inside me. "Adalynn?"

"What? I'm sorry Logan I dropped the phone," I say lamely.

"I just want to make sure you're doing okay with everything. I worry about you when I'm gone."

"Logan, it's just a sprained ankle, I've suffered from a lot worse over the years. You don't need to worry."

"You know that's not what I'm talking about, Addie."

"Yeah I know, I was just trying to make you feel better. I. AM. FINE." I enunciate each word so that he knows that I mean it.

When he doesn't say anything for awhile, I pull the phone away from my ear to make sure I didn't accidentally hang up. Wouldn't be the first time.

"I just worry about you, Addie, you're all I have left."

I know that Logan doesn't tell me this to make me feel bad, but I can't help feeling worthless regardless. Our family is dead because of me. I don't need the reminder, it's not something that I can easily forget.

I choke out, "I know," before my throat starts to close.

I know that Logan can hear the pain in my voice because he curses. "That's not what I meant, Addie, and you know it!"

Swallowing a few times, I force myself to breathe deeply and let it out slowly. "I know, Logan, it's fine, it's the truth." He tries to interrupt me, but I cut him off. "Look I just took my meds and I'm really tired. I'll call you tomorrow. I love you."

Please just let me off the phone, Logan, I can't handle this right now.

"Yeah of course, love you too, baby girl."

I hang up. Before Jax can say anything I whisper, "Can you take me home now please?"

The last thing I want to do is fall apart at work. Getting lost in the sweet smell of the bakery while decorating cupcakes doesn't have the same effect on me as it did minutes ago. All I want to do now is curl up in my bed and get lost in the memories.

He must see how much I'm dying inside because he nods and works on cleaning up. I close my eyes, and by the time I open them again, the kitchen is spotless. You can't tell that we've been in here for almost two hours. It's almost laughable how easy it is to erase something. I hear Jax speaking to Sam, but they're too quiet for me to understand anything being said.

The cab ride is a blur. I'm barely aware of his arms around me while the endless amount of guilt suffocates me. As Jax helps me out of the taxi and into my apartment building, I'm losing my mind. I want to be strong enough, but I'm sinking fast. The memories that I work so hard to keep buried are rushing to the surface.

My body trembles from the emotional pain I'm intentionally causing myself. The memory of waking up in the hospital with Logan by my side is so powerful that reality disappears. I'm suddenly back in that bleak hospital room while he struggles to tell me we're all we have left.

I woke up a little over twenty-five hours ago, but I haven't really been here. I've been in and out of sleep the entire time, trying to piece together what happened, but my mind won't let me. Everything is confusing.

Logan sits in a chair beside my bed, clutching my uninjured hand. I know that whatever he is going to say is bad. Really bad. He has tears in his eyes and he hasn't talked about our parents, or Hadley. Not once. Every time I bring them up, he just shakes his head.

I have no idea what he means. "No" as in he doesn't know yet because they're not stable yet, or "No" because . . . I won't let myself go there. I already know our dad is dead, there's no way he could have survived.

My body convulses as I remember all the blood. The broken glass. No, he didn't survive. Even though I know that he's dead, I knew it before someone rescued us, I still pray that I'm wrong.

I allow myself to hope for the best, that maybe by some miracle he did survive like the rest of us. That they were able to stop the bleeding and give him a transfusion. He had to have survived, I can't live without his help.

He's my hero.

My dad didn't die.

He wouldn't leave me.

"I-I-I don't know how to tell you this . . ." He stops talking, tries to compose himself.

I whisper, "Logan it's fine, we'll get through this together." I wait for him to nod. "Now tell me what it is, how's everyone doing? I haven't seen Hadley since they put her in a different ambulance. Is she doing okay?"

I struggle to speak because my throat still hurts from not using it for two weeks. He holds out my water for me to sip. I swallow a few times, testing my throat. I wonder if it will ever stop hurting; even with all the meds they have me on, everything aches. It's as if I'm reliving the accident without realizing it and I'm going through all of that pain, and desperation to escape again and again.

After I am able to speak again without it hurting so much, I ask the question that I'm dreading. "Are Mom and Dad . . . ar-are they okay? Di-did they make it?" That had to be the hardest question I have ever had to ask. I was barely able to put the words together.

Logan doesn't say anything for awhile and when he finally does, I wish he didn't. Ignorance is bliss.

"They didn't make it."

The tears in his eyes fall while I just stare at him, shocked. He squeezes my hand tightly but I hardly notice.

"Does Hadley know yet?"

When Logan looks into my eyes, his face full of so much remorse, it's then that I know.

"NO! NO! NO!" I scream over and over again until a nurse hurries in and gives me a sedative. The last thing I see before my lids close is the unmistakable torture in my brother's blue eyes.

I did this.

He's alone because of me.

I killed them. I killed Hads.

The memories begin to float away as Jax whispers, "It's gonna be okay, I'm here, Ads," and suddenly I'm in the present again. The memory was so strong I started screaming, not just in the flashback. My entire body quivers and I feel like all of the air has been sucked out of the room. It takes me a moment to realize that we're back in my apartment. I have no recollection of riding the elevator.

Jax holds me tighter to his chest and tells me, "Take deep breaths in and out for me."

I'm barely able to hear him, I have no control over my mind right now. I'm sucked back into the past. It's a welcome pain.

Connor and Jax wait by a nearby tree outside the cemetery gates. I can't open the car door. If I open it, it's real. I want to stay in here and pretend that this is a nightmare, that I'm still asleep in the hospital.

The sun shines, it's a perfect day in Southern California. Not even the wind blows. Today should be a perfect day, but instead it's the worst day of my life. Today I have to come to terms with what I failed to do.

Logan reaches over and clutches my hand. "I'm right here, I'm not going anywhere."

He pulls me into a hug, but I barely feel it. I'm numb. This isn't real. It can't be. Logan gets out of the car after letting me go. I make no move to take off my seatbelt. No, I'm not ready, I can't do this.

I lock the car door. No, I won't go through with this. If I don't face it, it's not real. They're not dead. I'm going to wake up any minute now. I refuse to believe that I killed my family.

My voice is hoarse as I whisper the first words since the nurse sedated me days ago. "No, they're not dead."

A knock on the door stops me from having a full-blown panic attack. Turning my head, I see Jax. Logan stands in the front of the car with Connor. Logan looks how I feel, utterly broken.

I did this.

I broke him.

I destroyed our family.

I'm struggling to breathe when Jax says, "You're stronger than you think, Ads. YOU. CAN. DO. THIS."

He unlocks the door, opens it and kneels in front of me. He sets the Stargazer Lilies on the floor next to him before he fits my hands in his. As he says, "We're all here for you, you're not alone," my eyes are transfixed on the bouquet at his feet. When did we pick those up? How long have they been in my hands?

He lifts my chin, pulling me out of the silent battle between forgetting everything, and not wanting to ever let the memories go. The pain in his sad eyes resemble mine. I caused him pain, too. All I do is hurt people with my selfishness.

"Don't, Ads. This is not your fault. Don't blame yourself for surviving."

Surviving. Yes, I'm a survivor, that's what the doctor told me, too. Too bad I feel like I'm dead inside. I ignore Jax because I don't want to fight. If I tell him what I'm really thinking, we will just argue. I'm too tired to fight with him. I'm tired of everything.

"This can't be my life . . . it can't. I can't . . . I-I-if I go with you, it will be real, they will really be gone . . . I don't know how to live without them."

Jax squeezes my hands. His voice breaks as he says, "It's already real, Ads. It already happened, you can't change that. You need to do this, we don't need to rush, we can go when you're ready."

Jax doesn't say anything else and neither do I. There's nothing to say. I know he's right. This is real and I have to face it. Deep down I know that I have to do this, I just don't know how. I feel like I shouldn't be allowed here, I shouldn't get to say goodbye to them, it's because of me that they're dead. After minutes of sitting in the car with my hands clasped in Jax's, I finally nod.

"It's time." I whisper more to myself than him. If he's surprised at hearing me speak, he doesn't show it.

My legs feel like Jell-O. Jax supports most of my weight. If it wasn't for him I would have crumbled to the ground. Logan and Connor walk from the front of the car to where Jax and I are standing.

Logan's tear-strained face would break me if I wasn't already dead inside. "I'm ready."

Logan nods. I cling to him with Jax grasping my free hand as we make our way to our family's graves. I hate that I'm making them all relive the pain. I wish I was strong enough to say goodbye on my own, but I'm not. I wasn't even strong enough to save my family.

When Logan told me that our family was dead, I didn't cry, I haven't cried a single tear since I woke up in the hospital two weeks after the accident. But when we reach their graves and I see Hadley's name etched onto her headstone, I lose it. I fall to my knees and bawl my eyes out. I gasp for breath.

The world around me disappears.

All that is left are three graves.

Three lives lost because of me.

"I did this," I choke out.

Logan crouches beside me to tell me something, but I don't hear him. I barely see him. I can only see the three headstones.

I cry for everything that I lost.

The mom that I lost . . .

The dad that I lost . . .

My little sister . . .

And finally I cry for myself . . .

The night of the car accident, I died with them. I never made it out whole. Now I'm just a shell of a person. I don't know how long I stayed like this, kneeling on the ground in front of my sister's grave, but eventually the world starts to come back into place. I'm still crying, silent tears now, even though inside I'm screaming. The pain is all-consuming.

When I look at my brother, I see how much I have broken him. Connor and Jax are in silent agony, watching our world fall apart and not being able to do anything but witness it, all because of me.

I did this.

The first thing I notice when I open my eyes is the stained-glass stars Logan hung above my bed. Jax's rhythmic strokes through my hair makes it easier to breathe. Even though I've been lost in my memories, he didn't leave. Being wrapped in his arms brings me comfort that I don't deserve. I feel his lips at the top of my head, but he doesn't say anything. He's letting me know that he's here for me while I relive the past. I squeeze him as tightly as I possibly can, hoping that the nightmares won't punish me tonight if he's here.

As I watch my stars twirl on the invisible string, I will myself to relax. Whenever my memories weigh me down, I come here. I can lay here for hours and have the beautiful stars make everything else disappear. It always reminds me of when I would sneak out and lay on my roof and stare at the night sky.

"I love you, Ads," Jax whispers into my hair.

My chest constricts painfully. How I wish he meant those words in the way I wanted. Without taking my gaze off my stars I whisper, "Love you, too."

We don't say anything else to each other for the rest of the night. Jax's fingers running through my hair lulls me into a heavy, dreamless sleep.

CHAPTER FOUR

Life was slowing getting back to normal. I went to work, saw my brother and Connor regularly, and tried to ignore the fact that I haven't seen or heard from Jax since he left my apartment three weeks ago. It's getting embarrassing how many times I have attempted to call him, but always hang up before the call goes through. Connor insists that Jax is busy with work, but my gut tells me that he's avoiding me.

I'm finally able to work-out again, which is good since it occupies my mind for a little while. I have a feeling Jax is avoiding me because of everything that happened. He treated me like I meant more to him again, which of course means avoidance at all cost.

Today I decided to surprise Logan with lunch since I know he's been working more than usual after taking so much time off to visit. I'm glad that I brought my iPad because my brother is working through lunch so that doesn't leave a lot of time to talk to him. I don't mind, of course I know that he's a busy man, and I couldn't be more proud of everything that he has accomplished. Trinity, has flourished since the guys started the business in college.

I zone out, thinking about our parents. I'm picking at my pasta without actually eating it when Connor sneaks into Logan's office and blows into my ear.

"AHHH . . . Holy shit!" I jump out of my chair, spilling pasta all over the floor in the process. I whirl around to an amused Connor.

I'm steaming! I hate that he always scares me. I'm about to rip him a new one when Jax storms into the office, looking like he is going to kill someone. Seeing him brings such a shock to my system that I'm barely aware that I'm blatantly staring at him. I have no idea what I was about to say to Connor.

Jax comes to an abrupt halt when he sees that I'm the reason for the obnoxious scream. Time seems to stop. Everything evaporates and the only thing that is left is Jax and me. The need to touch him is so powerful that my hand shakes from the sheer force of keeping it at my side and not reaching out.

Connor clears his throat, jarring me out of the trance. Logan types away at his computer, thankfully missing the encounter. It isn't until Logan notices the silence that his head snaps up.

"What's going on?" He studies the three of us.

Jax bumps his shoulder against mine, in a friendly way. "Ads is mad because she's a sore loser and I beat her at poker when I stayed at her house." He shrugs, smoothly lying. "I think she learned her poker skills from you."

After a few more minutes of awkward silence, Logan engages Connor in a discussion over a new technology prototype they are considering purchasing. I can't help but stare at Jax as if I'm seeing him for the first time. I've witnessed him lying before in the past, daily, but there's something about this time. Usually I can always tell when he's lying. This time, I can't. If I wasn't there, then I would believe him. Have I always been oblivious when it comes to him? Has he always been able to lie so effortlessly and I just now noticed? What else is he hiding?

I sit down on the leather sofa and attempt to ignore Jax. I can feel him watching my every move, making it impossible to ignore him. He shifts his feet as if he's trying to decide if he should leave or say something to me. My money is on him leaving. That's what he does best. Leave. Whenever we get close to each other, Jax disappears. Always.

Jax startles me when he answers whatever question my brother just asked and sits next to me. I'm the only one that notices when his finger grazes my pinky. Sadly I notice everything that Jax does.

Jax rearranges himself in his seat so that he's facing me. I focus on a black and white picture across from us as if it's the most interesting photograph in the world. After a few more agonizing minutes of Jax silently studying me, I finally give up.

After glancing at my brother and Connor to make sure they are still engrossed in conversation, I focus on Jax. "Are you going to just stare at me or do you actually have something to say?"

Jax gives me a rare smile. "Hi."

I huff out a breath. Hi, really that's all he has to say to me after three weeks of silence. "I'm out of here," I tell my brother as I stand.

"Want to meet at my gym later this week?" Logan asks as he engulfs me into a hug.

"Sure."

"Where you off to in such a rush?" Connor asks.

I meet Jax's green eyes for a second before turning to Connor. "I have a coffee date," I lie.

"With who?" Logan asks.

Crap, I didn't think this far ahead. This is why I'm horrible at lying. I toss out the first name I think of. "Kohen . . . the doctor who lives in my building."

At everyone's stunned expressions, I flee. I know they're about to shoot a million questions at me, questions I don't have the answers to. Because I can't help myself, I look over my shoulder before closing the door. Logan and Connor have returned to their conversation again. I have to force myself to keep moving when I see Jax. He's smiling. He *never* smiles. And he's choosing now to do it. He was supposed to be furious that I was going out with someone. *Of course he isn't mad. He doesn't care.* I rush to the elevators.

As the doors start to slide close, someone reaches a hand out to stop them from shutting all the way. So much for my hasty exit. Hopefully it isn't anyone I recognize, but I know it's highly unlikely since my brother owns the company. I keep my head down and let my hair cascade down the side of my face in an attempt from letting whoever it is recognize me.

Any attempts of being left alone fail. That someone who stopped the elevator doors from closing is Jax. Of course it is. It's always him. I'm so lost, I don't want him to see me like this. Not again.

He continues to press the open button as he talks. "I got this for you, and before you say you won't accept it, understand that I'm not taking no for an answer." He hands me a present with a purple ribbon. "Oh, and you're welcome."

It shakes in my trembling hands. I hate presents. I don't celebrate my birthday anymore. "I haven't even opened it yet. How do you know I'm going to even like it?"

He shrugs. "I know you." Then he steps away.

"You don't —" The words die on my lips as the doors slide shut.

When I get home, I stare down at the present, wondering if I can get away with throwing it out. Not likely, Jax will ask about it. I sigh, hating that he's does this to me every year. He's the only one that continues to get me birthday presents. Of course he says they're just gifts since he doesn't give them to me on my actual birthday, but we both know what it really is, and why he never gives them to me on May 21.

With shaky legs, I head over to the living room. I set the present on the table before going to the kitchen for a glass of wine. Phone! I hurry over to my bedroom where I left it. I'm stalling. Once I'm seated, I finally grab the present.

The first thing I notice is a note in Jax's handwriting.

Seven years ago you were consumed with swimming, you began to lose yourself. This helped . . . maybe it can help you find yourself again. It's time to live again, it's time to move on. I'll be here every step of the way.

-Jax.

Without seeing the gift, I know what it is. A camera. As much as I try to be angry with him for deciding it's time for me to move on, I can't. I wouldn't be able to without him pushing me. I want to ask him what he means by being here. I want him to mean it as more than a friend, but I know he doesn't. We're not those teenage lovers who sneak behind everyone's back to be together every chance we got anymore. Too much has transpired.

Taking a deep breath, I pull the camera out of the box. My eyes go wide when I realize exactly what camera he bought me. It's a SLR Leica. It's so expensive, I'm almost too afraid to touch it . . . almost.

My phone goes off, startling me. I plan to ignore it, but when I see it's a text from Jax, I carefully set down the camera.

Jax: You actually get a choice . . . Thai or subs.

Me: Yeah real big choice there. Subs.

Jax: Great choice, I already have them. Be there soon.

Me: Why do you even ask then?

Jax: So you think you actually have a choice.

Me: Thanks for the camera . . . You shouldn't have . . . but thanks.

Jax: Don't mention it. You're going to use it, maybe not tomorrow, but soon. And I can't wait to see you come to life again when you're behind the lens.

I smile as I set my phone down and I decide that I need music to fill the silence until Jax gets here. Picking the playlist *feelgood* on my iPhone, I hit shuffle and plug it into the Surround Sound. The first song has my head bumping, but it isn't until Sammy Adams *Only One* comes on that I actually begin to move. I jump around, shaking my butt, and whipping my hair back and forth. When the chorus comes on, I'm screaming about the one that is way out of my league with Sammy. Fitting.

Forgetting about all of my stresses, I dance it out. Cheap Trick's *She's Tight* comes on next and I'm lost in the music. I use a water bottle as a makeshift microphone. Closing my eyes, I go all out.

It isn't until I hear Jax sing, "I had a smoke and went upstairs," that I realize I'm no longer alone. Kill me now please.

Mortified, I turn around to see Jax mimicking my ass shaking. "Oh no, please don't stop on my account. I was enjoying myself."

I don't think that I can blush a darker shade of red even if I tried. I realize that I have two choices here: I can be embarrassed and stop, or I can let go for once and have fun. I go for option two and hand Jax the other "microphone." Shania decides to come on next. *Man! I Feel Like a Woman* is the perfect song to let go! Putting my arms up in the air, I twirl around and start singing along with Shania.

When the first verse of the chorus blares through the speakers, I strut up to Jax, turn around and grind my ass up to his pelvis. Walking a few steps, I shake my ass, bend over and touch my toes. I tilt my head to the side and wink at him. When his jaw hits the floor, I laugh. Men are so easy. Closing my eyes again, I let the music wash over me and give Jax the best floor show in the world. Of course I may be biased.

PJ Simas comes on next and to my surprise Jax lifts the water bottle I handed him and starts rapping to the song *Ocean Drop*. I double over in laughter because I have a Greek God in a suit rapping in my living room. Jax "drops it like it's hot" and I can't even breathe, I'm laughing so hard.

He holds out his water bottle for me when the girl starts singing. Smiling, I scream along. Singing is so overrated.

By the time our duet is over, I have tears in my eyes. Being the showman, Jax bows dramatically and I applaud him. Who wouldn't applaud him? He rapped the entire song, not missing any of the words.

"I can't even hide the fact that I'm surprised you know that song," I shout over Dirty South.

Jax saunters over to the speakers to unplug my phone. "Yeah, well same here. I can't believe I walked into that."

"Tell anyone and I'll be forced to feed you your balls," I say with a wink.

"By anyone you mean Connor?"

"Of course!"

"Don't worry, your dancing fetish is safe with me." I smack his arm. "You do realize they came out with this thing called Bluetooth Speakers, right?"

"You do realize that I'm going to have to hurt you if you dis my stereo system, right?" I counter.

"Touche."

Collapsing onto the couch we both lay here for a few minutes and catch our breaths. My abs will ache tomorrow. I can't remember the last time I laughed this hard. Without bothering to get plates, we dig into our sandwiches. We eat in silence, enjoying the food too much to talk. After I eat my sandwich and steal the other half of Jax's, I'm finally full.

"My lunch was thrown on the floor," I remind him.

"By thrown you mean you dropped it, right?"

"So Logan's surprise party," I say in a obvious way to change the subject.

We decide that we're going to rent out Logan's favorite restaurant and have his party the weekend of his birthday on July 12. Connor will take Logan out all day so that Jax and I can make sure everything is set up perfectly since I don't see the need to hire someone to do something that we are more than capable of doing. Jax, of course, objects but I don't care. This is my brother's birthday and I want to do everything. Jax doesn't have to try too hard to talk me into making Logan's favorite cake from one of my mom's recipes for us four and then a bigger one for the party. I'll use any excuse to bake.

This year the "after party" will be at Connor's which is perfect since Connor's place is closest to the bakery. Every year for anyone's birthday we always celebrate an "after party" of just the four of us. Of course mine is the only exception to the rule since I refuse to celebrate my mine.

A knock on the door causes us to look in the direction of the hallway.

"Are you expecting someone?" he asks with a hint of unease in his voice.

I shake my head and before I can get up, Jax strides down the hallway. He beats me to the door. I just *love* how he makes himself at home and feels the need to answer my door. I give him a mock glare that he ignores. He's squeezing the life out of my poor door. Confused I focus my gaze away from Jax and to the delivery man.

There are a million and one things that the delivery man could have brought up. The vase in his hands does not fit into the million and one category . . . at all. I gape at the flowers, unable to move, let alone breathe. My head spins. I'm getting lightheaded just standing here.

Who would be so cruel to send me Stargazer Lilies? I ignore the delivery guy as every memory I try to repress comes crashing down.

Hadley twirls around in our dance studio while our mom plays the piano . . . Hadley spins in her favorite yellow dress with the biggest smile on her face . . . Hadley's first recital . . . Everyone in our family giving her Stargazer Lilies . . . Hadley . . .

Hadley sprawled lifeless on the stretcher while the paramedics try to bring her back . . . Stargazer Lilies engraved on her headstone . . . All because of me.

Blinking back tears that threaten to spill over, I notice that I'm no longer standing in the doorway but sitting on the couch with a worried Jax crouched in front of me. I can't believe I just lost it in front of Jax. Again! I must have blacked out because, for the life of me, I can't remember how I got to the couch.

Great, now Jax is going to realize how crazy I actually am. Crap, Logan! If Jax called my brother and told him what happened, Logan should be bursting through my door any minute now. So not what I need!

"Ads, it's okay. You're here, you're fine. Just breathe for me, baby," Jax says in a calming voice I have only heard from him once. The funeral. The memories start to come back, but I fight them off. I won't lose it in front of Jax. Not again.

Watching him closely, I mimic Jax's breathing because I'm unable to perform the most basic task in the world.

"Sorry." I have to clear my dry throat so that I can talk above a pained whisper. "Sorry, Jax, you didn't need to see that." Much better. I almost have full strength in my vocal cords again. "I'm fine, I promise. I just wasn't expecting to see those . . . st-star . . . flowers." I choke up. I can't even say the name of the stupid flowers.

"Shut up," Jax says calmly but with an edge still to his voice.

Startled by his outburst, my head snaps up to see Jax steaming.

Venom drips from my voice. "Excuse me?" I can't believe he just told me to shut up.

"You heard me, Ads, I said shut up." Before I even have a chance to open my mouth, Jax drags me off the couch and pulls me on top of his lap. "I don't need to hear any explanations. I know why you just completely shut down on me, I get it. So stop. If you open that sexy mouth of yours, it better not be to explain or to apologize, do you understand?"

I can only nod because I'm shocked that Jax knows why I broke down and gets it. Not that I should be surprised, Jax knows a lot more then he lets on. Right when I start to lean into his embrace, I shove his arms away and stand up.

"Thanks, Jax, but I need to be alone right now." I hastily retreat to my room and I hear a faint, "Shit," from Jax. I slam my door, hoping that he takes the hint and leaves.

Sinking to the floor, I try to shut it all off. I can't believe I was stupid enough to think that I could change, that I could be me again. That I was dancing around my apartment without a care in the world, as if I hadn't killed my family. I can't do this, I need to shut it off. It hurts too much.

I rise and make my way to my closet until a crippling pain from the guilt brings me to my knees. The memories start flooding back full-force. I can hear Hadley's laughter as if she's sitting right next to me. God, I can't do this. I need to get out of here, away from Jax, away from everything.

Forcing my legs to cooperate, I open my walk-in closet. After blindly changing into the first work-out clothes my hands touch, I'm out the door. I jump from foot-to-foot as I put my socks on while walking. Not an easy task for someone like me. I snatch up Logan's Columbia sweater I stole from him and then my Nikes that are still by the front door where I left them. I'm about to leave, but then I remember my phone is still in the living room. Ugh!

I'm relieved when I find my living room empty. I collect my phone from the coffee table and slide it into my armband. Before I can even leave the living room, Jax blocks my path. Great. I study my bright pink Nikes because I can't face him right now. Why couldn't he just leave? Was me telling him I need to be alone not a big enough hint?

"Where do you think you're going, Ads? You can't just go out and run right now in your condition."

It would have been better for Jax to slap me across my face. Anything would have been better than saying "my condition" as if I have some contagious disease.

I'm no longer staring intently at the floor. I'm glaring at Jax. "MY CONDITION? WHAT CONDITION WOULD THAT BE EXACTLY, JAX?" I yell. Taking a deep breath, I try to calm down. I'm anything but calm as I say, "I am going for a run. I can't be here right now, Jax." I shove past him towards my escape.

Jax follows, closing on my heels to the door. This would have been so much easier if he just left.

Turning around, I whisper, "Please don't tell Logan." I leave without another word.

As I wait for the elevators to escape to Central Park, I try desperately to forget Jax's expression. I wish that I was strong enough to turn around and reassure him that I'm okay, but I'm not. Instead I step into the elevator, and as the doors close, I feel like I'm making a mistake, but I can't go back in there. I can't face Jax right now even though everything in me is telling me that I need to be with him.

I'm so distracted that I don't even realize that I'm not alone until I see movement to my left. I ignore the person behind me and concentrate on the emptiness inside of me.

"Well, this is a pleasant surprise. How are you Adalynn?" a deep husky voice asks, startling me. I know who that voice belongs to.

Putting my mask perfectly into place, I swing around toward Kohen. "Hey, I'm doing great!" Too cheerful, I need to take it down a notch or it will be obvious that I'm anything but great. "How are you?" God, I couldn't be more awkward if I tried.

The doors open before Kohen has a chance to respond and like the socially inept person that I am, I flee without saying anything else. It's better for him if he thinks I'm strange, then any interest he has in me will disappear. I don't need to start anything with Kohen, well anyone for that matter, especially Jax. I deserve to be alone. I like it. I need to continue with the life I made for myself. I learned a long time ago that I can't trust myself, let alone anyone else. Nobody would want the real me anyways.

I almost reach the doorman when Kohen comes running up to me. *Just keep walking. Ignore him.*

"Want some company while you run? I'm the perfect workout buddy."

Why can't everyone just leave me alone?

"I actually prefer to run by myself," I answer in a bored tone. Finishing my bitch act, I pat his shoulder while I patronizingly say, "But, hey, no hard feelings, you can try that line with the next chick you see." I turn and walk away. "Thanks for the offer," I toss over my shoulder before leaving the building.

I head across the street to Central Park with the heaviness of despair coursing through my veins. Later on, when I'm back to myself, I know I'll feel guilty. I make a mental note to apologize to Kohen the next time I see him, which should be easy considering we live in the same building.

I slide my phone out of my armband and I click on Marilyn Manson's *Sweet Dreams*, before putting it back. As the music blares I wonder what sick fuck sent me those flowers. It couldn't be any of the guys. They know better than that. So if not them, then who? I turn the music up and I finally get the chance to do what I've wanted since the flowers arrived at my place . . . escape.

CHAPTER FIVE

On my third mile through Central Park I slowly allow the memories to roll in. Whenever I let the memories come back it reminds me of the person I once was, everything that I lost, and why I don't deserve happiness. This is why I continue to put myself through this unimaginable pain, so that I can never forget, so that I can never be happy. I don't deserve to be happy.

There is only one memory that I can never relive . . . the day I lost everything. Whenever that memory comes barreling through, it feels like I'm in the ocean with the waves crashing down on top of me, the surface always out of reach. I pant, on the brink of collapsing into despair.

I stop running and use all of my energy to push that memory away. I can taste metallic even though I haven't cut my mouth . . . the memory is that strong. *Breathe in . . . out.* Bending at the knees, I take slow calming breaths. When the white spots fade from my vision, I run again. The surroundings of Central Park change from pavement to grass; soon it's as if I'm seeing my old backyard with the swing, and the Olympic-size pool my parents had built for my tenth birthday, to a memory that I've repressed for far too long, tugging at my consciousness, reminding me of time I thought was lost . . . a happy time with Hadley.

"What's wrong, Hads?" I ask my frowning baby sister.

With fresh tears in her eyes she mumbles, "I can't come to your birthday party."

"Why not?" I sit down beside Hadley on her bed. I nudge her with my shoulder when she doesn't answer. "Come on, you can tell me anything."

"Promise you won't laugh?" She hiccups.

"Promise."

She twirls her thumbs. "Everyone is going to make fun of me because I can't swim."

A laugh escapes before I can stop it. "Sorry," I say when she glares at me. "Nobody would dare laugh at you, Hads." Even though I know she's lying, I still tell her to put her suit on.

"No!"

God, even at six she's stubborn. "Come on Hads. We have two hours before anyone gets here. That's more than enough time."

"Enough time for what?" she asks cautiously.

"For me to teach you how to swim, obviously!"

She's jumping off her bed and racing towards her dresser before I can even finish my sentence.

"You really mean it?" she asks as she starts to put on her bikini.

"I can't have my favorite person not at my party." Her smile is breathtaking. She's going to be a heartbreaker when she's older. I actually feel bad for all of the boys.

"Really?"

"Of course."

Within an hour, Hadley is swimming better than Ariel the mermaid. I know that swimming wasn't really an issue since I've been working with her on her skills all summer. She was worried that I was going to ignore her; all she needed was some one-on-one time with me.

"Ready for the party?" I ask when it's obvious that she doesn't need help at all.

"Can we swim some more before everyone gets here?" Hadley ask as she paddles away from me.

"Of course!" Logan yells before jumping off the diving board to join us.

Dad takes a picture of the three of us in the water. When he sets down his camera, I get a brilliant idea. And by brilliant, I mean hilarious.

"Dad can you look at my finger? I think I have a splinter."

"From swimming? Doubtful," Logan says. I wink at him and he catches on immediately.

Logan climbs out of the pool as our dad comes closer to the pool to inspect my finger. Logan circles behind our father. When Dad gets to the edge of the pool, I kick off the wall in perfect timing with Logan.

"Andy!" our mom shouts from the doorway as Logan pushes our dad in. We're all laughing when our dad surfaces.

By my fifth mile, I force myself to turn around. Swimming used to be the most important part of my life. At age ten, I knew that I was destined to be a swimmer. There's some days where the pull to be in the water again is so fierce that I find myself itching to smell the chlorine-filled room, but I'm never able to open the door. I haven't allowed myself to touch the water, even with my toes, ever since I tried to kill myself five years ago.

Finally reaching my apartment building, I force all of the memories away. I need to face the mess I left up there and hopefully Jax won't think I'm a total lunatic. As I press the elevator button, I find myself questioning my sanity and Liv's. Maybe she's as crazy as I am for thinking I can move on with my life. I can't even receive Stargazer Lilies without a meltdown. Maybe with time I can prove her right, or I'll just prove my new theory of us both being out of our minds.

I'm surprised to find Jax pacing my living room. The second he notices me, he rushes to me. Right when I'm about to open my mouth to ask him why he's still here, I realize that I smell . . . bad. Holy B.O. I need a shower, quick, if I'm going to be around him.

"I need to jump in the shower . . ." I hesitate. I want to ask him to stay, but I don't have the right to ask.

"I'll be here when you get out," Jax says, reading my mind like always.

I return his smile before making a quick dash to my bathroom with the single thought of my Midnight Pomegranate body wash from Bath & Body Works. I smell so ripe there could be a rotting corpse in my apartment and you couldn't tell the difference. Okay, maybe not that bad, but close enough.

I turn the shower all the way to hot before slipping off my Nikes. It isn't until my drenched workout clothes are on the bathroom floor that I notice my swollen ankle. Because my mind was absorbed in my memories, I didn't even realize my ankle was hurting while I was running. It's not the first time this has happened either and I know it won't be the last.

Stepping into the steaming shower I welcome the pain from the scalding water and my throbbing ankle. The water burns my skin, turning it a nice shade of red, to the point that I want to yelp, but I hold it in. Instead I force my muscles to relax, enjoying the pain the hot water brings. It's easier to deal with the physical pain right now than the emotional pain from my memories.

No, I'm not that girl anymore! Disgusted with myself and my thoughts, I quickly adjust the water to a much more normal temperature. I tilt my head back and let the water stream down my back while rubbing my hands through my long hair. I lather shampoo and right as I start to lean into the water again, there's a knock on the door. I could bang my head against the wall right now. I pretend that I don't hear him come into the bathroom and continue to shower like he isn't here. I'm not ready to face him, let alone talk to him yet. *What are the chances that he will just go away? Not big.*

Once the shampoo is washed out, I squeeze conditioner into my hand and massage it into my scalp. The shower is made of glass, I know he can see me even with all the steam. I'm tempted to ask him to make me forget about everything, but instead I remain silent.

"I got you a cupcake so hurry up or it might be missing by the time you get out." With that, the bathroom door swings open and he leaves before I can ask him if he knows who sent the flowers.

I rush through the rest of my shower, not because of the cupcake, but because I know it's time to face Jax. The cupcake is a bonus, of course. I dress in leggings, a cami, and my favorite rose colored sweater of my mom's. Lifting the soft material to my nose, I inhale deeply. I can almost smell the fresh floral scent my mom always smelled like. For a split second I pretend that she's here with me and not in a box six-feet under. I'm happy, then the second is gone and I'm back to reality.

Jax is back to pacing my living room again. I clear my throat, ready to explain myself, but Jax's utterly lost expression stops me. He takes two long strides and then suddenly I'm in his arms. He hugs me tightly. I struggle against his hold; I can't handle the way he always makes me feel like we have more than friendship. It's not fair that it can never happen. I keep struggling a pointless battle against his iron-like grip.

Very slowly, about the speed that ice melts off of glaciers, I fall lax into Jax. He never loosens his hold on me; if anything it gets tighter the more I relax into him. He rubs my back in a soothing manner. When I finally mold to him, he picks me up and sits on my couch. He drapes my legs over him in a way that has me practically sitting in his lap.

A few minutes go by in a comfortable silence before I murmur, "I'm sorry Jax. I lost it when I saw those stupid flowers and I just—"

Jax's large hand covers my mouth.

"I already told you not to apologize. YOU. DID. NOTHING. WRONG." Sighing Jax runs a hand through his hair. Collecting himself, he says in a much calmer voice, "I get it more than you can possibly understand, Ads. I know who Stargazer Lilies remind you of. I know all of this is too much for you on most days . . . but being blindsided with something like Had's flowers . . ." His voice trails off as he gets a distant look in his eyes. I know that look, he's remembering something. I wonder if he's picturing me setting the flowers onto her grave.

"I didn't throw them away. They're in your room . . . where they belong." He continues to say something to me, but I don't hear him. I'm somewhere else.

"Stay with me, Ads. I'm here. Talk to me," Jax begs quietly before pressing his lips to mine. All of my senses come to life, everything disappears but Jax. He brings me back before I'm gone.

"Thank you," I mumble against his lips. Jax winks. My face heats up. "Not for that. You're always here for me. So thanks, Jax, for knowing what I need more than I do." I kiss his cheek. "Thank you for not throwing them away like I would have done," I whisper into his ear.

Jax holds my hand in his. "I'll always be here for you, Ads."

"I know," I agree because I don't doubt him. Whenever I needed him most, Jax has always been here. I couldn't imagine my life without him in it.

"Did you know when Hadley was two, that's when she first fell in love with Stargazer Lilies?" I ask even though I already know the answer.

"She would always go to such lengths to get her way."

"That's putting it mildly." I surprise us both by jumping off the couch. "I'll be right back."

"Take your time." Jax knows exactly what I'm going to do.

I need to see the flowers that remind me of my dead baby sister. I need to do this. Each step closer to my bedroom, brings me closer to everything I chose to forget. When I finally reach my doorknob, my breathing is rapid. I wish my brother was here. I don't think I can do this by myself. I'm not strong enough. I can't move. My knuckles whiten as I firmly squeeze the doorknob.

Jax comes up behind me, his hand covers mine. "You ready?"

He didn't leave me. "Yes," I say with a shaky breath.

Together we open the door. Jax holds my hand again. The warmth from his fingers helps center me. As usual, Jax is right. Hadley wouldn't want me to act like her favorite flowers are a bomb ready to explode. No matter how painful this is, I need to do this. *I can do this.* I chant in my head.

My gaze instantly goes to the flowers sitting on my nightstand. I have no idea how I missed them when I took a shower. I feel them pulling me toward them. Jax doesn't let go of my hand while we approach my nightstand.

The pink petals are vibrant against the white backdrop of the walls of my bedroom. Some of them haven't fully bloomed yet. Hadley's favorite thing, she would love to watch them grow, to open up. She thought it was magical. The way she view the world was extraordinary. She saw the beauty in everything.

I rub the yellow tentacles in the center of the bulbs, dyeing my finger tips yellow. It's exactly what Hads would do, just to one of them. Their powerful scent already fills my room with their fragrance. I used to hate that, I always thought these were the type of flowers that needed to be outside. Now it's as if I have a piece of my little sister back, I don't want to part without them, without Hadley.

"I'm so proud of you, Ads," Jax says, breaking the silence.

Without taking my gaze off them, I attempt to lighten the mood. "Now that you got your way and pretty much forced me to face my fears, you can go now. I know you need to get up early for your meeting, and besides, I'm getting kinda sick of seeing your ugly face."

"Ugly? Me? Come on, Ads, we both know I'm the hottest man on the planet. I have women falling all over themselves just to catch a glimpse of me."

I try to hold a straight face, but I can't. "You're impossible."

"Ah, but I got you to smile."

"When are you leaving again?" I quip.

Jax takes my face into his hands. "How are you doing?"

"Better than I thought," I say truthfully.

"I really don't want to—"

"Jax, I'm a big girl. I actually don't need you to look after me all of the time."

"If I don't, who will?"

"Go home already," I say, ignoring his question.

Walking Jax to the front door, I have the sudden urge to keep him here. I don't want him to leave, I don't want to be alone. I quickly throw away that thought. I don't need to spend anymore one-on-one time with him, it just confuses me.

"Bye, Ads."

I don't say anything to him as the door closes because I'm afraid that I'll ask him to stay. Definitely not something that needs to come out of my mouth.

The next day, I wake up and smile when I turn over to see the beautiful Stargazer Lilies on my nightstand. It feels amazing to smile at something that used to bring delight to Hadley without getting stuck in the past. For the first time, I realize there's a note attached to the flowers. I'm not even a little surprised that I missed it yesterday. Anticipation killing me, I lean over and grab it.

It's been 3 weeks & I still can't stop thinking about you. If you feel the same, let's see where this can go.

-K. D.

He sent me the flowers. Wow, I never would have guessed that. God, I'm such a bitch! I wonder if I should call him to apologize for yesterday, but decide against it. I don't want to give him the wrong idea. I'm not interested and it's better for him to learn that now then think he has a chance. Even if Jax wasn't in the picture —well he's not technically— I still wouldn't give him a chance. Sure, I'm attracted to him, what woman wouldn't be? But it doesn't change anything. My heart will forever belong to Jaxon Chandler.

I get up and take a quick shower. Taking advantage of the perfect weather, I choose one of my favorite sundresses with a cutout heart on the back and my beige Steve Madden's to complete the look. I curl a few pieces of my naturally curly hair, apply mascara, add a light coat of rose color lipstick, and I'm ready to go. After retrieving my phone off the nightstand, I pick up Kohen's note and slip it into my purse.

Deciding to skip breakfast and buy a smoothie, I'm almost ready to leave when I spot the camera bag Jax bought me. Without over-thinking it, I quickly grab it and walk out the door.

Smoothie in hand, I browse at a few stores to buy supplies for Logan's surprise party. Two hours later, I have everything that Jax and I will need, and much more. I'd rather be overly prepared than realize too late that we're missing something. I want the party to be perfect for Logan. He deserves it.

After a cab ride back to my place, I drop off the bags in the living room and close the door. I'll put everything away later, it's too nice of a day out to be stuck inside. Looking to kill an hour until I meet the boys, I head over to Central Park with my camera bag still in hand.

Cedar Hill is my all-time favorite place in New York. I always come here when I feel like the world is crumbling down on me, so it's the perfect place for today, even though I doubt I'll be able to take any pictures. I play with the zipper and remember the first time my dad bought me a camera. He wanted me to try to get into something other than swimming. Apparently it's important to have more than one thing to love.

If only he could see me now.

With shaking hands, I reach in and grasp my new camera. I have so many mixed emotions right now. I want to remember how I've felt being behind the lens, how I share the same passion as my dad had, but I can't help feeling guilty.

The last time I ever held a camera was the last day I ever saw my family. If I take a picture, I won't be able to share it with my dad anymore. I don't know if I'm ready to move on with this chapter in my life yet. The day my dad took me to buy my first camera was one of my favorite times with him. He was able to see that I was missing a creative outlet, even if I didn't see it myself.

I'm afraid that if I pick up this camera, I won't feel the same, everything will be different, and I will lose what my dad gave me that day. I don't want to taint that memory with my demons.

Another fifteen minutes pass before I'm finally able to talk myself into capturing one simple picture. I can take one picture without ruining everything. I stand up and examine the area. I spot a butterfly landing on a flower a few yards away. Bringing the camera up to my face I focus on the scene before me. With a shaky breath, I press the button to forever imprison the image before me. As I view the digital photo, I feel a weight has lifted off my shoulders. I feel like I've just found a piece to my soul again.

Without realizing it, I start snapping away. I capture the scenery, a couple holding hands, and an older woman reading a book underneath a tree. I click until the memory card is full. As I put away the camera, my phone rings. Startled, I notice that two hours have flown by and I have several missed calls from Logan and Connor.

Crap, I'm so late. I jog towards the exit to catch a cab.

After sitting in traffic, I'm at the boys' office in Manhattan with our burgers. I promise the security guards that I'll bring them cupcakes from the bakery tomorrow before I swipe my ID to access the elevators.

Gloria, Connor's assistant, stops me from entering my brother's office. "Hi Addie, Mr. Evans informed me that you will be having lunch in his office today. Your brother will join you two shortly."

"Thanks Gloria. Have a great day!" I say before opening Connor's door.

Ignoring the fact that Connor is on the phone, I whisper, "Mr. Evans, your lunch has arrived."

Connor holds up his index finger, the universal sign for one minute. "Are you the boss or am I?"

I cringe, I know that tone. I feel bad for whoever is on the other line. Giving him a knowing look, I steal two waters for Connor and I, and a Gatorade for Logan from his fridge. Setting them down on his glass coffee table, I open up the bags. I place Connors burger and fries in front of him before drawing mine out of the bag.

"Exactly. So either do what I pay you for or I will find someone else to do your job." He eats a fry. "Last time I checked, it's not my problem. It's yours."

I shake my head and mouth "be nice" to him which he ignores.

"I expect a copy on my desk by the time I walk in tomorrow morning." He hangs up without waiting for a response.

"I'm so glad that you're basically my brother," I state as he joins me on the couch.

"Me too, if I wasn't, you wouldn't have a cool brother," Connor says with a mouth full of fries. "You know you would love to work for me."

I ignore his last comment. This isn't the first time he's suggested it.

"If you have to say you're 'cool,' you really aren't." Connor waves me off and digs into his burger. By dig in, I mean devour. He's done with his burger before I'm able to take more than three bites.

"Someone was hungry."

"I may have worked through breakfast," Connor says with a shrug.

I don't say anything back. There's no point reminding him that he has an assistant that can order him breakfast. We've had that talk so many times I'm tempted to record myself reminding him how important it is too eat just so I don't have to repeat the speech. Connor takes being a workaholic to a whole new level. He practically lives out of his office. He has a suite discreetly tucked away to the right of his desk that he uses regularly.

For some reason I think about the note from Kohen that is burning a hole through my purse. I want to get Connor's opinion on the Kohen thing before Logan comes in because I know my brother will make a big deal out of nothing. I open my mouth to bring it up, but quickly close it. I don't even know where to start, until now, I haven't been interested in anyone but Jax.

I thought I didn't want to see where things could go with Kohen, hence me being a complete bitch to him the other day, but after using the camera Jax bought me, I have a new urge to take Liv's advice. I need to live again. And it's not like Jax will be my boyfriend anytime soon. Maybe it's time to see what else is out there. I fiddle with the straps of my purse, coming up with a brilliant idea. If I have Connor, the man whore, help me, maybe Jax will find out. I wonder if he'll be grateful that I'm not lusting after him anymore or if he'll be jealous. I hope for the latter.

When I peek at Connor, he's already staring at me with his eyebrow raised. I reach into my purse and hand him the note. After reading it, he passes it back to me without saying a word. I swear, he constantly makes me want to give him a high-five in the face! Glaring at him I return the note to my purse.

"Really, you're not going to say anything?"

He leans back onto to the couch, and stretches his feet in front of him. "What would you like me to say, Addie?"

I could smack him right now. I'm tempted to just drop it and ask Logan. Who am I kidding, that's not an option and Connor knows it. He's my only option since there's no way I can ask Jax. Ha! I'd rather get my brother's advice. And Logan wouldn't give me any advice, he would lock me in a tower, away from the much older doctor.

Knowing he's just going to drag this out as long as possible, I spit out, "Well, do you think I should go out with him or not? You don't have to be a jerk about it and purposely mess with me."

Connor doesn't even have the decency to pretend to be apologetic. "If I don't mess with you, who will?"

"Can you help me out or what? I'm really confused, I'm kinda out of my element in case you didn't notice."

"Okay, okay, Addie relax. You caught me by surprise, I couldn't help it. I would have been less shocked if the note contained that address to where you hide dead bodies instead of someone asking you out . . . again."

"Body."

He frowns in confusion. "What?"

"You said 'bodies.' It would be body. As in one body. Yours."

"Ha ha ha Addie. But in all seriousness, if you're asking for my permission then, yes, you have it."

"Really?"

"Yes, Addie you don't need my permission or even Logan's. Don't you dare tell him I said that." I nod in total agreement. "The question isn't if you should go out with him, it's do you want to? Do you want to finally see who else is out there? Or do you want to continue to play head games with a certain tattooed man we know?"

"You know?"

"It's you and Jax," he says simply as if it's the most logical answer in the world. I raise my eyebrow, begging him silently to go on. He does. "Anyone with eyes knows."

I gulp. "Logan?"

He shakes his head. "I think Logan chooses not to see it because you're his little sister and Jax is his best friend. But when he does find out, make sure I'm there so I can restrain him." He laughs. I don't find the image of my brother and Jax fighting as amusing.

"When did you—" The question dies on my lips as Logan strides into Connor's office.

His eyes immediately find my camera bag on the floor next to Connor's desk. As Logan gives me a hug, I can see the questions forming in his head. I'm grateful that he doesn't voice any of them. As much as I want to tell my brother why I was late, I can't. I know he will make a big deal out of this and I'm not ready to acknowledge the significance of today. Not yet anyways.

When Logan is almost done with his burger he asks, "Do you want me to pick you up or just send a car tomorrow?" I give him the what-the-heck look. "The Annual Masquerade Ball we always put on, to raise money for rare diseases, it's tomorrow. The same ball I've reminded you about at *least* once a week for a month now. The same ball that I knew you would forget about, like you do every year." He mocks exasperation.

How do I forget about this every year? It's mind-boggling that my brother hasn't strangled me yet.

I scrunch up my nose. "I didn't need you to explain yourself, dear brother. I'm irritated that you assumed I forgot again. How could I with you reminding me all of the time?" I think I'm convincing enough, but just to make sure I add, "Oh and not to make a big deal or anything but I already have my dress, shoes, and a mask." I throw up my hands. "But no big deal or anything."

As I talk, I realize how much I have to do in such little time.

Logan grunts at my antics. "I won't even pretend that I'm not surprised, Addie. I thought for sure you forgot like you do every year." Shaking his head, he addresses Connor. "Well shit, I guess Jax won the bet after all."

Connor groans as he explains, "Our dear brother here has been making a big deal about how you would forget yet again. So Jax, of course, bet Logan a small sum that you wouldn't forget. He kept going on and on about how you actually would have your dress and everything by tonight. It was annoying how he was defending your honor and whatnot."

"What!" I say in mock outrage.

"I'm with your brother on this one, Addie. I can't believe you remembered. You have the worst, and I mean the worst memory when it comes to planned events." Connor ties his long shaggy blonde hair into a knot at the back of his head.

"Man, I kinda want to ditch the rest of the day. I do not want to run into that smug bastard," Logan tells Connor.

"Well, then I guess next time you won't bet against your sister!" I say.

I can't imagine how I can possibly get myself out of the hole I've dug myself into. There's no way I can find a dress last minute. Not for an event of this stature. The only option is for the earth to open up and swallow me whole. If I don't want to be so dramatic, I can always wear my dress from last year. They're men, they won't notice . . . I hope.

"Oh shut up. Like you would have bet any differently."

I don't have time to listen to them. I have a dress to find. I make an excuse to leave. After giving my brother a hug, I ask, "How much was the bet anyways?"

"I'll see you tomorrow night, Addie," Logan says, ignoring me, which only piques my interest.

As Connor gives me a hug he whispers, "Let me know when and where if you decide to take the hot doc up on his offer," into my ear so only I can hear.

Once I'm in the cab I quickly calculate that I have about six hours and tomorrow morning to find something. This is New York, I've totally got this. Will my plan work? Will Connor blab to Jax? Only one way to find out. With that thought, I find enough courage to stick to my game plan and text Kohen.

Me: Hey it's Adalynn. Sorry about yesterday, let me make it up to you . . . dinner on me?

I get a text back from him within seconds.

Kohen: One condition

Me: And that would be . . .

Kohen: Dinner's on me. How does eight sound?

I contemplate if that's enough time or not. Doubtful since I'll need to jump in a quick shower and reapply my makeup from spending the rest of the day shopping. I'll need at least an extra hour to make sure I'm presentable for the first date I've had in six years. I force myself to stop thinking about that and text Kohen back.

Me: Make it nine and you have yourself a deal ;)

Kohen: Great. See you tonight.

As the cab pulls up to the first store, I hold back a groan. I am in no mood to shop. I have a date to prepare for and I'm in desperate need of at least one bottle of wine to help my nerves. *I'll have more than enough time tomorrow before the ball.* With that settled, I close the door and tell the cab driver my address. He doesn't hold back his grunt of irritation. As he veers into traffic, I call Connor.

"Miss me alr—"

"So I have a date tonight at nine."

"HOLY SHIT!" Connor says so loudly I have to pull the phone away from my now sore eardrum.

"It's not that big of a deal. You were the one that told me I should take the hot doc up on his offer."

He lets out a breath. "Yeah, but I never thought you would. Holy shit," he says again but in a much more normal tone.

"Am I making a mistake?" I ask after a moment of silence.

Connor doesn't even hesitate. "Don't Addie, don't go there. Don't talk yourself out of this. Kohen is a great guy, granted I've only met him that one time but still. He even asked you out in front of all of us. He gets major points for that."

My face heats up at the mere mention of how Kohen asked me out in the emergency room hallway. "I'm not talking myself out of it."

"Tell your bullshit to someone who believes it. You're going on this date and you're going to have fun, even if I have to drag you there myself."

"Well, okay, then, I guess I'm going. Twist my arm, why don't you."

Connor laughs. "Seriously, though, I think this is a great idea and I don't think you could find someone better than the doc. Obviously I'm taking myself out of the equation because that just wouldn't be fair."

"Obviously," I say dryly.

"What about Jax?"

"What about him?" I ask.

"So you're going with avoidance? Let me know how that works out for you."

"Connor . . ." My voice dies off. I have no idea what to say to that.

The driver idle at the curb of my building. Connor breaks the silence. "Look, I've got to go, but let me know where you're going, and if you need another pep talk, I'm just a phone call away."

"This was a pep talk?"

"Yes and you're welcome. Gotta go. Love you, sis."

"Love you, too."

Even though he's more annoying than not, I still love him with all my heart. All jokes aside, he's serious when he needs to be and can always make me smile even when I'd rather not.

Hours later, I find myself standing in the mirror, not really remembering how I was able to get ready, but somehow I did. There's no evidence that I'm nervous; it's shocking how I'm able to mask my emotions so well and show the world what I want them to see. I want to pretend like this isn't a big deal, even if I'm freaking out inside.

The woman staring back at me is beautiful. There's a fire in her violet eyes. Her long brown hair cascades down her back in curls, and she's wearing a simple creme top, paired with designer black skinny jeans, and red booties. She seems perfect, she's me, but I'm anything but perfect. Is this how Kohen is going to view me? Perfect, my life in order, happy? Do I want him to see the real me?

No, I don't. I'm nowhere near ready for that and I doubt I'll ever be. This is a first date, a date to see if it gets under Jax's skin, nothing more. I don't see how Kohen and I will have anything in common. He's older, put together, and smart. The more I think about it, the more intimidated I feel.

Maybe it's not too late to cancel.

CHAPTER SIX

I pick up my phone to cancel for the hundredth time tonight. I even get as far as pulling up our text thread before locking it. Each and every time I do this, I remember how alive I felt being behind the camera lens. That's the only reason why I don't go through with any of the excuses I keep making. If I'm able to do that, then I can go on a date with a decent guy. Hopefully Connor can help with the nerves.

Me: I'm going to throw up

Connor: Don't be dramatic. YOU ARE GOING so don't even try to back down

I'm about to reply when there's a knock on the door. My whole body stiffens.

Me: Crap he's here. What do I do?

Connor: Just a guess but I would say . . . open the door.

Connor: Breathe. Relax. Have fun. In that order.

Doing as Connor says, I take several deep breaths and will myself to relax. After another minute of trying to calm down and failing, I trudge to the door. My fake persona is firmly in place as I swing it open.

Kohen holds the most exquisite bouquet of ranunculus I've ever seen. Not knowing what to do, I stare at him, wondering not for the first time why a guy like him could possibly want to go out with me.

Kohen clears his throat and extends the flowers. "These are for you."

Nervously, I take them. "Thanks, they're beautiful. They're actually one of my favorite flowers. I like quite a few kinds." I force my mouth shut to keep from rambling.

I wave Kohen inside so that I can get a vase for them. He follows silently behind me into the kitchen and watches my every movement.

"I know," he says once I'm finished arranging the flowers.

"Huh?" I ask, confused.

"I knew they were your favorite flowers," he says with an easy smile.

"Should I be worried that I have a stalker?" I ask with a laugh. I'm slightly serious.

"Ha hardly. You just seem like a ranunculus type of girl." He shrugs. "Lucky guess."

He moves to stand in front of me. "You look beautiful, Adalynn. I don't think that I could ever get bored looking at you." Without warning, he gives me a lingering kiss on the cheek.

The elevator ride down is filled with awkward silence. I can't stop myself from stealing glances at Kohen. I chew my lip, a nervous habit of mine. This is the first time I'm alone with a man besides one of the guys in six years. Okay, not exactly if I count the gym incident. Why did I agree to this date in the first place? Oh that's right, because I'm a child and want to make Jax jealous instead of acting like an adult and confronting him. So now I'm on a date with someone that I don't really have any interest in. Points to my stupidity.

The elevator doors slide open, distracting me from telling him I can't do this. He rests his hand on my lower back while he leads me out of the elevator and into the parking garage. He steers me towards his BMW. Like a true gentlemen, he holds his door open for me.

I wait for him to speak, but when he doesn't I snag his iPhone. "May I?" Before he has a chance to answer, I start going through his music. I can always tell a lot about a person by their music choices.

Kohen is a good sport. "Sure . . . oh and I hope you like pizza, I know this amazing place called Frank's, it's to—"

"Die for," I finish for him.

"You've been there?"

I place my hand over my heart. "I LOVE Frank's. I have to have at least a dose of the yummy goodness once a month."

Kohen shows his dimples. "I'm glad I can help."

"You're two for two." I can see that he's about to ask what I'm talking about so I elaborate. "With my favorites. Two for two."

Kohen chuckles, but it seems a little strained. "The first one was a lucky guess on my part."

"And this one?"

He surprises me by clasping my hand. "We both have excellent taste." The way he says it makes me think he isn't talking just about our pizza preferences.

I pick a Journey song before I reach for my phone with my free hand and text Connor. My fingers hover over the keys. I want to defy him and prove that he doesn't need to know where I'm going. I can protect myself. Besides, Kohen doesn't seem like the serial killer type. I give in only because if I don't tell Connor where we're going, he will tell my brother, and I do not need Logan finding out about this, only Jax.

Me: Eating pizza.

Connor: Where?

Me: At the only place that I eat pizza.

Without waiting for a reply, I slide my phone back into my clutch. The rest of the short drive, we listen to music. I'm surprised that Kohen's music is an almost identical copy of my iTunes.

"We have a lot in common," I tell him as he opens my door.

"Oh?"

"Well, besides both of our excellent choices in pizza parlors, we like the same music . . . give or take a few bands."

"Really?" he asks.

"I know, I was shocked too. I thought I was going to have to give you a lesson in music."

Kohen laughs. "Do that a lot?"

I'm not even surprised when the hostess addresses both of us by our first names. It's obvious that Kohen is as much as a regular as I am. I search my memory, but I come up with a blank. I don't remember seeing him here.

"I did, but now my brother and his friends have graduated from my class so I don't need to give them lessons anymore," I say once we sit down.

"I'm guessing they just added a playlist for you on their phones."

I bite my lip to keep from grinning but fail. "Of course."

We both laugh. I'm pleasantly surprised how easily conversation flows between us. I'm glad that the first date I decided to go on in six years is with Kohen. I think if I went out with anyone else, it would have been beyond awkward. It helps that we have a lot in common, but I doubt it would really matter since Kohen is so easy to talk to.

I'm working on my second slice of pizza when for some reason my skin breaks out in goosebumps. My eyes find their way to the door. I gasp loudly when I see who walks in.

Logan, followed by Connor, and lastly Jax.

I'm somehow able to swallow the bite I just took without choking to death. I glare at the guys as they approach our table. Terrific. Kohen pauses mid-sentences when he realizes we have company.

"I'm sorry," I whisper as the boys stop at our table.

I can't tell if I want to die from embarrassment or kill Connor for telling Logan and Jax. Both will be perfect. I should have gone with my gut and not told him where I was going.

Connor puts on a lame attempt to feign innocence. "Wow, crazy running into you two here."

"Yeah, we wouldn't have come if I'd known you were going out on a date." My brother shrugs. "Too bad you chose not to tell me. We could have avoided this awkwardness."

"Yeah, too bad," Jax says with so much sarcasm it's impossible to believe him.

Yup, kill me now. Kohen raises an eyebrow, but I ignore him to glare at three soon-to-be dead men. To my absolute horror, my brother and Connor both sit down on Kohen's side of our booth, blocking him in. I shake my head at Jax as I extend my legs on my side of the booth.

He shrugs before sitting down on my legs. I don't know if I'm more upset that they crashed my date or that Jax seems so blasé.

"Ow, get your fat butt off of me!" I say more angrily than I should. Jax doesn't even notice how upset I am.

"If you moved your legs, you wouldn't be getting squished."

Too many witnesses.

"Fine!" I shout.

Jax leans up so I can drop my feet back under the table where they belong. I want to breathe in relief that he's not touching me anymore, but I can't. I despise being this close to him and not being able to touch him. That weekend at my apartment comes to mind and I have to forcibly drink my wine to keep from reaching out to him. Probably not the best move on a date with someone else.

The waitress arrives with three more waters. "Can I get anything else for you three?"

"No," I say at the same time that Jax says, "Yes."

The poor waitress's eyes bounce back from me to Jax and back at me again.

"No, we're good, thanks though," I inform her.

As the waitress leaves, Jax gives me a smug grin. "Fine, have it your way." And before I can say anything, he picks up my wine glass. I yank it from him mid-sip, spilling wine on his tailored shirt.

"I don't even feel bad!" I say when he looks from the stain to me.

He glares at me and I glare right back. I will not be the one to back down first. Someone coughs not too discreetly, but we both ignore him. Jax raises his eyebrow, silently challenging me. It isn't until I hear Kohen clear his throat with obvious annoyance that I snap out of the trance Jax has put me under. When I turn my head, my brother is studying the three of us; Kohen, Jax, and me. I cast my eyes down to my plate.

"So help yourselves, there's more than enough to go around," Kohen says with forced indifference.

Ignoring the three men that have decided to stay and make this the date from hell, I look at Kohen. "So you were about to tell me why you chose to be a neurologist before we were rudely interrupted."

"How old are you?" Jax shifts in the booth. His hand grazes my thigh. It's only a whisper of a caress, but it's enough to ignite my entire body.

"Thirty-one come July."

Jax noticeably stiffens. "Don't you think you should date someone more your age?"

My brother's baby blues meet mine. I silently beg him to leave. I nod from the table to the door. Twice. Logan is either being obtuse or ignoring me.

"So, about that career choice . . ." I trail off uneasily.

Talk about awkward silence.

Kohen seems a little uncomfortable as he clears his throat. "Oh . . . right . . . eh . . . well, my mom died from a brain tumor when I was twelve so I think that's the reason why I chose neuro instead of a differently specialty." He fiddles with the Parmesan shaker. "I guess when I was little I thought that I could prevent what happened to my mom from happening to someone else and it just always stuck with me."

Wow, and I thought this date couldn't get any more awkward. Clearly the boys weren't expecting this either from the looks on their face. I have no idea what to say to that. I thought I was staying on an easy topic. Guess not.

Reaching over, I squeezes his hand. I see Jax's fist tighten from the corner of my eye, but I ignore it and focus solely on Kohen. "Your mom would be very proud of you."

He squeezes my hand back. "Thanks," he says quietly before taking a long drink from his wine.

The guys help themselves to pizza and Connor places an order for an extra one. He eats more than anyone I have ever met.

Connor clears his throat and faces Kohen. "From what I hear, you're a pretty decent neurologist, as in one of the best in the country. I'm positive you're able to prevent what happened to your mother from happening to someone else if it's in your power."

I stare at Connor, wondering how he knows this, but I quickly decide I'd rather not ask in front of Kohen. I have a sinking feeling it involves a certain P.I. that I know Logan is fond of. Instead I sit back and watch while Kohen gets the third degree from Logan, Connor, and Jax. I'll be surprised if Kohen wants to go out with me again.

Dinner is almost over and I'm beyond surprised that I haven't stabbed anyone yet. There were a couple close calls, though. It's still early, so who knows, someone will more than likely get stabbed, all because Connor couldn't keep his big mouth shut. I give Connor a little kick under the table, but my temper gets the best of me. I kick him harder than I expected. Too bad, I guess he'll learn to keep his mouth shut next time.

"Ow," Logan says as he bends to rub the shin that I thought was Connor's.

I don't even bother giving my brother an innocent smile. "I would say my foot slipped, but that would be a lie."

"I guess that will teach me not to crash your dates."

"Too bad you couldn't figure that out a lot sooner, you could have gone home without limping," I snap, hoping that he'll see how insane he is for crashing my date.

Then again, I don't really have anything to be upset about since I've been able to witness Jax's reaction firsthand. Maybe I should be thanking them? Never.

Suddenly Connor starts pushing Logan out of the booth. "Well, we'll take that as our sign to leave. I don't want to be bleeding by the end of the night."

I narrow my eyes at him, but follow Connor's lead and shove Jax out of my way. Luckily he is already getting up because I wouldn't have had any hope of moving him without his help. I wasn't joking when I said he had a fat butt. It's sexy as hell and rock hard but still, his muscles weigh too much.

Connor pulls me into his arms first. "You're going to pay for this," I threaten into his ear.

Connor turns away from my scowling face to see Logan and Jax saying goodbye to Kohen. "Sorry, but Jax was over when you texted me," he whispers.

"And what happened?" I whisper back.

He rubs his hand through his hair. "Because once he saw your name, he stole my phone and the next thing I know we're on our way here. Your brother came over just in time to tag along."

"You couldn't have stopped them?"

"Look, I'm sorry. I thought it would be better if I dragged Logan here with me so it wouldn't just be you two and Jax." He gives me his puppy dog pouting lips.

I hate how easily it is for me to sympathize for him. With his pouty lips and sad eyes it's hard to stay mad at Connor and he knows it. He uses this look every chance he gets. Each and every time I fall for it. Even when we were kids.

I nod so that he knows I'm no longer mad at him before hugging my brother. Jax steps back as I move over to him. I sit down, feeling more than awkward. He doesn't deserve a hug. He's the reason why I'm on what can only be described as the worst date in history.

"Really?" Jax asks with his arms open.

Who does he think he is? He's the one who just stepped back when I went to give him a hug and now he's demanding one?

I ignore him. "Bye," I say only to my brother and Connor.

Jax surprises me by sitting back down and telling Kohen, "Sorry for crashing your date. I had to make sure your intentions were good. I promise we won't crash the next one." I can't help but notice that there isn't an ounce of jealously seeping through his voice. Maybe I imagined the jealousy earlier? I mask my disappointment with a smile.

"Assuming there's a next one," I accidentally say out loud.

There's no point in pretending when there isn't a spark between us. Kohen was a fun distraction before the guys showed up, I'll give him that.

"Oh, there will be," Kohen says with a twinkle in his eyes.

Jax turns and gives me his full attention. "Are you ever going to forgive me?" he asks sweetly.

So sweetly I almost break. Key word . . . almost. Then I realize he's asking about more than just tonight. Maybe it's wishful thinking on my part, but I honestly believe he's asking if I'll ever forgive him for not stepping up. That's something I can't forgive. Instead of saying exactly that, I play along more for the benefit of everyone else.

"That depends . . . can you honestly tell me that you wouldn't do this again?"

He doesn't even seem a little guilty when he answers, "Nope."

Fixing my eyes solely on his, I abandon my mask so he can see I'm talking about more than tonight. "Then nope, sorry Jax, that's just something I can't forgive. Pretending just doesn't do it for me."

Connor attempts to break the tension bubbling between us. Too bad his joke is told to deaf ears. The only thing I can hear is my heart beating too rapidly. Something that happens quite often when I'm near The God.

Connor and Logan linger around our table, clearly ready to take off, but Jax doesn't notice. As much as I know giving into him will make Jax leave, I can't. I stand my guard. "How can I possibly forgive something that you don't even realize that you're doing?"

Jax stretches his arm and drapes it over my shoulder. I notice Kohen tense in my peripheral. "Stop speaking riddles and tell me what's wrong."

I want to scream in frustration. I want to scream that he's the problem. I want to shout that I love him. Instead I say, "Let's just pretend I said I forgive you so you'll leave me to my handsome date." I give Kohen the same sweet smile Jax gave me seconds ago.

"Ads—" He starts, but stops. I would give anything to know what he's thinking right now.

Jax pulls me into his side and kisses the top of my head. My entire body is on fire. All I want is Jax. Kohen tenses again so I pull away. So not cool to have another guy kiss me even if it's as innocent as Jax kissing the top of my head. Which if I'm being honest with myself, I wish the kiss was anything but innocent.

"Bye Jax," I say breathlessly.

Looking directly at Kohen he says, "Bye Ads. See you tomorrow night."

I rub the bridge of my nose. Only Jax would act like an ass when he crashes my date. Games. That's all this is to him. Since the beginning, all I've ever been is a game to him. I finally go out on a date and he crashes it just because he can. Jax believes he can do whatever he pleases. I wish I could tell myself that I'm done with him and his games, but that would be the biggest lie. I doubt I'll ever give up hope on us.

"Ignore him," I tell Kohen once they leave.

"Well tonight didn't go as I expected."

I force out a laugh, understatement of the year.

"It was still amazing though," Kohen goes on. "I can't wait to take you out again, Ads."

"Adalynn," I say automatically.

"I'm sorry, I just thought since Jax called you Ads and your brother and Connor call you Addie that you prefer a nickname."

Why couldn't I just keep my mouth shut? "Sorry it's just . . . just something that only Jax can call me." So not true, but I don't want to dwell on the fact that the only other person who can call me Ads is dead.

Kohen studies the dessert menu. "It's okay, Adalynn," he says quietly.

He sounds as if I wounded him. I can't even pretend to care. Ads is off-limits to everyone, that will never change. It's better for him to accept this now.

"I'm sorry, it's something I can't really explain. You can call me whatever you want, just not Ads."

"And will you ever tell me why? If not, it's okay."

For some unknown reason, I tell him as much of the truth as I can. "There's stuff about me that you don't know, things that are too heavy for a first date."

"Heavier than my mom?"

I can only nod.

"Okay, so Ads is off the table. Don't worry I'll think of a nickname for you that only I can use."

"I would like that." I lie because I have no idea what to say.

The waitress surprises Kohen by informing us that the check has already been paid. I would have been surprised if Logan didn't pay it, he can't help himself. Kohen's jaw tightens and his gaze becomes hard for a second before he relaxes and is back to the sweet man he was a second ago. I ignore that he's bothered by my brother paying for our meal. I shake my head. Men. No wonder why us women are the superior sex.

When we get back into the car, the wine kicks in and I'm struggling to keep my eyes open. About a block away from the restaurant, Kohen reaches over and start to run his fingers over my hand.

Suddenly Kohen is taking my off seatbelt. I realize that we're back in the parking garage. Crap, I slept the entire ride home, I'm the world's worst date.

"Sorry I didn't realize that I was so tired," I say as Kohen helps me out of the car.

He brushes the hair from my face and gives me a quick peck on the lips. "There, all better."

All I can do is stare wide-eyed at him. I can't believe he just kissed me. I touch my still, tingling lips. I've only ever had Jax's lips on mine. I feel as if I betrayed what we had somehow. I follow Kohen to the elevator banks on the ground floor of the parking lot. When it arrives, he holds his hand in front of the doors and lets me go in first. He presses the button for my floor.

Not wanting to do the awkward goodbye at my door, I stand on my tiptoes, and kiss him on the cheek. "Thanks for tonight," I whisper into his ear before walking out of the elevator and down the hallway to my apartment.

I unlock my door and throw my clutch at the wall. Tonight didn't go as planned. At least Liv will be happy. She'll be thrilled with all the changes in my life: the camera, the date, sticking up for myself. That's something, I guess. I wish I could at least fake happiness, but my mood is anything but happy. I feel more disappointed with tonight's events. I was sure Jax would be raging in jealousy. I need to stop expecting too much from him.

I stumble to my bedroom. Too exhausted to wash my face, I strip out of my clothes and crawl into bed naked. Curled up in bed, I think about everything that Kohen said to me. I know it must have taken a lot to open up about his mom, especially in front of the boys. The trust that he has given me tonight makes me want to throw up.

I used him to make someone jealous and he's genuinely interested in me. I have to be the worst person in the history of the world.

CHAPTER SEVEN

I wipe my sweaty forehead before I toss the paper towel in the trashcan. The rich fragrance of sweets fill the hot air. I love the back room, well except for tonight, as the air-conditioner stopped working an hour ago. Thank goodness it was close to closing, or customers would not have wanted to eat their treats here on this humid June evening.

"Bye guys," I say to Sam and Clark before leaving.

"Bye sweetie," Sam yells back.

Clark rushes over in his white apron with the twins' handprints on it and gives me a hug. "Those new cupcakes are amazing. And that frosting . . . Mmm, it's to die for. One of these days I'm going to force you to show me your magic." He squeezes my hand. "Seriously, Addie, you have a wonderful gift in the kitchen. Sam is adding them to the menu!"

"That's great!"

His beard tickles my face as he embraces me. "Bye, dollface," he says before returning to the back to finish cleaning.

I hail down a taxi so I can ambush the guys at Logan's while they're working out in his home gym. My ire rises the longer I sit in the backseat, thinking about last night's events.

I pace the lobby as I wait for the elevator. I won't be surprised if I leave an indentation in the hardwood floor from pacing back and forth in the same spot. I wish that I had restraint over my temper, but there's no use. I'm crackling with anger. I'm thankful that all three of them work out together.

I march into his foyer, making my presence known when I shout for my brother. I hear him hastily coming down the stairs. I lean against the wall while I wait for him.

He holds his hands up in surrender. "Look, that wasn't my idea. I didn't even know you were going to be there when we left."

I fold my arms over my chest. "Really? You expect me to believe that you, my overprotective brother, who needs help I might add, didn't know I was going to be there with Kohen? Oh please, Logan, give me some credit, this has your name written all over it! I can't believe that you would allow Jax to go this far."

He grins even wider now. "Come on, Addie, you know I wouldn't actually crash your date. I do have limits."

"Yeah, the only limit you have is not putting a GPS tracker in me."

"Only because that would be illegal."

I shove him hard but he doesn't move so I punch him in the shoulder. "OH MY GOD! You're unbelievable! I'm mad at you."

"Yes, but not for long, you can never be mad at your favorite brother, remember." I hate that he's right I'm not mad at him anymore. "Honestly, though, Addie, it wasn't my idea. Jax said he wanted pizza and was out the door before I could even finish opening it. The only choice I had was to follow. Besides, it's not like I knew you were going to be there. I was just as surprised as you."

"You really didn't know?" I ask, my temper gone. Well, more on a low simmer until I find Jax.

"If I knew you were going to be there with a date, I wouldn't have gone. I truly do have limits, not much of them, but I still have them."

"Right, you draw the line at tracking devices."

"Because they're illegal," he says with a chuckle. "This all could have been avoided if you just told me about the date."

My anger is nearly nonexistent until my dear brother opens his fat mouth again. "You have to admit, it was pretty hilarious that we crashed your date though." He actually fucking laughs as if it's funny. I'm not laughing. "The way you 'accidentally' poured wine all over Jax." More snickering. "The kick to the shin was a little much though, sis."

And just like that I'm fuming all over again.

"A little much? A little much!" I shout. "Do you know how stupid I felt with you guys there? You're the one who makes such a big deal about me 'living my life again' and when I finally start to, you crash my fucking date.

The first date I've had in SIX YEARS LOGAN! SIX YEARS! Do you even get how monumental this was for me? And you're fucking laughing right now?"

Logan attempts to rein himself in by biting his cheek to not make it obvious. He's used to my tantrums by now, but still. This is not a laughing matter. Granted, it wasn't his idea to crash my date, but he could have insisted on leaving once he realized what Jax's master plan was.

I snap my mouth shut. I'm lashing out at the wrong person. My brother doesn't deserve my wrath. I should be upset that they crashed my date, but I'm more upset that my plan didn't work. I wanted Jax to be seething in jealousy and he couldn't even give me that. No, that jerk was just messing with my head for his own amusement. Why did I have to fall for The God?

Out in the corridor, the elevator doors slide open. Perfect timing.

When Connor comes into view, I storm up to him, push him as hard as I can in his chest and snap, "YOU!"

Connor eyes widen and he swallows loudly. "Yeah, I kind of deserve that."

I throw up my hands in frustration. "I don't understand how you could possibly think it would be okay to crash my date . . . a date you talked me into."

"You talked her into going?" Jax's demanding tone bounces off the walls as he comes to a stop next to Connor.

I glare at the man that used to tell me all of his secrets. Jax shakes his head and continues to stroll into the in-home gym.

"Really? You think you can just walk away from me after last night?" I demand as I follow him.

He ignores me as he sets down his bag by the door. I can't help but stare as he slides off his shirt and begins to stretch. If it's a tactic to distract me, it almost works. The only reason it doesn't is because I know we won't be alone for long. I can't allow Logan to notice anything between Jax and I. Jax is already punching the bag without his hands wrapped when Connor and Logan come in.

I move towards Jax. "You really have nothing to say to me?"

He doesn't take his eyes off the black bag.

"Fine!" I shout as I move in front of him, right as his clenched fist flies toward me.

His fist freezes a breath away from my face. His gaze finally meets mine. I kind of wish he wasn't looking at me anymore. He's pissed. He grinds his teeth together. Logan and Connor are yelling at my stupidity, but I ignore them. I knew Jax would stop, he wouldn't hurt me physically, no he saves his torture for the emotional games he plays with me.

"WHAT THE FUCK IS A MATTER WITH YOU! I could have hit you!" he spits out as he pushes me out of the way.

I shrug. "I got your attention."

"Whatever," he says under his breath and moves to do pull-ups.

I hate that I have to force myself to be aloof around him. His muscles tighten with each lift, beckoning my eyes to follow the movement. I shake my head and march over to Connor and Logan who are doing crunches on the red mat.

"I'm leaving." I hover over them.

Connor nods. "Jax has been in a weird mood all day, ignore him."

"Fully intend to."

Logan stands and hugs me. "I'll pick you up at eight."

I look at him, confused. "Eight?"

He and Connor sigh. "The ball."

"Right. Okay I'll meet you in the lobby."

Crap, the stupid ball . . . the ball that I don't have a dress for yet. The same ball that Jax will be attending. I swallow the uneasiness that is starting to take over. I do not want to see him tonight.

I flip Jax off as I fling open the door. Just because I have to be nice to him tonight doesn't mean I can't get out all of my hostility now.

"Wait, Ads," he says as he rushes to his discarded bag. I ignore him.

I stride out of the penthouse and towards the elevator, hoping that he doesn't follow. He does. The doors slide open. I hit the 'L' button then repeatedly hit the 'Close doors' button. I sigh in relief when they shut in Jax's stunned face. It isn't until I'm outside, breathing fresh air, that I realize he was bearing a white box in his hand. Whoops, I hope that wasn't an apology. Too late to find out.

"Ads! Wait!" he shouts, out of breath, as he storms outside where I'm trying to hail a cab.

Crap!

"What do you want?" I ask without turning around.

He steps around me. "This is for you."

By the time I glance up from the white box in my hands to Jax, he's gone, running back inside. Leaving me. Typical. I shake my head as I open it. I gasp when I see the most beautiful mask I've ever seen, in the most vibrant turquoise I have laid eyes on. Shades of gold, blues, and green twirl around the entire mask with a gold trim. Satin ribbon of the same shades weave together along the top of the mask. The deep blue feathers above the right eye remind me of the ocean. Without even putting it on, I know how well it will complement my complexion.

It's absolutely perfect.

I close the lid, cradle the box in my arm, and I lift my free hand. A cab stops in front of me. As the taxi waits in New York traffic, I send a thank you via text to Jax. He doesn't respond. For some reason, I open the lid again. It isn't until I take the mask out that I see the note.

You're so full of crap. Good thing I think ahead and knew you wouldn't remember the ball tonight to save your life.

Leave it to Jax to give me such a romantic gift and ruin it with a simple note. I can picture him in his office writing the note with a smug smile.

As soon as the car pulls up to the curb, I sprint into my building and jump in the cold shower, with only one thought: finding the perfect dress to match the more than perfect mask Jax bought me.

I dry off then wrap a towel in my hair and make my way to my dresser to fetch a pair of leggings and an oversized shirt. Comfy is always best when I'm on a shopping mission. I'm slipping on a pair of La Perla panties when I hear my front door open. I don't remember locking it before making a mad dash to the shower. I freeze mid step and wait . . .

I know the rational response would be to finish dressing to see who just walked in here, or better yet, lock my bedroom door and hide. I choose neither and decide to wait, naked with one leg in my panties, unable to do anything but close my eyes and stand as still as the Mary and Dickon statue in The Secret Garden in Central Park. Someone turns the door handle.

Maybe if I don't see them, they won't see me? Man, why can't I still be as naive as a child?

My body breaks out in goosebumps and not from the cold. I can feel his gaze on me; I know who I will see. I take a deep breath before opening my eyes to confirm Jax standing in my doorway with a similar white box on steroids in his hands.

As he slowly scans my body, the box drop to the ground. I feel as if its his hands roaming my body instead of his eyes. My body hums with need, need for Jax. In a trance, I drop my arms to my side and welcome the fact that Jax is blatantly staring at me. If he wasn't so sexy I would laugh. His eyes can't seem to find a spot to look at, they keep jumping from my boobs, to my flat stomach, to my legs, and finally to my bare pussy.

"Why are you here?" I ask breathlessly.

"I wanted to see your face when you open this," he says as his gaze roams over me.

I love every second his attention is solely focused on me. I feel like I'm on fire just from him devouring me with his eyes. I feel sexy because of him. When he runs his tongue over his bottom lip, I stare at his mouth. I want to run my tongue over his lips. Who am I kidding, I want to run my tongue over his entire body. I want to trace every line on him with my tongue.

My heart pounds so hard I'm sure it's going to stop working. I'm positive that he can hear my heart from across the room. I force myself to drag my eyes away from his more than welcoming lips. His gym clothes cling to his sweaty body. Yum, Jax and sweat. I bite my lip as I remember when I licked him clean after practice when I surprised him at NYU. I pause over his rock-hard abs, visible through his wet white shirt. I force my eyes to keep traveling, only to have them stop again at the huge bulge.

Transfixed I continue to stare at his hard on, imagining what it would feel like to have him between my legs again. I gasp at the same time that he steps towards me. I stand here, waiting to see what he will do. After a few more seconds, which feels like hours, he takes the last two steps so that he's standing right in front of me. I lean my head back so I can look up at his handsome face. The exact second our irises meet, I know he feels it too. And just as suddenly, Jax turns around and walks out of my bedroom without uttering a single word.

Stunned, I stand here like an idiot and listen to my front door open, close, and him locking it with his key. I don't know how long I wait in my room with one leg still in my panties, but eventually I pull them into place. Reluctantly I saunter over to the gigantic box that Jax carelessly dropped. *So much for seeing my face while I open it.* Sitting Indian-style, I stare at the box as if it's a bomb. I think I know what's in it, and if I'm right, then I don't want to open it.

Manning up, I slowly lift the lid and peel the tissue paper away. My breath catches at the exquisite Monique Lhuillier gown. I hold the dress up to reveal an embroidered cap sleeve gown in the exact shade of turquoise as my mask and with gold embroidery on the entire dress. It has a tiered train with tiny green flecks on the bottom. It matches my mask perfectly!

Carefully I lay the dress down across the bed before returning to the box on the floor. Shuffling around the tissue paper, I find what I knew would be there. Another notecard in Jax's handwriting.

This dress will not do you justice . . . I still look forward to seeing how beautiful you make this dress look tonight though.

I almost melt at his words, but then I remember the little incident that just took place. I hate this hot and cold game Jax always plays with me. I'm tempted to wear another dress just to spite him, but this one is so amazing that it deserves a night out. And okay, I kinda want to see Jax's face when he sees me in it tonight.

I rummage through my dresser and grab the first oversized shirt I see, realizing it's one of Jax's old soccer jerseys that I've collected over the years. I contemplate switching it out for another one, but quickly dismiss that idea. There's something about wearing his clothing that relaxes me; however, tonight it does the exact opposite. Instead of feeling the calm that his presence brings me, even if it's via an old shirt, I feel anxious.

Two hours later, I French braid my bangs back, and use bobby pins to make a bun. I leave a few curls down to frame my face and I'm happy with the end result. It's a chic updo that doesn't take much effort. After spraying my hair into place, I work on my makeup. I use a dark eyeshadow and do smokey eyes, then add a little gold glitter, and finish up with eyeliner and mascara. I add a little blush and lastly I paint my lips a deep crimson.

Carefully I slip Jax's jersey off of my head and toss it onto the bed besides the dress. I admire the gown for a few seconds before putting it on. The corset top fits like a glove and makes my boobs pop up with the perfect amount of cleavage and then some more, but luckily the embroidery still makes me look classy. I slip on my nude peep toe Louboutin heels and the gold clutch that I laid out earlier that matches my dress perfectly. I have five minutes before I have to be downstairs for the car. Quickly, I put on the earrings that Logan bought me from Paris last year, grab my mask, and head towards the elevators.

As soon as the elevator arrives at the lobby, my heart skips a beat . . . I don't think I've ever seen anything as breathtaking as the sight before me. Holy moses, I'm afraid to blink because I don't want The God before me to evaporate if I do. I've seen Jax in a tux several times, more than I can count actually, and each time he looks like The God, but this time it's just too much. It almost hurts to look at how beautiful he is. Almost is the keyword.

His back is to me as he talks on the phone. I've only seen his side profile and I know when he turns around I won't be able to keep my eyes off him. When I see two passing guys stare at me, I blush and slowly step to Jax.

Noticing the two unblinking men in front of him, Jax slowly turns around and pauses mid-sentence. I stop and beam in awe. I can't believe someone can possibly look this good. It's truly unfair Jax doesn't even notice the effect he causes me when he's in a tux; heck even breathing, this man affects me. Blinking, as if coming out of a daze, he walks my way while I continue to gawk at him, wishing that he was mine again.

He stops in front of me and I have to work hard at keeping my distance. All I want to do is launch myself at him and rip his shirt apart to reveal that chiseled body he's hiding underneath his tux. Tonight will be impossible if he's going to look this good.

Slowly, painfully slowly, he twirls one of the loose curls that frame my face. With his other hand, he strokes from my cheek to my jaw with the tip of his index finger. I bite my lip, forcing myself not to take his finger in my mouth and suck it . . . hard.

He groans so quietly I almost don't hear him. "I have no words to adequately describe how heart-stopping beautiful you look, Adalynn."

Blushing scarlet red, I smile up at him. "You clean up pretty nicely, too."

He offers me his elbow and I eagerly wrap my arm around his. Without another word to each other, we exit my apartment building to the waiting car. When I sit down, Jax helps gather the small train of the dress before closing the door and going around to the other side.

Noticing the empty limo I ask, "Not that I'm not thrilled to see you or anything, but where's my brother?"

Jax ignores me and reaches into his pocket to retrieve his vibrating phone. "Hmmm . . . well this should be fun. Yeah I already got her. Yeah, see you in a bit, we're just leaving."

I give him my no-nonsense stare when he hangs up.

Sighing dramatically he says, "Logan has some last minute things to take care of so I offered to take you."

I laugh. "So you're my knight in shining armor, Jax?"

He rolls his eyes.

I'm debating what to say now since we're sitting in traffic in awkward silence when a thought hits me. "Wait, what last minute things? Logan didn't mention anything today."

Jax looks momentarily panicked for a whole half a second, but he quickly masks it with the unreadable expression that he uses when he's trying to hide something from me. "Guess he doesn't tell you everything. You know, kind of the same way you withhold information from him."

For a second I think he's referring to us, though his sudden hostility baffles me. Then he adds, "You know how you told him about your date with the good doctor and all."

And the lightbulb finally comes on. So that's why he is so cold with me all of a sudden. "You wouldn't be jealous, would you?" I ask, knowing full well that he is, even though he won't admit it.

"Hardly," Jax says.

Jaxon Chandler is jealous. There's a first for everything I guess. If only he knew that he has nothing to envy. It's him; no matter what, he will always be it for me. Too bad I can't tell him, I have my own demons and I know Jax will never have the courage to take this further. He's never been able to. That's why we sneaked around when we were teenagers, because of idea of making our relationship public freaked him out.

"I know it's popular belief that I tell my brother everything in my life, but I actually don't tell him about the men in my life," I say in the most condescending voice I can manage. I give him a glare that would kill a lesser man on the spot, but of course The God beside me just glares back.

Yeah, that's right, Jax, I said men. Plural. Suck on that. If Jax wants to keep playing the hot and cold game, then fine, I'm all in. I shift in my seat and look out the window, trying my hardest to ignore the seething man beside me. Everyone wants me to live again, to find myself, so fine, I will. The old me would never allow Jax to continue pulling this crap and frankly I'm tired of it. Enough is enough.

I don't know if it's the recent events or how this magnificent dress makes me feel incredibly beautiful, but I can't wait for the Rare Disease Charity Ball. I'm going to embrace myself tonight and I won't let Jax giving me whiplash stop me from having a good time.

Once we arrive, a quick surveillance of the room shows me that I might have options. It seems that every single man here is checking me out, some to their dates' disappointment. All thanks to the gorgeous dress Jax bought for me. My attention drifts to the ceiling. It's covered in lights, as if they want it to appear like the night sky. Of course I think of my brother. I know he's had a hand in this. I'll have to compliment him once I see him. I turn. My "date" has mysteriously disappeared within the crowd. I do, however, spot the place to boost up my courage, a short distance away. There also happens to be a sexy guy leaning against the bar ogling me.

I'm still at the bar flirting shamelessly when I feel his eyes on me. I know he is somewhere close. I choose to step up my game and ignore him like I've been doing since we arrived.

Setting my hand on the stranger's bicep, I lean closer than necessary to whisper, "Are you going to just flirt with me or are you going to ask me to dance anytime soon?" I lean back and gaze into his brown eyes and bite my lip suggestively.

He places both of our champagne flutes on the table, then takes my hand and whispers, "It would be my pleasure Ms . . .?"

I lick my bottom lip and say in what I hope is a sexy voice, "Let's not get into names." I wave my hand vaguely around the room. "Defeats the theme for tonight."

His eyes get heated and I'm suddenly regretting my decision to flirt with a complete stranger. Maybe this wasn't a good idea. I feel his presence closing in on us and I know that I'm making the right decision after all. Jax keeps leaving me frustrated and I know this is the perfect idea.

I'm accompanying the handsome stranger to the dance floor when we see Connor and one of his blonde bimbos blocking our path. Connor is dashing in his tux and Phantom of the Opera mask. His date for the evening, if you can call it that, reminds me of all the stereotypical blondes that everyone hates. I bet her voice is even annoying. I refuse to learn her name since she will be gone by tonight . . . or within the next few hours, they never last until the morning. I look pointedly from his date to him. Connor just shrugs as if to say, "she's hot."

Connor leans in, gives me a quick kiss on the cheek. "You look beyond words tonight Ada—"

"Thanks!" I say much too loudly so he doesn't reveal my name to the stranger. "Have you seen Logan?"

The stranger beside me shifts nervously on his feet. I think it could be because of the person glaring daggers at him close by. I choose to ignore both and focus on Connor.

"Logan won't be able to make it tonight, actually. He kindly told me at the last minute so that I would have the short car ride over to prepare my speech."

I do the most ladylike snort. "I'm not even going to pretend to feel sorry for you. I would say something along the lines of, you can always talk your way out of anything and you'll do great, but let's face it, you don't need to hear it. I'm sure you hear how great you are from the endless women on your arm."

The bimbo, who was ignoring me and doing everything in her power to gain Connor's attention, scowls at me. I smirk in response. There, payback for the whole crashing my date thing.

Without another word I yank on the stranger's hand again and lead him to the dance floor. He pulls me into his arms and starts spinning me across the room. I have to admit, Mr. Mysterious really knows how to move. When he spins me back into his arms, I realize I'm having fun. He moves his hands to my lower back, which of course makes me step on his toe with my heel.

"Crap! Sorry."

"It's fine." Without taking his eyes off my mouth, he begins to descend for a kiss. Instinctively, I turn away at the last second so his lips graze the side of my cheek.

I can tell he's irritated that I dodged his kiss, but I ignore it and continue to dance with him to another song. As the chorus comes through the speakers, his hand starts to roam again. I have no idea why I turned away at the last minute. I wonder if it has anything to do with Kohen, or worse with Jax. I tell myself I'm just not the kind of person to kiss random strangers.

I want to pretend to be the confident person I used to be, but I'm not her, I can't pretend. Not even wearing a mask can transform me into a different person. When the song ends, I thank the stranger for the dance when I feel him behind me. My whole body breaks into chills. I know if I turn around, I will come face-to-face with Jax. I'm not ready, but my body doesn't want to listen to me anymore. I slowly turn around toward the one person that I want more than anything.

I'm taken aback when it's not Jax. This is a new stranger. The man staring intensely down at me wears a blood red mask that covers his entire face, except for his lustful lips. He looks like the devil; the mask even has horns at the top. I blink a few times, expecting this devil mask to disappear and a simple black Casanova mask to take its place.

Automatically, I take his offered hand.

Mr. Secretive pulls me close so there isn't any space between our bodies. I can feel his hard muscles underneath his tux. My breathing has become embarrassingly noticeable, and I'm pretty positive that my skin is on fire when his hands start to roam my bare arms. I look up at his face, trying to see his eyes, but with the lack of light on the dance floor, it's impossible to tell the color.

I'm so confused, everything in me tells me this is Jax. He's the only one who can ignite my skin, that makes my whole body burn. But my mind can't process why he's in a different mask.

Because this isn't him. This is Mr. Secretive.

He still hasn't said anything and I don't want to break the spell he has me under. He continues to grind his groin into my pelvis with the beat of the music, making it painfully obvious how aroused he is. By the pool of moisture gathering in my panties, it's safe to say I'm in the same boat as him. The song is almost over when I get a quick whiff of his cologne.

And I know without a doubt who's behind the mask.

I shouldn't have doubted myself. I knew it was Jax before I turned around. I know him. My body knows him. I can feel him even from across the room. It's as if my body, my soul, wants to haunt me forever. To torture me some more by reminding me what I can never have.

Jax.

CHAPTER EIGHT

Reaching up, I thread my hands through his velvety soft hair. I pull his head down to me and press my lips to his. Jax releases his hold on my hips to cup my face as he deepens the kiss. I meet his tongue eagerly, loving the taste of him. I nibble on his lip and he growls into my mouth, turning me on even more. He's the one to pull back first. I smile when I see he's as breathless as I am. We've both just run an imaginary marathon.

The smoldering look he gives me makes me shiver. I've never wanted anyone as desperately as I want him right here, right now. Without thinking long enough to talk myself out of it, I grip his hand and lead him off the dance floor. If there wasn't people everywhere I would be sprinting with him to the nearest closed door. I weave us through the crowd and out to the hallway. I pull him along while I find somewhere for us to be alone.

The first door we come to is locked. Same thing for the second one. We both sigh in relief when the third door opens. As I tug him in after me, my heel catches on the rug and I start to fall, but his grip on my hand saves me. He holds me to him as if he's afraid to let me go. Spinning me around, he roughly slams his body into mine, banging my back into the wall. His hands are everywhere.

Oh God . . . his magical hands skim the side of my body. He then squeezes my hip. I'm positive that I'll have a bruise there tomorrow. I bite my lip to suppress my moan, too afraid to break the silence because I don't want anything to stop this. There's a reason why he hasn't uttered a single word. It will break the spell, it will give him away. I don't dare stop him. If this is the way he wants to talk, then who am I to stop him. I love our new communication skills.

I manage to slide his tux jacket off his sculpted shoulders, but when he starts kissing my neck, I lose it and grasp his biceps to stay upright. I try to stay quiet, but it's impossible, it feels too good.

"Oh . . . God . . . Ahh," I moan out loud.

He makes the hottest noise I've ever heard in the back of his throat. Even the sounds he's making are turning me on. I want him and I want him now. I push him off me with as much force as I can manage. The puzzled look he gives me makes me smirk. He thinks I'm stopping this. Ha! No way that's happening. It's been too long since I've felt him inside me. I lock the door.

I yank his shirt roughly out of his tuxedo pants and drag him towards a nearby chair in the room. I push him down. He sits in the chair and then slowly slides down the zipper on the side of my dress.

His eyes never stray from my face. The intensity in his stare makes me feel like the most seductive woman in the world. Knowing that he finds me beautiful gives me the courage to let my dress fall to the floor. I stand in my Louboutin and La Perla purple lace panties. Nothing else.

Jax's gaze slowly leaves my faces as he takes in my naked breast, my tight stomach, barely-there panties, and then finally my toned legs. I move slowly to him, closing the distance between us. After the last step, I'm standing directly in front of him, ready to melt just from him watching me. I've never felt so wanted, so cherished in all of my life. He hasn't even touched me yet, but I can feel him all the way to my core.

It suddenly dawns on me that I'm out of my element. I haven't been with anyone else in six years. Jax has continued to sleep around with women who know exactly what to do in and out of the bedroom. I'm not them. I've only been with Jax. Standing in front of him in just panties, my newly found courage melts away. My mind races. Is it possible to forget how to have sex?

Luckily Jax takes the lead. He runs one finger from my left hipbone all the way to the right. With one look he gives me back all of the confidence that was drifting away. He's showing me that he needs me as desperately as I need him. It's his eyes, they give everything away, they always have. That one finger leaves goosebumps in its wake. I'm ready to convulse when his other hand traces the outline of my flat stomach.

"Please," I moan loudly.

Jax chuckles as his hand falls away. I'm not even a little ashamed when I whimper in protest. I'm done with his games. They went out the window when I locked the door. I don't want to go slow, the last six years has been leading up to this moment.

I straddle his lap while I unbutton his shirt. I bend my head down so I can press my lips to each inch of skin that I expose. He finally breaks the silence by letting out a moan. It's my turn to chuckle. I slow my pace of removing his shirt just to make him as frustrated as I am. Too bad, Jax plays dirty. He roughly presses me harder into his lap. His erection hits me exactly where we both want it.

I give up trying to tease him and rip his shirt open. Buttons fly in every direction. My panties get drenched just from the noise of the buttons scattering on the marble flooring. I can't wait for what's going to come. He yanks his arms out of his shirt, eager to be rid of it. I take advantage of the fact that he's leaning forward, into me, and press my breast into his face.

Jax groans loudly when I tug his hair to direct his mouth to my sensitive nipple. Too bad, Jax has other plans in mind. His head falls back as he smirks at me. It's a smirk that tells me who is in charge. Him. I doubt I was ever in charge in the first place.

He licks a trail all the way from the middle of my breast to my neck, then nips at my jaw. I'm panting as I rub my clit on his rock hard cock. My breathing is embarrassingly fast and I'm positive that he can hear the loud thumping of my heart. He kisses each corner of my mouth and when he is close enough to my mouth that I can feel the heat from his breath, I try to kiss him but he pulls back with the smug look that I secretly love. I don't love it now. Right now I hate it. Glaring at him, I pull his hair hard, and angrily kiss him.

His stupid smug smile reminds me of all the times he has given me whiplash lately. I want to make him pay. I want him to be the one to beg. I want to rip off our masks and stop pretending. I want him to know that I know it's him, that it will always be him. I'm done with all of these charades. Resolve made, I unlatch my hands from around his neck and get off his lap.

Jax's grin immediately disappears. He opens his mouth then closes it again. I can tell that he's on the verge of saying something so I give him the biggest smirk in my book. That's right, he can't talk. If he does, all of this will drift away.

I have him. He knows it and so do I. I lick my lips and slowly drag my hands up my body and cup my breasts. I'm thankful that there's enough light in here to see his green eyes darken. He makes a move to stand, but I shake my head. I run my hands through my hair and untie the bow and let the mask meet the same fate as my dress.

Without saying anything, I plead with Jax to do the same. I want this so badly, but I know I won't be satisfied unless he is here with me, really here. I want Jax, not someone in a mask.

I wait for what seems like hours, but it's only seconds. After about a minute, our awkward standoff is over. Jax shakes his head before tilting his head down so that I can't see his face. My mouth drops open. I can't believe he is so afraid to actually be here with me.

With fake confidence, I pick up my dress, raise an eyebrow at him, and when he doesn't make a move towards me, I step back into it. I turn my back to him and zip it up. Once my dress is in place, I pluck my mask off the floor and put it back on as if I'm perfectly fine. I take a few calming breaths before turning around to face him again.

I see the anguish in his eyes, but I don't care. He had his chance. Heck, the jerk had me naked on his lap. Okay, nearly naked, but still, my barely-there panties hardly count. I walk over to him still sitting in the chair, watching every move I make.

I trace his lips with my finger before saying, "Don't worry, Jax, this wasn't even good enough to remember, so it definitely isn't good enough to mention again."

He sharply inhales like I punched him in the gut. I spin quickly on my heel to flee, but not before I say, "This devil mask suits you better than the other one you arrived in. Have a nice night." I unlock the door and storm out with my head held high.

I lean on the door to collect all the different emotions racing through me. Ready to throw up, I clutch my stomach. I've made a fool of myself. Of course The God wouldn't truly be with me. I'm so stupid. My body shakes as I try not to pass out. My lungs aren't working correctly. Slowly, I count backwards from ten like Liv has told me to do when I'm hyperventilating. It seems to work on my third attempt. The sick-to-my-stomach feeling dissipates, replaced by anger.

I can't believe he just sat there and didn't do anything. I'm proud of myself for realizing that I couldn't finish what I started unless he was there with me, even if the moment was beyond wonderful. I give myself a mental shake. No, it wasn't wonderful, it wasn't real. It was just more games.

I'm need to head back to the party so I can leave. I don't want to be here anymore. Then I hear something crash against a wall in the room I just left and a loud, "Fuck." I turn my head so that my ear is to the door. Absolute silence. This is stupid, I don't need to stand by a door all night, listening to Jax lose it.

I take a step away, fully intending on leaving the party, when the door swings open. A pissed off Jax, still in his mask, looms in the doorway. He stares at me with his mouth agape. I watch him, waiting to see if he will do anything. I'm not even a little disappointed when nothing happens. Shocker. I march down the hallway, this time not stopping, when I hear him cuss again.

I've almost to the crowd when I feel him behind me. An involuntary shudder runs through me when I feel him press against me. He wraps one hand around my waist and pulls me tighter against him so there's no space between us. I bite my lips hard enough that I taste blood to keep the moan in that is begging to come out. He still wants me, I can feel the evidence pressing against me.

"Come with me," he whispers into my ear before tracing my earlobe with his tongue. This time the moan escapes. I barely manage a nod before he's dragging me towards the exit. We leave through a back door. His car waits with his driver holding the door open for us, as if he was expecting us.

"Pretty confident."

He raises my hand to his mouth and kisses the inside of my palm. "Hopeful," Jax corrects.

He helps me in and gathers the small train again before closing the door and going to the other side. We sit in silence. My mind races to the point that I can't focus on anything to say. I have no idea where we're going, but as long as I'm not going home alone, I won't complain.

Not wanting to look out the window or at The God besides me, I opt for closing my eyes. I feel him shift closer to me. Everything in me screams for me to open them, but I can't. I know if I face him, I will see the regret in his eyes because he doesn't want this, our time has passed. I'm just Logan's little sister now. He won't ruin his friendship with my brother for me. Sadly, I can't even fault him for that. I'm not worthy of him taking a risk on me.

Cupping my face, he turns me towards him. Acting like a stubborn child, I squeeze my eyes tighter, refusing to open them.

"Please look at me, Ads," Jax pleads.

I almost sigh at the way he whispers his nickname for me, but instead I shake my head.

"Fine." And without any warning he crushes his lips to mine.

I try not to kiss him back because my emotions are still rattled from earlier. I lose what little self-control I was holding onto when Jax bites my lower lip. It's an instant turn-on. I kiss him back with everything I have. I want him to know how much he means to me, how much I've wanted this. I'm about to straddle his lap when he pulls back abruptly.

I open my eyes to see what the heck just happened, and when I see that stupid smug grin, I want to punch him.

"There's those beautiful eyes." He winks at me. He surprises me by untying my mask and throwing it onto the floor. "No more masks." He then tosses his away too.

"No more masks," I repeat.

I beam at him before launching myself at him, kissing him hard. He groans loudly as he gathers my dress around my hips. He licks my neck before pressing his mouth back to mine. I moan into his mouth when his tongue meets mine and dig my nails into his shoulders.

Framing my face with his hands, he aims that intense stare that only Jax can manage pulling off. "Stay with me?" he asks.

I nod while saying, "Of course," right as the car stops.

He smiles so brightly that it reminds me of a child's smile after Santa has visited. When he gets out of the car, he speaks to his driver before helping me out. Gripping my hand, he kisses the back of my palm, and then leads us into his apartment building.

The elevator seems to take it's time carrying up to the top floor. Jax quickly tugs me into his penthouse, never letting go of my hand as he leads me into his bedroom. The only noise in is very sterile bedroom is my heels clinking on the hardwood floor. Although his bedroom is impressive with the dark oak bed, matching dressers, and an abstract painting on his far wall, it always reminds me of an expensive hotel. It's just so clean, everything in perfect order. If I move one thing even slightly, he will know. His panoramic wall, that leads to his private balcony, shows the glistening lights from the city.

My smile drops when I turn around to see Jax holding up one of his cotton T-shirts for me. Um, so not what I was expecting him to grab. I raise an eyebrow at him in question.

Jax laughs and tosses the shirt at me. "For you to sleep in."

Yeah, so not gonna work for me. I move out of the way so the shirt falls to the ground in front of me. I unzip my dress while saying, "Thanks, but I'll just sleep in what I always do." I drop the dress to the floor.

Jax's eyes darken in an instant. He runs a hand through his hair and says through clenched teeth, "Put the shirt on, Ads."

Aw, he's serious. How cute.

"Make me," I taunt.

I step out of my heels and leans over his bed so he has the perfect view of my ass. Keeping my back to him, I start to slide my panties down my legs before sitting on his grey duvet. When I look at Jax, his mouth is securely attached to the floor.

"I sleep naked, but by all means, Jax, put the shirt on me."

Rubbing both hands roughly down his face he mutters, "Fuck" so quietly I almost don't hear him. Then he takes three long strides to his bed. Jax wraps his hand around my ankle and drags me to him, making me fall onto my back. He caresses my calfs with his fingertips. His hands don't roam higher than my knees and his eyes don't stray from my face. He's enjoying watching me squirm around, beyond frustrated for relief.

"Someone is overdressed."

Jax looks down at his open shirt, revealing the sexiest abs in the world that I plan to trace with my tongue shortly. "Well, since you started ripping my clothes off of me, don't you think you should finish the job?" he asks in that deep bedroom voice of his.

Mmm, just his voice is a turn on. If it wasn't for the huge tent in his pants, I would hate how much he effects me. It's painfully obvious what he does to me. As if on cue, his eyes drift from my face to my open thighs. He licks his bottom lip in such a way that I imagine his tongue on my clit.

"Wider," Jax commands. I obey without any thought.

All of the sudden Jax's lips are everywhere all at once. I can't hold back any longer. I moan loudly and thrash against his sheets when his mouth gets dangerously close to my inner thighs.

"Yes . . . Please . . ." I pant when Jax starts to nibble on my inner thighs. He's so close to my throbbing clit that I can feel his breath on my dripping wet pussy. He's so close but so far away at the same time.

"No!" I shout, not caring in the least how I sound when Jax dips his tongue in my belly button.

His eyes meet mine. "You want me to stop?"

I can only manage to whimper at him when he starts kissing a path up my body. He misses my aching breast as he makes his way up my neck. He gives special attention to my neck, making me moan embarrassingly louder. He kisses a wet trail of small kisses from my jaw to my mouth. Automatically my hands tangle into his silky hair as he kisses me long and hard.

"I need you," I whisper into his ear.

"You have me," he says as his mouth presses to my burning skin.

I moan in protest when he leans off of me and stands. The words die on my suddenly dry lips as I watch him unzip his pants. He pulls them and his briefs down at the same time. My mouth waters at the sight of him.

"Six years has been too long," I mutter.

He bends down and grabs a condom from the pocket of his discarded pants. My breathing becomes nonexistent as he rolls it onto his impressive length. *Is it possible that he's gotten bigger? How is he going to fit?* All thoughts float away as he drags his naked body on top of mine.

He kisses me passionately. "Are you sure?" Jax swipes the hair out of my face.

I have no words. I nod.

"I need to hear you, Ads."

I moan into his mouth as his hands play with my pussy lips. I swallow twice before I'm able to get my mouth to work. "I want this, I want us, Jax."

My heart beats double time when he stares into my eyes. He opens his mouth, but I kiss him, stopping whatever he was about to say. I fear that he's about to tell me something that he can't take back.

My body trembles as we become one. I whimper in pain, but it's soon swallowed up by Jax's tongue. He goes slow, and runs his hands down my sides. He pulls out to the tip and eases back into me. It's torture, but I never want it to stop, it feels too good. He brushes my sweaty hair out of my face and then interlocks our fingers. Jax brings his mouth closer to mine, but doesn't kiss me. Our face are so close together we're breathing for each other.

"Oh . . . God . . . " I moan loudly.

He wraps one of my legs around his waist, allowing him to go deeper. He grasps one of my hands and uses his free one to rub my clit. It's too much. I tremble as I hold my release in.

"Let go," he whispers into my ear before nipping on my earlobe.

I'm losing myself in Jax. I never want to be found as long as he's with me. I fight off my release. I can't go without him. He must see exactly what I need because he squeezes my hand and kisses me, stealing my breath away.

"I'm there, Ads. Let go," he says against my lips.

I stare into his dark eyes as everything else disappears beside us. The only thing I can hear is Jax breathing heavily. I can feel his beating heart, it matches mine. I bite his shoulder as we climax together. I'm vaguely aware of his weight on top of me as I come off the high only Jax can deliver.

He kisses my nose, his signature kiss for me, and rolls off me. He walks into the bathroom and I smile to myself when I hear the water running. He returns to clean me up with a warm towel. The first time we slept together on the night before my sixteenth birthday, I was embarrassed when he did this, but each and every time we were done he would always insist on cleaning me up. I'm glad that things haven't completely changed between us. Once he's finished, he crawls over me, and pulls me into to spoon me.

Kissing the back of my neck, he whispers, "Good night, Ads."

I'm barely able to mumble, "Night." The eight letter words that I wish I could say to him are on the tip of my tongue, but they never come out. I don't want to ruin this moment. I have no idea what tomorrow will be like, but tonight I'm happy in the arms of the man I love.

The sunlight streaming in from the panoramic windows wakes me up. I'm disoriented at first, but once my brain wakes up, too, everything from last night comes rushing back. I can't believe that I was brave enough to take control, or rather pretend to take control, of the situation. Jax never really gave me the control I thought I had. I can still feel his hands on me. I loved the way he touched me, leaving my skin on fire, desperate for more.

I open my eyes, but then close them for another minute or two against the glaring sunlight. Once I'm able to remove the pillow from my face without wincing, I roll over. I expect to feel Jax beside me, but instead my hand touches a cold bed. It's obvious that he's been up for awhile.

Not caring about the bright morning sun, I sit up hoping that I will hear him making breakfast or something romantic, but I already know it's wishful thinking. I'm not surprised when I'm met with silence. He's gone. The sinking feeling in my chest lets me know how very wrong I was about last night, but I don't regret any of it. How could I? I was finally able to have a small glimpse of how Jax really thinks of me.

Needing last night to mean something to him, too, I desperately search around the bed for a note that I never find. I'm not even ashamed that I lift each pillow and rip the blankets off the bed . . . twice. Still no note. Now the regret rolls in. I focus on how Jax made me forget about everything last night and made me feel. Really made me feel in the first time in . . . I don't even know how long. There's no way I can regret what happened last night between us even if it didn't mean the same to him. How could it?

My thoughts are everywhere and nowhere at once. I'm too distracted to notice anything but getting out of here as fast as I can as I hurriedly walk into the bathroom. Peeling the wrapper off one of several spare toothbrushes, I refuse to acknowledge why he has so many extras. I focus on the task at hand. I close my eyes while I brush my teeth because I don't want to look at myself in the mirror. I'm afraid of what I'll see in my reflection. As I open my eyes to spit, I spot a pile of my clothes on the sink with a note on top.

I pause, toothbrush in hand, and gape at the note. Without reading it, I recognize my favorite pair of shorts, and an old Ramones T-shirt, with a matching bra and panty set. I blush thinking of Jax going through my drawer just to find a matching pair. That's the only thing I don't have color-coordinated. I just toss them in my top drawer. Awesome. I have no idea how he was able to get all of this over here, but then it's Jax. He's capable of anything.

After getting dressed, I tuck the note in my back pocket and decide that I'll read whatever he has to say when I get home. I'm too afraid to read it while I'm here. Glancing around his room for the first time since I woke up, I'm not even a little surprised that my entire outfit from last night is missing. In its place is my favorite red purse and black Toms. At least he's thoughtful about my morning-after outfit. *Points to him.*

I paint a smile on my face that I'm not feeling as the elevator doors open. When I spot the doorman, I beam at him, my exit only a few footsteps away. As he holds the door open for me, I'm caught off guard to discover Jax's driver waiting patiently for me. I'm tempted to hail down a taxi just to spite Jax, but I don't want his driver, Henry, to think I'm mad at him. I really like Henry, always have.

Swallowing my pride, I close the distance between Henry and me. "Thanks, Henry, but can you do me a favor?"

"Whatever it is, consider it done, Adalynn," he says in his British accent. If he wasn't happily married, I have no doubt that he would be as big of a player as the boys.

"Next time call me so that you're not just waiting out here." He seems confused so I add, "I was just going to get a taxi. You didn't have to wait here to take me home, I'm a big girl."

If it's even possible, he looks more confused than before. He opens his mouth to say something but stops when the back door opens from the inside. I'm so startled to see Jax waiting for me that I nearly fall flat on my butt. And when I say nearly, I mean if Henry didn't step in to catch me, I would have been mortified.

"Why are you in the car?" I accuse more than ask.

Jax counters with a smirk. "Why aren't you in the car?" he asks while extending his hand out for me.

I smack it out of the way. "I got it." He gives me another one of his classic smirks and I roll my eyes at him.

Getting in the car was a lot easier than thinking of what to say to him. My mind tries to piece together an explanation, but I can't come up with anything to explain why he's sitting next to me. I give up quickly and cross my arms over my chest and wait. He obviously has something to say to me or he wouldn't be here.

I should have read the stupid note before I got into the elevator!

Following my lead, he leans against his door to fully face me, too. Right when I think he's going to say something, he winks. Actually winks! *What I wouldn't do to give him a nice hard kick to the balls.*

"Ouch. What has your panties in a twist today?" he asks.

It isn't until he places a hand in-between his legs to protect himself that I realize I said that out loud.

I just glare at him. I hate when he does that stupid raised eyebrow thing. I want to smile. Ugh, he's annoyingly charming. I need to wait him out. I'm not going to break under the pressure.

As he stares intently into my eyes like he did last night, the memories come crashing down. My face heats up as I blush a deep crimson, remembering everything that happened, and it suddenly gets way too hot in this air conditioned car. Needing a distraction from the staring contest, I take in his appearance for the first time today. Which of course is a huge mistake. Why didn't I just look out the window instead of at him? He's too hot for his own good. He's wearing his dark blue jeans that I know hug his ass in that sexy way only he seems to be able to pull off and a faded black Superman shirt that makes his green eyes stand out in contrast.

Looking back up at his face is an even bigger mistake. He's studying me in a way that makes me think he can see right through my soul. Remembering the way he drank me in last night right before his lips trailed up my legs, I bite my bottom lip to keep from making any embarrassing sounds. My body temperature rises. I'm positive that he can hear my heart hammering through my chest. He licks his lips and I let out a barely audible moan.

He isn't even touching me and yet every time his eyes sweep over me, I can feel it like a caress. I somehow find the will power to break the trance he has me under and turn towards the window. My body burns so I rest my forehead against the cold glass as I watch the city zoom past us. I can't focus on a single thing going on outside of this car. However, I'm more than fully aware of everything inside it. Without taking my head off the window, I can feel him stretch out his legs. He must have pressed a button because suddenly the privacy window slides up.

"Fuck it." Jax nearly growls and that's the only warning I get before he is on me.

His tongue takes full advantage of my gasp. His kiss is anything but gentle. It's almost like he's mad that he's kissing me and is taking it out on me. Fine by me. He can take it out on me whenever he wants if this is how he's going to do it. I dig my nails into his biceps, trying to hold on as he kisses me passionately.

I angrily grab his face and kiss him back. I take out all of the conflicting emotions swimming inside of me, out on him. We become each other's oxygen supply. He breathes me in and then breathes the air into my lungs. Repeat. We're both running out of air, but neither of us makes a move to slow down the kiss. We can't. It's all-consuming. The kiss starts to transform from sexual frustration to something more.

Something much, much more.

Something that terrifies me.

I pull away and study his face. I need to know that I'm not just imagining this. I need to know that he's feeling the weight of this just as heavily as I am.

He caresses my face and smiles at me. "You're my light," he says simply before kissing me again.

I know what he means because I feel exactly the same way about him. He's my light that shines through all of the darkness.

CHAPTER NINE

He guides me against the back seat and hovers over me. I know that he needs me to say something, but I can't. I have no words. I'm at war with my mind and my heart. I know what I want to say, but I can't tell him how much he means to me. I don't deserve to ask for more from Jax.

"Don't," he says as if reading my mind.

"I can't, Jax," I say, full of regret.

He knows that I can't do this, I'm not ready, but I can't seem to stop either. I've gotten so used to building walls, brick-by-brick, that it seems impossible to let someone in. Even Jax. With each brick that he has broken down over the years, another one replaces it. As much as I want to tear down all of my walls for him, I can't trust him to catch me. Every time I do, he disappears.

"Let go." I barely have time to process what he's saying before he's kissing me again.

Everything slips away with his hands caressing my face while his tongue tangles with mine in a soul shattering kiss. I'm almost out of air, but I don't dare stop him. Reading my mind again, he eases up and leaves a wet trail of kisses down my chin, then across my jaw, and then he's sucking on that spot right below my ear. I shiver as I dig my nails into his back. I bite my lip so hard to smother the moan that I cut it. He nips on the pulse point at my throat and I whimper.

"I want to hear you," he whispers huskily into my ear and I almost combust on the spot.

Holy-hotness, just hearing him whisper to me in that voice is enough to make me cum. I'm vaguely aware that we're still in a car. I try to be quiet but he rolls my earlobe with his teeth, making my last strand of willpower break. I moan loudly. He fondles my boobs over my shirt. I moan again, this time louder than the last. Jax forcibly grabs my face and swallows the rest of my sounds.

Not wanting to be the only one getting off, I finally manage to make my hands move to the hem of his Superman T-shirt, instead of clawing at his back like some wild animal. Knowing what I want, Jax lifts his body off me to help me take off his shirt, at least that what I assumed. When he doesn't remove his shirt, but instead puts it back into place, I know this isn't going where I thought it was.

"We're back to this?" I whisper.

He doesn't respond, either because he doesn't hear me or because he doesn't know what to say. I'm going with the latter.

I close my eyes because I know if I see him right now, I will more than likely punch him in his stupid, beautiful face. He moves his body weight off me. I sit up. He doesn't need to say it, to tell me that the moment is gone. He surprises me by reaching for my hand, but like the child that I am, I snatch it back and turn so that I'm facing the window again.

I don't need to say anything to Jax because he knows how I feel. If he wants to keep playing these hot and cold games with me, then fine. I'm done. *And he wonders why I won't let him in. Hmm that's a tough one.* I'm fine stewing in my anger all by myself, but when he chuckles, I lose it.

I turn around and surprise the both of us by slapping him across the cheek. I quickly get over my shock and close my mouth. I almost feel bad for how hard I slapped him. My palm stings and there's a clear handprint on his cheek. But then I hear his chuckle in my head and I get angry all over again.

On its own accord, my hand goes to slap him again, but Jax is much faster than I am. He captures my wrist before it can connect with its target. All of my pent-up fury comes rushing forward and I try to smack him with my other hand. Just as quickly, he's holding that wrist too. I can't help it, I laugh. Wrong move.

He's seething; his jaw keeps popping from clenching it too tightly. His entire body hums with anger, just like mine, but yet I can't stop laughing. He narrows his eyes at me, which would make a lesser woman feel intimidated, and I laugh even harder. I don't know what makes Jax more upset: me laughing at him or the fact that I slapped him. I'm gonna go with a little bit of both. His stern gaze reminds me of someone trying to throw daggers with their eyes.

Deep breaths. Control yourself. Repeating this mantra somehow helps me calm down.

"Oh God . . . It hurts . . . I better have abs for days," I say once I'm able to catch my breath.

I playfully nudge Jax with my shoulder. The games is us, and as much as I hate them, I would hate for him to play with anyone else.

He nudges me back and I know I'm forgiven. How? I have no idea. I caress his still red cheek. It's warm to the touch. I trace the outline of my hand with my fingertips. Before I even have a chance to apologize, he beats me to it.

"Don't, Ads. It's fine."

Because I just can't seem to help myself when it comes to hitting Jax, I lightly slap his other cheek. "I wasn't going to apologize for hitting you, jackass. You deserved it . . . I just didn't mean to hit you that hard." Sarcasm drips from my voice. I go to move my hand, but before I do, he bites my palm with enough pressure to leave teeth marks. "Yeah, you definitely deserved that slap."

As he moves closer to me, I notice that we're stopped at Central Park. I give Jax my what-the-heck face because I have no idea why we're here. I also have no idea how long we've been here because of course my full attention was consumed by The God-like creature next to me. I assumed he was taking me back to my apartment. Man, was I wrong. Maybe he didn't deserve that slap after all? No, he deserved it. He's had it coming for awhile now.

Jax smirks, gets out of the car, and offers me his hand once he comes around to my side. "Trust me," he whispers into my ear before blindfolding me.

I try not to panic when my world submerges in darkness, but my body isn't listening to me. I'm already sweating, my pulse beats rapidly. I'm positive I'm about to go into heart failure any second now. I can't seem to breathe in enough air into my lungs. I remind myself that I'm out in the open with Jax to ward off the full-blown panic attic that is about to hit from memories of the car crash.

Jax is with me. I'm safe. He won't let anything happen to me. Even as I repeat the words, I have vivid flashbacks from being trapped in the car that night. I can hear glass shattering, followed by an earth shattering scream, then silence. The silence is the worst. My body shakes involuntary. The memories reel me in and I lose the tiny hold I had on staying in the present.

I struggle to focus but something keeps blocking my view, making it impossible to see what is going on. I attempt to wipe whatever it is away, but my right hand isn't working correctly. I try again and instantly feel excruciating pain. I scream at the top of my lungs. I struggle to use my other hand but I can't . . . It's stuck. I black out.

When I regain consciousness, whatever is gushing down my face has begun to dry. I lick my lips and taste blood. It dawns on me what my face is covered in. Blood . . . my blood. I know it isn't good that I keep blacking out, and how much blood I've lost. The accident comes back full force and I'm suddenly aware of what's happening.

The blinding light . . .

Glass shattering . . .

Screaming . . .

I turn to the right to see Hadley's head down. She's barely breathing. I panic. "Hadley!" I scream.

I want to reach her, but I can't move. I'm trapped. The pelting of the heavy rain is the only noise not drowned out by my screaming. I can't see my dad but I have a clear view of my mom. She's hanging forward, not moving either. Darkness takes over again before I can scream for help again. . . .

I'm yanked back into reality when Jax's lips press firmly to mine. It takes a while to kiss him back, but when my lips finally move against his, he pulls back enough to whisper, "Stay with me. Don't go away again," against my lips and then he's kissing me again.

The memories drift away, but continue to taunt me at the edge of the surface, never letting me forget. Being blindfolded doesn't help, though knowing that Jax is here and understands helps keep the memories at bay.

"Trust me, Ads." he murmurs into my ear.

I think I nod but I'm not sure. His hand grips mine. He lifts our intertwined fingers to his lips and kisses the back of my palm. I take another deep, calming breath, welcoming the clean air. As I breathe in, I breathe out the smell of burnt rubber that exist only in my memory. Jax leads the way to an unknown destination. I have a sinking feeling that he's taking me to my favorite place in Central Park, but I have no way of knowing.

When I start to panic again, he squeezes my hand, letting me know that I'm safe. I focus on my breathing and the panic eases up. I know that we look ridiculous because we're barely moving and we keep stopping every few feet so that I can catch my breath, but I don't care. I'm conquering a fear of lack of control because of Jax. He's extremely patient with me, always whispering sweet nothings into my ear to remind me where I am. If I was with anyone else, I seriously doubt that I would be able to do this without being trapped into the past.

As he continues to lead me around Central Park, I finally relax. The tension in my shoulders subsides and with each squeeze of Jax's strong hand holding mine, my pulse slowly returns to a much more normal pace. Being blindfolded is still one of the hardest things I've had to do in awhile, but with each step, I feel stronger for being able to relinquish control to someone else.

Jax suddenly stops, spins me around and whispers, "Keep your eyes closed." He kisses my neck and removes the blindfold.

I tell myself to count to ten. The entire time I remind myself to be patient, to do as directed. When I get to five, the urge to take a quick peek overwhelms me. When I make it to seven, I shake my head, realizing that I'm not patient, far from it. Very slowly I open my eyes and see a very amused Jax sitting on an ocean blue blanket.

"I have to admit, I didn't think you had it in you to keep your eyes closed for that long. The world must be ending."

I ignore his comment and focus on the scenery. He took me to my favorite spot. *He knows me too well.* He has a blanket spread out with a picnic basket. His socks and shoes rest on the grass near the blanket. He's grinning from ear-to-ear. There's something about seeing him so relaxed, looking at me as if he couldn't tear his eyes away from me even if he wanted to, that makes my stomach flutter. Awesome, Jax has turned me into *that* girl. The girl that gets butterflies in her stomach just from a look. As hard as I try, I can't find a reason to not like the girl I'm becoming when I'm with him.

I take the three small steps to the blanket and stand over him so each leg is on the outside of his thighs. I make a point to cross my arms over my chest. "Well, were you just going to let me stand there all day with my eyes closed while you sunbathed?"

Jax raises his left eyebrow in that sexy way of his. Too quickly for me to gauge his intentions, he sweeps his arms out and hits me behind my knees so I fall forward on top of him. There's something about Jax that makes me want to hit him all the time. I sit on top of his thighs and boldly kiss him. Jax waves his index finger back and forth in front of my face. I pout for a whole nanosecond before he grabs my face with both of his hands and deepens the kiss that I meant only as a peck.

When we both pull away, we're breathless. My smile matches his. He draws circles on my bare thighs while I take the time to notice everything else he brought. Next to the picnic basket is my new camera bag and a book that's so damaged I can't even read what it is, but I know it's his favorite, *The Giver*. It was the last thing his mom gave him before walking out the door, never to be heard or seen from again. He took so much effort to make this happen and I slapped him. Why is he still here? I'm crazy with a capital C.

"I'm sorry." I kiss the cheek that I slapped.

Placing his hands on my shoulders, he drags me back so he has a clear view of my eyes. "It's fine. Don't worry about it."

"But—"

"It's FINE, Ads. Besides, I've had it coming."

"Who am I to argue with that." I barely have the words out of my mouth before he's tickling me. "Stop! Stop!" I try to squirm off him but it's useless. He's too strong. "I'm gonna pee my pants!" I shout through my laughter. He finally takes pity on me and kisses my nose.

"We couldn't have you peeing on me again now, can we?"

Again? He's crazy. I've never peed on anyone in my life. I ignore him and give him a quick kiss before leaning over to peer in the picnic basket. However, Jax quickly interrupts my attempts to eat by kissing me again. It isn't until my stomach growls that he stops. Jax reaches over and unpacks our lunch with me still sitting on his lap.

After we take turns feeding each other, Jax decides to bask in the sun. Our fingers brush against each other as he hands me my camera bag and I feel it everywhere. He smiles at me as if feeling the same thing. I have no idea how a simple touch, even accidental, can set my skin on fire. It's always been like this for me. I've tried to ignore it, but it's always there. Even if I wanted to, I could never escape him. He's a part of me.

I walk a distance away to take pictures of anything that catches my eye. I'm surprised that I'm able to get back into it as if no time has passed. Looking through the lens, I feel in control. I control what image I capture. When I take a picture of a little girl running after a little boy, I'm assaulted by memories of how I chased Jax when we younger. Glancing over my shoulder, I see Jax peacefully sleeping on the blanket, appearing much like The God that he is. So unfair.

I sneak up to him so that I can snap a picture of him completely relaxed. It's amazing to see him lying here without his usual frown. I'm lost studying the man that I've always loved through the lens, when suddenly I see nothing but darkness. Startled, I move the camera out of my face to see Jax's hand blocking the lens. He has an eyebrow raised in question.

Laughing I ask, "Were you awake the whole time?" He offers his hand to me. I take it and sit next to him.

"Of course. I love watching you, it's like you're in your own little world with this in front of your face." He holds up my camera, I assume to make his point, but he starts clicking away instead.

I shield my face because I hate getting photographed, but Jax rolls on top of me to pin me down. Relief washes over me when he relinquishes the camera. It's gone just as quickly after he captures both of my hands in one of his strong ones. He hovers over me with my hands stretched out over me head, away from my face.

"Okay, you made your point, Jax. You can stop now." I speak sternly, but I'm fighting back a smile.

Releasing my hands, he snaps picture after picture, and continues to tickle me with his free hand. I scream and try to wiggle out from underneath him, but it's useless. I'm his prisoner, powerless against him. Smiling wickedly, he leans down to trail his nose down my throat and back up. My breath catches. Dear God, that feels amazing.

"Jax," I moan quietly.

He's gone in the next breath, clicking pictures of me. My face burns up as I cover it with my arm. Jax leans in, lightly bites my arm in an attempt to stop me from shielding myself. He helps me sit up and continues taking pictures. This time he shoots both of us. We make funny faces, me kissing his cheek, him making me laugh, him looking at me fondly, and one of us kissing passionately. I love that he's captured all of this. It somehow makes it real, I will always have the reminder of today. The re-beginning of us . . .

His phone rings, breaking the spell. I groan inwardly. When he sees who it is, his entire body goes rigid, his expression darkening. I know immediately that it's Wyatt on the other line. That's the only person who can make Jax change from the happy-go-lucky person he was a second ago to an avenging angel. As he gets to his feet, his face fills with regret. He swipes his finger across the screen to answer and strides over to a tree.

I want to comfort him, to let him know that I'm here for him. I want to be here in every way that he's been here for me, but I can't make my feet move. I'm torn. Something is stopping me. I remember Jax not being here for me when I needed him the most. Before I can put the pieces together, the flash eludes me, as if the feeling never took place.

Needing a distraction, I turn on my camera so I can flip through pictures while I wait for Jax's return. I remember my dad and I developing the first pictures I took. The thought stirs a warm feeling inside me. I'm grateful Jax gave me that extra push to start doing this again. The first forty or so aren't that special, but I still can't seem to delete them since they helped get me back to this point . . . to being me. Each picture shows improvement. By the last hundred, it's easy for me to remember why I wanted to major in photography. When I realize that I only have about ten left, I notice that Jax still isn't back.

I put away the camera and reach for my phone to see if Jax texted. I have nothing from Jax, only missed texts from Logan, Connor, and Kohen. Before opening my messages, I shoot one off to Jax.

Me: Everything okay?

I stare at my phone, willing it to ring with a new text, but nothing happens. I open my brother's text thread instead of sending Jax another message that will go unanswered.

Logan: Lunch noon?

Logan: Up yet?

Logan: It's not normal how much you sleep.

Me: Why did you ditch me last night?

My phone buzzes in my hand.

Logan: Something came up. Did you get home okay?

Since I haven't been home yet, I keep the text as vague as possible. It's not like I can tell him I stayed over at Jax's.

Me: Still breathing c: See you tomorrow?

Logan: Ha Ha Ha. Connor said Jax took you home so I just wanted to make sure you weren't sick or anything.

All the air whooshes out my body as I quickly run through the night's events in my head. I can't recall seeing Connor when I was leaving with Jax. Even if Connor did notice us he wouldn't have recognized Jax with the different mask. Jax must have told Connor he was taking me home. Which makes sense. If Jax didn't say anything, that would have been suspicious. Nobody actually knows I went home *with* Jax. With shaking fingers, I text my brother back.

Me: Either that or I walked.

Logan: Funny.

Me: Thanks. I try.

I take the first relaxing breath since I replied to him. *He doesn't know anything.* That would have been bad. My body shudders. I ignore Kohen's text and read the two I missed from Connor.

Connor: You alive?

Connor: Call Logan before he comes looking for you . . .

I can't even go a day without Logan recruiting Connor to find out where I am. I contemplate banging my head against a tree instead of confronting my overprotective brother. The tree-banging seems like the less painful choice.

Me: Already handled . . . thanks?

Without even waiting for a response, I start packing everything up to search for Jax. Something is clearly wrong. I've just finished folding the blanket when I feel him behind me. I turn around. His face is ghostly pale, rigid, and if the clenching of his jaw is any indication, I know he is trying hard to stay in control. His eyes are the worst, void of the previous happiness and now haunted by his past, by his father.

As I step towards him to comfort him, he takes two steps back and raises his hands to stop me from coming any closer.

"I have to go."

And to my astonishment, he quickly picks up the basket with the blanket on top and walks away without another word. I stand staring, mouth agape, watching him leave me. Again. It's taking everything in me to keep myself from collapsing to the ground. Somehow I find the strength to keep standing, watching him. With every step he takes away from me, I wonder if I'll be enough for him. When he's almost out of eyesight, I know I need to fight.

For him.

For me.

For us.

After retrieving my forgotten camera bag, I take off running after him. Last night changed everything. I need to tell him that whatever that sick bastard said to him doesn't change anything, that he can lean on me. When I finally reach him, I'm hopeful. I'm finally fighting for the one thing I want most in this world. Jax.

"Stop. Tell me what happened. Don't shut me out." I slide my hands up to his face and force him to look at me. "We're in this together now, Jax. Lean on me. I'm not going anywhere. I'm yours." I wrap my arms around his waist, breathing in the most intoxicating smell in the world. Jax.

His entire body stiffens and his arms remains at his side. I move back to gaze into his eyes again. Almost wishing I hadn't with how much pain I see behind them. It's as if I'm staring at my reflection. I reach up to stroke his cheek again, but he flinches away as if in pain. He isn't here with me, he's somewhere far away. I know the signs all too well.

"Please talk to me, Jax. I'm right here. Don't shut me out," I plead to deaf ears.

He stares straight through me. Not knowing what else to do, I grab his face with both hands, lean on my tiptoes, and kiss him with all the love I have. Every agonizing second he doesn't respond, I kiss him back harder, unwilling to give up. A lifetime passes before I feel anything back from him. When he tentatively strokes his tongue with mine, I nearly sigh with relief. His hands go into my hair, pulling at the strands, angling my face to deepen the kiss. The rest of the world floats away. Nothing else matters. Nobody can touch us in this moment. The passion fades and the kiss turns angry. He's fighting this, fighting us. He's telling me goodbye with his lips. He tears his mouth away from mine and leans his head against my forehead.

"I'm sorry, Adalynn." He didn't use his nickname. Before he speaks again, I know this is over. "I can't," he whispers.

He closes his eyes and drops his hands from my face and walks away. I'm still struggling to make my brain work, but I somehow manage to reach out and stop him. He shakes his head and doesn't turn around to face me.

"Why?"

I have no idea why I'm even asking. I won't get an answer and Jax isn't one to disappoint. His silence rings loud and clear. I can't believe he won't even turn around to look at me. Last night meant nothing to him.

Reining in my temper, I demand in a deadly quiet voice, "Tell me Jax, I deserve to know why you're pushing me away, yet again." Nothing. "At least have the decency to look at me!" I nearly shout at him. Nothing.

I tramp around him and grip his face to forcibly make him look at me. When he finally opens his eyes and sees me, really sees me, I smile warmly at him.

"Nothing you can say will change how I feel about you Jax . . . I—"

He shoves me away, cutting me off.

"Enough, Adalynn. You can't fix me. You can't even fix yourself." Him punching me would have hurt less. "Leave me alone. I don't want or need you." Typical Jax-style, he leaves without another word, uncaring that he just gutted me.

If this were a movie I would chase after him again. I would show him that I won't give up, and he would be running towards me, too. He would tell me he didn't mean it and kiss me with everything he has. But this isn't a movie and I don't have enough strength left in me to chase after him and tell him I love him. *You can't even fix yourself.* His words drain me from any strength that I have, making it impossible to keep standing.

It's surprisingly easy to convince myself to let him go, that he doesn't feel the same for me. With my head down, I leave Central Park. Each step I take away from him, I promise myself I need to let go of this fantasy I've had of us together. I'm nothing to him.

Two weeks later I'm half expecting Jax to show up at the bakery. Each time the bell chimes upon someone's arrival and it's not him, it becomes increasingly clear that Jax is continuing to push me away. I kept telling myself he needed time and then we could go back to normal, and a tiny part of me hoped we could go back to being more. I replay the night of the ball on a continuous wheel in my head.

Every time I see him in passing, he avoids me. I finally force myself to stop trying to talk to him when it became obvious that he wasn't going to respond to any of my text messages or calls. I wanted to scream at the top of my lungs when I met the guys for dinner the other night, and as soon as I sat down, Jax made an excuse to leave. He shouldn't have bothered showing up, it's our weekly dinner. Of course I'm going to be there. *I need to move on.* That mantra is easier said than done.

I'm trying desperately to concentrate on booking a pirate-themed birthday cake for a customer, but I keep losing focus. I really need to pay attention to her, but I can't. She changes her mind every single time I'm almost done with the paperwork. My temper starts to awaken. I honestly don't know how many times I've crossed everything out because she's changed her mind. Ha, someone changing their mind on me. The irony is not lost on me.

I'm contemplating how illegal it is to poke her in the eye with my pen, or if it would be better to stab myself with my own pen, when a deep voice saves me from doing something extreme. I want to feign happiness at seeing Kohen, but I can't. Jax has ruined even the simple act of masking my emotions, like he's ruined me.

Despite my indifference, Kohen in scrubs is a sight to behold. He has an amused expression and it takes me a second to realize what's so funny. At first I think it's because he heard the customer, whose name I keep forgetting, but then it becomes apparent why he's standing here pleased with himself. He asked me something. *Crap . . . Think . . . Think . . .*

The girl glances up when she notices she doesn't have my undivided attention any longer and gasps loudly as she takes Kohen in. Yeah, who can blame her? It's pretty hilarious to watch her whole demeanor change. The bitchy side of her disappears and she's giving him a look that I can only describe as the come-fuck-me look. It's a look I have become very aware of from women when I'm with the guys. I have to turn away to keep from laughing in her face. Honestly, does she not have class?

When I face them again, she's narrowing her eyes at me. Okay maybe my coughing didn't cover up my laugh like I thought. Whoops. I don't even feel a little guilty. I peer at the form to see that her name is Amanda. *Ah, that's what it is.* Kohen beams at me and it makes me smile my first real smile all week. Well, the second if I'm being honest. The first was when I saw Jax sitting with the guys in the restaurant. I give Kohen the universal sign for five minutes before I try unsuccessfully to rush Amanda. I could always ask someone from the back to help Kohen, but I have a feeling that he would just wait for me anyway.

It's the longest ten minutes of my life before Amanda is on her way out the door, but not before she tries again to get Kohen's attention. She pouts when he shows no interest in her. A laugh slips out of my mouth. I'll make sure to remain in the back when she picks up her cake in a few days. The bell chimes, signaling Amanda's departure. I turn to find Kohen standing in front of me, leaning over the counter. My surprised gasp makes him smile.

"Hi . . . ?" I ask because I have no idea why he's here.

I haven't talked to him since our date, nor have I responded to his text messages. I've just deleted them without reading. I wouldn't say I was ignoring him per se, I was just hoping things with Jax would turn out differently and I didn't want to lead on Kohen if I pursued things with Jax. But now seeing him in front of me, looking way too good in his scrubs, I'm wondering why I didn't seek him out. He's exactly the kind of distraction I need in my life. And it's pretty clear that he likes me so that's a plus. I definitely don't need someone who's going to play the hot and cold game with me, I get enough of that from The God.

"Okay, feel free to turn me down." Kohen pauses to see if I'm going to stop him, but when I don't say anything, he continues. "I was hoping I could talk you into a quick lunch, but I have to get back to the hospital now, so how about dinner tonight? Anywhere you want, just text me the location, let's say seven?"

Before I can say anything, he gives me a chaste kiss on the lips. He walks out of the bakery, leaving me with my fingers touching my lips, fighting the urge to throw up. Why do I feel like I've betrayed Jax by letting him kiss me? It infuriates me to even think that. Seeing Kohen might be exactly what I need to get over Jax.

Hmmm . . . A little cocky assuming I'm just going to say yes. Well, it's a good thing I'm having dinner at Connor's tonight after therapy. Hopefully Kohen's ready for another dinner date with the boys because that's what he's getting, sans Jax, of course, since apparently having dinner with me is so appalling. At least someone wants to have dinner with my winning personality. I idly wonder if I should let Kohen know we'll be having company, but dismiss that idea. He's the one that assumed I didn't have plans so he can suffer through dinner with my overprotective brother and Connor. I text Kohen to meet me at the coffee place around the corner from Connor's.

CHAPTER TEN

When I step outside into the humid air, I see two cars waiting for me. Logan's and Connor's. *Because driving one car is so difficult.* I've never understood driving in New York, especially when they have drivers. You never know when the guys will have a driver. As far as I can tell, their current mood dictates being behind the wheel. Which is strange when I think about it because sometimes I get the impression that Logan fears being behind the wheel because of what happened to our family.

"Connor's taking you back to his place while I get the food."

I shake my head as I walk into his open arms. When I turn towards Connor, he slides off the hood of his car. He engulfs me into a hug. When I pull back, he clutches me tighter to him, refusing to let go. I bite him on his forearm.

He shouts, "Ow Addie! Only in the bedroom! How many times do I have to tell you?" as he rubs his chest. "Does Jax like it rough?" he whispers so only I can hear.

I don't know if I should reprimand him for risking that comment or if I want to kick him in the shin for bringing up Jax.

"Leave her alone, Connor! I swear if you were anyone else you would be dead for talking to her like that. Go with the jackass and I'll get the burgers."

I hug my brother. "Don't forget about Kohen's burger." I slide into the passenger side and yank the door from Connor's grasp to slam it.

Connor grins at me and faces my brother. The window is down so I can hear everything he says to Logan.

"She just sank her teeth into me and you're mad at me?" He claps my brother on the shoulder. "Don't worry, I'll get her to fall in line with all the others."

We ignore him. My brother shakes his head at Connor before leaving. I can't believe Connor has the nerve to say something about Jax in front of Logan.

"Love you too!" Connor shouts at him.

Logan flips him off before getting into his car and peeling out into New York traffic. I love my brother.

I give Connor the silent treatment the entire ride. He tries to make me talk by putting on the worst pop music in the world. And I do mean the worst! *I won't let it get to me. I won't let it get to me. Drown it out. It's just music.* I smile sweetly at him, not willing to play into his games. He turns it up even more. *I won't let it get to me . . . I won't let it—*

"God you're so annoying!" I snatch his iPhone and switch it to actual music. "Why do you even have this crap on here?"

"Just to annoy you," he says with a secretive smile.

"Right!" I go back to ignoring him.

"Come on, Addie, it was funny."

I yank my hand away. "Funny? Really? So telling all of New York your immature joke is funny to you? Or saying something about Jax in front of Logan? Sorry, your humor is lost on me."

"Don't be dramatic, Addie, it wasn't all of New York." He laughs at me.

"And what about the Jax comment?"

"What about it? Logan didn't hear me."

It's a good thing he's driving and not me. I wait for him to elaborate, ask more questions, but he never does. I'm kind of glad. I don't want to hear about Jax right now. I made the decision to move on. Or at least be distracted enough to attempt to move on.

"Gah I hate you, you do know this, right?" I mutter because I can't help myself.

He knows exactly what he's doing. He's making me think of his best friend right before I go out with someone else. As if I needed a reminder of Jax.

He stops at a green light and leans over to kiss my cheek, not caring in the slightest at the angry New Yorkers honking at us.

"Oh my God, it's green, Connor!"

"Tell me you love me."

How does he even have a license? "Fine, I love you, now drive."

"You wish is my command, sis." He pats my knee. "I'm sorry about that Jax comment . . . Just don't give up on him."

"What does that even mean?"

He shrugs and focuses on not killing us. The rest of the drive, the only thing on my mind is Jax. I hate that I can't stop thinking about him and I hate that it's Connor's fault for bringing him up. He tries to put his arm over my shoulder as we walk into his building, but I pull away. I'm still upset.

And then he gives me his sad face, complete with pouting lips. Even though I'm still irked at him for not explaining what he means about Jax, I lean against him, loving how safe he makes me feel. As much as I hate to admit it, I love Connor's *unique* sense of humor.

Once we're inside, Connor marches over to his kitchen and makes a sandwich. The only thing that he knows how to make without burning himself, or anything in the near vicinity. I settle onto a barstool.

My eyes are glued to his flat stomach as he inhales his turkey and roast beef sandwich. Logan will be here soon with dinner, but no, someone can't wait that long. It's amazing that Connor's not a whale with how much food he consumes. I'm about to tell him that he needs to watch his diet when he opens his big mouth, filled with the bite he just took. Someone didn't learn their manners when they were younger. I make a mental note to bring this up at Thanksgiving with his parents. It's always entertaining to watch Connor's mom treat him like a small child who needs his food cut.

"When are you meeting the good doctor? I still can't believe you haven't told him you're coming back here and not going on a date." He holds his fist out for a fist-bump. I shove it away and check the time on my phone.

"Crap, I have to go. I'm late."

As I scramble to stand, I trip over the barstool and almost fall flat on my face. Luckily Connor rushes to me and steadies me.

"The chair tried to kill me. Be back soon."

He chuckles as he walks me out. "Oh yes, it was my murderous chair and not my sister who can't walk a straight line sober."

"Be nice . . . so basically don't be you," I say before the elevator doors close in his face.

As I enter the coffee shop, all the chaos overwhelms me. How the heck am I going to find Kohen? I didn't need to worry, his beautiful smiling face stands out in the sea of people. He leans against the wall with two coffee cups in his hands. I fight the urge to wrinkle my nose. I hate hot coffee. I'm a frappuccino girl all the way.

As I make my way towards him, I notice that the majority of women are stealing glances at him or bluntly staring. Some women have no shame. Then again, I can't blame them. He's easy to look at especially tonight. He's sporting dark jeans and a white button-up shirt with the sleeves rolled up, displaying his muscular forearms. It's simple, yet sexy in a mouthwatering way. *Jax looks better.* My subconscious is nice enough to remind me of something that I'm very aware of. I don't care, I'm not comparing the two. I'm not that girl.

It isn't until I'm in front of him that I realize I've been gawking at him with my mouth wide open. I promptly shut it. His grin is sinfully sexy, with a hint of danger. I think it's forced though, he doesn't seem like anyone who could be dangerous. He's the boy-next-door. He extends his hand. I accept the coffee without making a face. Go me!

"Thanks." Tentatively I take a sip and I'm pleasantly surprised it's my one and only favorite hot drink.

Mmm, I love this chocolatey goodness. It seems too big of a coincidence for him to just guess my favorite drink. I open my mouth to ask him about it, but I'm struck speechless when he wipes a dab of chocolate from my lip and sucks his thumb into his mouth. Holy-hotness. Talk about a bold move. It's been too long since I've flirted with anyone besides Jax. I'm way out of my league when it comes to Kohen. Any man if I'm being honest. Flirting? Me? Ha, what a joke!

Leaning in so his lips brush against my ear, he whispers, "Mmm, Adalynn and chocolate . . . my favorite."

I would be lying if I said he doesn't affect me. I meet his azure eyes, attempting to figure him out. No luck. I have a sinking feeling he's not the man that he appears. He's wearing a mask, too. Can I make him take it off? Will I take mine off for him and open up to him? I seriously doubt it. I don't want anyone to know me. I like being isolated. *You sure about that?* I have no idea what I want anymore. I do know I need to make sure this man is real. I reach out to touch him, but I'm pushed from behind. I accidentally bump into Kohen and spill my boiling hot drink down my chest.

I suck in a breath. Fuck, that's hot. In a split second Kohen has me behind him in a protective gesture and is confronting some poor teenager terrified for his life. I forget about my boiling skin and focus on the scene in front of me. Kohen says something too low for me to hear and the teenager's eyes nearly bulge out of his head. Whatever it is, it isn't pleasant and is very unnecessary. I attempt to move in front of Kohen to apologize, but he's holding me behind him, trapping me. It takes all my willpower to not smack the back of his head to get his attention. He's making a scene. People are staring.

He leans into the guy's face and says something else. The teenager and his friends practically run out of the coffee shop. Kohen releases my wrist. His body shudders with the effort to calm down before he faces me. I'm expecting rage in his eyes, but he's composed as if he didn't just make a scene and scare the crap out of some poor kids. What just happened? If it wasn't for my sore wrist, I would think that I've imagined the whole thing. I look from my wrist, that has the clear indentation of his hands wrapping around it, to his face. The sadness I see there makes whatever nasty comment I was going to make die on my tongue.

Caressing his face I say, "Hey, it's okay, it was an accident."

He doesn't say anything. He lightly traces his index finger over the red mark on my wrist.

"It was an accident. Now let's go eat some burgers and watch a movie."

I nearly have to drag him out of the coffee shop. When we cross the street, I can tell he's coming out of his sulky mood. We're almost at Connor's building when he squeezes my hand, letting me know that he's back to normal and we're gonna have a good night. The jury is still out on that one, I still haven't told him we aren't having dinner by ourselves. Maybe he hates surprises like me. Only one way to find out.

I swipe the access card to the penthouse. Once the elevator start its rise to the top, it's clear I'm not taking him to a restaurant.

"Since I already know you don't live here, mind telling me where you're taking me?" Kohen asks.

Well, there goes the surprise. I wonder how he's going to take the news. I square my shoulders, preparing for battle. Here goes nothing.

"Connor's," I respond in a voice that would make any cheerleader proud.

He doesn't speak. I'm gonna say this is good news. We're almost at the top floor when Kohen breaks the silence.

"Sure that's such a safe idea?" I give my what-the-heck look. "Last time we tried this I'm pretty sure one of them was trying not to punch me."

Instantly, I picture The God's too gorgeous face. I force out a laugh, pretending like I have no idea what he means.

"You were the one who assumed I didn't have plans tonight, so now you have to suffer along with me." When the elevators open into Connor's foyer, I stand on my tiptoes and give Kohen a quick kiss. "Besides, nobody wanted to punch you."

Hand-in-hand, we stroll through Connor's penthouse while I hope that Jax shows up tonight. That would be the last thing I need, but I'm mature enough to admit that I want him to see me with someone else.

Before I give Kohen a small tour of the main level, I kick off my shoes because I hate the clicking they make on the marble floor. Besides, Connor's cleaning lady cleans too well; his floor is slippery. I may or may not have broken my finger slipping on it one time. I point out one of the bathrooms on the way to the kitchen. I fetch beers from the state-of-the-art-fridge before leading him to the living room where the noise is coming from.

From the corner of my eye, I notice Kohen studying the pictures in the hallway. I slow my pace but don't stop. He admires a black and white painting before striding to my side. He takes in the lavish decor as I lead him around Connor's bachelor pad.

The guys sit on the black leather couch, playing some sort of shooting video game. Guys. You would think at twenty-eight, Connor would grow up, but you'd be wrong. His place hints at the playboy that I've always known him to be. Connor settling down is as likely as me growing another limb.

Dinner runs smoothly. It was a little touch-and-go in the beginning with Logan and Connor interrogating Kohen. Once Twenty Questions were over and they were satisfied I could be interested in a decent guy, dinner becomes relatively normal.

Kohen jokes along with the guys. He even thinks Connor is funny, which surprises me a little. Connor's sense of humor is a lot like mine. You either love it, or you think he's an ass. Stealing my last fry, Connor looks innocently at me. Too innocently. Oh no, this isn't good.

"So Addie must *really* like you," Connor says at the same time Logan says, "She's trying to impress him, Connor."

"Why do you say that?" Kohen asks.

Logan and Connor wear the purest expressions. I don't buy it. I scowl at both of them, silently daring them to say something. I have my foot ready. I haven't kicked either of them all night. That's a success in my book. *The night's still early,* that voice in my head taunts. They nod at each other and have a silent conversation. I hate when they do that. Connor's grin nearly breaks his face in two. This is bad, very bad.

"Well, she was able to eat her entire burger while being a lady."

Logan nods in agreement. "Yeah, she didn't even stuff her face like usual, Connor."

"She must *really* like you," Connor says again.

I'm debating what excuse will get us to leave so they can't embarrass me any further when Kohen starts laughing with them. I was so consumed by not blushing that I missed Kohen making a mess of himself. I give him a grateful smile when I see the remains of his burger all over his face.

"Touché, you two are perfect for each other." Logan winks at me.

Connor picks some action movie that I've never heard of. Not surprisingly, it has the same plot of most movies about secret agents. Kohen and I sit together on one couch while the guys take the much bigger one. Kohen circles his arm around me and I lean into him.

I keep pretending that I don't notice every time Connor glances over, but I do. Each time I feel guilty and I feel as if I'm doing something wrong. I can't shake this feeling that I need to put some distance between Kohen and me. Logan comments to Kohen about the last scene. I can't even pretend to know what they're talking about so I tune them out. I stopped paying attention to the movie five minutes into it. Connor's scrutinizes me again. I force myself to ignore him and focus on the movie, but it's no use.

I stare down Connor, wondering why he's watching my every move. He gives me a sympathetic look and it becomes crystal clear why he's watching every interaction of my date. The lightbulb goes off.

Jax.

I hold in my humorless laugh. Everything leads back to the one guy who doesn't love me. I nestle closer into Kohen because I'm not going to second guess everything I do with someone who actually likes me. As I concentrate on the movie, Kohen runs his fingertips along my shoulder and down my arm. If I didn't feel guilty using Kohen as a distraction, I would enjoy his simple defiance of my brother and Connor. He doesn't seem to mind touching me in front of them. I hate that I want to push him away from me because I feel as if I'm cheating on Jax.

As the end credits roll, I mentally curse myself for falling in love with the damaged boy who trusted me to take care of him when he used to sneak into my bedroom growing up. Ignoring the questioning look Logan sends my way, I rise and collect my purse. I plaster on a fake smile when I face the guys. For the first time tonight, I'm glad Jax isn't here. He would be able to see right through me, and that's not something I want or need right now.

"Ready to head out?" I ask Kohen.

I can tell my mood change catches him off guard, but he recovers quickly. "Absolutely." He assures my brother, "I'll make sure she gets home safely."

Logan shakes his offered hand. "*Alone,*" he says in a brotherly tone that isn't necessary.

I could die of mortification.

Connor rescues Kohen from any more brotherly advice by smoothly slapping Logan on the back of the head. "What Logan means is, thank you for making sure Addie gets home safely."

Kohen forces out a laugh. "Yeah . . . no problem."

They escort us to the elevators and before Logan decides to join us, I rush to hug him and then Connor.

"Give it time," Connor whispers into my ear.

The cab ride to our building is long and awkward. Every time things start to get normal between us again, an image of Jax pops into my head, shattering our conversation. I tell myself it's because I haven't seen him in forever and I miss my friend. As the car pulls up to the curb, I almost sigh in relief.

Once we're in the elevator, I look up to apologize for my bipolar behavior, but the words stick in my throat. Kohen watches me with his dark, stormy eyes. Since words are nonexistent at this point, I try for another tactic. I lean up on my tiptoes and kiss him. His kiss is nothing like Jax's. Where Jax is passionate, Kohen is tender. I break away from the kiss as soon as I realize that I'm comparing the two.

Breathless Kohen, seems influenced by our kiss. His eyes are full of desire. I want to throw up. This is wrong and unfair to him. Luckily the elevator gods decide to have pity on me. They finally stop at my floor.

"Next time it will be a real date." I step out.

"I'll hold you to that. Good night, Adalynn."

I make it back to my apartment and sink to the floor. Why am I still obsessed with Jax after all this time? Why can't I just move on? Why can't I even remember the sensation from Kohen's lips on mine? Forcing myself off the floor, I concentrate on getting ready for bed.

Three weeks have flown by since that *unforgettable* dinner at Connor's. Liv is a thorn in my butt that I can't shake . . . not like I really want to, anyway. I've been seeing the change in myself and I won't jeopardize my progress. Kohen has become a permanent fixture in my life. We usually have dinner together unless he's working. Connor and Logan, Yankees season pass holders, invited him to a game. Liv seems pleased that I'm dating, she just cautions me to take it slow.

Luckily Kohen treats me with extreme patience. Which is great because every time things get interesting between us, I think of Jax. I have to concentrate on removing Jax from my mind, total mood killer. Kohen thinks I'm just not ready to take the next logical step in our . . . whatever we are . . . but the truth is I don't want to do anything with him that I will regret. I have a sinking feeling that if I'm with him, I'll be thinking of Jax. So until I no longer have to force my thoughts off Jax, I can't take that much needed next step. It's unfair to Kohen.

Jax avoids me at all costs. I'm not even worth the effort for him to nod in greeting. I hate that he's ignoring me. Sure, when I'm at the office he mumbles two words to me in passing if someone is around. I learned pretty fast to give up on conversation. If he doesn't want to talk to me, fine, I'm not going to beg him. I'm not a dog. Jax makes excuse after excuse so he isn't forced to be around me. It's a good thing Connor is aware of what's going on because he helps me distract Logan.

As much as it hurts to not have Jax in my life anymore, I know that him pushing me away is the best thing that he could have ever done for me. He's not my savior, and I need to stop thinking that one day we might end up together.

"Order ready for Addie," a server calls out, jerking me out of my thoughts.

I jump up from the bench and snag two salads for the lunch I'm surprising Kohen with, since he's working all night. He didn't take anything with him and he usually forgets to eat unless someone forces him to sit down. Lately I've become that person. I jog out the door and hail down a cab.

When I reach the hospital, a passing nurse gives me directions on where to find him. I head into another corridor and come across Kohen facing a young guy in scrubs.

"I know I'm sorry, it won't happen again," the man says, with exasperation.

"Sorry. That's all you have to say? I could have you fired for this!" Kohen shouts.

"I'm not going to make excuses, there are none. This won't happen again I promise." The guy's eyes bulge out of his head as if he's afraid. He doesn't know Kohen as well as I do because he wouldn't hurt anyone.

An older doctor steps out of a room and notices the situation unfolding. It takes him about a nanosecond to guess what's going on.

"It's an easily corrected mistake that happens with interns, Dr. Daniels. He won't let this slip by again and just to make sure it sticks, he's going to be doing grunt work for the next three months."

The older guys pats Kohen on the shoulder and walks away, leaving Kohen and the intern alone. When the other doctor is out of sight, Kohen grabs the intern by his throat and slams him into the wall. When Kohen has the intern's attention, he releases his throat but doesn't back away. Instead Kohen whispers into his ear. The intern can only nod because it's clear from where I'm standing that he's too terrified to speak.

I'm speechless. I know that I need to stop this from happening, but I can't make my legs move. I'm transfixed as Kohen tells him something unimaginable. I watch in horror as the blood slowly drains out of the intern's face. I can't even pretend to know what he's telling him. I release my death-like grip on the bag. The salads crash to the floor. Suddenly my legs move on their own accord.

Out of nowhere, Kohen backs away. I have no idea if I've yelled his name or if he heard my too-loud feet. The guy sinks to the floor. Immediately I squat down beside him, ignoring Kohen. I have no idea how much time has passed, but it feels like hours, not minutes. I can't believe Kohen reacted this way. I desperately want to know what he said that was so terrifying.

"Are you okay?" I ask like an idiot. Obviously he's not.

"Yes . . . Fine," the intern wheezes as he glares at Kohen.

Brave man. I help him rise and when he's finally able to stand on his own, I take a small step back, but keep myself in between him and Kohen. I don't know this guy, but I need to protect him. There's no telling what

Kohen's capable of. As I turn to face Kohen, the intern mumbles something under his breath that I don't hear. Kohen does.

In the next second, Kohen shoves me out of the way and slams the intern into the wall. I land onto the hard ceramic floor. I feel as if all air has left me. I can't believe I'm dating someone like Wyatt, Jax's abusive father. I swallow the bile rising.

It isn't until Kohen comes up behind me that I realize the intern is nowhere to be seen. I jump to my feet and put a good distance between us.

"Don't touch me," I warn.

I'm so mad at myself for not seeing the abusive man standing in front of me. My body hums with the anger coursing through my body. I'm furious with Kohen. I stalk away from him, leaving our lunch on the floor, but he stops me by wrapping his hands around my forearm.

"Ads, wait. I'm sorry, let me explain, please."

I don't know if it's the fact that I just watched him slam his intern into the wall, that he touched when I told him not to, or that he called me Ads, but for whatever reason I slap his face as hard as I can. Each one is reason enough in my book. Without another word, I flee.

The entire ride back to my apartment is a blur of every moment I've spent with him. I try to pinpoint times when I could have noticed his abusive tendencies, but I come up blank. It's scary how much you think you know someone, just to be proven wrong. Can you really ever know somebody?

After finishing a ten mile run through Central Park, I still don't have any answers. I don't know how I didn't see that Kohen is exactly like Wyatt. He has been nothing but perfect since I've met him. He doesn't even give off that too-nice vibe. He just seems to have the same amount of worries as everyone else.

With Jax's father, Wyatt, it was obvious since the first time I met him that he was a troubled man. He showed it in everything that he did. Even when I was little, I knew that there was something wrong. As a kid, Jax would cower away from his father whenever he raised his hand or made any fast movements. I feared him from the moment I met him and even more so the first night I saw what he was capable of; the night that Jax finally let me in, and shared his burden.

Stumbling down the hallway leading to my apartment, I'm so preoccupied that I don't realize someone is sitting beside my door until I trip over a pair of legs.

"Crap I'm—" The apology dies when Kohen leaps off the floor.

"Please, Adalynn, five minutes, and if you still don't want to talk to me, I will never bother you again."

I cross my arms over my chest and nearly yell, "Oh, so you expect to tell me some bullshit excuse that makes it okay to slam someone into a wall? Wow, this must be good. I can't wait. You now have four minutes. Go."

He runs his hands through his hair and down his face, exhaling loudly. He moves toward me, but when he sees me take two steps back, he gives up.

"Adalynn, you know me, I'm not the person you saw today. I lost it with Mike. I've been his mentor for so long I didn't even think to make sure he knew what he was doing and I failed him. I was more mad at myself than him for expecting too much, so early, and I lost it."

I roll my eyes and make a point to glance down at my phone to check the time. Times like this I wish I was wearing one of my watches.

"Simple mistakes like the one Mike made today can cost people their loved ones. Families can be ruined by one simple mistake."

Guilt washes over his face. Before his eyes cast down, I see the sign of unshed tears. It's almost enough for me to wrap my arms around him, but I need more from him. I stand frozen as I silently beg him to let me in, waiting for him to fill in the last puzzle piece.

"I know this doesn't excuse the way I handled everything earlier, but all I saw when he told me what happened was the doctors explaining to my dad that the brain tumor was inoperable and she didn't have much time. It was a simple mistake. If they were paying attention to the signs, they could have noticed it sooner and things may have been different. That's all I saw today, I didn't even realize what was happening until I heard you whisper my name."

I hate that I feel badly for him. For the first time, I can see how broken he really is, like me. He's not the perfect man I thought he was. More than anything, I hate that I can justify his actions. It's painfully obvious how hard it is for him to share this, yet he is. I have no idea why, I'm nothing special. But for some reason, he thinks I'm worth it. I let him take a timid step towards me. He stops when he is a breath away from me.

"I'm so sorry for what you saw today. As much as I want to say I wish you weren't there, I won't lie to you. I'm glad you were," he whispers.

"Why?" I whisper back.

"If it wasn't for you, I wouldn't have stopped. You saved me from making the biggest mistake of my life." Skimming his fingertips over my cheek, he gazes intently into my eyes. "I would never hurt you, Adalynn."

I don't know if it's that I feel like our shared grief connects us on some level, or his obvious regret for his actions that makes me forgive him. Covering the hand caressing my cheek, I lean into his touch.

"I'm so sorry for running off like that. I should have let you explain. I know more than most people about losing yourself to your past, Kohen."

Framing my face with his large, strong hands, Kohen asks, "Can you forgive me?"

"There's nothing to forgive."

Kohen kisses me as if he thinks I'm going to change my mind. Wanting him to believe that I'm here for him and to show him how happy I am that he opened up, I kiss him back with everything that I have. When he trails one of his hands down my neck, along my collarbone I pull back, breathless. His lust-filled eyes, reveal how he sees me. Beautiful. I open my mouth so I can slow things down, but he beats me to it.

"I'm going to go before I press my luck. I'll call you tomorrow, okay?"

"Sounds perfect."

After saying goodbye to Kohen with a few more heavy kisses, I head to my bedroom to get ready for bed. As I undress, it becomes disgustingly clear that I was just making out with Kohen covered in sweat. Yum, I sure know how to be as sexy as possible with men. No wonder he didn't try going further tonight. I wouldn't want to do anything with me, either. I step out of my sweaty workout clothes and climb into the boiling hot shower.

I can't believe how I treated Kohen earlier, I should have given him a chance to explain before fleeing. I know what he did was bad, but I shouldn't have overreacted and slapped him. Okay, so he deserved the slap, but comparing him to Wyatt was inexcusable. I should have never have let that thought drift into my head. Wyatt is a poor excuse for a human being whereas Kohen is nearly perfect.

Kohen has been nothing but nice to me. Everyone at work adores him, minus Mike. Ugh, my stomach clenches. I almost let Kohen go just because of a misunderstanding. Thank God he didn't just let me walk away from him. Letting me in and sharing his pain means more to me than he can ever realize. I'm so used to Jax shutting me out.

Kohen opened up to me even without the knowledge that I would listen. I can allow myself to plan things with him instead of always worrying he will leave without warning. He doesn't strike me as the type to let me go so easily. I smile. No, he sure doesn't. I pick up my phone.

Me: July 12 is Logan's surprise party . . . You in?

Within seconds my phone beeps, making me exhale in relief upon opening it.

Kohen: Love to :)

As I'm texting him back the info of when and where, he responds before I can even hit the send button.

Kohen: How old is the birthday boy going to be and what should I get him?

Me: 28 . . . I am so the wrong person to ask.

Kohen: You do know you're his sister, right? Who better to ask than you?

Me: I suck at giving gifts so if you want to get him something then you have to come up with it all on your own C:

Kohen: You couldn't suck at anything if you tried, but fine, thanks again for all the help.

Me: Welcome!

Kohen: Night Adalynn xoxo

I can't help the little chuckle that escapes when I read his last text. XOXO. So cheesy and high school, that I wrinkle my nose.

CHAPTER ELEVEN

Since the incident at Kohen's work, we've become a lot closer. I still haven't opened up to him about my past, but I make up for it by telling him about everything else. If he's proven anything in this past month, it's that I can count on him. To move our relationship forward, I've let him spend the night during the weekends. I don't know why we haven't had sex yet. Whenever we get hot and heavy, I always end up stopping it. I love that every time I do, he doesn't get mad at me or even say I'm a tease. He just pulls me in close and holds me all night.

Kohen is the only one who knows what I have planned today. It still amazes me that he was able to get me an interview. One night I told him that I wanted to do something with my business degree and the next day he's selling me on anyone's dream job. It's something that Logan would want me to do; he's never said it, but I don't think he approves of my current job. He will be thrilled if I can land the interview at Malcara Enterprises. I might be accomplishing his dreams today. For the life of me, I can't muster the excitement I should be feeling. I almost feel numb; I'm at the point between numb and feeling everything all at once. My heart races as I decide on the perfect interview outfit.

After pinning my hair into a knotted bun, I apply minimal make-up. Gazing at myself in the mirror, I untie the sash of my robe and let it fall off my shoulders to the ground. I slip into my white sheath dress and then slide my arms through the sleeves of my black blazer. Not a strand of hair is out of place, my lips bear a glossy shade of light pink lipstick, my violet eyes are accented with only mascara. I appear to be well put together, perfect.

As I sit in the back of a cab, I check the time to make sure Logan's in his morning meeting. I wait an extra five minute before I call Logan's assistant, so he can inform my brother to meet me at Liv's, instead of picking me up. If my overprotective brother knows that I'm on my way to an interview, it will be more than my nerves I'm worrying about. Adding Logan's would be too much for this opportunity, that arose thanks to Kohen.

Before I know it, the elevators open and I'm walking across the overly polished floor to the office of my hopefully soon-to-be boss and owner of Malcara Enterprises, William Malcara. If I can land this interview, I will be an assistant for the second largest marketing firm in the US. The first is Trinity. I square my shoulders back as I enter the impressive office, every step feeling as if I'm following my brother's footsteps instead of my own. I can't even think about what my own would be right now because I need to land this job. I need to prove to everyone that I'm not a kid anymore.

A receptionist ushers me down a corridor and introduces me. Mr. Malcara stands as I reach his desk. I shake his hand like my dad taught me. A firm handshake will go a long way in the business world, was his mantra when I was growing up. He looks as if he's in his early twenties, but I know he's in his late thirties from the internet.

"Have a seat, Ms. Maxwell." He directs me to the chair in front of his desk.

I hide my surprise that we're not moving to the conference style table to the left of his office. That's where my brother would hold an interview, Connor too. Jax wouldn't have bothered inviting them into his office. He would have them shown to the actual conference room.

"Thank you, Mr. Malcara."

My eyes scan the room and I notice that he is very much in love with his wife. Pictures of her, and of them together, fill his office.

"Can you tell me why you would want to work for me instead of your brother?" He gets straight to the point.

I was prepared for this question. I knew he would recognize my last name from his competitor. I get straight to the point. Mr. Malcara doesn't seem like the type for bullshit. I like that.

"If I wanted to work for my brother, all I would have to do is ask. I want to work somewhere where I can prove myself instead of being the owner's sister. Here, I can flourish and make something of myself. I can be an asset to your team. Working at Trinity I couldn't do that, and frankly I've never wanted to work for him."

He rubs his clean-shaven chin. "You have no experience in the industry except the internship you completed in college. Why should I choose you over any of the other candidates?"

I feel as if I'm going to battle for a job that I don't think I really want. I don't back down, though. If I want to prove myself to everyone, I need to start with him.

"I know the ins and out of this business. I may not have the experience that the other candidates will bring to the table, but I can bring knowledge and my willingness to learn. I can strive here, learning everything you teach me."

He almost smiles. "Doctor Daniels is a dear friend of mine and my wife. He is the reason why you have this interview. He spoke very kindly of you, that you will succeed working here, given the chance. Your chance is this interview. Wow me, Ms. Maxwell." He hands me a piece of paper.

There's a brief description of the company, its products, sales, and inventory. As I study the information in my hands, I know immediately I can do this.

"You have three minutes," he adds in a bored tone.

I only need seconds. It's numbers. Numbers I can work with. I set the paper back on his desk and stand. "I'm ready."

He waves his hand for me to start. I explain to him that the lingerie company is not utilizing the custom creations as much as they should. It's brushed over, not their focal point. It's something that gives them an edge compared to their competitors. They need to focus on growth as their one salon brings in more than enough to expand to another store. I spend another minute explaining their strengths before I give him my closing line.

"The market is there, they have done well this year. With numbers like that, I can see them expanding globally. They will have to want it, though."

"Interesting."

I almost deflate because I thought I nailed it, but then he smiles his first smile since I walked in.

"Everyone else needed ten minutes or more to point out what you noticed within seconds. I think Kohen was right about you, Ms. Maxwell." He stands up and offers me a tour.

"This will be your office," he says with a wave of a hand.

My office consists of a large desk, an empty bookcase that takes up the entire right wall, and two chairs in front of the desk. It's small but perfect. The walls are all glass, making it appear both larger and smaller at the same time. I don't have time to think about privacy because he's leading me out of my office and over to Human Resources. He points out my co-workers. Only one, a tiny redhead, looks up from her computer long enough to wave to me. Everyone else nods in my direction.

After an hour and a half of paperwork, my hand cramps. It isn't until after I talk to my boss Sam at the bakery, that I'm actually excited about my new life change. He isn't mad that I'm leaving. If I ever want a job all I have to do is ask. Now, I can actually say I'm looking forward to tell my brother and Liv. As the cab idles at the curb of her building, I have to stop myself from running into her office and gushing to Logan that I have a grown-up job. He can't treat me like a kid any longer.

My nerves reappear when I see Logan on his iPad in the waiting room, ignoring his surroundings. I wonder how he'll take the news. I don't want to fight with him. Hopefully he will see me as an adult and I can convince him that I don't need him taking care of me anymore. Yeah, that will go over well.

I patiently wait for him to notice my presence. By patiently, I mean tapping my foot of course. When that doesn't work to get his attention, I clear my throat. I'm rewarded with him setting down the iPad.

"Are you going to ask me why I'm excited or not?"

"I'm assuming your good mood is why you changed up today's schedule."

Barely taking time to breathe I say, "I had an interview and you are now looking at the new assistant at Malcara Enterprises. I already put in my two weeks at the bakery before heading over here."

He leaps to his feet within the next breath. "You can't accept a job from me, but you're working at Malcara Enterprises? I wouldn't have you working as an *assistant*." He spits out assistant as if it's a bad word.

I may not really want this job, but I'm proud that I landed it, especially since I have no experience. I nailed the interview. I knew Logan wouldn't be thrilled, but I thought he would at least pretend to be happy.

"I thought you would understand. I thought this is what you wanted. You're the one who wants me to have a real job." He opens his mouth, but I talk over him. "Working at the bakery wasn't good enough. Now being the assistant of William Malcara isn't good enough. What will be good enough for you, Logan?"

Two other patients and the receptionist eaves drop. I'm making a scene, but I don't care. I'm tired of him controlling me. If I was more level headed, I would stop, but I can't. I thought this would make him happy, maybe eventually I can be happy working there until I figure out what I really want to do. I want to do something with my life that I'm passionate about, but I've yet to find it.

"I just want what's best for you. If you want a job, you have one. You can work with Connor and learn firsthand what he does to keep our company striving."

I put my hands on my hips so he knows I'm serious. "I don't want to work for you guys. I see enough of you three as it is. I want to succeed on my own."

He mocks my stance. At 6'5" to my 5'4", he's much more intimidating with his hands on his hips than I am.

"I want you to succeed, too. Work for Trinity, Adalynn."

"No. I'm working for Malcara." I shake my head at whatever argument he's going to start. "Just be happy for me, Logan. I nailed the interview and landed a job at the best marketing firm."

"Second best."

I groan. My overbearing brother can be hard to handle sometimes. I cross my hands over my chest waiting for him to say something else that will dampen my mood. After a beat, Logan engulfs me into a hug.

"You're right. I'm sorry." He bends his knees so were at eye level. "I just want you to be happy. If working for Will or even for Sam will make you happy, then I want you to do it."

I nod.

"I'm so proud of you, Addie. I'll call the guys and we can celebrate tonight!"

My tight smile fades when I hear "the guys." As much as I want to celebrate, it will crush me if Jax doesn't show. He's been a part of my life for as long as I can remember. He hasn't missed a big event yet, and I don't want this to be the first.

"No, no, don't. Let's not make a big deal or anything until I actually finish a work week."

His phone is already in his hand and he's typing away, but he pauses to look at me. I need to think of something, fast.

"I mean, we're already playing poker tonight at Connor's so you can get me a cupcake or something to hold you over for two weeks."

Before he can say anything, I'm called into Liv's office. I fight the urge to give the receptionist a high five. Perfect timing as always. I nod so she knows that I'll be there in a minute before facing my brother again.

"Can we please not make a big deal out of this?" I give him the sad doe eyes.

He sighs dramatically as if I just asked for him to hand over the world to me. "Fine, you win. I won't make a big deal about it . . . yet. I'll see if Jax can change his plans tonight so we can have a small celebration."

I fidget with the strap of my purse. "I thought you said you'll wait?"

"I'll wait to throw you a real celebration, but there's no way in hell that we're not acknowledging this with a small one. This is a big deal, sis, even if you are working for the enemy."

He puts his arms on my shoulders and forcibly turns me toward the office door before I can say anything else. Perfect timing on his part because I don't know how much longer I'll be able to keep my pain masked by a fake smile. I know without a doubt that Jax won't be there. Even though this is something that I should have gotten used to by now, it's still impossibly hard. Will I ever get used to not seeing Jax? Will I ever be okay with him blowing off big events like this? No, I highly doubt that anything involving Jax will get any easier.

I sit down on one of the white couches in Liv's office and wait for her to start. Hopefully today will be one of those days that she occupies my mind with questions so I can stop thinking about Jax. I've been doing pretty well at keeping him out of my thoughts unless someone brings him up. Now I can't stop thinking about him, of course.

My mind is everywhere else but Liv's office. I barely can come out of my own depressing thoughts to tell her about the new job. I vaguely recall her telling me she's proud and knows that I will do great. Oh, I guess I did tell her, go autopilot me.

"Want to tell me what's going on in that head of yours?"

"Do I really get a choice?"

She doesn't bite. Not that I thought she would, she never does.

"Usually when you come in, I either have to pull teeth out of you to get you to talk or you're pretty forthcoming, it's always one or the other. I don't usually get the side of you when you're not really here. Well, not anymore."

"The way you describe me makes it appear that I have multi-personality disorder."

She ignores me. I fake hurt; my joke was pretty funny. I even used a psychology term and everything.

"What's going on? I thought you would be excited about the new job, but you look like someone just kicked a puppy. Are things with Kohen still going strong? Have things not gotten better with Jax?"

Deciding to just lay it out there for her I say, "Things with Kohen are good . . . well, great, actually."

"Then what is it?"

"It's just something Logan said right before I walked in that I can't stop thinking about. Which makes me wonder if things are actually good with Kohen, or if I'm just pretending without even realizing it. I'm so used to pretending all of the time, I guess it gets harder to distinguish between what's real and what's an act."

I pick at my perfect cuticles. "I'm happy about the job. It shows that I'm ready to get my act together and do something with my degree. I just . . . I don't know."

When Liv doesn't say anything, I stop examining my nails and find her staring at me.

"I'm going to guess the thing Logan said has something to do with Jax?"

My silence is enough of an answer. She knows about my past with Jax and the recent time we slept together. She knows everything.

"I don't think that you're pretending with Kohen, but only you can answer that question. From everything you've told me, and how I've seen you come alive lately, I know that Kohen has a lot to do with that. You have unresolved issues with Jax and until you get closure with him, you will always second guess yourself with Kohen."

I wait for her continue, but she doesn't. So typical. Something about the way she said closure rings true. I just don't want closure with him, it's so final.

"Really? That's all you have to say? That doesn't really help me out here. Obviously I'm aware I have unresolved issues with Jax. I thought he was ready to let me in, but I haven't talked to him in almost three months. How can I possibly get closure?"

Ugh, I feel like screaming in frustration. Instead I act like the adult I am and not the child I wish I was sometimes, just so I could get away with screaming at the top of my lungs.

"I like Kohen, I really do. I love how honest he is with me and how he makes me feel. I just wonder if it's okay to be with him when I secretly have feelings for Jax. It's just that I-I don't know . . . I'm so confused."

She nods, causing a strand of her honey colored hair to fall into her face. She swipes it behind her ear, displaying a beautiful wedding ring. Absently I play with my empty ring finger. I've noticed her ring a million times, I've never once felt anything towards it. Marriage is something I don't deserve. I haven't imagined sharing my life with anyone in a long time. Even now I can't picture a man at my side. But as I become mesmerized by her ring, I realize that I'm jealous. Olivia has a life with someone, like everyone else, and I'll never allow myself to have that. I don't know how. Do I even want that? Some part of me does, or I wouldn't be jealous of her. Liv's voice distracts me and I focus on her elegant white and black wallpaper on the far left wall as she continues.

"If you're asking if I think it's wrong for you to see Kohen knowing how you feel about Jax, my answer is no. You're not leading him on. You two aren't even 'exclusive' from the last I heard. You have nothing to worry about on that. Adalynn, you're only twenty-three, you don't need to have everything figured out right now. I don't even have everything figured out and I'm forty-five."

As she waits for that to sink in, the grandfather clock's ticking gets louder, absorbing my every thought. Everything floats away as I begin counting each time it swings to the left. I count all the way to twelve before she continues, capturing my attention again.

"Jax has been a part of your life since you were a little girl. Not having him in your life is going to be hard. You have to remind yourself not to call him when you have exciting news. Maybe it's time to share some of your excitement with someone else."

Even though she doesn't say Kohen, I think that's who she means. Which makes sense. If I want to take things further when Kohen, I need to rely on him more and not focus on who I can't count on.

Her hazel eyes plead with mine as she urges, "Don't shut down again."

I straighten up and shift into a cross-legged position. "Thanks, that actually helps, and you don't have to worry, it turns out that I actually like living life instead of pretending all of the time."

She smiles at me; I don't return it. Sometimes I wonder if I can ever really smile again. Sometimes I feel like I can, that I am, but then I realize that I was simply pretending. It's hard to notice the difference. I pick at my nails again, trying to gather my jumbled thoughts.

"I wish that it didn't hurt so much just to hear his name. When he walked away from me that day at the park, I had no idea that he was walking out of my life. I feel like I've been holding my breath since then and I can't breathe without him in my life. I want my friend back."

I bite my lip, a method of stalling I've always used. I rub my forehead, feeling a headache coming on. The words spill out of my mouth without any conscious thought.

"I'm afraid that if I never get my friend back, I won't be able to stop pretending. I hate that I count on him so much. I hate that it seems my happiness depends on Jax being in my life. The only time I'm not pretending is when he's near. Just his presence makes everything better. When he looks at me, really sees me for me, it's as if he shines light into the darkness of my life, chasing away every haunting memory from my past."

Thinking about how far Jax is from me makes me want to cry, which of course pisses me off. I refuse to cry over something so stupid. Welcoming the anger to center me, I stare past Liv and out the windows.

"I don't understand why he's doing this. He's put up this wall and I just want back in. I thought after everything we've been through together that he would always be here for me. Whenever I tried to run away from anything, he wouldn't let me. He was always pushing me to be better, to be more than I am, even when we were kids. I just can't believe he would let that go."

Liv gets up and grabs a black teddy bear from a chair in the corner. When she hands it to me, I raise my eyebrow at her in question, but take the dumb bear anyways. My fingers roam over the soft fur.

"Squeezing your frustration into him will help."

"Him?" My lips quirk up into a grin.

"Yes, him. Another patient of mine named him Mr. Bear."

A unladylike snort escapes me. "Fitting since he's a bear."

Sitting back down, she waits for me to continue talking about everything else running through my head. I give the bear a squeeze before I pour my heart out yet again and realize the stuffed animal does indeed help. Go figure.

"I don't understand how he can treat me like I don't exist. That I don't matter. I know he cares about me. I know I mean something to him. If I didn't, then I wouldn't be here. He wouldn't have been the one who found me that night in the pool, saving my life, if he didn't care."

I know I'm rambling, but I need to get this out. Liv watches me sit Indian-style with the bear in my lap.

"You never talk about that night you attempted suicide. The only thing I know is from your medical history. Are you ready discuss that night?" Liv studies me.

All of the air rushes out of my lungs. I know I shouldn't have mentioned anything. Just thinking about how weak I used to be makes me sick. I know that if I take this step and talk about that night, it will change me. I haven't been able to talk about it . . . ever. I don't want to be that weak, fragile girl I once was. I want to be strong. I need to tell my story, I need to really open up to Liv, so I can finally move past everything that happened to me six years ago. It's time I talk about the night I tried to make the pain go away for good, the night I thought I had nothing to live for, the night Jax saved me from myself.

"I remember feeling nothing at all. I wasn't sad or angry. I just was. It's kind of like all of the emotions I was feeling since I woke up and Logan told me our family was dead floated away. The only thing I had left was knowing that everything about me that made me *me*, was ripped away and I was the one solely responsible. I felt like my home had no meaning to me anymore because everything that I held dear was stolen from me."

I pause, trying to collect myself. It's crazy to relive how I felt back then, thinking that there was no other option. I never would have believed that I could be here, calmly talking about this. I never thought I would make it this far. I never wanted to. Now? I want to stop feeling emptiness and guilt all the time. I want to stop pretending and be truly happy. I have to believe that it gets better. If it doesn't? I don't even want to think about that.

"I knew that I was was never going to be able to ask for my dad's advice. I wouldn't be able to lean on my mom as my rock anymore. My little sister died before she was ever able to fall hopelessly in love and live her life. And it was all because of me. I'm the one responsible for all the pain Logan is suffering through."

As the memories and old feelings come back, I'm pulled from the couch to five years ago. I'm transported back to the pool the night I almost ruined everything.

The distinct scent of chlorine fills the cold air as I near the black gates. As I open them, I fill my lungs with my second favorite smell in the world. I gaze around to the water that brought me nothing but peace, up towards the white and red flags that made me feel like a champion, and all I feel now is despair towards the one thing that I cherished most in my life. It makes me laugh. It's a sound that I'm not accustomed to hearing, nor is it the sound my laugh used to be. Instead, it has a darkened tone to it. It matches my soul, how fitting.

It's chilly as I sit down at the edge of my high school pool. Putting my feet in the cold water, I instantly feel at ease. I'm finally doing the right thing for once in my life. I grab the bag of pills from my pocket, emptying the Norcos and muscle relaxers into my hand. The pills take up the entire space of my dainty hand. I try to remember why I've fought this for so long. I come up blank.

I watch the moonlight reflect off the water, the way it ripples as I move my feet through the Arctic water. Lifting my hands to my lips, I empty the pills into my mouth, and take a long swig of the water bottle beside me. Swallowing them all at once is a lot harder than I thought it would be. I'm glad that I went back to my car for water since dry-swallowing these would have been tougher than taking my tiny birth control pills.

I lay back on the concrete and look up at the stars . . . waiting for the medicine to take effect. The stars shine brighter than usual tonight. The North Star, the one that points you home, mocks me by burning the brightest. I have no home.

After a few more minutes of stargazing, I slowly sit up. My head feels fuzzy. As I stand, I wobble a little while I strip out of my jacket. I stumble my way to the diving board. I'm in my favorite suit. The one my mom bought me when I made varsity freshman year. Taking another deep breath, I step onto the diving board, get into the position that was drilled into me at a young age, and dive into the water for the last time.

I swim one, one hundred, stretching out all my muscles with each stroke. Committing to memory how it feels to have the water glide off of me, how my back tightens before each stoke. Even with my head hazy, I execute the freestyle perfectly. Closing my eyes, I savor every breath because soon I won't be breathing . . .

I take one final lap and then swim to the middle of the pool. I roll over onto my back and open my eyes to view the night sky. The white and red flags of Harvard-Westlake flap in the cold breeze. They used to bring me happiness, but now they only trigger agony. Every time I'm in the water I think of the last day, their last day, the day I lost everything. The white and red flags are the last thing I see before I allow myself to sink into the depths of the water. I hit the tile floor and blow out the rest of my remaining oxygen from my nose. I remind myself what I did and why I'm here. I'm responsible for my family's death.

I remember the first time our father, Andy, bought Logan a soccer ball, the first time our mother, Quinn, took me to a swim class, and the first time Hadley had a recital. All of these blissful memories are quickly replaced by the last haunted flashes I have of them, of everything that I lost.

As I watch the last bubble of my air supply hit the surface, I hear Hadley's screams. I begin to feel lighter as my body floats toward the surface. I don't fight the darkness this time.

Forgive me, I think before everything goes black.

I'm gasping for breath as if I was thrashing in the water instead of sitting on the couch. I don't even need to look at Liv to know that she's about to tell me it isn't my fault. I've heard it thousands of times before. It doesn't change the truth, no matter how many times I'm told. She tries to rationalize, saying something about survivor's guilt. I know she's right, but it's hard to believe her. I breathe deeply, filling my lungs with much needed air, before I tell her the rest.

"I woke up in the hospital after they pumped my stomach. If Jax didn't already call 911 before he even made it to the school, it would have been too late."

Just thinking about how close I was to succeeding makes bile rise to the back of my throat. What would Logan's life be like if I succeeded? Would his life be easier without me weighing him down?

"I don't know how he knew I would be there or that I was attempting to kill myself, since I didn't leave a note or anything. I was admitted into the psych ward once the doctors released me. The rest is pretty blurry." I welcome the way my chest expands as I gulp a breath of fresh air, centering me.

"I never allowed anyone to tell me what exactly happened when Jax saved me that night." I admit this as if it's a dirty little secret.

Somewhere in the back of my mind, I vaguely remember Jax visiting me, but the memory retreats as soon as it appears. I've blocked the majority of that time; remembering it now seems impossible. It feels like I don't have all the pieces of the puzzle. I need to talk to Jax. He's the one that holds all the answers. I just don't know if I want to hear them. Maybe it's better not knowing.

I'm thankful that Liv gauges my mood well enough to ask the easiest questions right now. I don't think I can handle the real ones. Those will be for another day.

"Why didn't you ask what happened and how Jax knew those things?"

I release my bottom lip when I realize I'm chewing on it. It makes a loud popping sound, breaking the silence.

"I don't know. I guess I never really wanted to know. I felt so ashamed for how weak I was when Logan was struggling with their absence, too."

"Logan was dealing with the loss of his family. Not survivor's guilt, at least not to the extent you were, Adalynn. You and your brother were, are, going through two very different things. You both lost your family that night, but he wasn't there. You are going through the loss of your family and survivor's guilt. You blame yourself, and keep everything that happened that night bottled up. Talking about it will help. "

I ignore her and focus back on the suicide. It's too soon to talk about the accident.

"I didn't want to ask Jax how he knew what was happening, how he found me, and all of that crap." I wave my hand through the air. "I just wanted to pretend like it never happened." If only.

Liv waits a second before she gives me the hard blow. "So you wanted to pretend everything was fine instead of dealing with the problem . . . What's stopping you now? I thought you were done pretending."

Check mate.

I hate that she's right, that she's always right. Sometimes it seems like she knows me better than I know myself. I pat the teddy bear, surprised to find myself clutching him close.

"I'm trying not to pretend anymore. I just don't see the point in getting those answers. I still tried to kill myself but Jax saved me." I shrug. "New information won't change anything."

"You're right."

She has my attention again. "I am?"

"Yes, but you'd be surprised what can change when you put all the pieces together, Addie. It won't change the events that happened, but how you feel might."

This session is getting too emotional for me, too real. I'm done, I can't take anymore of this. Not today. I set the soft bear beside me even though I secretly want to smuggle him into my purse and take him home.

"Okay, I'll keep that in mind."

"We're done for today, I take it?" Liv asks.

I nod before rising. "Thanks, I feel better talking about the whole Jax thing."

"That's what I'm here for."

Leaving her office, I'm surprised how true those words are. I am happy with how much we talked through today. It's helped my feelings toward the whole Kohen situation. I can finally stop playing ping-pong in my head with my emotions. The Jax thing will need to change and soon. He either needs to be in my life, even just as a friend, or not in my life at all. I refuse to continue tiptoeing around him, now knowing what's okay and what isn't.

When I reach the waiting room, I smile warmly at my brother, letting him know that I'm still in a good mood.

He opens the door for me. "I hope you're hungry because I have it on good authority your favorite food will be at Connor's."

"Starved."

Later in the car, he comments about how upbeat I am and how much it means to him to see that I'm happy again. Basically he spends the entire car ride being a big cheese-ball. I think it's more to make up for his behavior earlier about my new job. As quickly as that thought rolls in, I force it away. Logan isn't pretending because he feels guilty. He really sees a change in me. It makes a small blossom of hope build inside me. Maybe therapy is helping and I'm getting better. Maybe it's possible to move on from my past after all.

Soon we step out of the elevator and into Connor's penthouse. I hear the telltale signs of cooking. Crap, Connor cooking, so not good. Logan shares my horrid expression when he hears something banging around.

"We can still get out of here to eat something then come back before he notices," Logan whispers, reading my mind.

I'm nodding in agreement when Connor comes around the corner sporting a "kiss the cook" apron with a revealing swimsuit model, complete with red sauce all over the front. He glowers at us. Whoops, I guess he heard. I can't seem to find the urge to care at the moment. I've tried one too many of Connor's *attempts* at cooking, if you can even call it that.

"Not a chance, now get in here and tell me about the interview you had with the enemy."

Awesome, I'm starving and won't be eating anything edible for at least three hours until I get home. I know Logan is counting the minutes until we can both escape, too. Mutely, we follow Connor into the kitchen.

I'm startled when I see Kohen chopping away at the kitchen island. A wonderful aroma assaults my senses. I turn back to my brother. He's just as surprised as I am. Connor wears a shit-eating grin. I throw him down a few notches.

"Oh, relax Connor, we know you had help since the building wasn't on fire when we showed up."

Kohen holds up his hands, one hand still brandishing the menacing knife. "Actually Connor is doing most of the cooking."

I can't help it, I laugh with my brother. Connor cooking is too funny to picture.

"I'm serious."

We laugh again, earning a glare from Connor.

"I'm just instructing him on what to do," Kohen says with his charming smile.

Logan beats me to the insult. "Oh please, even with directions, the only thing he can make is either a sandwich or something that can be cooked in the microwave."

Everyone laughs, except for Connor. He hits Logan across the back of the head before resuming his post near Kohen. Logan sits in one of the barstools alongside the island to watch Connor attempt to make dinner. I pour myself a glass of red wine. I have to admit, I'm pretty impressed with Connor. He hasn't cut off any fingers yet and he's chopping the onions pretty fast, well fast for him at least. After taking a delicious sip of the fruity wine, I lay my head against Kohen's back.

I move beside him and lean against the counter. "Do you need any help?"

Kohen pauses long enough to give me the don't-be-stupid look before returning to his task. "No, just relax, baby, and let us men folk cook you dinner for your accomplishment today."

Jumping on the counter, I allow myself to relax while I tell them about the interview. Being so focused on retelling everything in perfect detail, I don't even notice that I've finished my glass of wine until Kohen takes my glass. I'm more surprised when he washes my glass and puts it away instead of pouring me another.

"I would like some more," I say quietly into his ear.

He shakes his head. "One is plenty."

"I would like another glass."

I hate that I'm whispering, but I don't want Logan and Connor a part of this conversation. It's embarrassing that Kohen is trying to dictate how much wine I can have. He sets down the menacing knife and stands in front of me. As he bends his head down to murmur in my ear, an act that looks like he's whispering sweet-nothings, my skin breaks out in goosebumps, and not the good kind.

"If you're thirsty, I will pour you a glass of water. You will not get drunk and embarrass me in front of your brother and Connor."

It's on the tip of my tongue to explain to him that two glasses of wine will not get me drunk, but when he squeezes my hand, harder than necessary I refrain. Instead I nod and finish telling everyone about the interview.

"I had a feeling I had it in the bag when he showed me where my office would be. He then asked if I was interested in looking around to see if I thought it would be a 'good fit.' Hello! It's Malcara Enterprises, of course it's a good fit, but obviously I didn't tell him that."

"Obviously," Connor deadpans.

I go on and on about how it seemed like everyone enjoyed what they were doing. How all of the employees seemed nice but busy. It isn't until Connor staking plates that I realize I left out the most important part.

"Connor, you would not believe how hot this girl is that works there." I bite my knuckles like I've seen him do in the past.

I smile, knowing I have his complete attention. I go for nonchalant as I describe the pixie woman that I immediately intrigued me.

"Tinkerbell, the nickname that I secretly gave her, is the hottest little thing I've ever seen. I don't know where she's from since I only talked to her for a second, but somewhere southern because she has that sweet southern accent." I say the last part in a butchered southern accent, that doesn't do her justice, but it gets the reaction I wanted.

Conner raises an eyebrow at me in a silent get-on-with-it manner as he prepares everyone's plates. I hop off the counter.

"Oh, and she's so out of your league," I say to Connor while I pass him to sit down at the cozy oval table.

My brother pats Connor on the back before joining me. He sits across from me, while Kohen sits beside me and sets a glass of water down by my plate. I have to remind myself that it's just wine, nothing to fight about, and bite my cheek to keep from saying anything. Conner takes the head of the table, muttering under his breath that I can't hear. This is going to be fun. I decide to poke the bear a little more tonight.

"What was that, Connor, I didn't quite hear you?" I ask.

Connor opens his mouth to speak, but Logan beats him to it. "So does Tinkerbell have an actual name or did her parents hate her that much?"

"Harper, but I think Tinkerbell suits her better."

Connor finally asks the question I knew he was going to ask; it was just a matter of time. "Vague much, Addie? What's her last name?"

As deadpan as I can manage I say, "Bell," as nonchalantly as possible.

Connor gives me a death glare.

Staring at him I say slowly, as if I'm speaking to a child, "You're a whore, so you won't be getting her last name because we know you will charm your way into her pants just to piss me off. So don't ask."

Connor's mouth hangs open. He closes and opens it again, then wisely shuts it. As the boys start talking about sports, I decide not to tell them they're wrong about their predictions. It would only hurt their fragile egos for me to nicely point it out.

I smile when I see how much Kohen gets along with my family, almost as if he belongs here by my side. He even played a basketball game with them the other day at the gym. I love that he likes to hang out with my family without me there. I love that he cares so much about me and wants to be a part of everything in my life. He's simply amazing. I know he plays a huge part in helping me heal, even if he doesn't know it.

I'm smiling like an idiot when I'm finally pulled out of my thoughts and notice that the room has gone quiet. Everyone is watching me. My face turns red from getting caught staring at Kohen. Awesome.

"Eh . . .What?"

From the look on everyone's face, it's obvious that I missed something, again. Kohen wraps an arm around my shoulder, bringing me closer to him, and kisses the top of me head.

"I have to go, babe. I'm sorry, that was the hospital."

I look at him, confused, because I honestly have no idea what's going on. Kohen pushes back his chair while saying his goodbyes to the guys. That's when it clicks into place.

"Wait, you're leaving?"

Whoever said there's no such thing as a stupid question has never met me. I fight the urge not to smack myself in the face. Of course he's leaving, he just said that. Kohen helps me out of my chair and engulfs me into a hug.

He breathes me in. "Yes, I'm sorry, enjoy your night though."

"Go and save lives."

I kiss him, forgetting that we're not alone, but Kohen hasn't forgotten because he pulls back before it gets interesting. Saying a final goodbye to the guys and thanking Connor for dinner even though he cooked most of it, Kohen rushes toward the elevator. After watching Kohen leave, I turn to help with the clean up. When Connor starts to collect the plates, I stop him.

"Go sit down and watch T.V. or something. We've got this."

I grab the plates out of his hands and make my way to the kitchen. Logan puts away the leftovers so I rinse off the dishes before loading them in the dishwasher.

Afterwards, Logan joins Connor in the other room for a beer. Once I'm left alone, I take my time cleaning up, wondering if I should leave or not. I know Kohen will check up on me to see what time I come home. I'd rather be home when he calls than explain to my brother why it matters where I am.

Even though I've cleaned the counter enough, I continue wiping it. I know I'm stalling and yet I can't stop. When the kitchen sparkles and I have nothing left to do, it's time to make my decision. If I stay, I'll have fun, Kohen will pretend not to be upset, and I won't go home to a lonely apartment. If I go, I'm doing it because of Kohen. I tap my foot, contemplating. I need to live my life for me and not someone else. Just to spite Kohen, I snatch a beer from the fridge before striding to the living room.

The feeling of something moving slightly wakes me. I feel someone's arm pulling me closer and I sleepily wrap my arms around his neck. I crack an eye open to see Connor's face. I close them again and drift to sleep, but wake when I feel him lay me on his bed. Connor fixes his blanket over me. Pushing my hair out of my face, he kisses my forehead.

"Get some sleep," he whispers.

I try to smile in acknowledgement, but I doubt my face is even working, I'm that tired. I squint through bleary eyes at my brother whose behind Connor. He runs his hand over his buzz-cut. He's so handsome, one day he will make a girl very happy.

"You're going to sleep here tonight, okay, Addie?"

I don't know if I manage to say anything before sleep takes over again. All too soon the sound of crashing and breaking rudely awakens me. I nearly fall out of bed. Rubbing the sleepiness from my eyes, I sit up. As soon as I take in my surroundings I notice that I'm in Connor's bed.

The chaos outside his bedroom door sends goosebumps over my entire body. I know who's out there. When his voice carries through the closed door, my body trembles. With a mind of their own, my legs swing out of bed and I'm suddenly standing next to the door. I pause with my hand on the knob. What am I doing? He shouldn't still have this effect on me. I'm so angry with myself, I have to stop from punching a hole in Connor's wall. I don't care what's going on out there.

I go back to bed, but pause mid-step when I hear another crash. I'm so tempted to open the door to face him, but the fear of him rejecting me again wins. So like the coward that I am, I pull the covers back. As I start to crawl into bed, Connor mumbles something, but I can't make out any of the words from here. I should have stayed beside the door.

"Why is Ads here?" The man that invades my every thought ask too loudly.

CHAPTER TWELVE

I gasp from the sound of my nickname on his lips, and the obvious threat in his voice. Connor mutters something that I can't hear because Jax is now yelling over him.

"WHAT DO YOU MEAN IT'S NOT WHAT I THINK? WHY THE FUCK IS SHE IN YOUR BED!"

Something hard smashes by the door and I'm out of bed, running towards the noise, hoping that Jax didn't throw Connor into the wall. When Connor talks in his scary calm voice, I stop myself from turning the knob.

"I'll let that pass, but if you try that again, your drunk ass will be on the floor. Now calm down and I'll explain."

Gah, the temptation to open the door is overpowering. I have to clench both hands at my sides to keep from reaching out. I lean against the door to hear better.

"She passed out on the couch. We tried to wake her, but she couldn't keep her eyes open long enough to stand on her own two feet. LOGAN and I decided to just let her sleep here, instead of trying to get her back to her place when she was PASSED OUT," Connor says with annoyance.

I can't help the little giggle that escapes. I slap my hand over my mouth to keep from groaning. What did Jax expect? For Connor and me to be doing the nasty in here? Yuck! That thought alone makes me want to bleach my brain.

I don't understand why Jax is so angry; he knows nothing between Connor and I would ever happen. I think of him as a brother. I get Jax wanted to come over here and hang out with his friend, but me being asleep shouldn't stop him. It's deadly quiet and I have a minor panic attack thinking I said something out loud. I'm relieved when Jax starts to talk, oblivious that I'm awake and hanging onto each word that falls out of his mouth.

"What happened to her?" he slurs.

It's unmistakable that he's drunk. I check the digital alarm clock. I've been passed out for a little over three hours. Connor asks the question that I'm dying to know. Thank goodness he can apparently read my mind right now since it's not like I can open the door and confront Jax.

"What do you mean what happened to her? I just told you she fell asleep. Would you like to know the exact time? Or what part of the movie? Maybe instead of hounding me, you should be sleeping it off."

I think Jax tries to whisper but fails. "How is she?"

Usually his raspy voice sends my blood into overdrive. It still does but for a different reason. Instead of turning me on like it usually does, I'm pissed off. Who the heck does he think he is? He can't disappear from my life and ask questions about me. If he wants to know how I'm doing, then he can grow a pair and ask me himself.

"Why don't you ask her for yourself tomorrow?" Connor asks him, reading my mind again.

Jax says something, but in his drunken state I can't make out the words. I nearly groan out loud, frustrated that I can't understand what he's saying and that I care enough to want to know.

Connor snapping, "No Jax leave it alone. She's asleep, and even if she wasn't, she wouldn't want to deal with you right now," makes me leap back, panicked.

There's shuffling and I know Connor has blocked the door. I fling myself on the bed, just in case Jax does come into the room. Connor's right, I do not want to see Jax right now. He's not in a rational state of mind. I lay down and try to steady my fast beating heart. Connor says something that I can't hear, but I'm able to decipher my name. *Please, Connor, don't let him come in here.*

I hear more shuffling outside then Jax pleading. "Please! I just . . . I need to see her, I won't wake her up, I promise."

"This is a mistake, Jax. You need to leave her alone."

"I can't."

"Then stop playing games. She deserves better."

"I know."

Minutes tick by before Connor says, "Be quiet when you go in."

That's my only warning before I hear the click of the door opening. I feign asleep, hoping that Jax can't tell I'm awake. My whole body feels on fire, just knowing he's so close yet so far away. When he halts at the edge of the bed, my heart is thumping, ready to jump out of my chest.

What I wouldn't give to open my eyes and watch him as he's watching me. When his fingers brush over my face, it takes all of my willpower not to lean into his touch. *I'm pathetic.* He traces my cheeks, then slowly he runs his fingers through my hair, like he used to do when we were younger after I patched him up. My breath catches as he brushes his lips across mine.

Thankfully Jax is too drunk to notice. He gives me a lingering kiss on my forehead before leaving. I wait a few seconds to make sure he doesn't return, but when their voices trail away, I know I'm good. I touch my still tingling lips. What the heck just happened?

I lay awake for awhile. It's almost four in the morning when I hear Jax leave. I'm so lost in my own thoughts that I forget to feign sleep for Connor. I wonder if I should act as if I'm just waking up, but I know he won't buy it.

Connor gives me a sympathetic smile. "Sorry, I tried keeping him out."

"I know, I wish I knew what was going on with him."

I scoot over in bed and pat the space next to me. He climbs in and raises his arm so I can cuddle into him. I feel mentally exhausted.

"Me too."

I don't say anything and relax into Connor. He dozes next to me and I lay awake with my eyes closed, thinking of everything and anything that involves Jax. I hate that I don't know how to fall out of love with him.

"How much did you hear?" Connor asks, startling me.

"Enough."

He lets out a deep breath but doesn't say anything. He gives me a reassuring squeeze. I drift off to sleep in the comfort and safety of Connor's arms.

I'm not gonna lie, this entire week I thought things between Jax and I would have been different. It's not like I'm asking for much, I just want things to get back to normal between us. But nope, he's been avoiding me even more, if that's even possible. I just want our friendship back. Especially now with my brother's surprise party this weekend.

After work I spend the entire day searching for the perfect present, but it's tough choosing something for Logan. He has more money than sense and whenever he wants something he goes out and gets it, which makes buying presents for him an impossible task. After spending two hours with no luck, I give up. I won't find anything at these stores. I return to my apartment, considering the entire trip back if I should buy him football tickets to his favorite team. Crap! I can't do that, that's what I got him last year.

Ugh, times like these is when I could ask my mom's advice. She was the best present-giver in the entire world. And then it hits me, I know what will be the best present for my brother. With a bounce in my step, I rush into my spare bedroom. When I'm standing outside the closet I take a few deep, calming breaths, knowing that I need to do this even though it seems like the worst idea right now.

Pulling open the doors to the closet, I see the box from my old life on the bottom shelf. I approach the box with shaky legs. I sit in front of it, but make no move to reach for it, not yet. I'm too afraid of what the memories will do to me. I hate that I know I need to do this. This is the only box I have from my old life. After the accident, this is the sole thing that I brought with me to New York. I've never been able to open it, and never been able to depart without it either. I have no idea what happened to everything else I owned. Logan took care of everything because I couldn't. I was too weak.

Closing my eyes, I blindly reach out for the box and trace the pattern in the oak lid. I trace over the seashell imprints my mother had made. Then, I trace over the ocean carvings across the length of the lid. I finally open my eyes and stare at the keepsake box my mother created for my sixteenth birthday. A year before they died.

I carry it back to my bedroom and rummage through my jewelry box for the key. After shuffling around a ridiculous amount of earrings, necklaces, and bracelets, I finally find the key with my watch collections. I hold it up as if I just won a marathon and the key is my prize. I walk over to my bed with the box, count to ten slowly, then count back from twenty, trying to gain the courage to open it. With nervous hands, I slowly unlock it.

I push the knickknacks out of my way so I can locate all the pictures. I find a stack with a pink ribbon around them, indicating my favorite photos of Hadley. I set those back in the box and rifle through the stack with the blue ribbon, Logan's stack. Knowing exactly which picture will be the perfect one for Logan's present, I quickly thumb through them. I pass the cliche ones of him as a baby and even a toddler. When I get to the pictures of his soccer days, I slow down, knowing I'm close. After about ten more pictures, I find the one I'm seeking.

Logan's first goal when he was about eight.

You can see our parents cheering for him in the background. My mom is pregnant with Hadley in the picture, and I'm on top of our dad's shoulders, clapping. I plan on changing the photo to a black and white shot. Then keeping everything out of focus except Logan and our parents. I may even keep them in color.

With that plan, I tie the stack back up and place them back in their original spot. My finger travels over the other ribbons, but decide I'll save those for another day. Today is about creating the perfect present for my brother. My hand come across a stray memory card that should be in the pouch with the other ones. After setting it on my nightstand, I lock the box, and slide it underneath my bed. Curious, I pick up the memory card again and turn it over and over in my hand. Finally I insert it into my camera and review the pictures.

The first shot is a closeup of a lane pool and I know immediately these aren't just random pictures from a swim meet. There are pictures I forced myself to forget. This is the memory card that someone else put in here when I wasn't "well." That's why it wasn't in the pouch.

These are the photos I took the last day my family was alive.

Holy fuck, I can't breath. Why couldn't I have left it alone?

I set down the camera and step back, wanting to be as far away as possible from those memories. Without any other thought but needing to release the pain, I run to my bathroom. On my knees I grab the razor blade I have taped underneath my sink. Lifting my shirt, I press the steel blade to my hip. When the first trickle of blood escapes, I realize what I'm doing and throw the blade across the bathroom.

Dropping my face into my hands, I will myself not to cry. *I will not cry over this. I'm stronger than this.* I try not to feel the relief that washes over me as I watch the trail of blood. As much as I wish that my action sickened me, it doesn't. I can't lie to myself. I already feel better. I ignore the signs that I still need help, and clean myself up. With shaky legs I get off the cold tile floor and trudge over to the discarded camera.

I force myself to view the pictures again. I have to do this. This is yet another step in the right direction. I want to remember them happy, all of us happy, together. I want to remember their last moments.

I load the photos onto my MacBook Pro and slowly start flipping through them. Because I've re-played that disastrous day in my head for the past six years, I know the perfect pictures for Logan's present are here. I just have to find them without falling apart.

After a couple more minutes of searching, I arrive at the picture of the guys from my last swim meet. Connor and Logan sport smiles, while Jax stares thoughtfully at the person holding the camera, me. Their arms encircle each other's shoulders, the best of friends. Jax is simply perfect. Even in a photo it's unmistakable how truly handsome he is. It physically hurts to look at him and realize that I lost such an amazing friend. I focus on his sad, tired eyes. For some reason I think it's because of me, but I can't remember why. There's something important I'm forgetting, but I can't grasp what it is. I don't pry too hard because I'm afraid of what I may reveal. Instead I continue flipping through the rest of the pictures, ignoring the truth that I need to uncover.

My fingers pause over the button to view the next picture; Logan has one hand on Hadley's shoulder. His other hand makes a fist pump in the air as they cheer me on at the end of my lane. This is the perfect picture. This was exactly what I was searching for . . . I'm so thankful to whoever captured this moment. Hadley looks stunning in her yellow shirt and creme tutu, making me have to catch my breath. She loved tutu's, always insisting to wear them with every outfit. She was thirteen when she died; she never even had a chance to live. She had such a promising future ahead of her. I still don't know how I can live without my kid sister.

She would be nineteen if it wasn't for me. I miss her so much that I'm riveted to the screen, not wanting to blink or even change the picture. I want to memorize everything about her. I love how she was bouncing up and down with excitement, her long blonde hair flying through the air. I love that I was the reason for this smile on her last day. She drove me crazy, but was able to made me smile when I felt sad. I was never able to stay angry at her for long. I miss her each and every day.

I click to the next one, wanting to finish this project before I can't handle it anymore. It's not until the last picture that I have to fight the urge to find the razor blade. It's of all of us, the family that is no more. Our parents are on the ends, Logan, Hadley and I in the middle.

This picture breaks me . . . like I broke them.

The darkness takes over as I stare into my parent's laughing faces. I feel guilty that I'm alive and they're not. They were my world, they were the type of parents that you read about in books, the parents that are always there for their children no matter what. They were always understanding. Even when we were fighting, I knew that I was lucky to have them. Of course at the time I didn't, but reflecting now, I know that I couldn't have had better parents. There wasn't a day that went by that I didn't know they would always love me.

I didn't have the horror of growing up in a crappy situation that some children face, like Jax. I was loved by them and everything they did, they did for us. I wish that I could still make them proud. I know that I haven't. Since the accident, I've let the happy memories of them fade away and be replaced by their last hours, my worst nightmare come to life. I've let Logan down, too. I need to remember that I'm not the only one who lost them that day, Logan did, too. He continued to live, to make them proud. I need to do the same.

I don't know how long I'm transfixed to the computer screen. It feels like hours, but I know it could have only been a matter of minutes when I finally I drag the three photos over to Photoshop.

Being as rusty as I am, it takes longer than necessary to edit them. It's like riding a bike, hard to forget the basics, and soon everything else comes back, just slowly. It takes me an hour to finish. When I'm finally done, I go to a local store to buy a few picture frames. I only intended to buy four, but I end up carrying twelve back to my apartment because I want to hang up a few pictures of my own. Hopefully they will make my place feel more like home.

After setting everything down on the table, I force myself to eat a granola bar even though I'm not hungry. I hear my phone chime with a text as I finish my last bite, but ignore it. Oops, I forgot to bring it on my errands. I'll check it when I'm ready for bed.

Crawling into bed, I set my alarm for the morning. Before I press the icon for my text messages, someone bangs on my door, making me jump. I watch in slow motion as my phone flies out of my hands and onto the floor.

Please don't be broken. Please don't be broken.

"Great!" I say when I flip it over.

A huge crack mars the screen, but at least it still turns on. Setting my now cracked phone on the nightstand, I jump out of bed fully intending to kick someone's ass. It's almost two in the morning. Too focused on wanting to murder my late night visitor, I open it without checking to see who it is.

Nope. That's gonna be a hard no!

I slam the door and lock it.

Too stunned to do anything else, I gape at the closed door. *Please let this be a dream.* I contemplate opening it again, but I quickly dismiss that notion. As much as I want to see him, I so do not need his games. I'm an emotional wreck as it is. I pace my bedroom with the thump of him knocking on the door as a constant soundtrack.

I'm thinking I handled that like a grown-up. Didn't want to deal with him, no big deal, just slam the door in his face before he can say anything. *Yeah, real grown-up.*

I climb back into bed, hating that I'll have to deal with him tomorrow at the party. Ugh. I throw the pillow over my head to drown out his constant banging. I don't care if he knocks all night, I will not open that door.

After another minute or two, blissful silence fills the apartment. Apparently my "grown-up" tactics do work. Go me! I smile then drop the pillow to the other side of the bed, ready to finally go to sleep. My smile disappears as quickly as it appeared when I feel the bed dip.

FUCK!

He's here.

CHAPTER THIRTEEN

"It's nice to see you too, Ads," he says with a chuckle. "Oh, and thanks for the warm welcome."

My body stiffens and I make a show of moving as far away from him as possible. Half of me is leaning off the bed; one sudden movement and I'll be on the floor. Not a good idea for an accident-prone person like me. I scoot a little closer to the middle so I don't tempt fate.

Hatred laces my voice. "Why didn't you just leave? You didn't catch the fact that when someone slams the door in your face, they don't want to see you?"

I sit up in bed and glare at him. I can't believe after all this time he is here, as if he hadn't slept with me and acted like I didn't exist. I hate that I'm completely and utterly aware of him. I hate that he smells mouth-watering, how sexy his stubble looks from not shaving in a few days, and how striking his green eyes are as they stare back at me.

"How did you even get in here? I don't want you here! LEAVE!"

I push him as I jump out of bed. He holds his hands up in surrender.

"Ads, just listen, okay? I didn't come here to fight." I raise an eyebrow at him and he runs his hand over his face. "Tomorrow is Logan's party. I'm here for that, to go over our plans."

He's here because of my brother, not because he wants to fix us. Of course. I don't even know what I expected but it wasn't that. Why couldn't he have just slapped me? It would have hurt less. In bitch mode, I cross my arms over my chest, and I smile on the inside when he glances down at the cleavage exposed in my sheer white tank.

"The plans are exactly the same since the day we made them. Since you've ignored all of my calls, I assumed that you didn't intend on helping. Kohen can step in on your part, which he will do happily."

His fist clench together at his sides. Good. I move closer to him so there is only an inch between us. I can feel the heat rolling off his body. I have to control myself not to react so I don't end up throwing myself at him.

Smiling sweetly up at him I ask, "Oh, and Jax?"

He blinks a few times as if coming out of a dream. "Yes?"

"Last time I checked, the name on my birth certificate says Adalynn not Ads. Try to remember that for the next time you decide to talk to me."

Shoving past him, I leave my bedroom and march all the way to my front door. I wait about twenty seconds until I hear him finally starting to follow me. When he gets close, I open the door and maneuver out of his way so he doesn't brush against me as he passes the threshold.

He looks as if someone just ripped out his heart and I'm glad. I will not be the only one hurting over his actions. He was the one who decided to leave me, to ignore me, after sleeping with me again. I'm done. I want him to know how pissed off I am. I will not let him just walk into my life with his sexy emerald eyes. That won't work this time. I won't be his doormat.

Jax pulls on fohawk, and begins to speak, but I cut him off, ignoring that he just used his nickname for me. "There's nothing more to say. The plans are the same and Kohen will help me."

I stop myself from closing the door. My eyes seek his. I wish that I had more self-control and can turn away from his eyes. His visible pain matches mine. I remind myself that this is his doing.

"I don't need you anymore Jax," I whisper.

I shut the door and lock it before he can mutter anything else. I sink to the floor, wondering if I just made the biggest mistake of my life. I know that I did the right thing, but at the same time I wish that I was a little nicer. He could have wanted to fix everything. Ugh! No, I will not do the whole "what if" game. I do enough of that without adding the Jax drama to it. If he was here for anything besides my brother's party plans, then he would have said something. God! That is all I am to him, his best friend's little sister.

I just wanted to be someone that he could love, I wanted him to want me as much as I want him. I don't even think we can get past this and become friends again. Then again, he's probably only been my "friend" because of my brother.

Pulling myself off the floor, I head back to my room with shaking legs.

After applying minimal make-up, I curl my hair and walk over to my closet. I select the sleeveless ocean blue Valentino lace dress, my studded nude Saint Laurent heels, and my matching nude Michael Kors clutch.

As I grab Logan's freshly wrapped present someone knocks on my door. With heavy footsteps, I approach it, I remind myself not to make this awkward. *It's just Jax. No big deal.* Only one of the many lies I'll tell myself to get through today.

I awkwardly hold the door open for him, but don't move out of his way as I stare at The God. Only he can make a simple pair of dark blue jeans and a navy long-sleeve polo with the sleeves pushed up to his elbows, displaying his tattooed arms, look sinfully delicious. My eyes travel the length of his body twice.

My tongue darts out to moisten my suddenly dry lips when my gaze meets his. He is so handsome I forget to breathe. He shouldn't be be this sexy; it messes with my emotions. I want to wrap my arms around him, bury my nose into his chest, and relax into the man that reminds me of home.

"Breathe, *Ads*, I'm not going anywhere," Jax says.

And just like that, my emotions are back in check. Maybe I should high-five him for helping me out? No, that would be awkward because then I would have to explain why. I go for option two. I attempt to shut the door, but his foot stops it from closing.

"I don't have time to deal with your crap today," I tell him once he comes inside.

Jax jaw tightens, a clear sign that he's uncomfortable. He does realize that he doesn't need to be here, right? Before I can voice this, Jax surprises me by closing the distance and wrapping me into a bear hug. I breathe in his all too familiar scent, welcoming the brief reprieve his presence brings me. Stepping out of his hug, he keeps me at arm's lengths. How fitting.

"You look beautiful, *Ads*."

I don't miss how he makes a point to enunciate Ads again. I take a step back. His arms fall to his side. "Shut up and let's gets this over with already."

I return to the living room to retrieve everything I need.

"Someone's in a chipper mood today," he says from behind me.

I hand him the presents and glare at him. "That could be because someone decided to break into my place last night. Oh, and that same someone scared the crap out of me and I shattered the screen on my phone!"

Jax's smile widens as if he's proud of himself. *It's not nice to hit. It's not nice to hit.*

"I don't know who you're trying to fool. We both know you attempted to walk and text at the same time and it fell."

He maneuvers away to avoid getting punched. Smart man.

"You're an ass."

He laughs. When we're in the elevator, he pats my head as if I'm a child. I remind myself to keep my hands to myself and instead focus on texting Kohen.

Me: Hey I won't be needing your help after all. Thanks though, I'll see you in a few hours. . . I'll be the one in the dress that matches your eyes.

I don't wait for a reply, rather I slip my phone into my clutch and watch the elevator descend slowly to the lobby.

"I love you too, Ads," he says as he strides out of the elevator.

I'm glad I'm behind him so he can't see that my steps falter.

Almost two hours later, we finally have everything set up. We even had time to deliver everything to Connor's for the "after party" that will be just the four of us. It's been a tradition for the guys since they were kids and I started crashing them after the accident. By crashing, I mean dragged, of course, but I've been going willingly after the first two years. The only reason why I didn't want to go in the first place is because I thought I was intruding on a guys' night type of thing.

As guest filter in, I text Connor asking their e.t.a. I want to make sure that we're all ready when he arrives with Logan. Jax and I worked too hard for the surprise to be ruined.

I find Jax talking up a leggy blonde, big surprise there. I tap his shoulder a little harder than necessary. "Connor said they'll be here in twenty, but I can see you're busy so I'll let everyone know."

I lean to the side and smile brightly at the blonde. Gosh, she reminds me of the skanks Connor usually bags. Jax rushes to my side when I start to walk away.

"Don't be silly, Ads, we're in this together," he says way too loudly, linking our arms together as if we're best friends.

Once we're away from Jax's blonde, I pull my arm roughly out of his. "Um no, that's not going to work for me. I'm not here to be your wing woman."

He laughs. Wrong move, Jaxon. I yank his face down by his chin so he's forced to look at me.

"I'm not here to help you dodge unwelcome sluts! Connor will be more than happy to fill that role for you." I pause, not wanting to make a scene. I stand up on my tiptoes so I can whisper into his ear. "We're not friends anymore. You've made that abundantly clear. I'm only putting up with you because of my brother."

Well, there goes all pleasantries. I didn't even know I was going to say all that. I opened my mouth and the words spilled out, my tone sounding more pissed with each syllable. Jax hisses in a breath as if in pain. I grip his massive bicep with my dainty hand, because I'm not done. I'm going to get all of this out now.

"If you want to go back to being friends, you can let me know. But until then, I'm only tolerating you because of Logan. That's it. I will not be your doormat anymore. I will not let you pretend to be here for me when we both know you'll leave again once the condom is off."

I step back, glad that I finally told him that it's not okay to treat me that way. I'm surprised how true every word is. I march to the opposite side of the room without waiting for a response.

The surprise goes flawlessly. I even surprised Logan and Connor by capturing the whole thing. Logan's delight when he saw the camera around my neck made me smile shyly at him. It's wonderful moments like when I'm taking pictures of everyone having fun that I'm reminded how great of a friend Jax has been to me.

He pushes me to do things that I would never have been able to do without him. It hurts that much more since he's been avoiding me all night. I know what I said was harsh, but it was the truth and I don't regret it. I just wish life were like a movie or a book. He would whisk me away to proclaim his unbreakable love. Or at least say he's sorry and that he wants to still be in my life. Of course neither will happen, life isn't that simple, or that cheesy.

Before my mind can carry on with more unrealistic expectations, Kohen pulls me into his side. I snuggle into him and kiss his neck. Without turning around, I sense Jax scowling at us. I can feel his eyes on me, like I've been able to all night. I rub my hand down Kohen's chest and make a show of slipping it into his back pocket. Pleased with my affection, Kohen kisses me square on the lips. Even the feel of his lips on mine isn't enough of a distraction from Jax's eyes boring into my back.

As Kohen helps Connor load the presents into the car, Jax joins them. Tension between him and Kohen has escalated throughout the party. I stand wide-eyed as Jax practically shoves a heavy present into Kohen's stomach. Kohen grunts, but surprises me by setting it calmly into the trunk. Still his back stiffens, all the muscles tight, anger radiating off him in waves. Jax's fist tighten at his sides, he makes a move to step closer but halts when Connor places his hand on his shoulder. Connor whispers to him, and then those green eyes are trained on me.

I become trapped by his predatory gaze. It feels as if I'm being drawn towards him. I'm vaguely aware of my feet moving in his direction. Jax attempts to step around Connor, but freezes in his tracks. It takes a few seconds for my mind to work again. I flick my gaze away from Jax's face to see Kohen seething. With no thought at all, my fake smile is in place and I march over to him. As I near him, I hope that he doesn't lose his temper in front of the guys. That would be stupid on his part. I sigh in relief as his begins to relax. He takes a deep breath and as he exhales, all the earlier tension leaves his body. He pulls me into him. I don't hesitate as I kiss him on his lips.

This kiss is unlike any of our past ones. It's possessive, forceful, jealous even. I feel badly that I'm the reason why he's acting like this. If I could get over my unrequited love, then we wouldn't be in this position. As I hear footsteps retreating, Kohen squeezes my hand until I yelp into his mouth.

"Do I need to remind you who you're dating?"

I shake my head. "I don't know what you're talking about."

His eyes darken and I know I need to say something to lighten the mood. I do not want to be the reason to ruin my brother's party. I swallow my fear and hold his hand again.

"I'm here with the only person I want to be with."

He gives me a charming smile, but underneath it hides something darker. I can relate. I'm not as well put together as the world thinks I am, either. He folds his arm around my shoulders and leads me over to my brother.

Logan stands near Jax's car, with the passenger door open. It takes a second to realize that he's waiting for something . . . me. For some reason, I know I'll be riding with Jax back to Connor's. My suspicions are confirmed when he waves his hand for me to get in. The one time Jax decided to drive one of his many cars and I'm forced to ride with him. Kohen stiffens beside me but luckily he doesn't say anything. I think it's because of my brother's presence.

"There's no room for you in Connor's car with all the presents so Jax offered to drive you over," Logan explains when I make no move to get in.

"I can take her." Kohen says.

"I thought you had to be at the hospital . . . five minutes ago." Jax leans over the center console to talk to us.

I give Kohen a quick kiss on the lips to stop his protest. Jax is right, he's late. He reaches behind me and shakes Logan's hand.

"Happy birthday," Kohen says.

Logan nods. "Thanks."

Kohen gives me a hug before helping me into the car. He closes the door with more force than necessary. As I watch him climb into the cab in front of us, my anger emerges. My hands shake at my side with barely controlled temper. I'm fed up with the games Jax likes to play. Jax has no right to treat Kohen like he did today. Kohen isn't the problem here; he is.

"You could have at least said goodbye to him."

"I'm sure the boyfriend doesn't mind."

Uncomfortable silence fills the rest of the ride. I hold my breath as much as possible because his scent wafts all around me, invading my senses. Thankfully the ride doesn't take as long as usual. When he parks in an empty space, I sigh in relief.

I jump out so fast that I nearly fall flat on my face, but I catch myself on the doorframe just in time. I don't wait for him. I stride to the elevator and press the button, urging it to hurry up. Since I've run out of all my luck today, Jax strolls up, ignoring that I'm trying to ditch him. He waits with me for the elevator to arrive.

When it does, we both enter. His arm brushes against mine and I fight with everything in me not to react. I bite my lip in agitation from my traitorous body. The tension in the air intensifies. It's now a mixture of anger and sexual tension. I hold my clutch up to my chest as a barrier and a way to keep my hands to myself. When the bell chimes, signaling we're at the penthouse, we both exhale the breaths we we're holding.

I run into Connor's as fast as my feet can carry me without falling on my face. Connor sets a beer bucket on the coffee table when I enter. Yes, an actual beer bucket, heaped to the brim with ice and beer. There's a stack of action-packed movies on the table. Of course he has the poker table set up in full view of his flat screen television. It's perfect!

Logan walks in with his hands full of junk food. I rush over to him and take the precious food out of his hands.

"Sit down, it's your birthday!" I give Connor my no-nonsense look. "He shouldn't be doing anything but having fun, Connor!"

Immediately I take charge of the evening. I order Jax to put a movie on and line all of our presents on the poker table. Connor attempts to help him, but I shake my head. He smirks and moves to take the seat that I saved for Jax, the chair furthest away from me. I shake my head again, but he ignores me and hands Logan his gift. As Jax comes to the poker table, he pauses mid-step when he realizes that he's going to sit next to me. I'm the only one who notices, since I'm the only one paying attention to everything he does.

I glance at my brother, wondering if I can play sick so I can go home. That thought leaves as quickly as it appears. There's no way I'm ditching just because I have to be near Jax. I can handle anything he throws my way. I scowl in Jax's direction. His eyes sparkle, as if he just read my mind, and I know that will take a lot of self-control to avoid a scene.

Jax winks at me as he takes his seat. His leg brushes against mine. I suck in a breath and frown at him. Our stare down is broken by Logan tearing through the blue wrapping paper. His face lights up when he sees whatever is inside.

"Thanks, man!"

He springs up and gives Connor a hug. Not a one-arm man hug either, a real hug. He must really like it.

"Well, are you going to show us what he got you or not?" I ask.

"Concert tickets to Cheap Trick the second weekend of November!"

I jump out of my seat so fast the chair falls to the ground. *Please say we're all going,* I chant in my head. To my relief Logan, holds out four tickets! All thoughts of Jax are momentarily forgotten. Until he picks up the chair. It doesn't escape my notice that Jax moves my chair closer to his. I eye him, wondering what his game is, but he doesn't give anything away.

"I think this present is more for Adalynn than me," Logan says, distracting me from The God I'm forced to sit beside.

"Oh shut up. You're the one who got me into them when we were little."

When Logan picks up Jax's present, Jax fidgets in his seat. I watch him from the corner of my eye, not wanting him to catch me staring. Hmm . . . What can be in the bag? Logan's mouth drops open as he removes an old shirt. He sits there, immobile.

"An old shirt? Really Jax you couldn't get him something better than one of your old jerseys?" Connors asks him.

I agree with Connor. I mean, come on, Jax has more money than anyone I know. Anything else would have been better than that. Still silent, Logan slowly turns the jersey around so I can see it better. My breath catches. Holy shit.

"Is that really his?" I ask Jax.

Connor gulps loudly. He seems ashamed from his comment earlier as he studies his beer with a forlorn expression.

Jax looks more than uncomfortable as he runs a shaky hand over his face. "Yeah . . . if you want something else, I'll get you anything you want . . . I just . . ."

He stops his rant when Logan sweeps him into the biggest bear hug I've ever seen. Can Jax even breathe? Composing himself, Logan sits back down and traces the number twenty-three on the back with his finger in awe.

"How did you get this?" Logan and I ask at the same time.

It's our dad's jersey from when he played soccer in college. The one signed by everyone on his team the last year he played.

"I went through your storage in California. Found it and brought it back . . . I thought you would rather have it then it being kept somewhere in a box," Jax explains.

WOW! I'm speechless and so is my brother. I don't know what's in storage since Logan dealt with all that, but I can only imagine there are millions of boxes everywhere. Give or take. I don't even want to think about how much time that took. It's incredible that he did that especially with his work schedule. He is an amazing friend to my brother and I think I just fell in love with him a little more.

"When?" Connor asks.

Jax shrugs. "I've had time lately and I wanted to give you something meaningful. Not that Cheap Trick tickets aren't."

"Thanks man," Connor says sourly.

Jax winks and I can tell Logan is getting all choked up.

"I don't...I don't...even—"

"Don't even worry about it. Happy birthday," Jax says.

Knowing my brother needs a mood-lifter, I hand him his present. Naturally, I wrapped it in the brightest shade of neon pink wrapping paper I could find.

"Really Addie? They didn't have any other color?" Logan accepts the box from my hands.

Giving him my cheesiest smile, I say in a sing song voice, "Nope, they only carry this color. I know it sucks!"

"Oh I'm sure that's why, not because you've enjoyed giving me presents wrapped in pink since we were kids."

"Why break tradition?"

We smile at each other. Logan tears into it and slides the lid off of the box. He picks up one frame after another, not saying anything. He sets each frame on the table and stares at them. I hold my breath. The guys can now see exactly what I got him. They look at the pictures, to Logan, to me, and back to Logan again. It's eerily quiet and I can hear Logan's heavy breathing from across the poker table. When I glance up, my brother blue eyes are pinned to my face.

I can feel how much pain he's in now because of me. I can't believe I'm such an idiot. Of course he doesn't want a reminder of everyone that isn't here on his birthday. I open my mouth to apologize, but stop when I see his eyes glistening with tears. Crap! I'm the worst gift-giver in the history of the world. I really thought he would love this. I turn away from him, and run though ideas to flee without being insensitive.

Emotions . . . I can't do them.

Logan slowly stands and makes the few steps around the table to me. Bending down so we're at eye level he whispers, "Thank you."

He says it so earnestly that I immediately feel better.

"I can't put into words how much this means to me, sis. I love it." He folds his arms around me. "I'm so lucky to have a sister like you."

I hug him back just as fiercely. "That's good since you're kind of stuck with me."

Logan excuses himself to use the bathroom, but I think it's more to rein in his emotions than anything else. Connor glares at Jax and I.

"What?" we ask at the same time.

"Maybe next time you two do a themed gift, let me know, okay?" he jokes.

I don't find it funny, but I laugh alongside Jax anyways. I was thinking the same thing earlier when Logan opened Jax's present. He bumps his shoulder against mine. He's being playful, hopefully attempting to sweep whatever this is between us under the rug. That's what I'm going to believe he's doing, anyways. I'm tired of fighting with him. So he slept with me and then fled. *Wouldn't be the first time.* I give him a small smile so that he knows I'm done with all the hostility between us.

It's almost three in the morning when we're all more than ready to leave. We've played way too much poker and drank even more. Thank goodness for taxis, or we would all be crashing here tonight. Logan leaves his gifts except for mine. He refuses to keep them here and retrieve them in the morning with the rest of the presents. Drunken logic, got to love it. I peer at Connor and Jax with my head held high. It there was a competition for best present, I so would have won. They both know me too well because they shake their heads at me.

Connor says, "You cheated with pictures!" at the same time Jax says, "It's not a competition, Ads."

"Obviously since I blew you guys out of the water. You're just mad, Evans, because you're a sore loser. Bring your A game next time, Chandler," I taunt them.

We all laugh as we make our way to the lobby after saying goodbye to Connor. I stop in my tracks when I notice only one taxi. I stand next to my brother, glaring at Jax.

"Why is there only one taxi?" I ask him.

"We're going to share a taxi," Jax says as if it's obvious.

"You and me? Why? You don't live near me."

"We're gonna make sure you get home safely," Logan says.

"You two do realize I'm not a child, right?"

Logan sighs loudly. "Get in the car, Addie."

I really, really do not want to be crammed in a taxi with Jax. That does not sound like a good time to me especially in my drunken state. I'll do something to embarrass myself. I know it.

I stomp my foot. "No! I can get home all by myself. Thank you very much." The words jumble together. Stupid alcohol.

They both laugh at me. Screw them! I will not ride with Jax. I refuse! Jax's eyes widen and he shakes his head in frustration. Logan stops laughing and stares at me and then Jax in question. Crap! Stupid alcohol, I said that out loud. I can only stare open-mouthed at my brother, hoping that he doesn't piece together what's happening with his little sister and best friend.

"Why can't you ride with Jax? What did he do?" He asks the other question to Jax, stepping closer to him.

This is not good. Jax chuckles. Does he have a death wish? I seriously think there's something wrong with him.

"Ads is just mad because she shattered the screen on her phone last night and blames me instead of her two left feet."

They both turn towards me. I open my mouth to tell him off, but stop. He wins, I can't yell at him because if I do, then Logan will know something is up. After a few more choice words, I follow behind my brother and sit in the middle of the taxi.

"Nice save," I whisper to Jax.

He nods but doesn't say anything. Maybe he's back to ignoring me? I would ignore me, too. When the cab takes off, my eyes drift shut. I feel my body being moved, but I can't open them to see why. I feel protected. I rest my head on something hard and welcome the pleasant woodsy scent.

I count to five slowly, hoping that I'm dreaming, but I know I'm not. I'm not that imaginative, I can't dream up Jax's scent. I've tried and failed. As soon as I breathe in his scent again, my brain wakes up from its drunken slumber to let me know I'm in Jax's arms. I open my eyes and I'm met with the most beautiful green eyes in the world. Just being this close to him makes me moan in pleasure. His jaw tightens.

I hear the distant click of my door unlocking and become instantly aware of my surroundings. Logan attempts to hold the door open, but settles for leaning against the doorframe for support. I'm not surprised by my brother's drunken state. He shouldn't have done those shots with Connor. Logan barely makes it to the couch before passing out. Guess he'll be sleeping here tonight.

I am surprised how sober Jax appears, though. When we reach my bedroom, I struggle out of his arms, wanting to be as far away as possible from The God, but he grips me closer to his chest. I want to stay here forever wrapped in his arms. But reality is a bitch and this isn't a dream. I don't belong in the safety of his arms.

"Put me down," I demand quietly.

Ignoring my protest, he continues to carry me.

"Jax, please, I just want to go to bed. You're going the wrong way."

He flips on the light to my bathroom. I squeeze my eyes closed and bury my face deeper into his warm chest. That was bright. He finally lets me go and deposits me on the counter. I watch him make himself at home in my bathroom. He squeezes toothpaste on my toothbrush, runs it under the sink, and holds it in front of my mouth.

To my shock he says, "Open."

I'm too stunned to do anything but obey. His complete focus is on my mouth. I sit immobile while he brushes my teeth. I'm so entranced as he takes care of me that I barley notice that he's stopped brushing my teeth.

He points my toothbrush towards the sink, humor evident in his eyes. "Spit."

I want to spit in his face, but I of course I do what I'm told. He rinses off my toothbrush when he's finished, then puts it back in its rightful place. He grabs my make-up removal cloths next. I put my hand up to stop him.

"I'm capable of doing this myself, Jax."

He swats my hand away, takes my chin in his huge strong hand and starts wiping off my make-up. "I never said you weren't," he says once he's done.

Thanking him, I slide off the counter but he moves too fast and suddenly I'm in his arms again. I sigh dramatically, trying to pull off the "I'm annoyed sigh" but it comes off more as a moan than anything else. Lovely.

"Just so you're aware, I can actually use these to walk." I kick my legs to prove my point.

He chuckles as he nears my bed. I think he's going to set me down and leave, but nope, that would be too kind of him. Instead he drops me on my bed. Roughly.

"Ouch," I say in mock anger.

He laughs as he strides to my dresser to get me something to sleep in. If I wasn't fully aware that my brother is in the living room I would taunt him by stripping, but instead I settle for studying him. He wears a smug grin when he gives me a jersey. I don't even need to see it to confirm it's one of his. Wanting to get rid of his stupid smile, I stand up and turn away from him. I'm done being waited on.

Glancing over my shoulder at him I ask in a sultry voice, "Get the zipper?"

His Adam's apple bobbles up and down a few times before he reaches out slowly to unzip my dress.

"Thanks," I whisper.

I saunter into my closet with the jersey in hand. I strip out of my dress, unhook my strapless bra, and slide a long shirt off the hanger. Once I'm dressed, I throw his jersey into my hamper before rejoining Jax in my bedroom. When I say walk I mean stumble since I'm still drunk. When I finally reach my bed that I swear has moved, it dawns on me that I didn't grab boy shorts to sleep in. Awesome. I start to stand, but the stupid floor starts to move. What the heck is that about? Jax steadies me and bends down so his face is lined with mine.

"Get into bed before you hurt yourself, Ads."

I close my eyes to prepare myself for what I'm going to say next. He couldn't have just left me to fend for myself, could he? No, of course not. Jax lives to confuse the crap out of me.

I whisper, "I'm not wearing any panties . . . can you help me to my dresser so I can grab some boy shorts please?"

He sucks in a breath. He clenches his jaw so tight I'm sure it's about to break, and he runs a hand over his face. His eyes darken. At first I think he's turned on, but that changes when I notice how pissed off he is. Why is he mad? He's the one that wouldn't let me get up.

Without a word he spins on his heels, makes his way to my dresser and grabs the first thing he sees. He tosses it over his shoulder and surprise, surprise, the boy shorts land right next to me. Ugh, why is he good at everything without even trying? I yank them on. I open my mouth to thank him but he's already gone. Shocker.

I shake my head, annoyed. I clamp my hands over my mouth and take slow deep breaths, willing myself not to throw up. When the wave of nausea subsides, I lay down in bed. I don't even bother huddling underneath the blankets. I'm way too tired. I close my eyes and pass out.

CHAPTER FOURTEEN

I finally start at Malcara Enterprises today. I'm buzzing with excitement. Yesterday I may or may not have gone a little overboard in the shopping department for new work clothes. I'm a girl, what can you expect?

After I style my hair into a side bun, I put on a light shade of shimmery grey eyeshadow to make my violet eyes pop, a little eyeliner and mascara to finish it off. I select a light shade of pink lipstick. Bam, my face and hair are done in a matter of minutes.

I step into my Derek Lam fitted silver dress. It's chic and business in one, perfect for my first day! I forgo jewelry and slip into my Michael Kors suede booties. Gripping my red Valentino tote bag, I rush to the kitchen to snag a breakfast bar and a water. Stuffing both in my bag, I dash out of my apartment.

My morning is full of playing catch-up. Which is perfect for me. I'm a fantastic multitasker. I'm given no direction, well not if you count "here's all the papers that need to be dealt with." My boss did add that I can ask questions if I have any, but me being stubborn, I chose to ignore that last part and figure everything out on my own. I'm almost done with everything when Tinkerbell strolls out of her office towards me. I smile warmly at her.

"Lunch is in about thirty. I have the perfect place for us to go," she says as she continues on her way.

My mouth drops open in surprise. I thought she was going to ask me to do something for her, not invite me to lunch. Well, demand is more like it. I see her smack her hand over her face before she stops and turns around with a guilty expression on her face. I raise an eyebrow in question.

"I'm so sorry. You probably already have plans . . . I just thought since you're new and everything."

I laugh at how quickly she can switch from commanding to uncertain. Tinkerbell to the core, I swear!

"That sounds great. Just come get me when you're ready to go to lunch, Ms. Harrison." I use her last name because I don't want to sound unprofessional.

The look of horror that washes over her face tells me before she says anything that I should have gone with her first name.

"No need for last names with me. Call me Harper. Never Ms. Harrison."

Harper takes me to a little hole in the wall diner that I would have never known was here without her. Once we open the heavy wood door, I fall in love immediately. There's a homey vibe to this little Mexican place. We grab the only table available, and both order water, mine with ice, hers without. Our server brings chips and salsa and takes our orders.

After eating a chip Harper asks, "How do you like Malcara so far?"

I tell her all about my first day, and how much I like it. "Ask again at the end of the week, though."

She laughs at my joke. After the server delivers our meals, I moan when I take the first bite of the burrito. Holy crap! Tinkerbell gives me a knowing look.

"Best Mexican around. Told you."

We launch into girly topics after a few bites and I learn that she may beat me on the whole over-spending gene by a landslide. She loves clothes more than me and that's saying something. I love that she doesn't bring up any family questions so I skip over those, too. However, I do ask where she's from, I mean the woman does have a southern accent.

Laughing she says, "I'm from Alabama. I'm surprised it took you this long to ask. It's usually the first thing somebody asks me."

We argue over the bill, but she's quicker than I am.

"It's your first day. Besides, you can get the next one."

I smile, realizing that I've just made my first friend since high school. I think this is bigger news than my job. I can't wait to tell Liv at therapy today.

After we get back to work, I don't see Harper until we're leaving for the day because she's been stuck in meetings. I finish closing up my computer files, stand up, and collect my things. I say a quick goodbye to my boss, William.

"Have a good night, Adalynn. You did a great job today. Oh and before I forget, whenever you make travel arrangements for me please email a copy to my wife or she'll kill me."

"Of course, William, goodnight."

I close the door, happy that I have an amazing boss that is so devoted to his wife. He is a firm believer on not pulling all-nighters at the office just so he can get back in time for dinner. It's refreshing to know that actual people work here and not robots.

Harper follows me into the elevator and we make small talk about our plans for the weekend while we ride down to the lobby. Apparently we're having a girls' night. I'm excited and a little nervous; the only girls' night that I know of are what I see in movies. Hopefully it's not full of drunken one night stands, because that is so not what I'm about.

"We'll only be drinking. Promise," she reassures me when she sees my expression.

"In that case, then I can't wait."

Liv's receptionist gives me a quick wave as I enter the waiting area and directs me into the office. Liv is already in her chair, ready to start today's session. I sit down in a huff, dropping my purse on the floor while I apologize for being late.

"How was work?"

As much as I didn't want the job before, I'm glad that I felt my brother pushing me in this direction. The only downside of being a career woman is this sensation that I'm missing something, I can't shake it. I want to tell Liv this, but I hold my tongue. I have a sinking feeling that I know what I really want to do, but I'm not ready to face that obstacle yet. So instead, I tell her the truth about my day but omit what's on my mind.

"It was fantastic, I was so busy! If I wasn't doing a million things at my computer, I was running around the office. Plus my boss is really nice. Oh and I made a friend, she reminds me of Tinkerbell."

"Your co-worker reminds you of a Disney fairy?"

I nod. "With a southern accent too. Her name is Harper. She's crazy and you would love her."

We talk about the changes in my life for twenty minutes. I think we're just gonna keep it light today, but she drops her famous bomb like always, catching me by surprise.

"With all of these changes, new job, new friends, and getting back into old stuff like photography, have you thought about getting in the pool again?"

I twirl my thumbs back and forth. Ironically, it's a calming gesture I picked up in swimming.

"No," I say in a way that hopefully stops her from pushing, but I know she will. She always does.

She sets down her notebook on the coffee table in front of her and I know she's about to get serious.

"Stop me if I'm wrong. You never thought you would be behind the camera again because it would remind you too much of your father. In a negative way, correct?"

I nod, hating where she's going with this.

"You finally did when Jax pushed you by buying you a new camera. It brought back good memories, the memories that you refused to remember. Now you're taking pictures, even looking through your old photos and going through your things from before the accident. The same things you kept telling Logan to throw away. He never did and you always kept those objects close to you."

Avoiding her scrutiny, I direct my attention to the window. She has a point, but I still don't want to be hearing this.

"Addie, swimming can bring back happy memories, too. Just think about it."

I continue to stare out the window. "Swimming is different than taking pictures. Taking pictures didn't kill my family." I lock gazes with her as I say the last part.

She doesn't say anything at first. Then after a minute or two she says, "Neither did swimming. A horrible accident killed your family that night. You had no control over what happened, Adalynn."

I jump out of my seat and grab my purse, ready to leave.

"This is too much for today. I have to go."

I make my way to her door but stop when she adds, "Addie I'm not going to apologize for saying that. It's the truth and you need to stop blaming yourself. I understand why you need to leave, just think about everything we discussed."

When I get home, I need to take my mind off everything before I lose it. It's time for a much needed run. Running always helps me when I feel like this. I can just leave it all on the pavement. I opt out of running outside because it's too dark. Reluctantly, I get changed and go to the gym in my building. The treadmill will have to do. After my warm-up I increase the speed so I can sprint. I need to feel the burn. I need to focus on that instead of swimming, and all its reminders.

It takes six miles before my body loosens up. I'm dripping in sweat, my breathing is heavy, and my legs burn from being out of shape. I need to start running more, I've been too distracted. I welcome the heat working its way up my thighs. I focus on the fire building in my calfs, enjoying the reprieve. Another three more miles, I'm done. I'm barley able to cool myself down. I over-did it, but I couldn't have stopped until I reached this point. When I get in these moods, I'm a machine. I push my body into overdrive, relishing the pain. I dry the sweat off my face and arms before I wipe the machine clean. I leave the gym. Like a beacon, I find myself in the last place I want to be right now.

The pool.

I smell the chlorine and close my eyes. I can picture myself gliding through the water with every stroke. The water has always been a way to escape. Every time I would inhale a whiff of the chlorine, or make the first dive off the block and into the water, it was like coming home. All of that is gone; it's just a fading memory now.

I take one final deep breath, I turn around and walk away as I remember the old red and white flags.

The week flies by. It's now Friday and I can't wait for work to be over so I can enjoy my first girls' night with Harper. It's crazy that I have a girlfriend to engage in girl talk. I will admit to being sexist on that part, but there are just some things I can't discuss with the boys, especially since most of it involves Jax.

I haven't spoken to Jax since the night of Logan's party, which isn't a surprise. Connor has been Connor and has texted me nonstop about taking Harper and me to lunch ever since I sent him a picture. I love teasing him, but we both know he doesn't have a chance with her. She isn't the bimbo one night stand type. I may bring her over for Sunday brunch, though.

Bumping her shoulder into mine, she points her head in the direction of my desk. "Someone has a secret admirer."

I look up from my phone and follow her line of sight to a huge bouquet of peonies. I stop mid-step when I realize they are from Jax without even seeing a card. I know they're from him because nobody else knows these are my favorite.

Harper reaches the flowers before me since I'm frozen to the spot. "Do you know who they're from? There's no card." She continues to search around my desk as if a card will magically appear.

I nod. Of course Jax wouldn't write a card; he's not talking to me, not even in letter form. Bending to smell the flowers, I decide that I'll wave the white flag. I shoot him over a text.

Me: Thank you, they're beautiful and make me smile whenever I look at them.

I even add the white flag emoji at the end. I'm surprised when I glance up from my phone to see Harper casually leaning against my desk. She isn't fooling anyone. I know exactly what she's after. I was hoping that she would just leave it be, but she won't be derailed. I should have known better.

"Why do I get the feeling that they're not from Kohen?"

I shrug. "I have no idea," I grumble but then admit, "They're from Jax."

Harper smiles at me and strides away as if she just won something. I just shake my head at her. I lean over my desk to smell the flowers. I can't believe he did this. Peonies are my all-time favorite. He remembers silly things like this. I check my phone again, willing it to show me I have a new text message, but I'm disappointed. *He's probably just busy.*

I've forced myself not to check my phone for one hundred and twenty minutes, not that I'm counting or anything. That's enough time, right? He didn't text back, no big deal. I don't care in the slightest.

As I drink my water, my phone buzzes on my desk. I force myself to swallow my sip and calmly reach for my phone. I square my shoulders, take a deep breath, and slide the unlock on my screen. My whole face lights up when I see it's from Jax.

Jax: Welcome, Ads. I have a chocolate cupcake with your name on it whenever you're free.

I bite my lip, contemplating what to say. Of course I want to say something along the lines of, "I'm free whenever you are," or my personal favorite, "Can I eat it off of you?" but I know there's no way in hell that I will ever be able to say something like that to him. I also don't want to seem too eager to hang out. His mood swings are worse than a woman on her period. I decide to ignore his text for now and get back to work.

An hour later I'm shutting down my computer when my phone beeps again. Glancing down at the screen, my face falls.

Kohen: I miss you. Date after work?

Me: Can't. Have plans with Tinkerbell. Remember?

I'm not gonna lie, I'm a little annoyed that he asked again today. He called me this morning and he sent me a text asking the same question I answered this morning. I just don't see how he can forget, especially since this is all I've talked about this week.

Harper comes over to my desk. She frowns when she notices that I'm worked up.

"What's going on?" She hands me my flowers as I rise.

As we step into the empty elevator I give her a quick run down about Kohen's persistence.

When we reach the lobby she says, "Men are stupid. For some reason they think we need to be at their beck and call. But don't worry your pretty little head over it, Addie, soon we will be drunk and your problems will float away on the dance floor." She even shakes her hips at the last part.

I laugh when an older man walks into a wall because he was watching her instead of paying attention to where he was going. When we part ways, promising to meet in a few hours, I can't help but wonder . . . how much trouble are we going to get into tonight?

Stepping into the nightclub, Basement, I gaze around the mass of people and wonder how the heck I'm going to spot Harper in this crowd. I should have listened to her and met her outside or someplace easier than this chaos. I walk around aimlessly for ten minutes until I realize, when in doubt check the bar.

She's most likely to stake out the bar nearest the door to watch for me. So I head in the direction of that one, which also happens to be the most crowded with men. I shove a few men out my way.

"Holy shit!" I say out loud when I realize they're clustered around a hot woman in a gold metallic short dress that fits her like another skin.

Fuck, I'm not even into girls and I'm turned on. I would seriously consider switching teams for her. She stands on the bar pouring drinks into men's mouths. Wow, they actually let people do this at clubs? I thought that was only in movies. I can just see from her chest down because a tree of a man hulks in front of me.

Sighing I step around him and look for any flash of red. Out of the corner of my eye, I see the flash of her red hair that I've been searching for and turn towards the bar. My mouth drops open.

"Holy shit!" I say again.

Harper beckons me with her finger. A man helps me onto the bar. I shake my head at her, but I open my mouth as she tilts the bottle to my lips. As the alcohol burns all the way down my throat, I have only one thought. *Tinkerbell is the best kind of trouble.*

Someone inserts a key in the elevator and says, "He's expecting you, so stay here and he'll come get you."

I press my hands to my face and try to gather enough strength to figure out what's going on. I think I focus enough to see a black dancing arm. Wait, that doesn't make sense. A dancing arm, what is that? I need to focus. Where am I? More importantly, where am I going? I'm in a elevator so I must be going home.

Bed.

That sounds amazing. Wait, Tinkerbell! I laugh when I hear myself shout her name out loud instead of saying it in my head. Vaguely, I remember her saying something along the lines of not using her nickname at work, while she was helping me into the lobby. Oh man, did I call her Tinkerbell? A lot? Whatever, she must not have hated it too much if she helped me inside the lobby.

"FUUCCCKK!" I shout when I realize where she left me.

I start pressing the down button, but the stupid elevator keeps going up.

"No! This cannot be happening!" I say a lot louder than I intend just as the elevator doors chime open and a devastatingly handsome god smirks at me.

"Nice to see you to, Ads," The God says.

I throw up on him.

OH . . . MY . . . GOD . . . please let this be the worse nightmare in the world. From the sour taste in my mouth, I know it's not. I refuse to open my eyes. If I don't see it, this didn't happen. His fingers wrap around my forearms and he steers my drunken self out of the elevator. Hopefully he's nice enough to avoid the vomit. I really wouldn't blame him if he made sure I stepped in it.

I force air into my lungs and slowly exhale, trying not to throw up again. So not what I need right now. We stop walking, I hear Jax moving about, but I refuse to open my eyes. This is just a horrible nightmare. This isn't real. There's no way I'm unlucky enough to end up at his place when I'm this drunk. The world isn't that cruel, is it? Yes, yes it is.

"Are you going to throw up again because I would prefer if you did it in my toilet instead of on me next time," Jax says from behind me.

Refusing to acknowledge his close proximity, I swallow a mouthful of air that's dripping in his scent. I'm relieved that I'm just dizzy, no longer nauseous.

"Maybe I'm not that drunk, maybe it's just you that makes me sick," I say in a teasing voice I don't think I pull off so well. For the life of me, I can't seem to care.

Jax leads me to his couch and orders me to sit. Leaning back, I try to focus on exactly how I ended up here. Rubbing my palms over my eyes, I concentrate as hard as I can but I can only pull up a slight memory of Harper asking if I wanted to see the boyfriend or lover.

God, I don't think I've ever been this drunk in my entire life. She should come with a warning label. I have to ask her for the details. My phone. I can ask her now. I open my eyes and I'm happy to see my purse attached to my shoulder. Thank goodness! Somehow my purse jumps from my shoulder to the floor. Hmmm. When did my purse start moving on its own? I reach for it, but gravity is a bitch. I fall flat on my face, nearly hitting my head on the coffee table. This is going to hurt tomorrow. I struggle to sit up, but my body isn't cooperating. I attempt three more times before giving up. Laying on the floor seems like the better option anyway. This isn't so bad, I think I'll sleep here.

I dream of flying through the woods. It's so vivid that I can smell it. I inhale the smell of fresh air, oak trees, and home.

"If I smell bad I blame your little gift," someone chuckles into my ear.

My eyes snap open. "So that wasn't a nightmare then?"

Jax brushes my bangs out of my face. "More my nightmare than yours. I've never been thrown up on, and as much as I love everything you do, I'd really rather you not do that again."

I hate that I know we're in Jax's bed. Ugh! The man lives in a huge, over-the-top penthouse, he couldn't have stuck me in one of the many spare bedrooms? He reads my mind or maybe I spoke out loud? It's hard to tell at this point.

"Didn't want you to throw up in your sleep and drown in your own vomit."

I roll my eyes, but on the inside I'm smiling. I wish I wasn't this drunk, though. Okay, so maybe I'm not drunk anymore, but my head is fuzzy. Jax reaches behind him and offers the most beautiful thing I've seen besides him this morning. A glass of water. I smile appreciatively at him before I chug the entire glass. Yup, classy should be my middle name. I gaze out his panoramic window, and to my surprise, it's dark. I turn back to Jax, startled.

"Please tell me I didn't sleep the entire day away."

He gives me the don't-be-stupid look. "No, you've only been out for a little over an hour."

I slap my hand over my face and mutter, "Oh."

He gently lifts my hand off my face, leans close enough to where our noses almost touch. I hold my breath, remembering I threw up, and watch his mouth as he says, "It's not like we haven't slept together before, Ads. It's not that big of a deal."

I push him off me and brush off his nearness with a laugh. Trying to play off that my heart didn't just stop.

"So how drunk are you still?"

I do a quick measure of everything. "Just a little buzz going on."

I stare at my hands, not knowing if I should get out of his more-than-welcoming bed and go home.

Jax laughs. "Yeah, I think you threw up everything on me and sobered up after that. It's pretty impressive how much you were able to get on me with one shot."

I growl at him from under my breath and say in a not-so-nice tone, "Oh shut up, you act like you've never thrown up from drinking before."

Jax, of course, won't let me live this down. That would be too nice of him.

"Of course I have. I've never had the pleasure of throwing up on someone, though. That, my dear, goes all to you."

I stick out my tongue at him.

"How's the doctor?" he asks with disdain.

I shake my head. "You really want to talk about Kohen?"

He opens his mouth, a witty comeback on the tip of his tongue I'm sure, but stops when I challenge him with a raise of my eyebrow. His finger traces over my frown lines, and then he shakes his head, as if to get rid of an unpleasant memory.

"How was your first week?" he asks to change the topic.

I give him a tight smile and tell him everything. He seems mesmerized as I talk. I tell him how the flowers are on my nightstand so they're the first thing I see in the morning. He tells me about a few business deals he's pursuing. It astounds me how intelligent Jax is. He should be, though, he's the only person I have ever met who has skipped a grade in elementary school. I listen, just as mesmerized.

"I don't know exactly what to say other than I'm an ass. I know I don't deserve it after everything, but I want things to get back to normal between us."

I give him my first real smile since I oh-so-kindly threw up on him. "I would love that!"

I know he probably means normal as in friends, but I secretly hope he means something more. As soon as that thought flies through my head, I get pissed off at myself. I need to let this stupid infatuation with him go. It was a fling, nothing more. After chastising myself for a bit longer, I relax against him again and enjoy our usual banter. I even open up about therapy. He's always been a great outlet to confide my sessions with Liv.

Jax, being as blunt as I am, lays into me. "You know she isn't wrong, Ads. Olivia has a point, if you're able to do things like photography, you can handle getting back into the water. You even went through your old stuff."

He bumps his shoulder into me, beaming proudly at me. I blush.

"It's not that big of a deal, Jax. It's not like I went through everything. I just knew what I wanted, where it was, and got it without looking at anything else."

"Don't sell yourself short."

"Just telling it like it is," I say with a shrug.

He scratches the sexy scruff on his jaw and watches me. His eyes widen as if the lightbulb just went off inside his head. The God jumps out of bed and goes over to his closet, which is so big it should be considered another room. I mean, come on, how many suits can one man own? It's pretty impressive, actually. Jax emerges from the closet with the plum tie I bought for his birthday last year. His sinful look makes me squirm.

"Now we're talking." I whisper seductively.

His eyes darken and his step falters. He shouldn't be allowed to look at me like this, it's dangerous to my health. I open my mouth to say something that I know will get me into trouble tomorrow, but all words evade me.

"Game?" He dangles the tie in front of me and uses his husky bedroom voice that sends tingles low in my belly.

My mouth falls open, but I quickly recover. "To wear your tie?" I ask him, skeptical.

He holds his other hand out to me, the one without the tie. I hesitate, wondering what he's up to, but I place my hand in his strong one, trusting him.

He takes me hesitance as something it's not because he leans in, brushes his lips against my ear and whispers, "I dare you to trust me, Adalynn."

I suppress a moan from escaping, but it's impossible to control the goosebumps. I just hope he thinks they're from the cold and not because of him. Jax stares into my eyes and I get captivated into his dark green ones that seem a little darker tonight. Everything floats away. Suddenly it's just a boy and a girl in their own little world, a place without any pain, a place where they will always have each other. But my vision goes dark and the boy and the girl are gone, the same as that perfect world.

His fingertips trace my cheek. I take a deep breath as reality crashes into me.

"It's just another blindfold, Ads. I'm here with you, nothing is going to happen that you don't want," he says soothingly, relaxing me with his words.

I draw another deep breath before I nod. How did girls' night end up with me at Jax's place with his tie acting as a blindfold? His fingers glide over my face once more. Slowly, painfully so, his fingers trail down my neck to my shoulder blade, down my forearm, and finally to my hand. He interlocks our fingers together. My breathing is erratic. Jax drives me crazy with just the tips of his fingers, a whisper of a promise that I want to hold onto. I hate the effect he has on me.

Giving my hand a gentle squeeze, he pulls me along and I blindly follow him. He keeps a strong hold of my hand, letting me know without words that he'll always be here. It makes being blindfolded much easier this time. I know his place as well as mine so when we reach the foyer, I panic.

"Um, Jax, I'm not going anywhere like this." I plant my feet to the ground, unwilling to move.

He rests both hands on my shoulders and I know that he's staring at me. "And like this, you mean without shoes I'm guessing?"

Oh man, I forgot I'm not wearing shoes. Not the first time I forgot something so vital with this Adonis near. He's going to make me say it, that jerk. I square my shoulders.

"The tie," I say through gritted teeth.

Jax laughs as if I'm the best comedian in New York. I wish I could see him right now because I have no doubt that he is doubled over in laughter. He lifts my hand to lead me along, but I keep my feet glued, not moving an inch.

"Nobody will see you at this time of night. Don't worry, Ads. Now move your ass!" He slaps my bottom hard.

I jump, startled from the force of his slap. I rub my palm in circles over my now sore butt. "That hurt!"

It didn't, it actually felt good . . . really good. Jax chuckles while he steers me out of his place. The moment my feet touch the cold floor of the elevator, I remember my lack of shoes.

"No shoes remember?" I point down at my bare feet that I can't see.

He slips his arm around my shoulder. "You won't need them."

I pull away a little, tilt my face up at him and give him a stern look. Well, as stern as I can manage being blindfolded.

"I am so not walking around barefoot!"

"You're not walking, I'm carrying you."

That's all the warning I get before Jax lifts me over his shoulder at the same time that the elevator doors open. I start to protest until Jax slaps my ass again, harder this time. I moan into his ear and bite his back.

Holy-hotness, what does this man do to me?

"You're making a scene," he taunts but his voice betrays him.

He's affected just as much as I am. I only stop because I have to focus on not convulsing on top of him as he marches on his merry way. I could care less about a making a scene. Plus I highly doubt we're making one at this time of night.

"I had a completely different scenario going on in my head when I saw the tie."

He sucks in a ragged breath and ignores me. I smile, I knew he would.

I open my mouth to ask how much further, but close it when I realize how close our faces are in this position. He squeezes me tighter to him, simultaneously bringing my face dangerously close to his. Not good. The need to kiss him grows so overpowering I have to bite the inside of my cheek.

"Someone needs to learn patience."

His voice sends tingles down my body. My heart skips a beat before stopping all together. I wish I could see his face right now. I would be able to read him a lot better.

"How long have you known me?" I ask.

"About sixteen years now, give or take."

"And in all of those years, have you ever seen me be patient?" I ask in a serious tone.

Jax fights off his laughter, but it's hard to hide when his chest shaking from suppressing it. "No, I guess you haven't. Maybe you should start working on that."

I pinch the inside of his arm. "Maybe in the—" All words escape me when I realize where we are.

No, he wouldn't do this to me . . .

I will never forgive him for this . . .

I hate him . . .

CHAPTER FIFTEEN

My entire body tenses, my heart races into overdrive, and I start to sweat. *Don't panic, you could be wrong. He wouldn't do this to you.* I try to convince myself that I'm wrong about my whereabouts. With each word I say in my head, I know I'm not able to fool myself. Even without being able to see, my body recognizes where I am.

I hold my breath for as long as possible to protect myself from inhaling the scent I know is here. I count in my head, wondering the entire time how Jax could do this to me, especially blindfolded. He's done questionable things in the past, but this is beyond fucked up, even for him.

I get to thirty when I feel Jax move again. My body stiffens even more, but I still don't say anything. I refuse to breathe. Forty-one, forty-two, forty-three. *Jax is out of his mind. I need to leave.* Fifty-five, fifty-six, fifty-seven.

My lungs hurt from lack of oxygen. I know I don't have much time until the inevitable happens. I breathe in deeply, hating him with each lungful of air.

When I have my breathing under control, Jax lowers me to the ground, keeping a hold of me until he's satisfied I won't fall. More than done with this blindfold, I start to untie it from around my head. Attempt is more like it, since my hands shake so badly I can't loosen the knot.

"Calm down, Ads. I'm right here." He covers my hands with his to stop my maddening movements.

I try to move my hands under his, but it's useless, he's too strong, too overpowering.

"Ta-take . . . ti-t-tie . . . off," I stutter as I concentrate on calming breaths. "Please, Jax, I can't do this," I finally manage to spit out after a minute or two.

He removes my hands away from the back of my head and rubs my arms up and down in a soothing gesture. I hate that it works.

Leaning his forehead against mine he says, "Listen to me, I know this is impossible for you, but I also know you need to overcome your fear."

A dry humorless laugh escapes me. "Me afraid of water? Really, how is that even possible? I know how to swim better than most fish!" I shout.

"You're not afraid of the water, Ads, that's impossible for someone like you. You're afraid of all the memories the water will invoke. You're afraid of remembering all the happy times." He pulls me into his arms and hugs me tightly. "You're afraid of wanting to be in the water, afraid of wanting to swim again, of enjoying it."

"I hate you."

"You're afraid if you get back in the water, you won't be able to get out and you won't be able to punish yourself anymore." I suck in a breath as if he punched me in the gut. "You force yourself to hate the one thing that you've always loved because you think it's the only way to punish yourself for surviving when Andy, Quinn, and Hadley died."

I punch his chest. "I HATE YOU! I HATE YOU! I HATE YOU!" My voice breaks, but I don't stop hitting him. He lets me.

My arms drop lifelessly to my sides while Jax holds me to him, rocking us gently. I shake my head as if just that simple act will create a barrier from his words.

"You're wrong," I whisper, voice hoarse from screaming.

"Prove it," Jax says just as quietly against my forehead.

My next breath comes out shaky. My legs tremble. Luckily I'm leaning against the solid rock that is Jax or I would be on the floor. I don't know how much time passes, it feels like seconds, but I know it's minutes as I stand in his strong embrace, borrowing strength.

"Fine."

I feel his smile against my forehead.

Fine? You can't do this. What the fuck is wrong with you?

Sealing my fate, I open my eyes and blink from the sudden brightness. Once I can focus without seeing spots, I realize that the lights are normal, I was just squeezing my eyes for too long. I stare at my bare feet, needing another moment before this becomes all too real. Oh look, my nail polish is chipped. Yeah, that doesn't distract me at all. Jax waits by my side while I gain the courage to do something I never thought I would ever consider doing again.

You can still run. No! I've been running for the past six years. I need to do this. I'm forced to come face-to-face with my worst nightmare . . . a pool.

My feet move on their own accord, and bring me to the edge of the indoor pool in Jax's building. There are five lanes, and at least a 15 person spa to the side. It's nice, it's also the only time I've ever been up here. I usually make an excuse to not join the guys at the pool. They stopped asking over the years. They got the hint that I don't like being around large amounts of water. Well, everyone except Jax, of course. Speaking of Jax, where did he go?

I scan the area. My mouth falls open as Jax removes his shirt and throws it on a lounge chair piled with two towels. Holy-hotness, I so did not think he planned on us getting in. Okay, maybe I did, hence the minor freakout, but I didn't realize I'd get in a pool with a half-naked Jaxon Chandler.

I don't even care when he turns around and sees me drooling on myself over him. It's impossible to close my mouth. I must look like a coke junkie without her fix. I can't focus on one particular part of his anatomy. My eyes roam as fast as they can over his body; his muscular chest, down to his defined abs that I've mapped out with my tongue, and finally over his long arms covered in tattoos. His artwork is so sexy, especially since you can't see it when he's dressed for work. It reminds me of a treasure hunt that I want to explore. I want to find 'x'.

It's amazing how he can make all of my problems float away.

Jax struts to me with the biggest shit-eating grin I've ever seen. Can't blame him, though, I would look like that too if someone stared at me how I'm staring at him. I watch the way his muscles move with each step. It's mouthwatering.

"Are you ready? Or do you need me to walk around a little longer for you?"

"That depends . . ."

"On?"

"If you're going to give me a little show."

To my amazement, he turns and wiggles his taut butt for me. I laugh even though the thought of going into the water makes my throat start to close. He knows exactly what he's doing . . . distracting me . . . it's working. I force myself to relax and seem aloof.

"Oh please don't, if I have to watch you shake that big fat thing you call an ass, I may throw up on you again."

Jax presses his lips together to fight his smile. "Yes, that's what you were doing, trying not to throw up, not trying to control yourself from throwing yourself at this sexy body." He points to his rock hard eight pack in case I forgot it was there. I didn't.

Hesitantly, I follow Jax to the steps of the pool, firmly holding onto his hand. When his foot touches the water, I pull back to stop him.

"I can't," I choke out.

Jax gives me the most breathtaking smile. "Yes you can, Ads. Trust me."

I bite my lip. *I can do this.* I inch toward him. *This is for them. This isn't for me. Make them proud.* I place my shaking hand back into his and take the final step, the first step into the heated water. *I'm doing this for me.* I close my eyes and relax into Jax. I let him guide me into the warm water. At the second-to-last step, the water reaches my thighs so I gather up my—

"Where's my dress?" I ask when I realize that I'm not wearing what I arrived in tonight. Instead I'm in one of his button-ups.

When did he change my clothes? How did I just now notice?

"I didn't want throw-up on my sheets. Plus you kind of smelled."

What a load of bull. I didn't throw up on myself. No, Jax had that pleasure. Arguing with him would be pointless, though.

"Thanks."

I yank the stupid clean, wonderful-smelling shirt to my panty line and continue walking into the pool with Jax.

"You ready?" he asks into my ear. I nod, letting him lead me deeper into the water.

Tears fill my eyes when we reach the middle of the pool, but I quickly squeeze them closed, refusing to let them fall. I will not cry, I never cry. Taking a deep breath, I dive underneath the water with Jax by my side.

Memories assault me so quickly it's hard to concentrate on a single one. I let go of Jax's hand and sink the rest of the way to the bottom until I'm at the pool's floor. I relive the first time I ever saw the ocean, swimming in my backyard, training, and when I would sneak into our pool at night during a rainstorm with Jax.

My hair floats around me. I move my hands back and forth in front of me and smile at the feel of my hands gliding in the water. Suddenly my peaceful moment is broken and I'm pulled to the surface.

"Adalynn, are you okay?" Jax shouts as he runs his hands over my face and down my throat to check my pulse.

I laugh at his absurdness. "Really, you're checking my pulse? What's the matter with you?"

I splash him with my feet as I backstroke away from him. I love how easily my body remembers the movements of the strokes, effortlessly carrying me away from him. Jax gives me a puzzled look as he studies me. Then a smile spreads across his luscious lips.

"You were down there for a pretty long time. I didn't like it."

"Ah caveman style and everything? You must be serious." Doing a quick flip-turn, I come up for air a foot away from him. "Relax and enjoy yourself for once, Mr. Always-So-Serious."

Jax looks behind him with that sexy one-eyebrow-raised thing he does and says, "I know you aren't talking to me like that," in that bedroom voice of his that sends chills all the way down to my toes.

Treading water, I smirk at him. "What are you gonna do about it?"

I turn over and sprint back to the wall with Jax racing behind me. If I can make it to the wall, I can get out and dive over him. He won't be able to catch me. I flip over to my back and do two backstrokes. I have more than enough time. I laugh as I reach the wall. This is fun. Before I can pull myself out of the water all the way, Jax captures the back of his shirt I'm borrowing.

Fast bastard.

Jax gets out of the pool after a while and watches me float around in nothing but my bra and panty set. I didn't see the point of swimming with his wet shirt. I smile up at him. From here I can see that his eyes are the dark shade of green that I love, the one that reminds me of a lion about to attack. I know he won't, he won't cross that line with me, not here. It's bittersweet. I love that we have our friendship back, but I hate that we can't be more than that.

I'm so grateful that he made me do this, that he pushed me when I was ready even though I didn't know it. He was right, I was punishing myself for my family's death. I refused to do the one thing that brought me so much joy. It's hard to believe that I've denied myself this feeling for six long years. Swimming is a part of me, the missing piece that I refused to acknowledge.

I know I will never compete again, that part of my life is over. It left the minute my family died. For the first time since that night, I can honestly say I'm okay with that, I know it will never be the same without them. At least now I know that I can go to the ocean or a pool without having a meltdown. Hmmm. The ocean, I miss it. Maybe I'll take a trip there soon.

God, this feels so amazing. I could float around all night like this. The memories that I feared would come back never do. The only memories are the happy ones, the ones that I forgot.

I sink down to the bottom of the pool again, one of my favorite places in the world. It's so quiet. It's peaceful, beautiful. It's like everything drifts away while I'm under here. This is the place I missed most of all. This is my happy place.

When I surface, Jax waits at the edge of the pool with his feet in and a towel in his lap. I swim towards him. I brace both hands on the outside of his legs, and peer up at him.

"Thank you for pushing me to remember who I am again and for everything you do for me, Jax."

His fingers travel over my shoulders. Then, in a move so fast I don't see it coming, he grips my underarms, lifts me out of the water and sets me on his lap. I go all too willingly. He drapes the towel around my shoulders and rubs it into my skin. Jax twirls a strand of my wet hair.

"I didn't do anything. This was all you, Ads. You did this. You faced your fear." He kisses the tip of my nose. "I only helped you realize what you already knew." He tilts my head up by my chin. "You are the strongest person I know, Adalynn. One day you'll see yourself how I see you."

I melt into him. He continues to dry me with the towel, rubbing circles into my back, making me fall asleep.

Stretching my arms over my head, I yawn. My left leg bumps into something warm and solid. My eyes fly open. I don't see my stars hanging over my bed. I know this plain white celling. Crap! Slowly I turn my head to see a bemused Jax in bed beside me.

"I know, I know I look amazing in the morning, but you don't have to stare, Ads," he says as he flexes his arms out in front of him, making his muscles pop.

Man! I can't catch a break with this guy. It's so unfair for him to look this good this early. Silently I curse The God. I have the sudden urge to punch his stupid smug grin off his face. I resist, barely. Forcing my gaze away from his delicious pecs that belong on billboards everywhere, I pointedly look him up and down.

Sassily I say, "You know the room down the hall and to the right have a much better view than this one. Maybe next time you could put me in that one."

"Yeah, I should do that next time. Besides, then I wouldn't have to fight you off in your sleep."

My mouth drops open.

"Don't worry kiddo, I was able to keep you at bay and get some sleep."

Kiddo? I glare at him. He laughs, finding me amusing. Wonderful.

He gets out of bed and makes a show off striding to his bathroom in just his black briefs. Yup, my mouth is fully agape now. I'm pretty sure there's now drool on his blanket, but I don't care.

All I'm able to do is gawk at him dumbfounded as he walks into his bathroom and closes his door. Groaning, I slam my head down, clutch the closest pillow and scream my frustration into it. Jax's mouthwatering smell hits me unexpectedly, which shouldn't be that big of a surprise since I'm in his bed clenching his pillow to my face, but it is. I throw the pillow across the room.

Stupid boy.

Stupid tattoos.

Stupid green eyes.

I hear the shower turn on so I decide it's safe to sneak out before he notices. My emotions run wild, too wild to be around him right now. Everything he has done confuses the crap out of me. One minute I'm nothing more than his best friend's little sister, the next it seems I'm something more, much more. I can't deal with this right now.

I open his drawer where he keeps his workout clothes. I steal a pair of basketball shorts, then pull down a black hoodie from a hanger and change. I spot my clothes and shoes from last night on the bench in front of his bed. After picking up everything, I rush out of his bedroom.

I call down to the lobby for a cab so I don't have to hail one in what looks to be the outfit from a one night stand. After hanging up, I write him a note.

Thanks for last night.

I want to say something more, but I can't force myself to go through with it. Everything about last night was perfect. Because of his insistent pushing, I have another piece of myself.

After placing the note on the coffee maker, I leave. Just in time, too, because right when I reach the elevator I hear him calling my name. As the doors close, I sigh in relief. I don't know which Jax I'll get if I stay. I can't deal with the cold and distant Jax, especially after last night.

An hour later, I lock myself in my apartment and sag against the door. After a minute of sitting on the floor, I force myself into the living room. I drop everything on my coffee table, grab my phone from my clutch and go into the bathroom for a much needed bath.

I strip out of Jax clothes, and draw the perfect bath, complete with bath salts and oils, in record time. Sitting on the edge of the tub, I go to text Harper. Immediately, I see I have a ton of missed calls and texts. Crap! Hopefully Harper is okay. I frown at the missed calls from Kohen. Using my index thumb I scroll up, up, up, and up some more. Missed calls from him fill my entire call log.

What . . . the . . . fuck . . .

I have voicemails . . . all twelve are from Kohen. I tap my foot as I listen to the first one, hoping he isn't seriously injured.

Hey babe, just wondering how your night is going. I miss you. Call me when you get back. Okay . . . bye.

The next one is ten minutes later.

Hey still haven't heard anything from you. Just checking in to make sure you're okay. Call me if you need anything.

How cute, he's worried about me which makes me the worst person in the world. While he worried about me, I ended up at the penthouse of a guy that I secretly love. Fantastic, I'm an amazing person. They should make a shrine in my honor. With that sarcastic thought, I press play for the next voicemail that occurred five minutes later.

You and Harper must really be having a great time at girls' night. Why aren't you answering any of my calls or returning my texts? I'm worried, please let me know you're safe when you get a chance. Okay, well I guess I'll talk to you whenever you decide to call me back. Bye.

I listen to the next one that comes twenty minutes later.

Hey, I know I've called a lot, but I'm just worried about you. I wish you would at least text me back so I know you aren't lying in an alley somewhere. I really hate it when you ignore me like this. Call me when you get this, or the other messages I've left.

When have I ever ignored him? Oh yeah, that's right never. Reluctantly I press play on the next one.

Adalynn, where are you? It's almost eleven. Are you planning on staying out all night with that girl that you just met? Be safe, please.

Okay, if you're trying to piss me off it's worked. Now call me back before I have to go look for your drunken ass. Thanks!

I'm a little taken aback from the last voicemail. I know I could have checked my phone when I was out, but I was having a good time. I didn't want to be that chick with her hand glued to her phone all night. I hate that chick. Plus, I didn't know he would be so worried about me. It's not like I was going out by myself or that I was in a sketchy area. Whenever I do call him, I need to explain that it's not okay to blow up my phone like this. I pinch the bridge of my nose in frustration while I listen to the rest of the messages.

Addie, I'm sorry for the last voicemail. I'm a little on edge. I don't like that you're out there drinking without me to protect you. It makes me nervous. Please, please babe call me back when you get this.

Thank you for not calling me back all night or even responding to any of my text messages, I really appreciate it. I guess I'll see you on Sunday if you're not still ignoring me. Hope you and your friend had fun tonight, at least one of us did.

I just stopped by your place, why aren't you answering the door?

It's three am and you're still not back.

Call me.

It's now five am. I guess I'll get off the floor and go to back to my place to wait for your call. Hopefully you and your best friend that you just met made it back to her place since you're obviously not coming back to yours. Call me.

Slapping my hand over my face, I groan. Tossing the phone down, I shut off the water before it overflows. Instead of lowering myself into the tempting bath, I retrieve my phone to text Kohen.

I don't bother to read the several texts he sent last night. There's no point, I just listened to it, I don't need to read it, too. I feel badly enough for how irresponsible I was last night for not texting him and letting him know I was okay. Of course he would worry, he's that type of guy. The guy that cares deeply and is considerate to others. Opposite of how I was last night.

I type a few different responses without sending them. I have no idea what to say. It's not like I can tell him I was with Jax. Yeah, I doubt that would go over well. I want to be honest with him, but at the same time I don't. I know I didn't do anything to feel guilty about, but after listening to how upset he got, I can't help but feel remorse for sharing a bed with Jax.

Sighing in defeat, I send him a text as close to the truth as I can manage. There's no way I can call him, I'm a coward. I remind myself that he doesn't need to know the rest. I was hanging out with a friend. No big deal.

Me: Hey! I just checked my phone. I didn't even think about checking it last night when I was out. But I had a lot of fun at girls' night with Tinkerbell!!! I'm sorry I worried you. I'll make it up to you. Promise . . . How about after brunch we go out just you and I? My treat . . .

Kohen: Did you spend the night at Harper's? How does a date at the carnival sound?

I chew on my lip, contemplating telling the truth. I ignore his first question and hope he doesn't get mad.

Me: Can't wait. See you then.

I wait a minute to see if he texts me back, but he doesn't. After setting my phone on a towel near the tub, I finally step inside. Oh sweet baby Jesus, this feels heavenly. I will my body to relax, to shut my mind off of the drama that surrounds me, and relax in the tub.

Saturday has come and gone with little-to-no stress. Kohen made me dinner at his place and is taking me to a carnival today after brunch. I'm way too excited. I haven't been to a carnival since I was a little girl. I was all for ditching out on brunch, but Kohen insisted. Plus, I want everyone to meet Harper.

I lean against Kohen's shoulder as we walk to the restaurant. He reaches out to open the door for me. Always such a gentleman, this one. I see a blur of red before someone tackles me into a hug. I fall back against Kohen and he steadies me while Harper hugs me.

"Nice to see you too," I say once I'm finally able to breathe air into my lungs.

She lets go, extends her hand to Kohen and singsongs in her southern accent, "I'm the best friend, Tinkerbell, but please call me Harper." I laugh. "You must be the boyfriend that I've heard so much about." I stop laughing.

I catch myself from dropping my jaw on the floor and glare at the traitor in front of me. I can't believe she said that to him. Great, now he'll think I'm serious about him. Am I? Nope, definitely not . . . at least yet. I am, however, ready to kill a tiny redhead that I know.

Kohen laughs and pulls me back to his side. "One day I hope to be introduced as her boyfriend, but until she's ready, I'll just keep her around for arm candy, Harper."

I kiss him on the cheek before glaring at my former best friend. She ignores my obvious irritation and links her arm with mine as we stroll to our table. I stop dead in my tracks when I see Jax. Why is he here? Just to torment me? Probably.

Harper peers back at me when she notices that I stopped walking. She follows my gaze to Jax, her mouth pops open. She looks back at me with wide eyes and mouths, "Lover?"

I nod. Sighing, I square my shoulders and grip her arm a lot tighter than necessary. Here goes nothing.

CHAPTER SIXTEEN

I can't hide my shock from seeing him. As much as I don't want to admit it, I stayed up half the night worrying about him coming today. I knew I would get these stupid butterflies in my stomach. It hurts to see him sitting here so casually.

"So the lover's here, things just got interesting!" Harper whispers into my ear.

Jax is the first to rise, followed by my brother, and lastly Connor. To my surprise, Harper stops mid-step and Connor seems confused at first, then bemused when he glances from Harper to me. Maybe I should have sent him a picture of her face instead of just her body. Kohen halts with me. Everyone is deadly silent as we watch the two.

Connor looks as if he just won some kind of contest while Harper turns a little green. I'm about to break the tension and ask her what the hell is going on, but she composes herself. She holds her chin high and introduces herself to everyone. I stand with Kohen, baffled.

Harper pauses with her introduction when she gets to Connor. Which of course piques my interest. *Do they know each other? What is going on?* The questions run wild in my head, but I force myself to remain calm and nonchalant.

She keeps her hands firmly at her sides. What I wouldn't give to drag her aside and demand answers.

"You must be the playboy that I've heard so much about," she practically sneers at him.

Logan spits his water all over the table, getting a little on Connor, who doesn't notice. The only thing he's aware of is Harper. This is not good.

Retreat, retreat, I want to shout at everyone. Kohen holds my chair out for me, but I don't sit. I'm too busy watching the car wreck happening right in front of me.

"And you must be the little fireball I've heard a lot about." He rubs his chin with his thumb and index finger. "Do you go by Elizabeth or Tinkerbell these days?" he asks in a condescending tone.

Elizabeth? Who is he talking about? I stare at Harper, wondering why she would give him a different name. She flexes her hand as if she wants to punch him. Not a common response from the ladies when it comes to Connor. They love his easy personality. Then again, he's usually nice.

We're halfway through brunch when I finally can't take it anymore. Everything has gone smoothly, except that Jax refused to pass Kohen the pepper. I steer all conversation away from Jax and Kohen in an effort to keep the peace. I restrain myself from kicking Jax in the shins. Doesn't Jax realize that he's being obvious? Luckily Harper and Connor keep the attention on them. They first made it a point to ignore each other, but now they're egging each other on. The elephant in the room needs to be addressed, now.

"Okay what the hell is going on? Do you two know each other or something?" I demand.

I'm met with silence. My brother coughs, covering his laugh. He has insider information, I know it. Their silence is all the answer I need, but I push anyways. Patience has never been my thing.

"Well?"

"No," Harper says at the same time Connor says, "Yes."

She glares at him, but doesn't elaborate. I cross my arms over my chest. My brother mouths something to Connor, but I can't catch what he says. I'm a horrible lip reader. Another few awkward minutes pass in silence before Connor sighs dramatically and clears his throat. Harper looks like she is about to punch him.

Raising his mimosa for a toast Connor says, "This one that you call Tinkerbell, Addie, hit me with her car almost a year ago and I haven't seen her since. Oh, and she also went by Elizabeth back then." He tilts his champagne flute towards her then to me. "Thanks for making friends with the enemy."

I was so not expecting that. I was thinking they slept together and he never called her back. Not this! Everyone speaks at once. I sit speechless, gaping at Harper. This is why I'm the only one who sees what she's about to do. My mouth drops open.

She pours the entire pitcher of water on Connor's head. Then, to shock us all, she slaps him across the face. I don't mean a little girl slap you would expect from someone her size, either. Nope, a bitch slap so powerful everyone in the restaurant winces. It's eerily quiet. I think everyone is too afraid to speak. I know I am. She leans over and whispers something to Connor that nobody else can hear. His jaw pops in anger.

Plastering the fakest smile I've ever seen she says, "Your womanizing friend has greatly exaggerated, as I'm sure he does to get women into his bed every night, even though he can't really perform as he would like everyone to believe."

Jax and Logan double over in laughter. The kind that shakes their entire bodies. Kohen seems as uncomfortable as I feel. I opt for a smile because I don't know what's about to happen. This can go either way. Harper surprises me yet again by standing and collecting her purse. She embraces me.

"I should say I'm sorry, but we both know I would be lying. I have to go though, I'll see you tomorrow at work."

She says goodbye to everyone. Connor cleans himself up with the hand towel our waiter brought him.

"Memorable as always, Evans."

How does she know his last name? Connor looks way too pleased with himself. Why is he smiling? Something is seriously wrong with him. We watch Harper leave the restaurant. Jax gives Connor the third degree before I can.

"That's her?" he asks.

"Have you seen her since that night?" my brother asks Connor, who nods at Jax.

Okay, clearly I'm the only one out of the loop. Awesome, my favorite place to be. I point the end of my butter knife at Connor's face and give him my best you're-going-to-be-dead-if-you-don't-answer-me look.

"I swear, Connor, if you don't tell me what the hell just happened, I will not be held responsible for my actions!"

Connor rolls his eyes. "Oh please, Addie, you've never been threatening. Now put the knife down before you hurt yourself."

Gleaming with pride that I got my way, I set down the butter knife and make a show of folding my hands on the table, like an eager child ready to learn.

Glancing at my brother, Connor answers his earlier question. "Yes, this is the first time I've seen her since a year ago. I didn't even know she lived in New York and she has that southern accent so I assumed she was visiting. She never gave me her last name so it's not like I could track her down."

He laughs and looks at me. "She didn't even give me her real name."

Okay, I'm as confused as can be. Kohen wears a bored expression. How? I have no idea. I can't believe Harper left without explaining. I listen intently to the rest of Connor's story.

"I was leaving work one night when the car in front of me smashed into me out of nowhere, then took off without waiting for the light to turn green."

I clench my teeth. It's hard not to be upset that Connor never shared this story. Guess we're not as close as I thought. I make a mental note to bring this up later and focus on not lashing out. She smashed into someone and took off? That hits too close to home. I shake my head. I have no idea how I didn't know this. How could I be friends with someone who would flee the scene of an accident?

"I did what any rational person would do when someone hits them and takes off. I followed her. I almost got hit by an oncoming car for speeding through the red light, too."

Connor pauses to collect himself, I'm sure. I squeeze Kohen's thigh to avoid launching myself at Connor to demand more information.

"I raced in and out of cars until I found the one that hit me. I followed it for an hour out of the city when it finally pulled up to a gas station. I waited until she was already out of the car and pumping gas before I pulled up. I don't think she realized I was following her, until she saw me pull up to the pump behind her. She screamed when I opened my door, but stopped when she saw me."

He pauses again and I can tell he's thinking of what to say next. I swear, if he's making this up I am going to gut him like a fish. Something's telling me he isn't, though.

"She immediately apologized saying that she thought I was someone else. I could tell that she was still freaking out. She kept glancing around as if she were searching for someone. Then she leaned into her car, grabbed her purse and gave me a wad of cash. A wad of hundreds to be exact."

I eye him closely, looking for any signs of dishonesty. I can't find any. She did this, she really took off. I want to give her the benefit of the doubt, but it's hard after everything I went through, what my family went through.

"Being the gentleman that I am, I didn't take her money. I offered to buy her coffee so she could explain what was going on, but she refused. I told her I wouldn't let her go until she at least told me her name. She got in her car, rolled down the window and said, 'Elizabeth' before she sped away."

He regards me. "I know what you're thinking, Addie, but it's not the same. Don't make her out to be the bad guy. She needs you. I don't know what happened, but she was scared that night. Terrified actually. Frightened enough to back into my car at a stop light. She thought I was somebody else. That's why I spent the majority of last year looking for a ghost. I needed to make sure she was okay."

I know without a doubt that he's telling the truth. Connor wouldn't joke about something like this. Harper and I will be having a serious conversation tomorrow. If it weren't for Connor explaining how scared she was, then her and I would be having a different conversation. Now, I just needed to make sure she's okay, too.

It takes all my remaining self-control to finish brunch and head with Kohen to the carnival instead of seeking out Harper. I know that if she wanted to talk, she would have said something to me. Hopefully she'll be ready tomorrow. Until then, I push all of this to the back of my mind. It's time to enjoy a day at the carnival with Kohen in Manhattan.

Hand-in-hand, Kohen and I walk up to the ticket booth. I tell myself to forget about wanting to be here with Jax and to have fun with the man that wants to spend time with me, the man who isn't afraid to be seen with me.

"Someone is a little excited," he observes.

I twirl myself around, using his hand to spin me. Laughing, we amble to the first ride, my personal favorite . . . bumper cars. Showing our wrist bands to the attendant, we head over to separate cars. I, of course, pick the pink one. Kohen chooses the black one across from mine. I smile wickedly at him.

"You're going down." I even give him two thumbs down to stress my point.

The music fades away so the attendant can review the rules. When I notice Kohen watching me, I wink at him.

I ram into Kohen and laugh as he maneuvers his bumper car in-between mine and the others, taking the hits for me. Maybe I should have informed him that this is a game and I can't get hurt? The ride ends far too quickly for my liking. Kohen slings his arms over my shoulder while he reminds me about all of the other rides and cotton candy. Yum!

We go on rides for the next few hours, hitting everything twice, some three times because I'm a little kid at heart. I'm surprised how easy he makes it to forget about Jax, and everything else. I'm enjoying myself because of him. After we go on the Zipper, we're both in desperate need of refueling. As we stand in line for food, I contemplate opening up to him, to an extent. Right now seems like the perfect time.

Kohen orders burgers, fries, and one large coke to share. He leads me to an empty bench away from the crowd. We eat in silence. I can't help but wonder what it would be like to date Jax in the open, for it not to be a secret. Kohen takes my hand into his, raises it up to his lips and kisses the inside of my palm. It's hard not to notice the nonexistent goosebumps. If he was Jax, my skin would be on fire with a simple touch like that.

"So I've told you all about growing up as an only child."

Crap, I know where he's going with this. Even though I've been considering opening up to him, I haven't been able to get the words out. I didn't know where to start.

"How was it growing up with Logan? Has he always been so protective over you? I swear, sometimes I don't know if I should be more worried of Logan's approval or *Jax's*."

I brush off his dislike for Jax with a laugh. It comes out forced, like the way he's forcing a smile even though we're talking about Jax. I need to change the subject, it's been clear that Jax is not something we discuss.

Okay, I can do this. He's given me the perfect opening. I decide to only mention the good parts. I'm not ready to share the accident, not yet.

"Logan was impossibly protective of Hadley and me." I can see the surprise on his face, all of the questions, but he composes himself and lets me finish. "He included me in everything he did when we were younger. He would even make the guys watch *The Little Mermaid*.

"When Hadley came along, we would play dress up with her. She loved to remind us that we were her real dolls. Jax and Connor were even roped into attending her tea parties and dressing up. We were all forced into tutus and tiaras."

Kohen stiffens at the mention of his name which I ignore. I chuckle, remembering walking into the house after practice with all three sweaty soccer boys in different shades of pink tutus and tiaras, drinking pretend tea with stuffed animals. Hadley was around six or seven so the guys were thirteen, I believe.

I don't say anything for awhile, as I remember what lengths we would all go to make Hads happy. After a few minutes of memories floating through my mind, Kohen breaks the silence.

"And your dad?" he asks tentatively.

"My dad, Andy, was extremely strict when it came to his little girls and boys. I think that's where Logan gets it from and why he's fond of running background checks."

Kohen forces out a laugh that doesn't reach his eyes.

"Don't worry I'm sure yours came back with flying colors, or I wouldn't be allowed to see you," I say to ease his noticeable tension.

He grins at me, but again it seems forced. I shouldn't have said anything, hopefully it doesn't ruin our day. Right as I open my mouth to apologize for my brother, even though I'm not really sorry, Kohen shakes his head and recovers from his sour mood.

"And Jax? Has he always been this protective over you, too?"

There is no easy way to talk about Jax. Just thinking about him makes my heart beat a little faster. I choose to ignore why. This is not a conversation I want to have with Kohen.

I shrug. "He's been Logan's best friend since I was seven. I was always around. I guess Jax forgets that I'm not his responsibility. Old habits and all that."

He takes ahold of my hand again. "You're a wonderful package to be a part of, Adalynn. They're lucky to have been in your lives for so long."

His words should be endearing, but I feel like he just stabbed me in the gut. All I can think about is Hadley's lifeless body while I was unable to help her, watching as the paramedics fought to bring her back. She's in the ground while I'm not. Why? She deserves to be here, not me. I force these disturbing thoughts away. Time for a change of subject.

"Do you know anyone that would love to buy me cotton candy and win me a bear?"

He makes a show of looking around. "I think I might know the right man for the job."

I help him collect our trash. I flee to the cotton candy vendor, hoping being in the crowd again will help chase away the haunting memories. He buys me a huge bag of pink cotton candy and I dive right into it. Tearing off a piece, I feed it to him. He pulls my finger into his mouth and sucks the cotton candy off it. Slowly he allows me to drag out my finger, but not before he bites the tip. Now would be a perfect time to give into him and forget about Jax.

"Mmm, best cotton candy I've ever had."

I force the images of Jax's naked body away. Picturing him is what makes my face heat up, not Kohen's sexual advances.

Kohen plays three games of shooting cans off moving objects so he can win the biggest stuffed animal here. It happens to be a brown bear with a pink tutu around it's waist and a tiara. Fitting. Kohen holds the stuffed animal out to me.

"It's perfect!" I say. "What should we name her?"

Kohen rubs his chin as if in deep thought. "What makes you think it's a girl?"

I glare at him.

He gives me an innocent expression, but I know better. "What? It looks like a manly bear to me."

As I balance the overly large bear on my hip, Kohen draws me to him. When his lips touch mine, the memories fade a little more, into the distance. I back away before he can turn it into something much hotter.

"How many manly bears do you see wearing a tutu?" I don't wait for him to respond. "Of course it's a girl!"

"So just because it has a tutu, it's a girl? I'm pretty sure you know a few guys that like to wear tutus and tiaras."

I can't help it, I snicker. He always know how to evoke a smile from me.

"Well, when you put it like that."

"How about Mac? That's a manly name for a bear like this."

I choke a little and tense at the name. Hadley's teddy bear, her favorite teddy bear, the only one she slept with every night, the one buried with her, was named Mac. How does he know? It can't be a coincidence, could it? I'm about to ask him, but think better of it. It's just a name, I'm analyzing this too much.

I force my voice to work. "It's perfect."

Out of every name in the human language, how did he pick Mac? It's not like it's a common name for a stuffed animal. *It's just a coincidence.*

"I can't believe you haven't been on a Ferris wheel before," Kohen says, breaking through my mental freakout.

Did I tell him that? I can't summon the mind power to search through our conversations from today. Obviously I did or he wouldn't know. I give myself a mental shake. I'm over-thinking everything. I need to stop before I voice my crazy thoughts of him being a stalker and ruin our day.

"Yeah, I know, but my mom would never let us ride them when we were younger and I haven't been to a carnival since . . ." I trail off, not wanting to go there. "So hopefully this doesn't break and we don't fall to our deaths like my mom was always afraid of."

"Your mom sounds like a lot like my mine. My mom wasn't the biggest fan of this ride either."

When we're seated on the Ferris wheel, I'm sandwiched between him and the stuffed animal that comes up to my knees.

Clutching my hand, he whispers, "Relax, Adalynn, this isn't going to break, we won't fall to our deaths. I promise I won't let anything happen to you."

Easier said than done. I yelp in surprise when the ride moves, making Kohen chuckle. It stops to let on the next passenger.

"See, that wasn't so bad," he says into my ear as we move again.

He trails small open mouth kisses from my ear down my throat. My breath hitches. He's trying to distract me and it's working. He slowly kisses my nose, my closed eyelids, both cheeks, and as we reach the top he kisses my lips. All my crazy thoughts earlier about Kohen disappear as I open my mouth to him. Slowly, oh so painfully slow, he strokes his tongue with mine. He keeps the kiss slow, sensual, barely touching his tongue with mine.

"Open your eyes, babe."

I gasp in surprise when I see the breathtaking view. I almost feel like we're floating being up this high. I have a clear view of the city lights from here. I want to look down, but I know that will be a mistake. Instead I stare, mesmerized at the setting sun reflecting off the water in Central Park. It feels more like a dream than reality.

"It's beautiful."

The last remaining thought of Jax floats away as I look into the horizon. I can't believe I've never done this before. And that I'm sharing this experience with someone as special as Kohen. I lean against him and we enjoy the view in silence at the top. As the ride descends to let us off, I think this is the beginning of us, and the end of Jax.

"Want to stay the night?" I ask when we reach my door.

He nods as he closes the distance between us and brings his mouth down to mine. I force myself to turn my head so I can unlock my door. Kohen takes full advantage of my exposed neck, making it impossible to concentrate on the task at hand. It takes me six tries until I'm finally able to insert the key.

CHAPTER SEVENTEEN

The door bursts open as Kohen eagerly pushes me inside my apartment. Dropping my purse, I turn to face him. His mouth captures mine so fast I gasp. His mouth is powerful, punishing even. I can't even kiss him back, I stand helplessly as he steals my breath away. He runs his hands down my arms to my waist and picks me up. Automatically I wrap my legs around his waist and kiss him back just as fiercely as he's kissing me. He carries me through my apartment heading in the direction of my bedroom. Perfect.

I moan into his mouth when he bites my lower lip. Somewhere in the back of my mind, I know I shouldn't be doing this, but it feels too good to stop.

Tongues fighting each other, we finally reach my room. Slowly, Kohen releases me, dragging my body down his strong one, letting me feel every one of his muscles with my body. I squeeze my thighs together, hoping to stop the moisture gathering in my panties. I only make it worse.

He brushes the hair out of my face. He bends down so that his mouth hovers over mine, but doesn't move closer. I stretch so I can close the tiny distance between us. He backs away.

"I love you. God, Adalynn I love you so much. I've loved you for so long, since the day I first saw you."

Breathing is nonexistent. I so did not expect him to declare his love for me when he opened his mouth. Why did he have to ruin this? I push away from him and sit on the edge of my bed. This can't be happening. He doesn't really know me. He can't love me. I examine his face and see that he believes he really does love me.

I'm going to throw up.

I press my hand to my mouth and will myself to take small deep breaths. *He isn't down on one knee. He just said 'I love you,' no big deal.* I know people say this all the time, but not to me, this feels wrong, he isn't Jax.

I need to say something, but I can't. Every time I open my mouth to speak, it feels like someone poured cement into it, making it impossible. He cups both hands around my legs and rubs them. After several awkward minutes of silence, he pulls his hands away from my legs and begins to stroke my face.

"Babe, it's okay. I know it's too soon for you. You don't have to say it back. I want you to say it when you really mean it, not because I said it." I hear the sincerity in his voice, "I couldn't wait any longer. I need you to know that I love you, that I've always loved you and I always will. I want to be the person you love, the person you want a future with. I'm willing to wait as long as it takes to hear those words for you, Adalynn, because you're worth it."

I give him a tight smile and nod since I'm incapable of speaking. Everything he says is perfect, what I've always wanted to hear from the man that loves me. I've just always pictured that the man confessing his love for me would have green eyes, not blue. It hurts that the image I've had since childhood has disappeared with Kohen's words. This isn't fair to him. I should be ecstatic that he loves me, but the only thing I can think about is the green-eyed God.

Kohen is the type of man that I should be in love with, the man that my parents would admire. He's the type of man to plan a future with, to grow old together. Maybe one day, he can be that man for me.

"I think in time I can fall in love with you, too."

Kohen opens his mouth to say something, but I stop him with my lips. I don't need anymore words tonight. He takes control of this kiss, too. I can feel the extent of his love; he's showing me with his mouth how much he cares. I pull away first because I can't go further. He frowns so quickly that I would have missed it if I wasn't paying attention.

Without any direction from me, Kohen gets up off the floor and heads over to the dresser where I keep my old shirts. He grabs an old jersey, one of Jax's, and sets it on the bed beside me. "I'm going to get us some water while you change for bed, my love."

I swallow the bile rising up.

He kisses my cheek. "If you want me to go, I understand."

His words register when he reaches the threshold. "No, please stay," I whisper to him before he leaves my room.

Kohen returns right when I'm coming out of the bathroom from doing my nightly routine.

"Hey," I say lamely to fill the silence.

He runs his fingers through my hair. "You're the most beautiful woman I've ever seen. You take my breath away, Adalynn."

I rest my head against his chest. "You're too good to me. I don't deserve someone like you."

He tilts my head up. "You deserve anything and everything you want, Adalynn. We belong together, never doubt that."

I force my lips to turn up into what I hope is a smile at his affectionate words. I wish I loved him and I could say it back, it would be the perfect moment. This is the moment I should realize that I love him, too, and jump into his waiting arms. Sadly, I don't, at least not yet.

"Can you wake me up when you're ready to go? I want to swim a few laps before work," I say when he sets the alarm on his phone.

Kohen nods. Snuggling in behind me, he drapes his arm over my stomach and tugs me close to him.

"I'm glad you're finally getting back into the water, my love."

I turn so that I'm facing him, lying my head on his chest. "Thanks." I press my lips to his bare sculpted chest.

"Addie, time to get up," someone coos into my ear.

I rub my eyes with the back of my palms before turning over and grunting my response. Nope, way too early.

"There's a lane somewhere with your name on it," Satan says again, ignoring that I do not want to get up.

"Huh?"

Kohen kisses my exposed neck. "Someone mentioned they wanted to do a few laps before work. Now time to get up or you won't get a chance before you have to leave."

Ah, that's what he's talking about. Painfully, I open my eyes. "Just so you know, you remind me of the devil in the morning."

He bites my neck at my pulse point, making me yelp. He hauls me up so I'm sitting in bed. He's dressed for work looking like the handsome doctor that he knows he is.

"How are you so excited to be up this early? No, wait, don't answer that. Let me guess, you've always been a morning person?"

He gives me a quick peck on the lips. "Yes, now get up. I have to go or I'll be late, and I know if you don't, you'll fall sleep the instant I leave."

I want to say I won't, but let's be honest, there's a real good possibility I will do just that. I force myself out of my warm bed that's calling my name, begging me to stay in for another hour and sleep.

I plant my hands on my hips. "I'm pretty capable of functioning without a babysitter."

He kisses my pouty lips. "Of course you are, my love."

"Get to work so I can go workout."

He gives me a mock salute. "Yes, ma'am."

Once he leaves, I check the time and groan when I see it's almost four. As in, not even four in the morning yet. *Sleep or swim, sleep or swim?* I repeat the question over and over again. The need to swim is too powerful.

Ten minutes later, I stretch my cap onto my head and slide my goggles into place. As I do a few calf-raises, I stare at the dark blue tiles at the bottom of the pool. Positioning both feet at the edge, I bend down at the waist, take a deep breath, push off and dive into the water.

My muscles relax into the rhythm that they are so accustomed to, even after all these years. I glide through the water, breathing every seven strokes. Quickly I reach the other side of the pool. My body goes through the motions of a flip-turn. I don't need to think to swim, never have. Swimming is to me as breathing is to everyone else. I'm meant to be in the water.

As I swim, I stop reflecting about what Kohen said last night, and the inevitable drama between Connor and Harper. I forget about Jax. I focus on my strokes, my breathing, and just let go.

Everything floats away. Everything is silent, it's just me and the water, no place I'd rather be. I feel more myself than I have in years. I push myself, enjoying the burning of my legs, my arms heavier with each stroke. I push myself even further, I'm sprinting now. I lose count of how many laps I've done. When I finally can't swim any longer, I stop. My arms feel like they're going to fall off any moment, and my legs feel like they're made of lead. I miss this sensation of being utterly spent after a workout, and enjoying every second of it.

After a long shower and an omelet, I hail down a taxi. I pull my phone out of my purse.

Me: You. Me. Wine. My place.

Tinkerbell: YES please! Want me to bring the wine?

I'm about to text her back that I already have some, but her reply beats mine. And then she texts again. And again.

Tinkerbell: Oh and what time? I can bring dinner?

Tinkerbell: Actually let's cook together!

Me: BEST IDEA EVER

After work, I leave my door unlocked so Harper can walk in when she arrives. After changing out of my work clothes and into a pair of shorts and a tank, I wash my make-up off my face and put my hair into a messy bun. I head into the living room to put on girl music. I love listening to music while I cook. I reach the kitchen right when I hear the door opening.

"HERE!"

"In the kitchen!" I set two wine glasses on the counter.

She comes wearing a smirk grasping a wine bottle in each hand. That smirk I know all too well. "No! I will not be hungover at work tomorrow!"

She laughs while she plucks the corkscrew off the counter and opens a bottle.

"I'm serious!"

She hands me a glass. "Relax, we probably won't even polish one off. The other one is for next time."

I hold my glass up to toast. "To many more next times."

"To many more everything."

I already have everything laid out on the table for pesto pasta and a wedge salad. I'm making the pesto from scratch and she's cooking everything else. I can tell that she's making an effort for small talk, anything to keep the conversation away from the elephant in the room. I wait until we're both two glasses in as I have a feeling we'll both need it.

"So . . . about the other day . . ."

She finishes the last touches on our meals, hands me my plate and gulps a long drink of her wine.

"Just so you know, I thought you were going to wait until after dinner to bring that up. I should have known better, though. You don't have the patience for that." She sets her plate on the marble bar countertop.

I roll my eyes, but don't disagree. She digs into her pasta and spins the barstool around so that she faces me. I follow her lead.

"Keep in mind it's not that big of a deal. What did he tell you guys yesterday?"

She doesn't deny anything as I retell her the colorful story Connor told yesterday. Once I'm finished, I sip the merlot and wait for her to share her side.

She looks anywhere but at me. And in this moment I see the scared woman Connor painted a picture of yesterday. She chews on her bottom lip, and her hands tremble. Her green eyes are vacant. The lively person that I've come to love is gone, replaced by a stranger. I squeeze her shoulder reassuringly.

"It's okay, Tinkerbell, you don't have to tell me." I use my nickname in hopes to lighten her mood. It works, barely.

"No, it's okay. It isn't that big of a deal, honestly. Okay, so that night something happened that, putting it mildly, scared the shit out of me. I shouldn't have been driving."

Her hands shake violently, so I clutch them in mine. After a minute or two they stop.

"When I looked in my rearview mirror, I thought I saw someone from my past. I didn't see Connor's car, I saw somebody else's. I panicked and reversed into him and fled."

She plays with her food in an attempt to gather her thoughts. I have that habit too! This story is like a nightmare. I possess my own demons so I understand seeing something that isn't really there. I have a gut feeling her demons are more real than mine.

"I sped away as fast as I could. I drove for miles without a destination until I was almost out gas. Surprise, surprise, Connor pulls up behind me. I almost maced him. Thankfully, right before I did, his face registered just in time."

Man, if she maced Connor that would have made my year! Connor being maced by a chick is something nobody would ever think would happen, and a spectacle that everyone would want to see. Maybe I can persuade her to do it if the chance ever comes again?

Harper continues in a rush, getting her words out so quickly that they jumble together.

"My face was covered in dry tears and mascara. I felt horrible that I slammed into someone's car and left. Who does that?"

I don't answer her. I think she's asking more for herself than for me to answer her.

"I was so scared, I needed to leave, to be by myself. For some unknown reason I knew I could trust him and that he would protect me. Which made me panic even more because I've never felt like that before. Stupid, I know."

"No, not stupid. I know exactly what you mean."

I can't fight the sick feeling in my gut that she was in serious shit that night and still is.

"I didn't want to tell him my real name in case he was working for . . . I mean if he wanted to tell the police. So I threw money at him, the money I was going to use to get a . . . to use for my new place. Yeah, for my new place."

Okay, so she happens to be the worst liar in the history of the world. There are worse traits than being a lousy liar. It would be cute if I wasn't dying to know why she had a wad of cash. I also know that she has lived in the same apartment since she's moved here. I want to ask who she was running from, but I don't. It's hard to open up to someone so I won't push it. Not yet anyways.

I can tell that she is reliving that night instead of sitting at my bar eating dinner. I've been forced to relive my past so many times, it's easy to recognize the signs.

"We haven't known each other long, but I'm here for you, okay? For whatever you need. You can tell me anything and I will never judge you. Trust me, I am the last person to pass judgement on someone."

She rises and dumps her still full plate of food in the trash before rinsing it. I finish my last bite and follow her lead of cleaning up.

"I know and thanks! I mean it, I haven't had a girlfriend since I moved here. Everyone seems so fake here, but that's kind of the appeal of the city. You can be whoever you want to be here."

Yeah, I know exactly what she's talking about. The allure of the city is hard to miss.

"Same here. So friend, are you going to tell me what that money was really for, or what? I mean, come on, let's be honest, you're a horrible liar. The worst actually."

Her hands tremble again. I squeeze them, feeling guiltier and guiltier for pushing her as they continue to shake.

"A gun," she says simply as if buying a gun is everyday conversation. "An untraceable gun."

My head whips around to face her so quickly I actually kink my neck. "What?"

She doesn't look guilty anymore, she looks darker, scary, a complete stranger from the happy-go-lucky Tinkerbell I know and love. "I had to have a gun that couldn't be traced. Don't worry, though, everything is fine now."

Yeah, that sounds convincing.

CHAPTER EIGHTEEN

I'm busy at work again, but unlike my usual multi-tasking self, I'm finding it exceptionally hard to concentrate. I'm still baffled by Harper's revelation last night. She wanted to buy a gun. As in, she wanted to shoot someone. Okay, okay she didn't tell me why she wanted a gun, she changed the subject as quickly as humanly possible, but why else would she need a gun? An untraceable gun to be exact. Did she buy it? I'm losing my mind! I can't stop seeing her face when she uttered, "a gun." Out of all the times she couldn't keep her mouth shut, she chose that time to be quiet. Really? Once again I'm distracted. Hence the reason why I'm skipping lunch the second day in a row.

Shaking my head, I get back to work. Three more hours and I can meet Harper for dinner. I'm excited for a low-key girls' night. Who knew there was such a thing? I need to get her advice on the whole Kohen-loves-me thing. I could always talk to Liv, but it's different talking to a friend compared to my therapist. Plus, I know she's itching for more information on the Lover and Boyfriend front as she likes to call them.

I love how close we're getting in the short time we've known each other. It's hard to explain, but I feel like I've been waiting for a friend like her my whole life. I've always been friends with guys, that's why I've never really been able to have many girlfriends.

After work, Harper and I head towards the subway to go to this little pub. We could have taken a cab, but when she found out that I've never been on the subway, she was dragging me behind her. It's not that I have anything against the it, I just hate being confined and in dark places, since the accident.

I will not freak out. I can do this. People ride the subway every day. I notice my hands are quivering. My mantra isn't working as well as I thought.

As we get closer, she keeps glancing back and asking if I'm okay. Am I okay? That's gonna be a hard no. I resemble a scared kitten right about now. I'm sweating and I can't focus on one thing. I'm trying really hard to control my breathing, but even performing that simple task seems impossible.

She links her arm with mine. "Hey, it's okay, we can take a cab or even walk if you want to get fresh air. We don't have to do this."

I try to give her a reassuring smile, but I think it comes out more as a grimace. I go for nonchalance. "No, really, I'm fine. I need to ride the subway eventually." I didn't pull it off from the expression on her face.

"I'm sorry, Addie, I didn't realize you were claustrophobic."

If only she knew the extent of it.

"No, really, it's fine. Besides, you can buy me a drink if I make it through this."

We board the subway without incident. The trip is over before it even started. Way faster than taking a cab at this hour. I wish I wasn't having a minor heart attack the entire time so that I could've enjoyed it. I've always wanted to ride it.

At least I didn't black out from fear, there's that. I also didn't get trapped inside my head. That's both refreshing and sad when I think about it. It's refreshing to know that I can do something as simple as riding a subway, and sad that this won't be the last time I have to fear whether I can handle something.

As we saunter into the Irish pub, I can feel waves of energy bouncing off of everyone. Live music flows through the speakers.

"This is amazing!"

She steers me to a nearby table in the center of the action. "I can't believe you've never been here! How have you survived?"

Survived? Interesting choice of words. I focus on the band on the stage in front of us and sway my hips to the uplifting beat.

"I haven't." I meant it as a joke, but it rings with more truth than I wanted to give.

Harper has an amazing instinct on when to push for more information. Now is not the time and she doesn't ask. I'm thankful. She orders for us since she's a regular. She knows what is best and I'm not that picky. As long as it's edible, I'll usually eat it. Besides, when I peer around at the other tables, the food looks mouthwatering. I don't think there's a wrong choice here.

After she returns from the bar with a pitcher of beer and two glasses, she asks, "Okay dish, what's going on with you and that unbelievably hot doctor?" Her southern accent rings heavy in her voice as she fans herself, making me choke on the sip of beer I just drank.

Luckily me coughing up a lung, maybe even both, buys me enough time to ponder what to say. "Eh, he loves me?"

Her smile slips. "And I'm taking this is a bad thing because?"

I down another swig of beer. "No, it's not bad. It's just . . . I don't know . . . Wrong somehow? I don't know how I feel. I don't love him, but maybe in time I can? It's complicated."

"Said every girl on earth." She brushes red bangs out of her face and stares at me for a second as if trying to figure out what to say. "Complicated by the lover, perhaps?"

I glare at my "supposed" friend. "Jax isn't my lover!"

She gives me a look that is only best described as I'm-so-not-buying-what-you're-selling. "Yes, and I don't have red hair or fantastic tits!" she says at the same time our food arrives.

The poor guy. His face reddens. I focus on the plate he sets in front of me. I bite into the sandwich and moan. The thing melts in my mouth. Yum! I take another bite before I even finish my first one. Classy, I know. I could lick my plate, it's that good.

"So you've been seeing the doctor for a few months now. How's the sex? Obviously decent if you're keeping him around . . . Wait! Who's better, him or the lover?"

I choke on my sandwich. I have no idea how to respond. I scan the room in hopes that I will somehow find the answer. Before I can say anything though, she beats me to it.

"Wait, you two haven't had sex yet?"

"No," I say hoping she drops it. She doesn't.

"No? Why not? It's not like you're a virgin."

I blush. I may not be a virgin, but I don't have much experience since I've only slept with one person.

Her mouth falls open. "You're a virgin!" she says too loudly, right when the band decides to end the song. Making everyone in close proximity able to hear her. Fantastic! Kill me now, please.

I cover my face in my hands and shake my head. "No, I'm not a virgin." I drop my hands and stare past her while I admit for the first time to anyone besides Liv, "Jax and I used to sleep together."

"Wait, you've only fucked Jax?"

God, she's crude. I nod while I chew on my lower lip.

She wiggles her eyebrows. "Recently?"

I shrug. "A few months ago."

"Wow."

I nod. "Yeah."

I resume eating while Harper thinks about my sex life, no doubt. Hopefully she drops it, but I doubt I'll be able to escape without telling her more. Her smile confirms my suspicions. I sigh as I wipe my mouth on a napkin.

"When did you two start dating?"

So we're still on the Jax thing. I can't blame her, if I was in her shoes I would be wondering the same thing. I bring the Heineken to my dry lips. I swallow a long pull of beer to help with the sudden desert forming in my throat.

"We've never dated. It wasn't like that for us. And no, before you ask, Logan doesn't know anything about it."

"Okay, A, for effort. Really good try on not telling me the complete truth." She claps her hands. "Bravo, it really was a nice try." She applauds me again.

Why am I friends with this chick again?

"Seriously, though, what's the real story?"

I know that I have to tell her. She won't let it go. Plus it might feel good getting this secret off my chest. I play with my napkin. I need to be doing something while we have this conversation. Things are about to get heavy. Heavier than she's expecting. I decide to just lay it all on the table, no pretense.

"Jax had a terrible childhood. Since I was nine, I would sneak him into my room at night. Over the years, our friendship turned into something more. He was my first kiss, my first love. The night before my sixteenth birthday, he flew back to California from NYU and surprised me. I lost my virginity under the stars to the man I loved that night."

I shiver as I remember him showering me with kisses to wake me up at midnight. It was the best gift he ever gave me.

"Our entire relationship was a secret. I couldn't tell anyone that I'd spent almost every night with Jax since we were children. He wouldn't let me share his secret. We hid everything from my family. During the day he was just my best friend, but at night, in my room we were always more."

I grip my stomach as a painful memory ripples through me. I can't grasp it, I don't want to. Something in the back of mind warns me I'm not ready to remember, not yet. I shake the memories away and share the rest of our story to Harper.

"Something happened to me six years ago, and no, I don't want to talk about it. I lost myself and Jax along the way. For the last six years, I've shut down on everyone and everything."

Wow, not dark at all. It's the truth, though, and I'm tired of hiding. It's exhausting pretending to be somebody you're not, always painting a smile on my face when all I want to do is scream.

"I did the basics. Enough to get me through the day. I lived day-by-day. If you can count what I've been doing living. I shut myself out from the world and Jax for too long. I've always thought that I would end up with him, but he doesn't want to be in the picture. Now I'm trying to find the person I used to be." I shrug. "That's my story."

"That's just a chapter in your story, Addie. Your story isn't finished yet."

We clink glasses in a toast. "To writing our stories."

Harper links her arm through mine as we leave the restaurant. I'm assaulted by the night chill as soon as she pushes through the door. Luckily Harper was smart enough to bring a jacket, me, not so much. I rub my hands up and down my arms for warmth and watch as she summons a cab. As I step closer to her for body warmth, I step in gum. Yuck. There's a trashcan not two feet away. She supports my arm as I attempt to wipe the gum onto the grass.

"I can't stop thinking about what you said earlier," she says while holding the cab door open.

Please don't ask. Please don't ask. I'm not ready. Soon . . . Just not yet.

"I understand feeling trapped, for wanting to find yourself. More than you know. I want you to understand that whatever happened to you six years ago changed you. You will never be the same person you once were. Remember that while you find yourself, Addie. Don't focus on trying to be the girl you were, but be the woman you are now."

She wraps me into a tight hug. "I think that the woman you are now is inspiring. I think you've already found yourself. You just need to see what everyone else does."

My throat tightens from the sincerity of her words. All I can do is watch as she climbs into the cab in front of mine. The entire trip back to my apartment, I think about what she said to me.

At the end of the week I meet Kohen for a movie night. We settle in our seats and he offers me his bag of popcorn. My disgusted face must be answer enough because he sets it in his lap again.

"I'm a kettle corn person through and through," I whisper, earning a chuckle from him.

I feel my phone vibrate in my pocket, but I choose to ignore it. I've come to realize that Kohen hates when I answer my phone on dates. I should have turned it off like I usually do, but I forgot. My mind is still elsewhere.

I snatch my phone from my pocket to do just that. The opening credits are rolling in, and I don't want to be the girl whose phone goes off during the movie. That girl sucks. I have every intention of turning it off without looking at my missed text but my thumb has other plans. Before I realize what I'm doing, I'm staring at the unanswered text from Jax. I gulp down my Pepsi as I read it.

Jax: I miss you. Let me fix us, Ads. Come over.

My heart stops working as I re-read the text. I'm so entrapped in it that I don't even feel Kohen's breath on my neck as he reads over my shoulder. Before what's happening clicks into place, he rips my phone from my hands. All I can do is gape wide-eyed at Kohen as he slides my phone into his pocket. My mouth moves but no words emerge.

He stands and holds his hand out for me.

"What about the movie?" I ask stupidly.

After a quick scan of the theater, he forcibly yanks me up by my hand. I glare at him as I sit back down. I make a point to appear comfortable even though my body hums in anger. How embarrassing! I can't believe he's acting like this over a text. Granted the text wasn't the best, but it's not like Jax confessed his undying love.

"Get up, Adalynn." Kohen commands quietly, but I don't miss the threat in his tone.

I raise an eyebrow. "You took me to the movies, so you can either sit down and enjoy it with me, or you can leave without me." I shrug. "Your choice."

"Adalynn don—"

"Kohen it's simple, sit down and let's enjoy the rest of our night. You're making a bigger deal out of this than there needs to be." I tug on his jeans. "Please don't ruin our night because my *friend,* who I haven't seen in a few months, said he misses me. It's not what you think."

I'm surprised nobody has yelled at him for blocking the screen. As if reading my mind, Kohen glances around the darken theater again. He huffs loudly and settles in a chair two seats away from me. Mature.

The movie starts before I can demand my phone back. Wanting to change the night around, I lean over to caress his hand with the tips of my fingers. He turns his head to me and shoots me a glare before facing the screen. I roll my eyes as I adjust myself in the chair.

If someone were to ask me what the movie was about, I couldn't tell them a single thing. It could have been in a foreign language and I wouldn't have known any better. Because instead of enjoying the new comedy, I focused on the fact that Kohen made no move to sit next to me. He acted as if I wasn't even there. He's punishing me for something I have no control over. It's not like I can tell Jax, someone who's been in my life for sixteen years, that he can't text me.

Silence fills the ride home. He keeps me tucked under his arm in the backseat. Every time I ask if wants to talk about it, he ignores me. When the cab pulls up to our apartment building Kohen tosses cash onto the seat and jerks me out of the taxi. Actually fucking tugs me out of it. This has to be about more than Jax just texting me. Looks like I won't have to wait too long to get to the bottom of it. After dragging me through the lobby and into the elevator, Kohen pushes me against the nearest wall.

"Are you going to tell me why you lied to me?"

"I didn't . . ." I trail off at the pressure of his fingers digging into my skin.

"DO. NOT. LIE. TO. ME."

With each word, he squeezes me harder. I nod but don't say anything. I don't know what to say.

"What's really going on with you and Jax?"

"Nothing!" I say, glad that I can tell the truth.

He squeezes me tighter. I force myself not to react. I'm used to pain. I've inflicted pain on myself. This is nothing. I can handle this. I can handle Kohen when he's irrationally upset over nothing. Well, not nothing since I'm the reason why he's jealous in the first place.

"I've been hanging out with you more and Jax has been busy with work. We keep missing each other when I go to dinner with Logan and Connor. We've been friends for sixteen years, he's my brother's best friend. He's always going to be in my life. The sooner you realize this, the better for us. I will not put up with you acting like this."

His dark blue stormy eyes soften and I know he believes my lies. He blinks as if finally realizing he has me pinned against the wall of the elevator. He releases me and steps back.

"Adalynn, I'm so sorry, baby. I . . . I didn't mean to hurt you. Please believe me."

He lightly runs his fingers over my fresh bruises, then covers my cheeks with his hands. "I could never hurt you, Adalynn. I love you." He trails kisses down my nose to my lips. "I love you so much, Adalynn. I'm so so sorry, baby."

The pain in his voice hurts me more than the bruises. I know all about doing something you wish you could take back, but you can't. I know all about hurting the people you love the most. I know all about wanting to change the impossible. I feel his pain as if it's my own.

I stroke my hands up and down his strong chest. His muscles tense underneath my hands. I stare up at his handsome face so he believes what I have to say.

"I know, I know you didn't mean it. You didn't hurt me. You could never really hurt me Kohen."

I lean up on my tiptoes, pull his head down with my hands and bring his lips to mine. In this one kiss I convey that we are all right, that I don't blame him, and I'm not mad at him. We separate from each other when the elevator opens on my floor.

"You have nothing to be sorry for."

He attention fixes on my bruises. I need to make him feel better. If he leaves like this he will only focus on the bruises, on hurting me. I don't want that. I want to invite him in, to stay the night, but I think it would be best if we slept at our own places tonight. Not because I think I'm afraid of him, but because I think he needs time to himself. Another reason I don't invite him in is because as much as I try to hide it, whenever he's in my apartment I feel like I'm betraying Jax.

I'm ridiculous, I know.

I give him a long hug. I know he needs this reassurance before he goes back to his place. I force myself to relax into his embrace, something that's harder to do than normal.

He kisses the top of my head. "I better go."

I nod against his chest. After another minute of being in each other's arms, he gently scoots away. Instead of kissing me in a way that will make my toes curl, he barely brushes his lips against mine.

"I love you, Adalynn. Never forget that."

I remain silent. I don't feel the same. He retreats into the elevator without another word.

A few minutes later, I do my nightly routine. I avoid the mirror. I do not want to see the bruises taking residence on my forearms. I can feel them. I don't want to make a big deal out of nothing. Before I crawl into bed, I delete Jax's text thread. I'm moving on with Kohen, I don't need my past with Jax interfering with my present. Suddenly feeling as if all my energy has been stolen away, I'm pulled into a dreamless sleep.

CHAPTER NINETEEN

The next morning as I'm dressing, I stand transfixed, staring at the bluish bruise of Kohen's fingerprints on my forearms. I lightly touch the bruise. It's tender, but not as bad as it looks. My relief is short-lived when I realize that I'll have to wear something to cover it up.

With heavy footsteps, I sort through every blouse I have, which is a lot. After five minutes of eyeing the dress I really want to wear today, I select my creme pencil skirt and my Diane Von Furstenberg deep green long sleeve blouse.

"This will have to do." I say a silent goodbye to the dress.

Spreading everything out, I change into a La Perla matching bra and panty set that are white with a gold lace trim. I'm feeling better about my outfit choice already as I slid the bra into place. This see-through number is one of my favorites.

At work, I'm busy typing an email when I feel someone staring at me. Glancing up, I spot Kohen walking towards my office with a exquisite bouquet of red tulips. I ignore the curious glances coming our way, and meet him at my glass door.

"What are these for?" I breathe them in. "They're lovely!"

He gives me a quick peck on my cheek. "They're incentive for a beautiful brunette to go to lunch with me."

I glance down at my watch. He's just in time. "Okay, give me a minute to finish everything up here. Then I'm all yours."

I let my boss know that I'm heading to lunch and give a quick wave to Harper as we pass her office on our way to the elevator. She barely notices us as she taps her keyboard. It's a busy day for her. I make a mental note to bring her back something.

Kohen interlaces our fingers together as we stroll to a nearby sushi place. He hasn't said much since we've left Malcara Enterprises. As we take our seats in the crowded restaurant, I break the silence.

"Are we okay?"

He lets out a long breath. "I should be asking you that." He runs his hand roughly down his face. "I'm so sorry, Adalynn. I can't believe I did that. I never intended to hurt you. I promise that I—"

I cover his mouth with my fingers. "Stop, Kohen. I told you last night, you have nothing to be sorry for and I meant it. Believe me. I'm fine." I slide my fingers from his lips to caress his cheek. "You. Did. Not. Hurt. Me."

It takes a while for him to give me his first real smile since he showed up at my work. I give him a lingering kiss on the lips and turn my attention to the menu.

"Great, now feed me. I'm starving!"

He follows my lead and picks up the menu. "Your wish is my command."

After an enjoyable lunch, I head toward the restroom. I can't help but notice that most women keep stealing glances at our table. I doubt that they're staring at our empty plates. I love that he is oblivious to everyone in the restaurant. His sole focus is me, always me. He makes me feel cherished.

I'm fully aware of the cheesy smile threatening to split my face in two when I walk into the bathroom. I ignore the two women checking themselves out in the mirror and go about my business. They talk about the usual things ladies discuss in the bathroom.

"Do you like my hair this color or do you think I should go back to being blonde?"

I ignore their conversation while I wash my hands.

"He has the most striking green eyes I've ever seen."

I, of course, think of the green-eyed man that I know. As I dry my hands, I hear something else that makes me stop. Turning, I face the one who just mentioned Trinity.

"I'm sorry, I couldn't help but overhear you." Because you're louder than a blow-horn. "You wouldn't happen to be talking about a man named Jaxon, would you?"

She immediately sizes me up. I do the same. I hate that her hair is practically the identical color as mine. Yes, she should go back to being a blonde. She does not pull off being a brunette well. Scratch that, she should keep it. She could stand putting on a few pounds. I'm sure if she turns too quickly she might snap in two. Would that be a bad thing? Her stupid skinny jeans and low cut shirt that shows off her ample breasts, make me want to throw something at her.

My eyes blaze as I stare at her, unwilling to back down. I need to know I'm paranoid and that the world doesn't revolve around Jax. Well, besides my world that is. Thankfully her friend pities me and turns her attention from her phone to me.

"I believe his last name is Chandler, but I'm not sure. Why? Are you his girlfriend or something?"

Both of them check my left hand for the ring they won't find. I laugh, but I'm dying inside. "Oh no, nothing like that. He's my brother's friend. That's it. I was just wondering."

Wow, small world. Out of all the restaurants in New York, I have to be at the place where one of Jax's one night stands shows up. Wonderful. Today just keeps getting better. As she flicks her hair over her shoulder, I realize that I've seen her before. I squint to make sure. About two months ago, I saw her leaving Jax's office. Has he been seeing her all this time? What about everything that happened between us? Did he leave me to choose her? Sweat bathes my forehead. I might be sick.

"Oh wow! Do you know what his favorite food is? I'm planning on surprising him with dinner tonight." She holds up a white card, his penthouse access card, and my heart breaks a little more. "We've been together a while, but his food preference hasn't come up before." Her friend snickers, making my no longer beating heart crack a little more. The slut continues to talk, unaware of the silent agony she's putting me through. "I thought he would love the surprise with how busy he's been with work this week."

Over-share much? I concentrate on not lashing out at her. I can't figure out why it would be such a horrible idea to bash her face into the mirror. Ah, her friend. Witness. Don't need that. I swallow the huge lump in my throat.

"Nope, sorry. We're not close. Like I said, he's my brother's friend, not mine."

Without waiting for a response, I turn on my heels. I can't even believe how upset I am over something like this. This is stupid. I'm stupid. I know he dates. Well, fucks is more like it. Hearing about it in a bathroom and realizing that he's been seeing her for a while now, is so much worse than I've ever imagined. I think I might throw up. Thank God that slut didn't go into details. I wouldn't be held responsible for my actions.

How can he sleep with her? Is she his girlfriend? I swallow the bile in my throat. No, Jax doesn't do girlfriends, I remind myself, but I don't believe my own lie. If she wasn't his girlfriend, why would she have the access card to his place?

I guess I finally know why he hasn't attended our weekly dinners. I should feel relieved that he isn't avoiding me, but I don't. If anything, I feel worse, much worse. I can't believe that I thought he wasn't coming around because of me. Could I be any more self-absorbed?

I need to scream. I hate that my heart is crumbling. I thought my heart was shattered, nothing left to break. I was wrong.

As I walk back to the seating area, Kohen types on his phone with an anxious expression. It evaporates when he spots me. Salvaging our lunch date is impossible.

Good thing I've perfected the art of acting. Anyone looking at me will see what I want them to see. I'm just a girl on a date with a boy. Laughing at his jokes that I don't hear. I touch his arm at the right time, showing we're intimate. I make sure that this is what he sees. Nothing else. From a typical outsider, it's the perfect picture.

From the inside I'm slowly dying. My entire body is wound so tightly, I can feel every individual muscle tense. I force my muscles to loosen up so that Kohen doesn't notice how stressed I am. My heart was pulled out of my chest and dumped onto the dirty cold tiled floor of that bathroom. Somehow my blood continues to pump, keeping me alive so I can torture myself with images of Jax and the slut. Kohen disappears. Behind my eyes is the vision of a naked Jax and a leggy brunette who isn't me.

I'm suffering on the inside. Perfect on the outside. It's a role I play well. A role I haven't played in a while. A role that I miss. I miss pretending to be perfect. I miss not reacting, not allowing anyone to see the real me, not allowing anything to hurt me. I miss being numb.

Kohen appears in a much better mood as we leave the restaurant. Me? I'm ready to drown a particular brunette. Thankfully Kohen doesn't notice my rotten mood. As he leans in to kiss me, I step away and force a cough.

"Are you getting sick?" Concern fills his voice.

"No, I think I swallowed a bug or something."

He pulls me into him and checks my head for a fever just in case. He kisses my forehead.

"Call me later?"

"Of course."

I watch his cab drive away. Clutching the doggie bag for Harper tighter than necessary, I head into work. I try to calm down enough so that nobody notices a change. *I don't care. It's not a big deal. People fuck all the time.* I wish my body could stop trembling. Will the pain in my chest ever go away?

I slam my bag on my desk. I glance around to make sure nobody notices. I'm in luck. Well, until I see Harper to the right with a raised eyebrow. I shake my head at her, point to her office and mouth "food." She mouths "thanks." I'll tell her about lunch when we go running tonight after work.

Harper waits in my living room while I change into my workout clothes. I usually don't run with a jacket, but the new accessories on my forearms leave me no choice. All of my long-sleeved workout clothes overflow the hamper. So I'm stuck wearing a purple razorback tank with a built-in sports bra and my black running jacket. I change into my black running shorts and snag my Nikes from my closet. I wash all my make-up off my face, before heading to the living room.

We walk across the street to Central Park and stretch. After about five minutes of jogging in silence, Harper squints at me, a question written all over her face.

"What?" I snap.

"I was just wondering how long until you tell me about your pissy mood after lunch." She picks up the pace. I easily keep up.

"I don't know what you're talking about," I say a little defensively.

Harper doesn't say anything at first. I don't know if I'm relieved that she dropped it, or not. Do I want to talk about it? I know I should.

I try to focus on the run. The feel of my feet hitting the pavement with each step. I'm doing everything I usually do. My mind usually shuts off by now.

As we jog, I concentrate on breathing in air through my nose, out of my mouth. A slow burn works its way up my calfs. It's still not enough to shove the image of Jax and the troll out of my head. I need to push myself harder. That's the only way. I need to feel the pain. I need to overwork myself.

I quicken my pace again. I'm almost sprinting. Harper doesn't break stride. She's sweating a little more than me and breathing a little harder. I can tell she isn't used to running like this. She's more of a marathon type, not a sprinter. I want to tell her to go at her own pace, but my mouth won't work. I doubt she would, anyways.

I push myself to the breaking point. It's the only way I know how to shut it off, to stop picturing them together.

Again I increase my pace. I can see Harper roll her eyes at me before she matches my stride again. We're both sprinting. My arms hurt, my thighs burn, but they're not on fire. I want the fire. I need to keep running until I can't anymore. I need the small distraction, if only for a second.

Harper surprises me by going even faster. Sweat drenches her yellow tank. I'm not much better. Sweat drips down my spine and I use my jacket-covered arm to wipe perspiration off my forehead. My blood pumps so hard I can hear it in my ears. They start to ring, making any other noise impossible to hear.

I won't last much longer. It's okay, the images are almost gone. I'll have my reprieve soon. Harper huffs and puffs alongside me. A little more is all I need. I can feel everything starting to slip away. It's as if I'm physically leaving my troubles on the pavement with each step. With each pump of my arms, the pain of my broken heart lessens. In its place is the burning of my legs.

I unzip my jacket, needing air or I might pass out. My jacket flaps in the wind. I bring the corner of my jacket up to my chest to wipe off sweat. Harper increases her speed. She has a lot more stamina than I realized. We're now running as fast as we can. If I don't stop, tomorrow will be hell. I don't, I keep pushing. Finally, everything is gone. No more Jax. No more leggy troll. No more broken heart. Just breathing.

I glance at Harper to see how she's doing. She's ready to faint. She's lathered in sweat, her face cherry red, and her breathing erratic. I know I look the same. I slow down. Sense finally kicks in and I realize what I'm doing. I'm killing myself over a guy. A guy that doesn't even want me. I won't be that girl. I'd rather save the torture I force upon my body for something real, something that matters. Jax doesn't matter. He never really did.

She looks relieved when I slow our pace again. We're now back to a fast jog. A little further, she begins a fast walk. I follow her lead. Two minutes later, we both stop. Waists bent, hand on our knees, we both struggle for air. I toss my water bottle on a patch of grass. Harper follows suit and stretches her hamstrings.

We don't say anything to each other. I think she is waiting for me to start the conversation. Clearly she knows that's not my regular running routine, something is on my mind. I'm glad that she gives me time to come out with it. She understands that I don't like to feel backed into a corner. I can't function that way.

When we finally gain strength, we trudge to our water bottles. Harper collapses on the ground and doesn't move. She just closes her eyes. If I didn't see her chest rising and falling with each heavy breath, I would think she was dead. I do a quick stretch with my arms. Hopefully if I stretch enough, I won't hate myself tomorrow for overdoing it.

I rinse out my dry mouth before sipping from my water bottle. I want to drink it all, but that will give me cramps. Harper heaves loudly and sits up. She chugs her water. Without any grace, I drop down right next to her. I stare at the trees in front of us. I know I need to tell her. Now. Quick and painless like ripping off a Band-Aid.

"I had the great pleasure of meeting Jax's current slut. Today. At lunch," I tell her point blank.

Harper's surprise quickly morphs into anger. She pretty much is spot-on to how I felt in that bathroom. I still can't believe how little the world is. I can't even put into words how small I felt sitting on the toilet listening to the troll tell her friend about Jax.

"Back up. Who is she? Where were you? And how do you know she's sleeping with Jax?" I don't even have time to answer her before she's shooting off a new round of questions. "Most importantly, have you talked to Jax? When do you see him again?"

My hands rip out the grass. I force them to lay flat on the ground as I fill her in. I was kind of hoping she wouldn't ask that question. The answer makes me look like a psycho. I sigh heavily, and lay down. I stare up at the sky, different hues of purple and pink with a splash of red. I wish I had my camera to capture the scene in front of me. Its beauty is so simple, it's magic.

"I asked her if she was talking about Jaxon. Her friend answered me. Even asked if I was his girlfriend. When I told them that I was just his friend's little sister, the troll stopped looking at me like I was a threat."

"Please tell me this story ends with you throwing something at her, or at least calling her a troll to her face?"

I love her. I shake my head. "I wish."

"What happened next?"

I tell Harper in detail everything that happened. Even the parts I didn't intend on telling her; feeling like my heart broke into tiny little pieces, how angry I was at myself. Surprisingly, I tell her about pretending, about making it seem like I was perfect on the outside, even though I am far from perfect. It's amazing how easy it is to bare my soul to her. As much as I keep telling myself to be quiet, words continue to flow out of my mouth.

"Nobody's perfect, Addie," Harper finally says when I'm done.

"I know that. It's just . . . I don't know. Hard to explain, I guess. I hate when people can really see me. See how broken I am. I hate feeling like everyone can see how easily I can shatter. I guess that's why I do it. It's become easier over the years pretending to be someone I'm not. It's easier to become the person I want the world to see than the person I really am."

"I think letting the world see the real you is better than pretending to be someone you're not. If anyone doesn't like the real you, then that person doesn't deserve to be in your life, Addie."

Harper lays down on the cold grass beside me. I don't know how to respond. I don't like people getting to know me. Probably more from fear than anything. Just something else I need to work on. I want to be the person that tries, not the person that gives up because something horrible happened.

My family wouldn't want me to give up my life. They would want me to live, to enjoy life. For them, I need to try. It won't be easy, something will tempt me to return to the dark shadows, but this time I will fight. I want to stay in the light. I don't want the horrors of my past to trap me in the dark.

Harper sits up again. Dusk has fallen. Time to head back. I need to soak in a hot bubble bath for at least an hour to relax the muscles I over-worked. Which makes me think of making Harper work just as hard. A thought I don't like.

"I'm sorry about the intense run. I promise next time it won't be like that. I kind of lost myself in my head." I hold out my hand to help her up.

She takes it. "It gives me an excuse to go to the spa and get a nice, long massage."

I grab both of our waters and toss Harper hers. A spa day and massage sounds wonderful. I haven't been to one in almost seven years. Since Hadley and I worked our butts off to surprise Mom with a day at the spa. My dad found chores around his office and at home so we could earn enough money for Mother's Day.

"We should make a day out of it. I can make reservations for this weekend if you don't have any plans," she says, reading my mind.

"It's a date. My treat," I tell her because I know her. She will insist on paying.

We argue back and forth as we leisurely walk back to my apartment. Cabs and town cars fill the street. A large group of people wait for the crosswalk. As we crossing the street, I get a brilliant idea. I'll force her to spend time with Connor. She told me she doesn't feel worthy, not in so many words, but I know that's how she feels. I want her to know she is worthy, of anything and anybody. I'm going to give her a push in the right direction.

"Fine, I'll let you buy." I wait to see the smile that she saves for when she's won. She is so wrong. "One condition. You have to go somewhere with me, no questions asked, and wear what I put you in."

She pretends to contemplate the deal, but I know I already have her. She isn't one to back down to anything. She's not that type of girl, if she were, we wouldn't get along as well as we do. If only she knew what I was planning. This is going to be fun. I hate that my part of our-soon-to-be-deal won't happen for a few more weeks. I hate waiting.

"Deal!" she sings as she holds her hand out for me to shake.

"Deal!" I say just as enthusiastically.

I control myself and only dance in my head. I can't let her think there's more to my master plan. I can't wait for her to find out the truth. Hopefully she doesn't dump water on me, I know that's her go-to move. Water will not go well with the couture dress I will be wearing.

"How do you know that the two of them are sleeping together?" Harper asks, pulling me out of my thoughts.

At first I'm startled, thinking she was reading my mind again. Then it clicks, Jax and the troll. That's what she meant. Not what I was planning. Which is good since I don't plan on her sleeping with her date. I just want her to know that it is an option, that she can have whoever she wants.

"Jax doesn't have any women friends he doesn't sleep with."

"I think there's more to the story. Maybe you should ask him."

I gawk at her like she's lost her mind. I mean come on, Jax is a man, if it's there in front of him, he's going to take it. With a woman like that, I have no doubt that she shows Jax exactly what she has to offer him.

"I saw the way he kept staring at you at brunch. I'm not blind, anyone with eyes can tell he wants you, Addie, and that he hates whenever Kohen touches you. Maybe he's sleeping around because he thinks he can't have you."

"Jax knows he can have me if he wants to. That's not the problem. You're reading into something that isn't there. Trust me."

"He kept sneaking glances at you the entire time. He needs to work on his stealth moves if he doesn't want to be so noticeable."

My mouth falls open a little. She's crazy. There's people everywhere in New York City and I befriended one of the crazies. Of course I did.

"You're the only one that doesn't see it then," Harper says.

I shake my head and sigh. "Trust me, I'm not wrong about this. As much as I wish I was. I'm not. He doesn't want me. He's made that fact crystal clear."

"Okay."

"Okay?" I ask, not believing she has given up so easily.

"One of us is right. Hopefully I don't have to wait too long to be proven right."

"Don't count on it," I mutter.

As we wait for the elevator to arrive, I hear her mutter something about Romeo and Juliet.

"Please tell me you didn't just compare my love life to Romeo and Juliet. You do realize that isn't even a love story, right? It's a tragedy that could have been easily avoidable."

She shrugs. "You can't deny that your love life has similar qualities from the story."

"Jax chooses to not be with me because . . ." I can't tell her about his abusive father, it's not my story to tell. I shake my head. "It's not because our families hate each other. Besides, where would Kohen fit in to all this?"

"Okay, I didn't say it was exactly like your love life. Just similar."

As I fetch my key I ask, "Did you get dropped on your head when you were a child? You do realize you pretty much said Jax and I are Romeo and

Juliet, everyone wants us together, but we die. Are you planning our deaths in the near future?"

She ignores me and tramps straight to my living room and collapses onto the couch. I follow her lead and sprawl in the chair beside the couch. Unable to get comfy, I struggle out of my jacket. After lying around for five minutes, Harper, rises and stretches. She could put the Energizer Bunny to shame.

"It's late, I'm gonna head home."

"Okay." I help her collect her things. "Let me know what time to meet you for our spa date."

"OH MY GOD! WHAT THE FUCK HAPPENED?" Harper yells as she grips both my arms.

I'm so startled from her outburst it takes a second to register what's happening. She stares wide-eyed at the dark bruises that appear worse than they did this morning. How is that even possible? Shouldn't they be getting better? I yank back my arms, and cross them, in hopes of covering the bruises.

"Nothing happened, it's fine."

"Nothing happened? NOTHING HAPPENED!" She grabs my arms again and turns them this way and that way, inspecting the damage. "There's fingerprints on your arms! NOTHING HAPPENED! WHO DID THIS TO YOU?"

I need to find a way to calm her down fast. She is about to explode. I have to extinguish this situation. If she thinks it's a big deal, she will tell someone. Then, it will definitely become a big deal.

"If you calm down, I will tell you everything, okay? Just relax and remember I'm fine."

She releases her hold on my arms, but gently touches the bruises with her index finger. A tear trickles down her cheek as if she can actually feel these herself.

"Did Kohen do this to you?" she asks quietly.

"It was an accident, I didn't even feel them. I still don't feel them. It looks worse than it is. It doesn't even hurt."

"A lot of women say 'it was an accident' until they can't say anything anymore."

"This is not one of those times. I promise. If he was actually hurting me, do you really think I would be okay with this? That I wouldn't immediately go to my brother?"

She leans against the wall. I follow suit. She doesn't say anything at first. Her eyes keep bouncing back from my forearms to my face. I can tell she's trying to determine if I'm lying or not. She kicks off the wall and stands in front of me.

"I'll believe you, this time. I don't know what happened and it won't make a difference if you tell me. I won't say anything to anyone because it's not my place, and if you say this isn't a big deal, fine, I'll believe you."

I sigh in relief, but she's not done.

"If he EVER lays a finger on you again, I don't care what you try to make me believe, I will make a big deal out of it and I will tell someone. I won't just stand by while your boyfriend uses you as a punching bag, Addie."

I know what she's saying is fair, but at the same time, it's not. It's not like Kohen hit me. He didn't even hurt me. I have been hurt a lot worse than this.

"Kohen isn't the type to hit a woman." I slip back into the jacket. "It isn't what it looks like."

"Every woman says that, you don't know what you'll do until you're in that situation."

"Well, it's a good thing I'm not in that situation," I snap at her.

I immediately feel like crap. I just lashed out at a friend. A friend that wants to be here for me and make sure I'm okay. I won't be getting the best friend of the week award.

"I'm sorry. I know you're just trying to help, but I promise you nothing happened." I engulf her into a huge bear hug. "Thank you for showing me how much you care, but I promise you, it's not what it looks like. Kohen is a good guy."

She squeezes me back tightly. "Fine, I'll drop it. Just promise me you'll be safe."

"I'll be safe, promise."

She gives me one more hug before leaving. I turn on the T.V. to drown out Harper's words that keep echoing in my ears. I switch it off when it doesn't help. I don't get why she would immediately assume the bruises were from Kohen. He's the last person I would suspect. It could have been anyone, a random person on the street. It could have even been Jax.

Groaning, I rub my temples with my palms. I can't believe I was stupid enough to take off my jacket. I don't want Harper treating Kohen differently, that will put everyone on edge and I don't want to deal with that drama. It's unnecessary.

As I attempt to sleep, without a shower, all I can think about is Harper's reaction. I dread them being in the same room together, and I hate that. I don't want to worry about her berating him, or her believing the worst if he gets upset in front of her. I know she's going to watch him, watch us, every chance she gets. I can't blame her because I would do the same thing in her situation.

My stars swirl around and around on their string from the breeze drifting through the open window. I don't remember opening it this morning, but my mind was elsewhere. I should close it, but I enjoy the fresh air. The city noise comforts me. It's as if I'm not alone.

CHAPTER TWENTY

Two weeks have passed by since Harper and I went running. Two weeks since I met Jax's latest troll in a bathroom. It seems like Harper avoids going out if Kohen will be there. Which he always is. I need to intervene.

"I swear this better be the last one!" Harper says, jarring me out of my thoughts.

I send an apologetic look to the sales clerk. "You act like we are at the dentist. You're trying on dresses, not getting a root canal. Calm down and put it on."

"I'm going to strangle you if I see one more dress."

I ignore her. One thing I learned about Harper, she can't stand shopping. Okay, so that's not entirely true, she can't stand shopping with me. Can't blame her, most people can't.

Harper emerges from the dressing room and poses in front of me. Wow. This is the one. It's spectacular! She fights her smile. I'm sure because she fears me forcing her into the dressing room to try on another endless pile of dresses. I wait before I tell her I love it. I keep my expression bored, not showing that I want to jump up and down.

I make a turn signal with my index finger. Her figure looks amazing! Men are going to have a hard time keeping their eyes off her. Mission accomplished. Her shoulders sag a little when she faces me again.

"Well?" she asks impatiently.

"That's the one!"

"Thank God! I thought I'd have to sneak out of here. I was afraid we would never leave!"

I grip my chest as if she wounded me. "And here I assumed you were dying to go shopping with me."

"Yeah, that was before I knew you had to try on everything in each store."

I shrug, not caring. "I'm not that bad. We didn't even get to that section yet." I nod to the left, proving my point.

"Okay, okay, you're right. We're done though, right?"

I nod.

"I'm starving!" she says dramatically as we leave the boutique.

Now here comes the hard part. I thought that I would sneak-attack a lunch between her and Kohen. What surprised me was when I heard Connor in the background. I have no idea why they're together. Kohen usually only hangs out with the guys if I'm there. I wonder if it was Connor's doing. It has to be, I don't see Kohen calling up Connor. Sometimes I think he's jealous of Connor. Gross.

"How about meeting Kohen and Connor for lunch? I told Kohen where we are and one thing led to another and we have a lunch date with them."

I chew on my lip when she doesn't answer. She hasn't brought Kohen up, and neither have I. It has kind of been an unspoken rule between us. And now I'm breaking it by making her go to lunch with him.

She turns away. "Sounds great."

She's still on the fence about Kohen. As much as she hides it, I can tell. I link our arms together and steer us toward the little cafe down the street. We spot the guys at the same time. It's pretty easy when every woman on the patio is doing her best to capture their attention. I'm not surprised Kohen ignores them; what surprises me is Connor does too.

"You sick?" I ask him.

"No. Why?"

I drop my bags down alongside Harper's, then I give Connor a hug, and Kohen a chaste kiss on the lips. Kohen pulls out a chair for me, always the gentleman. He and Harper exchange tight smiles. Interesting, does he sense her hostility?

"Oh, I just assumed you were sick," I say once everyone has sat down again.

"Again, why?"

"You know, because of all the women out here dying for the attention you're not giving them."

Both Kohen and Connor look like I started speaking a different language. Do I need to spell it out for them?

"She means she's surprised that you don't have your tongue down one of their throats yet," Harper says with a wave towards the surrounding women.

Now they understand my earlier comment. Connor, gives Harper his panty-dropper smile, complete with running the tip of his tongue over his top lip. Here's the Connor I was expecting.

"Don't be jealous, *Elizabeth*, you know I save it all for you," he says in a voice that should be reserved for the bedroom.

"I'd rather swallow my own tongue than have yours anywhere near my throat."

Connor leans in so that his lips are inches from her face. "I promise you wouldn't be saying that after I run my tongue up and down your throat."

I shake my head. This guy is asking for trouble. You don't mess with the devil, and she can be heartless when she wants. I've seen it, plenty of times on the opposite sex. It's never pretty, but always funny.

Harper swallows loudly. "Sorry I just threw up in my mouth." She sits back in her chair. "It's Harper, by the way."

"Not Elizabeth?"

And he wonders why she dumped water on him. What a mystery.

Lunch runs smoothly, at least until everyone has finished. Harper watches everything Kohen does, hanging onto his every word. And not in a good way. She's studying him, waiting for him to mess up. I've been trying to steer the conversation away from the two of them, but she has other plans.

"I saw a documentary on abusive partners last night," she says casually, but directs her eyes to Kohen.

I can't believe she just said that! Kohen surprises me by remaining calm. I can tell that he's nervous by the way his hand trembles slightly as he reaches for his glass of water.

"Any reason why you would bring that up, Harper? Is there a guy in your life that we should know about?" Kohen feigns concern.

She shrugs, but challenges him with her eyes. Harper stares him down until he turns away, to me. I shake my head, trying to convey my confusion. I can tell when his jaw tightens that he doesn't buy it. Time slows down in an awkward silence that doesn't break until Connor peers up from his phone, oblivious to the tension. At least I think he's oblivious until he engages Harper in conversation. I beam gratefully at him. He nods.

Kohen drags my chair closer to him and lays his arm on my shoulder. Harper gives a slight shake of her head in disapproval. I rub my forehead, feeling the pangs of a headache. Maybe lunch with them wasn't the brightest idea. When the bill arrives, both guys reach for it, but Harper intercepts it with her dainty hands.

"Have to be quicker than that, Evans."

Harper hands the bill over with her credit card to our waiter. Not bothering to even look at the price. She drinks the rest of her iced tea, happy as can be. She loves messing with Connor. She knows he hates anyone paying for him. I once made the mistake of telling her how he flipped out when I paid for lunch one time. Since then she has taken every chance to pay for him. I love it.

"Thanks for lunch, Harper," Kohen says through gritted teeth.

Letting her accent drip through her voice, Harper says, "You're most welcome," while she picks up her iced-tea.

Clearly these two don't mix well together. Hopefully that will change when she sees that he isn't a bad guy after all.

When the waiter returns, Connor smirks. The waiter casts his gaze to Connor when he speaks. "I'm sorry, Ms. Harrison, but your meal has already been paid for." He hands over her credit card without another word.

"Have to be smarter than that, Harrison," Connor says smugly.

"Well-played." Harper winks at Connor before putting away her credit card.

Connor gets up and bows. Actually bows. I groan as everyone watches the show.

"Thank you, thank you," Connor says.

"Okay, let's go before he really makes a scene," Harper says.

I pick up my bags as I get up and take Kohen's extended hand. Kohen and I start walking away from the table. We say good-bye after he reminds me to keep my phone on me while at the movies with Harper. I join Harper and Connor, who are in a heated conversation by his car. They're arguing about who's going to drive.

"Harper, we'll miss our movie, just get in the back. He doesn't let anyone drive his car," I inform her.

"Then why was Logan driving the other day?" Harper asks.

"What? When?" I turn towards Connor. "What the hell?"

"Yes, I let your brother drive my car. It's not a big deal, Addie."

I yank open the passenger door and slam it shut. Harper settles into the back without a word. I wait until Connor is situated until I drill into him.

"How many times? Has Jax?"

Connor shrugs. I can tell he is trying to decide if he should attempt lying, or tell the truth.

"Okay, so you're the only one I don't let drive my car."

"WHAT!" I scream.

"Come on, Addie, it's not that hard to believe. You're a nervous driver. Besides, it's not like you have a current license."

I tell myself to shut up. My voice has other plans, though.

"I haven't driven a car since I moved to New York. I've never been in a car accident!"

The minute the last sentence leaves my mouth, I clamp it shut. I have been in a car accident. I just wasn't the driver. That's what I meant, but that's not what came out. Luckily, Connor knows what I mean.

Connor seems lost. I know he is thinking the same thing. He remembers the last time I drove a car. I panicked and almost veered off the road because I couldn't stop picturing the accident. I haven't driven one since. I have never had the urge to get behind the wheel until now. Which means I have no right to be upset. But I am, I blame the stress of lunch.

"Adalynn, you haven't been behind a wheel in over five years. If you really want to drive, you can drive."

I hear Harper's gasp, but I don't look at her. I don't want to tell her about my fear of cars. At least not right now. Once there was a time when I couldn't ride in a car without having a panic attack. More times than I can count I ended up blacking out. I was able to conquer that fear. One day soon, I will drive a car again.

"Next time."

Connor sounds as surprised as I feel. "Really?"

I weigh my response before answering him. I know he's asking a lot more than if I'm ready to drive again. He's asking if I can handle it after everything. Before, I wouldn't have been able to handle it. Before when I would get behind the steering wheel, it would take me back to when I was trapped in the darkness. Cries unanswered.

"Yea I'm ready," I say quietly.

The heaviness of the last five minutes seeps through the air. Harper and Connor can feel it, too. I catch her worried eyes in the visor mirror. I give her a small smile. She squeezes my shoulder from behind me.

Connor pulls up to the AMC theater to drop us off. Before I unbuckle, he breaks the silence.

"Call one of us when you're ready to leave. I don't want you two walking around the city at night. You can even call Jax."

I know he's just looking out for me, but it still gets on my nerves. They act like I'm a child. They don't think I can take care of myself. Granted, I haven't been known to take care of myself over the years, but that's changed. I've changed.

"Fine," I say, opening the door.

I meet Harper on the sidewalk. We watch Connor drive away before we stand in line to buy tickets. I'm not in the mood to sit through a movie. Harper must sense this because she suggests skipping the movie for drinks.

"Lead the way," I tell her.

Harper and I are about four rounds in. When I say rounds, I don't mean beer. Nope, straight tequila. Tequila and limes to be exact. It's safe to say I'm buzzed. Digging into my purse, I grab my phone. I have four texts from Kohen and one from Connor and Logan in a group message. I hate group messages. Without responding to their reminders to be safe, I delete it.

I scan the area to see if Harper will be back anytime soon with our next round. We made a "no cell phone" rule earlier. I spot her at the bar flirting with two men. Because one is just not enough. Got to love her. I read Kohen's text.

Kohen: Where are you?

Kohen: When you gonna be home babe?

Kohen: Please don't ignore me again.

Kohen: Need me to pick you up?

Kohen: What did I say about ignoring me?

I peer up from my phone. Harper's chatting at the bar, but she will be back soon. I can tell she's bored. She's no longer touching one of their arms, and she has put space between them that wasn't there before. When she waves down the bartender, I begin to type out a message, then delete it. For some reason I don't want to inform him about my change of venue. Instead of being honest, I ignore his first question.

Me: Hey sorry just checked my phone. Hour or two tops. Are you still working?

The phone buzzes as the bartender passes Harper two beers and a shot.

Kohen: Okay. No, I'm out at dinner with Claire and her husband. Keep your phone on you, babe!

Me: Will do.

I set down my phone as Harper returns. The small shake of her head tells me that she caught me. She hands me a shot.
"Consequences for breaking the rules. Bottoms up."
I clink the shot with her beer. As I reach for the lime, she stretches across the table for my phone. I slap my hand on the table to stop her, but she's too fast.
"Harper don't, give it back."
She shakes her head. "I think someone needs a reminder that if they have a penis, then they can't interrupt girls' night."
My eyes widen in horror as her thumbs move over the screen. This is bad. I need to stop her. "Seriously, Harper, you made your point, now give me back my phone."
She offers me the phone with a wicked grin. Not good. I glance down. Crap! Kohen will be furious.

Me: If I'm out having a few drinks, please refrain from contacting me unless it's an emergency. I'm not going to check in every five minutes. If you have a problem with that, get over it. Enjoy your evening, I know I am.

I gasp. How could she do this? She knows this will create problems.
"You're seriously getting bent out of shape for me sending a joke?"

"You had no right to text him. He has done nothing but be nice to you." I stand up, ready to leave. "You need to get over your issue you with him, Harper. He's a nice person, he treats me well."

She rolls her eyes. "Last time I checked, bruises don't scream nice person."

I want to yell at her, but I can't. Harper has a point, but she's wrong. She doesn't see the real Kohen. He has only shown his vulnerable side to me. He's damaged like me, he has his problems, but so does everyone else. I can't fault him for that. He loves me.

"He isn't the monster you make him out to be," I tell her as I pick up my purse.

She doesn't seem convinced. "He hurt you."

"It was a misunderstanding."

"I don't trust him!"

I shrug. "You don't have to. You have to trust me." I glance around and notice we're making a scene. "I know you mean well, but causing problems between us isn't going to help. You need to get over this, for me."

"But what if—"

"No, Harper. You need to stop. I'm telling you, he isn't like that."

She searches my face for any sign of a lie. She finally nods. "You're right, I'm sorry, Addie. Stay."

My phone buzzes, I silence it. I'll deal with Kohen in a minute. "No, I'm going to call it a night. I'll talk to you soon."

She moves to stand but I'm already leaving. I'm still pissed at her for texting him. She could have gone about it in a different way. Instead, she tried to make Kohen angry, and succeeded if the continuous calls from him are any indication. I don't even have time to open the bar door before my phone rings again. I know I shouldn't answer, but I do. I'd rather deal with him when we're not face-to-face.

"I want you to leave now! I'm already on my way back to my place."

He isn't yelling, but he's mad. Yup, answering was the wrong decision.

"Look, it was a joke. Calm down or I'm not going to see you." I wait for a reply, but he doesn't respond. "I'm already getting in a cab. Meet me at my place so we can talk."

He hangs up. I throw my phone into my purse as I rave down a taxi. Once I'm settled in the backseat I rest my head against the cold glass. If he's not at my place when I get home, then fine, we can talk tomorrow. I'm not showing up at his apartment to explain myself. When the cab pulls up to our building, I see him leaning against the brick. I shouldn't have worried, Kohen isn't the type to run away from his problems.

I grasp the straps of my purse, and square my shoulders. He doesn't speak as he leads me into the elevator. It isn't until we're safely locked in my apartment that he breaks the silence.

"I don't want you seeing Harper anymore. She's a bad influence," he says calmly as he hangs up my coat.

"You honestly think you have a right to dictate who I spend time with?"

When he turns around, he's looking at me as if I'm stupid. "She hit someone. She didn't care if she seriously hurt them, she just took off. Now she's trying to start a fight between us. Why would you want to hang out with someone like that?"

My hands quiver while I listen to him. On a small level, I know he's right, but he's wrong about her.

"It was a fender bender, and she was terrified. It doesn't justify what she did, but I can't let one mistake ruin a friendship. If I did, would you seriously be standing here in front of me?"

His jaw tightens as his teeth grind together. I pissed him off. Good. He has no right choosing my friends.

"I just want what's best for you, Addie. I don't want you spending time with someone who could leave an accident without another thought. She's a bad person."

My throat feels dry because in any other circumstance, he would be right. But not now, not about Harper. She's a good person, an even better friend.

"She's my friend."

He leads us to my bedroom. Silently, we get ready for bed together. I assume the fight is over, but as I climb into bed, I'm proven wrong.

"Just be safe when you're around her. I don't trust her."

I don't say anything. There's no point in arguing with him. He joins me under the covers after setting the alarm on his phone. He pulls my head onto his chest and trails his fingers through my hair. As much as I want to, I can't make my body relax into him. Instead I kiss him so he doesn't think anything is wrong and face the other way.

His hand travels up and down my back. My body is at war with itself. It wants to rebel against his touch but it can't. He brings me comfort. Slowly, at the speed of ice thawing, I melt into his touch.

CHAPTER TWENTY-ONE

I add another five pounds to the weight machine. My arms shake from overuse, but I keep pushing, needing to focus on my muscles burning rather than the problems in my life. Kohen. Harper. Jax. In that order.

"Keep going like that, you're going to hurt yourself, sis."

"This is not my first time working out . . . I know, shocker."

My brother stops what he's doing and comes over to me. I'm too mad to care that I snapped at him. I ignore him as best as I can while finishing my current rep.

"For an athlete, you're pretty stupid."

I glare at my brother and move on to the next task. Squats. I hate squats. I sigh as I head towards the free-weight section of Logan's home gym. Clutching the bar, I notice that my brother switched the weight for me. This simple task makes my anger die down a little, but I'm still ready to kill someone. Sadly, my brother witnesses my anger firsthand. I guess we know whose the better sibling.

"I'm not an athlete," I remind him.

"Could have fooled me."

"Whatever," I say under my breath.

I know that Logan doesn't deserve me acting like this, I really do, I just can't help it. I'm so upset and I don't know how to handle it. I even did a few laps in the pool earlier, but that didn't help. If anything, swimming made it worse, because it reminded me of the root of the problem. Jax. It's always Jax.

My brother does pull-ups while he watches me. He would always do this when we were younger. He would let me lash out at him and then wait for me to spill my guts. That's not gonna happen this time. It can't. I'm mad because of his best friend. Not something that I think he will want to hear. Plus I can handle it on my own. I'm not a child.

I snap, "What!"

"Nothing. You ready to tell me what's wrong?"

I don't say anything. I turn my head in search of a distraction. I need to keep busy. I need to find something to take my mind off everything. I still can't believe swimming didn't work. That would always do the trick. It's because of Jax. He just had to be the one to get me back in the water. What a jerk!

I spot what I need in the corner. I eye my brother. He looks from me to the bag.

"We're wrapping your hands, first."

I mock salute him as I follow him over to the punching bag area in his private gym. I give Logan my hands so that he can wrap them up for me. When I'm all ready to go, my brother stands behind the bag and holds it for me.

"Lets see what you got, Ali."

I plant my legs how he's shown me and punch the bag as hard as I can. I'm not focused so the punch doesn't do as much damage as it should have. I hit the bag again, this time with the result that I want. I picture the one person that I need to hit right now.

I see Jax's stupid face instead of the black punching bag. I hit harder and harder each time. I imagine breaking his nose, hearing the crunch when my fist connects with it. I then land a kick. I can almost hear the grunt he would make if I landed it into his side instead of this bag.

"Adalynn, enough!" Logan snaps loudly enough to break through the mental image of me kicking Jax's avoiding ass. I finally texted him back and he never responded! He texted me first!

I bend down at the waist, throw the gloves to the floor, and start peeling off the wraps. When my hands are finally free, I drop my head into my hands and scream. I let out the loudest, most frustrated scream anyone has ever heard. It would have done Hadley proud. I crumble to the floor on my knees, exhausted.

Logan crouches next to me. He doesn't say anything, as he rubs my arm in a soothing manner while I let it all out. I scream for everything I lost, for my family, and for me. It's then that I realize that I'm not only mad at Jax. I'm mad at them, too. I'm mad at them for leaving me.

I'm mad at my parents and my sister. I'm mad that they're not here and I am. I'm pissed that I survived. I'm mad that I had to listen to them suffer for hours while I sat there helplessly, unable to do anything but listen to them die. I'm mad at the world for going on and not realizing they were suffering, that my family was dying.

My body trembles in silent sobs. No tears come out. I won't let them. Logan holds me tighter. Never saying anything, but saying everything in his embrace. I get myself under control after a while.

"Thanks."

"It's what I'm here for." He kisses the top of my head. "Ready to talk about it, sis?"

I used to be able to tell him everything, but I can't now. I want to, I really do, I just can't, not about this. I give him a small smile that doesn't feel right and shake my head.

"Okay then. Want me to guess?"

I narrow my eyes at him and get up. "I think our workout is done."

"Good idea." He hands me my water. "Now why don't you go work things out with Jax."

I spit water all over my brother while managing to choke at the same time. I was not expecting that. Logan smacks my back. I keep my back to him so he can't see my shocked face.

"Wh-what?" I squeak out when I can breathe again.

Logan doesn't answer me at first. I cross my hands over my chest and glare at my brother. I know what he's doing. He's stalling to lure a reaction out of me. I won't fall for it. That's what I tell myself, anyways.

"Well? Don't shut up now. I know you are dying to tell me whatever is on your mind!"

"Huh?" he asks, playing dumb.

I'm not falling for it. Not this time. If he wants to say something, he will. I dry the sweat off with a towel then fling it at his head. He ducks, used to my tantrums.

"Okay, well, I'm out of here."

"Bye."

I stop and turn to him. Mouth dropped to the floor. I was not expecting that. I know I should leave. I don't want to know what he has to say about Jax. I don't want to fall for his stupid trap. I do anyways.

"Spit it out already, Logan."

"Spit what out?"

"Don't be a child. If you have something to say, say it."

"Are you ready to talk yet?" he asks.

"Are you?" I challenge.

Together we sit on the floor against his panoramic window, with the view of the city behind us. I rest my head on his arm again and watch how the sun rays reflect off the punching bag's metal chain.

"Something happened between you and Jax, didn't it?" he asks.

I hold my breath. I don't want to lie to my brother, but I can't find the words to tell the truth. Saying yes would be so easy if things were different between Jax and I, but sadly things aren't. My brother takes my silence as an answer.

"You want to talk about it?"

I sigh heavily. "There's nothing to talk about because nothing happened."

I'm not sure what my brother knows, but I do know that I won't be giving any information out. Not about this.

"So you two just avoid each other for fun then?"

"I don't . . . He's the . . . Never mind, it doesn't matter. We're not avoiding each other."

Logan studies me, which of course makes me uncomfortable. He frowns. I would cut off my left arm to read his mind. I feel like my brother just tested me on something and I want to know if I passed.

"That's impressive."

"What?" I ask, regretting it as soon as the word slips out of my mouth.

"That you say 'it doesn't matter' like you believe it. Too bad I know something is going on between you two and you're not okay with it."

"We had a fight. We got over it. We're not avoiding each other, we just haven't been in the same room." He avoids being anywhere I am and doesn't respond to my texts or calls.

"You two aren't talking, and you haven't hung out in I don't even know how long. Clearly you guys aren't over it, Addie."

I don't bother objecting. There's no point. Jax and I aren't friends. That isn't going to change. I've given him every chance in the world and he still avoids me. It sucks, but I've accepted it.

"He misses you."

I laugh. "Right!" Sarcasm laces my voice.

"Even if he won't admit it, he misses your friendship. Ever since you guys had your falling out months ago, he's been different . . . lost almost."

I desperately want his words to be true, but sadly they're not. If they were, then Jax and I would have been able to get back to normal. We haven't and it's not from a lack of trying on my part, either.

"We were never that close," I say, even though Logan won't believe me. I don't even believe myself. "If he's lost, it's not because of me. I'm just his best friend's little sister. I've never been his friend."

I hate how small my voice gets. That is what I fear most with Jax. That he puts up with me for Logan's sake.

Logan gives me the-don't-be-stupid look. "You two have been friends since childhood."

"No, you two have been friends since childhood. I was the little girl that you let tag along."

Logan stands. I take his offered hand.

"You are as much of his friend as I am. He needs you in his life, Addie, and I know you need him, too." He gazes out at the city before he continues. "You two have been friends for so long. You shouldn't throw that away over something stupid."

"He told you why we got in a fight?"

"No, he didn't have to. Whatever you guys fought over is stupid if you two aren't talking. So swallow your pride and talk to him again."

I let out my breath. I thought Jax told Logan about everything that happened between us. I'm relieved he didn't. I don't think my brother would take it badly, but I'm sure he doesn't want to know that his best friend slept with his sister.

"It's not pride. He just doesn't want to fix things."

"He's your friend. Just call him."

"I'll think about it, that's the best I can offer."

"I'll take it. Now that it's settled, let's talk about more important matters," Logan says as he leads me to his living room.

Whenever I enter this room, one picture always steals my attention. The picture of our parents on their wedding day. They smile at each other, and in that one moment, the photographer captured the love my parents had for each other. It steals my breath away each and every time. I force myself to glance away and make my feet carry me to the grey couch.

"There's more important matters than Jax and I making up? No!" I grab my chest dramatically.

Logan shakes his head at me, but I know he thinks I'm funny. It's hard not to, I'm hilarious.

"The fundraiser tomorrow."

"Oh."

I don't know what to say. I know it's for a great cause. It raises money for foster care. My dad would be happy that we've kept it going, I just hate the looks I get from everyone there. I feel like I'm in that dream everyone has. The one when you show up to school naked and everyone points and laughs. Instead of being naked, I'm the girl who survived. Instead of laughing, everyone gives me sad smiles like they understand. They don't.

"So will you?" Logan asks.

"What?"

"You really need to stop spacing out."

"Yeah, yeah, yeah, I'm working on it." I roll my eyes at him. "Seriously, what's up?"

Logan runs his hand through his buzzed cut brown hair. A gesture I know well. He's stalling.

"I think you should give the speech this year." He raises his hands up to stop me from interrupting him. "Before you say no and give me every excuse in the book, just think about it."

"Besides the fact that everyone expects the speech to be by you, not me, I still can't do it."

"Why?"

"You do realize the event is tomorrow, right?" I ask him.

"Your point?"

"My point? Oh, I don't know, maybe that I can't write it, practice and in less than twenty-four hours give a speech that I'm not prepared for."

"Okay, I'll give you that, but what's the real reason."

Logan crosses his arms over his chest. I know he won't drop this until I tell him why I can't. My brother is stubborn.

"I just can't give the speech. I can't deal with the stares from everyone."

"You can do whatever you set your mind to, Addie. And they're not staring at you in the way you think. They're staring at you because they can't believe that after everything you've been through, you're still here. It's something we all admire, especially me."

"With a speech like that, I can't wait to hear what you come up with tomorrow."

"So you won't do it?"

I shake my head because that's my usual answer. Each year Logan asks me and each year I say no. I know he thinks this year will be different. So far this year *has* been different. I've been different. But it's still not the year for me to stand up in front of everyone and give a speech.

"Not this year, but maybe next year."

Logan thinks about it for a second. "Fine, are you actually going to stay and listen this year?"

"I promise I'll try. You know I hate these things."

"No you don't, you love them."

"No, I love the pretty dresses. That's about it. Everyone there is always so fake."

"And you wouldn't know anything about being fake in public?"

I shrug. We both know it's true. I'm not the only one guilty of that though, everyone does it. Nobody wants the world to really see them. They want that one special person to break down the walls and accept them as they are. The only difference between everyone and me is that I don't want anyone to break down my walls. I like them in their place. Without them I would be naked. Nobody has the patience to break down my walls anyway. With me, every brick that falls, another one comes back in its place.

After eating an early dinner with my brother, I return home. I still can't get over that my awkwardness with Jax is obvious to everyone. I thought we were doing a pretty good job acting like everything was fine. Guess I was wrong.

I know my brother is right. I should talk to Jax. I've avoided him as much as he's avoided me.

I tell myself this is the last chance that I will give Jaxon Chandler. That's what I want to believe anyway, but deep down I know it's bullshit. I will always give Jax every chance in the world. I wish I had more backbone when it comes to him. Maybe one day. Yeah, one day I'll be able to say enough is enough and mean it. Too bad today isn't that day. I send him a quick text, needing to get this over with before I lose my nerve.

Me: We need to talk . . . Can you come over?

Jax: Sure. What time

Not gonna lie, his quick response surprises me. Not as much as him agreeing to come over. I bite my lip, wondering if I should freshen up. I quickly shake that idea out of my head. I do not want to look good for him. I'm glad that I just got done working out with Logan. I'm definitely not looking my best right now.

Me: Now?

Jax: See you soon.

I sit on my couch and wait. A little less than twenty minutes later, I hear him outside my apartment. I wonder where Jax was because I know he wasn't at his place. It's not possible to get to each other's building in this short amount of time.

That's not the point. I need to focus on the matter at hand.

Calm and collected. No yelling. Just stay calm and collected. Calm and collected, should be easy right? From my spot on the couch I can hear him sliding a key into the lock. I stand, all previous thoughts vanish. I march over to the foyer.

"WHAT THE FUCK!" I say a little too loudly before he can even close the door.

"Hello to you too, Ads," Jax says.

Fucking cocky bastard. He walks past me to my living room and sits on the coffee table. I despise arrogant Jax. At least it's easier to stay mad at him when he's like this.

"Why do you still have a key? Never mind, it doesn't matter," I say when I realize that I never demanded it back. I blame The God for distracting me.

"What matters then?" he asks before I can finish my train of thought.

I point my finger at his face.

"Me?"

He slides his keys in his back pocket. If he didn't ask "me" in a way that sadly makes my skin ignite, I would be a little nicer. Too bad Jax is the only man who can make me want to kill him and kiss him at the same time. I am not going to be nice or easy on him. I may be losing it here, but I can't find the will to care.

I'm pissed. I'm outraged that he's hardly talked to me and just swaggers in here. Who does he think he is? I bite my lip in a way that I think is sexy and look him up and down. I watch him closely to see if I can ignite a reaction. All I want is a small one. Bingo! He swallows loudly and his pupils dilate. It's the exact reaction I wanted.

"Yes you," I say in a voice that I hope is seductive.

I know I'm playing with fire here.

"Me?" he asks again, this time his voice a little deeper.

I smile on the inside knowing that I got to him. I narrow my eyes at him. I'm done playing with fire now.

"Who do you think you are, Jaxon? We've barely talked in months. MONTHS! And you just walk in here like you own the place. Who does that?"

"Ads, calm down, it hasn't been months we just saw each other at brunch. Besides, I don't see why you're making such a big deal. I've always had a key and I've always used it. I don't see why you would care now."

"Calm down? Really, you want to tell me to calm down?" I shove him back a little. "A key to someone's place is either from a friend or a lover. You aren't my friend and you are definitely not my lover, Jaxon!"

I know I should calm down, but now that he's here, all sense has left. Did I even have any to begin with? *Not when he's near.*

"Talking is having a conversation. Not nodding your head and saying hello and goodbye to each other," I say with venom dripping out of my voice.

"We are friends! I don't know what else you want from me, Ads!"

"We're friends, really? Okay, Jax, since we're such close friends, what's been going on in my life? Because I have no idea what's going on in yours! That's not a friendship and you know it!"

Jax's silence angers me more.

"Exactly! You have no idea what's been going on in my life because you haven't been here! You've been avoiding me for no reason! We slept together again, get over it! I have!"

Jax opens his mouth to say something, but I talk over him.

"You want to know what I want? I want you, Jax! I want you in my life! I don't care about the stupid bullshit that happened between us. It was nothing and didn't mean anything to either one of us. I just want my friend back."

"Ads, I haven't been avoiding you. I've been busy with work and you know that we are friends."

"It's Adalynn! Not Ads!"

"Come on, Ads, don't be like this."

Jax makes an attempt to embrace me, but I step out of reach. His arms fall to his side. I will not let him walk all over me like this again. I deserve the truth.

"It's Adalynn, not Ads! We're not friends so you don't get to have a nickname for me!"

I shake my head when he moves closer. I know if he touches me, I will lose it. I will collapse into his arms and breathe in his heavenly scent. I can't do that. It can't be that easy, not this time.

"If you're going to lie to me than at least come up with a better excuse!" I shout.

"It is the truth! I'm not lying to you. I'VE BEEN FUCKING BUSY! Get over yourself, ADALYNN!" he shouts right back at me.

"You're not lying? Go fuck yourself, Jaxon! If you have enough time to take a shit you have enough time to send me a text to ask how my day was or respond to one of the millions texts I've sent you!"

Jax takes two long strides and gets in my face. I can feel the anger rolling off him. I know he's about to lose that self-control he's so big on. Good!

"Don't try to act all high and mighty, Adalynn! Talking is a two-way street! You can't blame this all on me!"

"You're right, talking is a two-way street. Too bad you NEVER PICK UP YOUR PHONE! It's kind of hard to carry a conversation with myself."

Jax pulls out his phone. "Really, when have you called me lately? I don't see any missed calls from you, princess!"

Do not kill him. Do not kill him.

"Don't you dare try to turn this around on me!"

I yank his phone out of his hand and throw it at the wall. His phone shatters. Well I guess I'm going to have to settle for killing his phone.

"Are you crazy!" he shouts at me at the same time I shout, "I have called you! I've given you every chance in the world, Jax. Repeatedly I've tried to fix us, but I can't do it alone!"

"Maybe I don't want to fix this, ever thought of that?"

I'm too shocked to say anything. I clutch my stomach as if he punched me. His verbal abuse isn't over, he's just getting started.

"The world doesn't revolve around you, Adalynn!"

"I know that!" I snap.

"Then act like it!" he shouts back.

"What are you talking about? "

"Nothing, forget it."

"No, I will not forget it! If you have something to tell me, then say it!"

Jax rubs his hand over his face. His voice is once again calm when he speaks. "Let's just talk later, we both said things we didn't mean."

"We've said things we didn't mean? Really? What did I say that I didn't mean? We're not friends since YOU have been avoiding me. I want our friendship back. There's nothing I said that I didn't mean, Jax. So please don't put words in my mouth."

"I can't do this anymore."

"What the hell are you talking about?" I ask.

He doesn't say anything at first. He gazes around the room. I know before he opens his mouth that it isn't good since he can't even look at me.

"Us," Jax finally says.

"There is no us, that's the point! You've been avoiding me so what exactly can't you do anymore, Jax?"

As soon as the words leave my mouth, I know. It's that little voice in my head that I was always afraid of. I know without a doubt what he's about to say, yet it doesn't make it easier.

"There isn't a friendship to fix because we've never been friends."

My throat is suddenly dry, but I manage to choke out. "We're not friends?"

"No."

The absoluteness in his voice helps me find mine again, "No? What am I to you?"

"Logan's little sister."

I land a perfect punch to Jax's jaw. I'm so pissed I don't feel pain in my hand. I'm not even satisfied when Jax stumbles back and I see the split lip. He rubs his jaw and wipes the blood on his shirt.

"All those nights I let you in my bed." I yell, remembering our time together. "I gave you my virginity! None of that means anything to you?" I shove him as hard as I can. "After EVERYTHING, that's all I am to you! Logan's sister! After all those times I patched you up when your dad beat the shit out of you, all I am is Logan's little sister!"

I desperately want to hurt him how he's hurt me. My body is screaming at me to hit him again, but it won't change anything.

"You're pathetic! Get out!"

"Ads, let me explain," he pleads.

I push him towards the door. He needs to leave now. I don't want him to see me crumble. I can't let him know how much he's killing me. I bite my lip to keep from begging him to not do this to us. The pain helps center me.

I square my shoulders as I turn to face the one man that has the power to destroy me. And he just did.

"My name is Adalynn. Don't call me, Ads again. We're not friends, we have never been friends. I'm just your best friend's little sister, remember?"

"I'm so—"

My eyes blaze as I dare him to utter another work. I don't need his apology. I need him to leave.

"Don't. I don't want to hear you're sorry. You came over and said what you had to say, now you can leave." I snap my hand out for my key. "Give me my key, please."

He had said the one thing that I always feared he would say. He must sense that he might get hit again because he sighs and reaches into his back pocket. My hand trembles as he sets my key into my hand. It feels like this, us, is finally over.

Jax spins on his heel and walks to the door. He hesitates before opening it. He rests his forehead on the door and sighs. After a few seconds, he finally opens it. I let out the breath I was holding. I was sure he was going to say something. Wishful thinking.

I can't believe he's just going to walk out. After everything, this is how it ends between us? I grip the door handle and glare at the one person I thought would always be here for me. I never thought he wouldn't be in my life. I thought I could always count on him. I guess I was wrong.

"I'm glad I can finally see the person you really are. I could never be friends with someone like you. So thank you, thank you for *finally* showing me your true colors." I slam the door in his face.

I slide to the floor. The rage from seconds ago starts to disappear. I feel empty without it, without Jax in my life. I rock back and forth, hitting my back against the door. Slamming myself into the hard wood. I wince from the pain and stop.

Closing my eyes, I replay everything that happened. I wish I could have done something different, said something different, to have Jax still in my life. It's unimaginable pain hearing the one thing you always feared was true. No matter how I look at the situation, I don't think I could have said or done something to change his mind.

I finally get off the floor and pick up Jax's broken phone. I throw it away. I know he'll have his assistant replace the phone in the morning. I wouldn't want to go buy a new one and pretend everything was normal between us.

My phone chimes in my bedroom. When I pick it up, I see that it's Kohen.

Kohen: Hope I don't wake you, but I wanted to tell you as soon as possible. I can't make it tomorrow. I have an emergency surgery I can't get out of. I already called your brother so he knows that I won't be taking you and he can pick you up instead.

I slap my hand over my face. I forgot about the fundraiser. I'll have to face Jax tomorrow. I will have to pretend like he didn't just shatter my heart. I won't let him see how devastated I am.

I need to get myself under control if I have any hope of confronting Jax tomorrow. I close my eyes in an attempt to calm down. Immediately I see Jax's face when he told me I'm just Logan's little sister. My mind won't stop replaying it.

I don't even care that Kohen can't make it. I would've been a terrible date because the only thing occupying my mind would be to stay calm and not show Jax how I feel. Kohen does not deserve the back burner.

Tomorrow night is going to be hell.

CHAPTER TWENTY-TWO

"Are you two ready yet?" Connor asks from the other side of my bedroom door.

Whose bright idea was it to have all of us meet at my apartment? I muse as I stand in front of my full length mirror.

Harper is in my in-suite bathroom, putting on her dress. I stare at my reflection. I seem different. My eyes are hard, they match my now impenetrable heart. For some reason when I smile, it's obvious that it's fake. It takes a few tries to get it right. When I'm finally able convert into the happy person that I need to be tonight, I uncap the new lipstick Harper bought me. It's a perfect blend of a soft rosy color that makes my lips pop, but not too dramatic.

"Wow! I don't think Jax will think of you as anyone's little sister, wearing that."

"Thanks, I think?"

"It's a compliment. One look at you and he will be fighting to get your attention."

"Why would he have to fight?" I ask her, studying my stunning Lela Rose gown in the mirror.

It's a fire engine red, off-the-shoulders fitted gown with a slight ruffled train. It shows all my curves. I feel beautiful in this gown. It gives me the confidence I will need seeing Jax tonight.

"Because every man in the room is going to want every second you're willing to give them. Besides, you're going to make that asshole work for it. I mean really work for it, I don't care how hot he looks, either!"

I mock salute her. "Yes, General."

"Oh, I almost forgot." Harper rummages into her clutch. "I saw this the other day and just had to get it. It's the perfect accessory to complete the look."

"Thank you! It's beautiful!"

Harper helps me clasp the diamond choker around my neck. It's perfect! Three rubies gleam in the center and diamonds encrust the rest of the choker. No wonder she insisted on me styling my hair in an up-do. She really does think of everything.

Her dress is bold enough to forgo accessories. I wish I was comfortable enough to wear something like her Jason Wu black see-through lace dress. It's a form-fitting number as well, with a tulle train. Only Harper can pull off a dress that is both provocative and conservative at the same time.

"You're welcome. Ready to go?"

"Yeah, I guess," I mumble.

"Hey, none of that. I won't have you being sad because your lover is an idiot."

"How many times do I have to tell you Jax isn't my lover?"

Harper shrugs. "As many times until you prove me wrong."

I groan. There really isn't getting through to her. She's stubborn. No wonder why we get along so well. I can't wait to tell her my surprise. I instantly cheer up.

"You look sexy, you know this, right?"

"All thanks to you!"

"No, that," I say, sweeping my hand in the direction of her body, "is all you."

"Thanks . . . wait why are you in such a good mood? I know you don't swing the other way so it can't just be my good looks."

I slap my hand over my face as if I just remembered something. "I forgot, I have a surprise for you, too!"

Her entire face lights up. It almost makes me not want to go through with it. Almost is the key word. I link our arms and drag her towards my bedroom door.

"You're not my date for tonight." I turn the knob.

"Huh? I thought Kohen wasn't coming?"

I open it and let her through first. Connor leans against the wall opposite my bedroom door.

"Oh no, he's still not coming, but you were never my date."

Harper stops and turns her head in my direction. "Who is then?"

"I am," Connor says huskily.

"Sure you are, stud," Harper says with a small laugh.

Harper yanks my arm, stopping my plan to flee to my brother. Logan stands in the middle of the hallway with his arms crossed over his chest. When I say grab, I mean she latches onto my arm with surprising force, not allowing me to move another step without her.

"What?" I ask in an innocent voice.

We all stare at Harper. It's easy to see the wheels turning in her head as she realizes I'm not joking. Her sweet smile makes me a little nervous. It's the kind that you just know means trouble. I'm hoping trouble for Connor and not me, but I don't think I'm that lucky. I know the fiery little redhead will have her payback on me soon enough. Letting go of my arm, Harper saunters over to Conner and wraps her hand around his offered arm.

"Well, let's go already, my date and I hate being late," Harper says as she leads the way to my front door.

"I'll hate whatever you tell me to hate," Connor responds as he opens the door.

She gives him a patient smile, one that a mother uses on a misbehaving child. "With lines like that, I wonder how I'm the lucky lady on your arm instead of your usual whores."

Logan manages to cover his chuckle with a cough. I don't even attempt to hide my laugh which earns me a glare from Connor.

"Oh, don't look at me like that! It was funny!" I say.

"And true, man," Logan pipes in.

Connor rides the elevator in silence as the rest of us make fun of him. Luckily Connor doesn't take anything personally, he even lets out a few chuckles as we leave the building and approach the waiting limo. I'm surprised the driver doesn't open the door for us; instead it opens from the inside. *Shoot me now.*

I want to imagine that my brother is bringing a date, but I know it's not a woman. The frown that Harper sends my way confirms what I'm thinking. Once I get inside the limo, I will have to face him. I'm not ready. I thought I would see him at the fundraiser. I was prepared for that. Almost.

I scan the area in hope that there might be another limo coming just for me. It isn't a real possibility, but fantasy is better than reality right now. I bend and pretend to fix my heel. *Not a big deal. Nonchalant. Easy.* Too bad pretending to fix a heel without an actual problem can't take all night.

Without anything else to stall the inevitable, I straighten up, and walk the last steps to the black limo.

"I'm guessing by the fantastic performance of stalling, you never talked to Jax?" Logan asks quietly in my ear.

"I don't know what you're talking about."

Harper gets in first, followed by Connor. I look longingly at my apartment building before climbing in. Logan sits next to me and gives me a small grin.

I keep my eyes away from the far end of the limo, where Jax is. Instead, I pin my attention on the amazing view outside. I pretend that it is the most fascinating thing in the world, that I've never seen the lights of the city before. I tilt my head as we drive through Times Square. Tourists roam the streets, bundled up on this cold New York night. I block out everything. I no longer care that I can feel Jax in here with me. All I care about is the world outside this window. That's the world I want to be in right now.

"Hello, earth to Adalynn," Connor says slowly enough that he almost spells out hello.

I nod in his direction so he know's I'm listening, but I refuse to turn away from the window. I will have to look away eventually, but eventually isn't this exact moment.

I sigh before facing Connor. He and Harper occupy the bench across from the bar, which takes up the entire right side of the limo. Jax is the furthest away from me, he's in the seat in front of the privacy mirror, but it seems as if he's the closest because he's directly across from me. I can feel his eyes on me, waiting for me to acknowledge him. I don't.

"Champagne?" Connor asks.

I swing my hand out, more than ready to get drunk. "Oh god yes!"

"Cheers!" Harper says too brightly.

Her presence makes the pain a little better. I'm glad that she is here, and is telling me she's here for me without words.

"To an amazing night!" Logan says beside me.

Connor slides his arm around Harper's shoulders. "An unforgettable night!"

I tune out her response and face the window again. As the limo makes a left turn onto an almost empty street, I wish that I was anywhere else. With autumn near, the leaves are changing into vibrant reds and oranges. Soon they will fall and people will forget how beautiful the leaves used to be as they collect dirt on the sidewalk.

"It's a good thing there isn't any water for Harper to throw at your ugly mug." Jax speaks up for the first time.

I can't help the way my entire body tenses from the sound of his voice. I ignore the rest of the conversation and sink back into myself again. I replay every moment I've ever had with Jax. The first time I saw him when I was seven, I knew that I would never be the same. I see every secret smile, every caress, every time he would sneak into my bedroom window when we were teenagers, and all the times he would fly back from NYU to visit me for the weekend.

The only thing that I'm aware of is when Harper switches my empty champagne flute for a full one. I'm so thankful for her right now. It isn't until my brother taps my shoulder that I turn away from the window.

"I take it from the tension between you two that you're still fighting," he murmurs.

He doesn't ask. He states it, as if there isn't any other option. Not able to lie to my brother, I shrug in answer.

"The talk didn't go well then?"

"It went . . ." I struggle for words, but can't find any. I decide to go with the truth. "It went as well as it could have I guess."

"Ah I see," Logan whispers.

I glance around to make sure nobody is paying any attention to us. Wrong move. My eyes seek out Jax's. He's nodding at something Connor said, but his gaze lands on mine. I'm ashamed to admit it takes a few seconds to shake myself out of a trance and glance away.

"You both are going to ruin a lifelong friendship from being afraid."

"You think you know everything but you don't, Logan. It's not that easy. Things with Jax are complicated. Nothing is as simple as you think it is."

I pause to collect myself. I need to stay calm and remember that we are not alone in the limo. Everyone else in here does not need to be part of this conversation. Heck, I don't even want to be part of this conversation.

I continue, "Afraid? Afraid of what? Come on, you seem to have all the answers so tell me. What exactly am I afraid of?"

"You're afraid of life. You're afraid of living because they didn't. You're scared of anything and everything that you can do that they can't."

I focus on life outside the window again. I remain silent. I see the city without actually seeing anything.

"You're wrong," I murmur so quietly I don't think he hears me.

"Prove it then."

My annoying brother taps my shoulder again. Tap . . . tap . . . tap . . . Over and over. Turning my head away from the window I glare at my irritating older brother. My anger rises. He's wrong. I've done everything I can to keep Jax in my life. Before I can help myself, words leave my mouth.

"I get that you care since it puts you in an awkward situation, but you should be having this conversation with him, not me! I already tried. He doesn't want to be my friend. He's only in my life because of you! So sorry, but you're not always right, Logan!"

I'm met with utter silence. It takes a second too long to realize that I raised my voice. Crap! I tell myself not to look at him but it seems like I can't control myself tonight. Jax's mouth hangs open a little, from shock I'm sure, and his green eyes won't meet mine. Logan says something, but I ignore him. As I watch Jax, it hits me that if I had any hopes of repairing our friendship, that is long gone. He can't even face me. I wish that I could disappear into the leather seats. We stop moving. Perfect timing, at least I can flee and get lost in the crowd. I follow my brother out of the limo.

After about an hour of mingling with Logan, I'm finally able to make a break for it. Well, for the table since I can't leave, at least not yet. Seizing a flute of champagne from the passing waiter, I pretend I don't see Harper waving me over. I need to sit down. I need a breather from everyone. I haven't seen Jax since we first arrived. Not that I've been searching for him or anything. He's probably with some slut in a closet. I don't care.

Weaving around people, I finally locate our table. I exhale when I see that nobody is sitting down yet. Useless conversations are the last thing I want to do. I have had enough of the fake bullshit people say to each other at these events to last a lifetime. I remind myself not to run as I move towards our table.

Pulling out my chair, I eye the exit. I want to get out of here. I need air. I force myself to stay seated instead of leaving. My hands shake slightly. I want to say it's from the lack of food and the champagne, but that would be a lie. My trembling hands and need to escape is because of Jax. Always him.

I can't stop rehashing last night in my head. It's been almost twenty-four hours, but it feels like only seconds have passed since he told me I'm Logan's little sister. Of course the man that I've been in love with forever wouldn't think of me as anything else except for his best friend's little sister. I thought he saw me, really saw me.

Little sister . . . little sister . . . His words are on a wheel that won't stop tormenting me. Just thinking about all those times that I let him in, when I closed out everyone else, makes me bite my lip to keep from screaming in anger.

"Are you okay?" Connor asks me.

I look to my right as he and Harper sit down. I'm not even surprised that I didn't notice them come over here. I've been lost in my head. I've been replaying every encounter I've had with Jax and attempting to view it from his perspective.

"Peachy."

"Sounds like it," Harper says.

"Oh shut up. Shouldn't you be out dancing? This one," I say, pointing to Connor, "is a fantastic dancer. His parents made him take dance classes when he was younger."

Connor makes a show of getting up and offering Harper his hand. "Please do me the honor of this dance, Ms. Harrison. Besides, I think Addie is going to be like this for the rest of the night."

"And please tell me, Connor, what am I being like?"

"Let's just say that you're not in the best of moods right now," Harper chimes in.

"That's a nice way of saying something else . . . I think the word you're looking for is bitchy," he says as he nabs Harper's hand and steers her away.

I run my finger over the table. Tracing invisible designs. Only Connor can call me a bitch and get away with it. That's because I know he never really means it. Connor treats me like the little sister that he's never had, but has always wanted.

Lights are once again strung to the ceiling. I stare at the twinkling ceiling for a long time. When I finally glance away, I try to find my brother. He's talking to someone by the stage in the middle of the room. I think she's the event planner. A waiter comes by and replaces my empty champagne flute. I move it away and sip the water in front of me instead.

My eyes land on Connor and Harper. I watch him swing her around the dance floor for two songs. She's clearly had lessons, too. They draw eyes to themselves with their effortless moves on the floor. When the third song begins, I trace patterns on the table again. With each second that goes by, I continue to think about last night.

Nothing, not even a ballroom full of people, can take my mind off last night. I wish that he told me how he felt in the beginning instead of waiting until now. He's led me on for too many years, playing games. I hate that I have to remind myself to be upset with him. I have every right to be, but at the same time I don't think I do. Yes, he's led me on, but I shouldn't fault him for not having feelings for me.

I need closure. I don't want to reflect on last night and always wonder what if. What if I said something different? What if I told him it's okay? What if I actually stopped loving him? Maybe then we could be friends. I already live my life full of "what ifs" with the accident; I don't want to do that for us, too.

Someone taps my shoulder. I open my mouth to tell Connor that I'm fine, but words fail me because it's not Connor. I know without looking over my shoulder that Jax is standing behind me. It could be from that simple touch that leaves my skin burning from his finger, or from his nearness that makes my skin break out in goosebumps. Either way, I know he's directly behind me.

"Dance with me, Ads."

Before I know what's happening, Jax pulls out my chair and helps me out of my seat. I stare at him, really stare at him, wondering what he's doing. I haven't seen him all night. I was sure he was with some leggy blonde without a brain. None of this makes sense, especially after last night.

"Why?" I ask quietly.

"Because you look too beautiful to be sitting here by yourself."

I'm too stunned to say anything. I'm barely able to make my feet function. If Jax didn't have such a strong grasp on my hand, I'm sure I would fall to the ground. When he says things like that, it's hard to believe that he just sees me as Logan's little sister. Good thing the replay of last night is still going on in my head to remind me.

I need to pull away, to save myself from more hurt. I tell myself to take my hand off his shoulder, but I can't. I'd rather hate myself later for giving into yet another game, and be around him one more time. I shut off my mind and bask in the warmth radiating off Jax's body. I let him lead me through a dance. Of course it has to be Coldplay. The stupid pianist mocks me by playing *Sparks*.

This is my all time favorite song by them because we would listen to it in my room late at night. And now I'm dancing to it with Jax. He drags me closer to him like he used to do in my bedroom. I close my eyes and pretend that we're dancing in my room again.

"I've never danced with anyone else to this song," he says, unaware that he's splintering my heart even more.

"Me either," I say without opening my eyes.

I know once I do, I will be lost. I will be trapped by his green ones. *Logan's little sister.* I can't let myself over-think this. He saw me sitting alone and sad. Of course he would ask me to dance. Jax isn't the bad guy he wants everyone to believe he is. Which is why it makes pulling away from him that much harder.

"I'm sorry. I can't. I know what you're doing. Thanks, but I can't."

I hurry away without another word. It's nice that Jax is being the better person, that he took time out of his night to dance with the sad little girl. I can't dance with him and pretend I feel nothing for him, that what he said last night is okay. It's not.

I jog off the dance floor. I rest against a pillar and squeeze my eyes shut. I won't be able to survive sitting next to Jax through dinner. It's too soon. I don't hear him come up behind me, but I know without turning around, it's him pressing against my back.

"Ads, please talk to me," he pleads into my ear.

"Please just go away."

I don't even open my eyes. I don't need to. He has been forever imprinted in my mind.

"Please just give me a chance to explain." He spins me around and grips my face in both hands. "Please just talk to me."

When I open my eyes, his sadness takes my breath away. I know this is my chance. This is the only chance I will get to not have "what ifs." This is the moment for closure.

I tear his hands away from my face. Him being this close is hard enough, I don't need him touching me. I lose every train of thought when he touches me. This is my time to tell him everything and walk away.

"You may think we were never friends, but we were, Jax. You were my best friend for sixteen years. You have always been here for me whenever I needed you." I press my fingertips over his mouth when he tries to speak. "You let me in once. I loved that I was the person you turned to when you needed someone. All I have ever wanted was to be here for you, to be the person you lean on."

I take a deep breath. I love the smell of Jax. If it was possible I would bottle up his woodsy scent.

"I may be just Logan's little sister to you, but you have always been my best friend. You saved me. When nobody else was there, you were. That's why it kills me to know that I'm nothing to you."

All the hurt from all his games rushes forward. I tell myself to leave, to not say another word, but I need to tell him everything. It's time for me to give up on any hope of us being together.

"All you had to do was tell me the truth eight years ago. But you didn't. Instead you chose to lead me on, knowing exactly how I felt about you. I've loved you for as long as I can remember, Jax!"

"I'm so sorry, Ads. I didn't mean it the way it came out last night."

"Please stop."

"No. You need to hear this. I need you in my life."

I refuse to believe his lies. "You don't want me in your life. If you did, you would have considered my feelings a long time ago. Instead you made me doubt being with Kohen. I could have lost someone who loves me because of you! But I'm nothing but your best friend's little sister to you."

"Even without Logan in my life, I would still need you in mine."

"We both know that's not true." I gather the folds of my dress as I prepare to leave. "You don't have to worry about Logan. He will never know. When we are forced to see one another because of my brother, we will be civil towards each other, but nothing more, never again."

Before Jax can say anything else, I walk away. I need to get out of here. I thought telling him how I felt would make me feel better. It doesn't. I head towards the stage hoping that my brother is still there. I smile in relief when I see him reviewing his speech.

"Addie, are you okay?" Logan asks when I reach him.

"No. Actually I feel like crap. I need to leave. I'm sorry."

I wish I was stronger. I wish that I could stay, pretend that I didn't just lose a piece of myself when I stormed away from Jax. I wish that I could stay for my brother. At least to hear his speech, but I can't. I'm at my breaking point and I need to leave before I lose it in front of all these people. Logan must see that I'm about to crumble because he nods and drapes his arm over my shoulder.

"Okay. I'll see you out."

"No, don't, you have the speech." I paint the smile on my face that I'm used to wearing. "I'll be fine, promise."

Logan eyes me, searching for signs that I'm lying. I hold my smile firmly in place. I don't let anything slip. I don't let the fact my world is collapsing around me show through the facade. I watch the band play as Logan searches for something or someone in the crowd. I focus on the woman playing the piano instead of the pain raging inside me.

"I'm going to kill him," Logan snaps.

I grab onto his arm to stop him. "Don't. I'm fine. This isn't his fault."

"You're hurt because of Jax. It's his fault."

I wish I could confess everything my brother, but I can't. I can't risk him losing a lifelong friend because of me. I couldn't do that to him.

"Please, Logan, just leave it be. Trust me, Jax and I are fine."

"Then why do you need to leave?"

I chew on my lip, hating that I'm going to tell him an even bigger lie. It's worth it. He can't ruin his friendships because my heart got broken. That wouldn't be fair to him.

"This," I wave my hand around the ballroom, "is too much . . . I can't handle it." I look away, hating how his face crumbles with sadness.

His baby blues lock on mine, as if trying to read something I'm not saying. Fake smile firmly in place, I kiss him on the cheek, and flee.

Even though I am nowhere near Jax, his scent lingers on my skin from his hot breath on my neck. I need to get out of here.

On the ride back to my apartment building, I replay what Jax said to me, how he held me tonight. Suddenly I'm standing in front of my apartment. I let out a long breath at the front door. If go in, I know I'll remember everything that Jax said to me the other night.

I vaguely remember unlocking my apartment. I slide to the floor. Kicking off my heels, I stare at my once blank wall. My new pictures make the place feel more like home and less like a hotel with my clothes hanging in the closet.

Studying the picture of my parents, I long for things to be different. I want to go back to a time that was simple, where my biggest problem was finishing my chores. I look at the photos of Hadley and Logan next. They're reenacting the final dance from *Dirty Dancing*. These are the pictures that remind me of home. These are the pictures that take me away to a better place.

I can remember capturing each of these moments in time. I remember how happy everyone was. How happy I was. I remember my family. I let these memories carry me away, back to a home with a family, and far from the reality where my family is dead.

The loud banging on my front door breaks through my reprieve. I slowly get up. I can't believe Logan left the fundraiser. Logan is usually pretty good at giving me space when I need it.

Jax's voice stops me in my tracks as I near the door. "Ads, I know you're in there. Let me in."

I stand immobile. I said everything I had to say to him. There's nothing left. I have no idea why he's here. *Please just go away.* Maybe he'll think I'm asleep and leave. Fat chance with him banging on my door. I can't sleep through noise that loud, and usually I can sleep through anything.

"Ads, open the door. Let me tell you what I should have told you last night. Please let me in, Ads."

I have every intention of staying right where I am and waiting him out. I tell myself that I'm just moving closer to the door to see make sure it's locked.

It's locked.

I knew it was. If I leave the door locked, he will just leave. We can eventually move past this. If I don't open this door, everything will return to normal.

I unlock the door.

CHAPTER TWENTY-THREE

I don't even have time to open the door all of the way before Jax rushes into the apartment. He has me pinned against the wall, kissing me in a matter of seconds. Stunned, all I manage to do is tilt my head back, welcoming his assault.

Jax makes the sexiest growl in the back of his throat before deepening the kiss. Winding my fingers into his soft, silky hair, I pull him closer to me, moaning when he bends down slightly and grabs the back of my thighs, lifting me up. Automatically my legs wrap around his waist.

Getting lost in the only man that I've ever loved, I don't even realize that Jax has moved us from the wall until he opens my bedroom door. Before I know it, he's laying me on my bed. Breaking off the kiss, he hovers over me, using his elbows to keep his weight from crushing me, and stares into my eyes with such longing.

The second that his lips leave mine, sense breaks through the heavy haze of lust. What am I doing? I can't do this with him. I can't keep playing this stupid hot and cold game. I will never be able to move on if I keep letting him take control, letting him take what he wants from me, and then leaving me behind without a second thought. I deserve better than this. I deserve better than what Jax can give.

He must have felt me stiffen because he hangs his head and sighs. The desperate expression he's shooting my way makes it hard to not embrace him. *We're not friends. You're my best friend's little sister.* The words play over and over again in my head. My eyes blaze as I push him off me and jump off my bed.

"I'm just Logan's little sister, remember?"

He swallows loudly, seeming pained. Good. I want to hurt him, just like he hurt me.

"Why are you here?" I don't even give him a chance to open his mouth before I lash out at him. "We're not friends, Jaxon. Remember? YOU," I point to him, "made that fucking clear the other night. I'm nothing to you. I'm just Logan's little sister. I have NEVER been anything but Logan's little sister to you!"

I shove him away when he reaches for my hand.

"No, don't you dare fucking touch me, Jax! You led me on, played with my feelings! You made me fall in love with you just to walk away! I can't believe I was so fucking stupid to believe that you actually cared about me."

I push past him, but he grips my waist, stopping me. I'm at war with myself; my body wants to stop fighting with Jax and to give in, but my stupid mind won't shut up. It keeps chanting over and over again, *you're my best friend's little sister.* I am so confused right now. I thought he said everything he had to say to me last night. I thought we were over for good.

Then it hits me.

Suddenly I have a new fear.

"No . . . No . . . Please . . . No." I take a deep breath. "This is pity," I whisper.

"What?" Jax asks

"You're here out of pity! That's it! You're here out of fucking pity!"

I can tell with each word that Jax is getting madder and madder. I keep talking, watching as he paces in front of me. His fists clench tightly. He opens his mouth and snaps it shut so hard I'm surprised he doesn't break any of his teeth. He's seething. Good. I am, too.

"OH MY GOD! I mean so little to you that you would come over here for a pity fuck! Fuck you Jax! I—" Jax covers my mouth with his hand.

"Stop talking now, Adalynn." He's vibrating with fury.

The only reason why I don't bite his hand and yell at him is because I've never seen him so angry before in my life. His body is shaking. If it was anyone else, like Kohen, I would be scared, but I know that I'm safe. Jax would never physically hurt me. He only hurts me by breaking down my walls and shattering my heart.

"You honestly think I'm here out of pity? You don't think too highly of me."

"Have you ever given me a reason to think differently?" I talk louder, blocking out his pretty words. "Why are you here?"

"You," he says simply as if that's answer enough.

"What does that even mean?"

"I'm always here because of you, Adalynn."

"What?"

I swear he's speaking another language. I have no idea what he's trying to say right now. His eyes never stray from me as he takes the few steps to me. I didn't even realize that I was stepping away from him.

Slowly, he softly trails his fingertips over my arm. The anger has gone. In it's place is determination.

"I'm here because of you, Ads. We're not friends. We've never been friends."

I open my mouth to tell him that he's already made that clear, but he places a finger over my mouth.

"Let me finish, okay? You've talked enough crap for the both of us lately. Now it's my turn."

I nod.

"We've always been more. My sweet Adalynn. I'm yours. I will always be yours. There isn't anyone else. There never has been. It's always been you. Just you."

I'm too stunned to speak. I have too many emotions coursing through me. I want to believe everything he's saying, I really do. I want to forget about the other night. Sadly, I can't. It's just words. It's always pretty words with him.

"I don't believe you," I say at last.

"I know, but I won't stop until you do. I'm done acting like I don't want you, you're the most important thing in the world to me, Ads. You're the only person who knows the real me, everything that I've been through, and you never look at me differently."

"Then why have you been pushing me away every chance you get?"

"Because I thought you deserved better than me. I never meant to play games with you, it was a way for me to be close to you and not risk losing our friendship."

I refuse to fall for his tricks again. "What changed?"

He hauls me closer until we're a breath apart.

"I did. I realized that sharing secret smiles, and a stolen kiss every once in awhile isn't enough for me anymore. I'm done pushing you away, Ads. I can't act like everything is fine when it isn't. We can't just be friends. I want more. I've always wanted more. I want to be everything to you, like you're everything to me. You're my sun, my moon. Ever since we were kids, you lit up my world."

My legs give out, Jax catches me. He's always here, catching me, being my knight in shining armor. I can't believe he's here, saying all these wonderful things. I don't know how many nights I've dreamed of him saying exactly this. I would fall into his arms and tell him I love him. That's what I want to do now, but I can't. If I tell him what I desperately want to say, I will be giving him all of me. I have one more small piece of my heart to hand out, and if I give it to him, he can break me. I know I won't be strong enough to survive.

"I'm sorry. God, you have no idea how sorry I am, but I can't, Jaxon. I would have given everything to hear you tell me all of this, but it doesn't matter anymore."

I'm ready to hammer in the nail and finally end this, but I stop short when I gaze into his eyes. His face falls. He knows I'm about to shut him out forever. Placing both hands on each side of his face, I softly kiss his lips.

Jax grabs me roughly and kisses me with everything that he has. He puts everything into the kiss. It's the kind of kiss that inspire poets. I kiss him back just as desperately. This is our last kiss. I know it, he knows it.

I'm not prepared for anything else.

Jax ends it, but doesn't move away from me. A final goodbye maybe?

"I love you," Jax says with such force I know he means it.

I drop all of my guards. I thought I was prepared to send him away, to give up on him. I wasn't. He's told me he loved me before, but I thought that was in the past. He's done nothing but prove me right over the years by pushing me away every chance he got. Now, he's standing in front of me, telling me the one thing I thought was unattainable, is within reach. He's within reach, if I'm willing to give him another chance.

His face pales. He just told me he loves me and I haven't said anything. I'm standing here like a mute. I love him. I know I love him. I've always loved him, but for some reason I can't find the words. He moves away from me, to leave I assume. I open my mouth to stop him, but nothing comes out. The moment his green eyes penetrate mine, I know he isn't giving up.

"I know you don't believe me. I've given you every reason not to, but I do. I love you, Adalynn. Loving you is as easy as breathing. I can't not love you. I've tried, I really have, but I can't. Please, give me a chance to prove my love."

My hands tremble at my sides. It's now or never. I can remain silent and he will walk away. Before I can convince myself to remain silent, my lips are moving. "I love you, too."

He sucks in a ragged breath. Okay, so that wasn't the reaction I was hoping for.

"You love me?" he asks quietly.

"No, the person behind you."

Jax bites his lower lip in that sexy way of his. Bending his head so his mouth touches my ear he whispers, "Say it again."

Barely able to fight the urge to repeat, *no the person behind you*, I give in and tell the man that I love what he wants to hear and a little more.

"I love you, Jaxon. Only you. I love that you're the one constant in my life. Despite everything we've put each other through, I love you. It's always just been you, Jax. It will only ever be you."

Jax leans his forehead against mine. Jax moves in to kiss me but I pull away slightly. There's still one more thing that needs to be settled before I give myself over to him . . . Well two things actually.

"There is nothing more I want to do right now than get lost with you all night, but I need you to clear up something for me."

"Anything, Ads, all you have to do is ask."

"Are you done shutting me out? Are you done running? If you're not, tell me now, because there will be no coming back to me if you leave me again. I can't play this game with you anymore, Jax. So if you don't think that you'll be able to stay, leave now."

"There is nothing that can push me away from you. Not even your brother. I'm so sorry for betraying your trust repeatedly. I love you, Ads. I want to be with you, nobody else. No more running, I promise."

I start to smile, but I realize that he didn't answer my first question.

"What about shutting me out? Are you gonna open up to me?"

"Are you going to open up to me?" he challenges.

I bite my lip, stalling. I would be easy to say yes, but I can't. I don't know how. I've kept everyone at arm's length for so long. It seems impossible to let even Jax in. What if I let him in and I lose him?

"I don't know how," I finally admit.

"How about we try together? It won't be easy for me to open up, either, even if it is to you."

"Perfect."

"You're perfect," he says huskily.

I roll my eyes. I've never known Jax to be this cheesy, but it sounds adorable coming out of his mouth. I'm pretty sure anything sounds adorable coming out of his mouth. All thoughts quickly float away as Jax presses his lips to mine. He traces my bottom lip with his tongue, seeking entrance. I open my mouth and moan when his tongue does devilish things to me. It's one of the soul-breaking kisses. A kiss that ruins you. I know I will never have a kiss this intense with anyone else. It's impossible.

I tangle my fingers into his hair. Jax bends and picks me up bridal style and carries me to my bed, as if I weigh nothing. Laying me down gently onto it, Jax breaks the kiss and memorizes my face by tracing my eyebrows, my cheeks, my lips, even my nose.

"I love you."

"I love you, too." I pull his face closer to me so that our lips are almost touching. "Now show me how much I mean to you."

Jax gives me his famous grin before kissing my nose, my cheeks, my forehead, everywhere except for the one place I need him the most. I groan in annoyance when he kisses around my mouth, never touching my lips. He's doing this on purpose.

"Patience."

"I hate you." I breathe heavily.

"I love you too, Ads," Jax says with delight in his voice.

Kissing a trail from my jaw line to my neck, he licks my earlobe, and makes me moan embarrassing loud. He moves back down to my collarbone, switching from wet kisses to licks, to my personal favorite, bites. God, the things this man can do with his mouth should be illegal.

It's because he has had a lot of practice. I hate that stupid voice in my head right now. I try to block it out, to stay here with Jax. It doesn't matter, they were all before me. I won't be one of those women that fault a man for their past. It's in the past. *How far in the past? A month? A week? A day?* Fuck. Without any conscious thought, I drag him up.

"What's wr—"

"I only had sex with you," I blurt out.

His fingers brush the hair out of my face. "I know."

"How?" I ask even though I don't want to hear the answer.

He's now frowning, which worries me. I know whatever he's about to say, I'm not going to like. He moves our linked hands so they're stretched over my head.

"Don't get mad. I mean it. I don't want to have to restrain you."

I nod.

"The only guy you were with in high school was me. I assumed you didn't get close enough to anyone after the accident. Plus I keep close tabs on you, as well as your brother when it comes to your dating life. I was getting a little nervous with Kohen being in the picture, but when we all hang out, you two never give off that intimate vibe."

"Wait. How do you know I didn't sleep with someone in high school after you left me? You were on the other side of the country."

Jax looks everywhere but at me. Whatever it is, isn't going to be good.

"Jax . . ." I prompt.

"I didn't leave you. I was at NYU. I was going to transfer to be closer to you and . . . "

"And what?"

A broken expression crosses over his face that I recognize all too well. Regret.

"And then we stopped talking. The accident happened and then you moved here."

There's something about the way he averts his gaze that makes me think he's lying. It doesn't make sense. There's no reason why he would lie to me. *But isn't there?*

"Is there something you're keeping from me?" I murmur.

For some reason I know there is, and I don't think I'm ready for the truth. A memory pushes it's way to the forefront of my mind, but I can't grasp it. There's a blockage, and something within me knows it's too painful to remember. I have my answer when he finally opens his eyes. They're filled with unshed tears. I shake my head. I've never seen him like this, so whatever it is, I don't want to know.

"Make me forget," I whisper before bringing his lips to mine.

It takes a second of coaxing until he responds. When his tongue caresses mine, my thoughts evaporate. The only thing left is Jax. I focus on the way my breathing matches his, the way his hand trembles slightly as he touches my bare shoulder. He's everything, taking away any painful memories. He deepens the kiss. Tangling one hand into my hair, he slowly runs his other hand down my body. I bite his lower lip while moaning into his mouth.

That seems to light a fire in him because he growls right before he bites my collarbone. Hard enough that I yelp in surprise, but gentle enough that it still feels incredible. I wither underneath him, trying to satisfy a need only Jax can fill.

"Jax."

"Patience," he says with that sexy bedroom voice of his that I love.

"Please," I plead as I unbutton his shirt.

Jax looks down at me with dark, hungry eyes before taking off his jacket and dress shirt. My eyes greedily soak up his naked chest while my hands roam his chiseled abs.

"This dress will look better on the floor." Jax whispers into my ear before nibbling on my ear lobe, making me moan in response.

The next second he's gone. Before I can protest, he drags me to him. He holds his hand out to me. I take it and he helps me stand. Before placing my hands on his shoulders, he trails kisses from my palm all the way up to my collarbone. He repeats this process with my other arm, making my skin break out in goosebumps.

This man is going to be the death of me.

He turns me around so that my back is to him. Then Jax starts rubbing my shoulder blades while kissing the back of my neck. I've never been this turned on in my life. Every part of my skin that he has touched is on fire.

Ever so slowly, Jax unzips my dress, pressing his lips to the skin he exposes. He's dragging this on, teasing me. I just want to be with him again. It's been too long.

"Please," I beg.

Jax ignores my pleas and finishes unzipping my dress while I squirm, trying to relieve the tension that has been building up. I'm surprised when my dress doesn't fall to the ground immediately. OH MY GOD. He's trying to kill me. I attempt to step away from him so that I can yank off my dress, but Jax's grip on me is unbreakable.

"I finally have you again, Ads. I'm going to take my sweet time with you. I'm going to etch your entire body with my tongue."

I'm about to say something in response, but every thought leaves my mind when I feel his tongue lick from the bottom of my spine to my neck. Holy-hotness.

"Let me learn your body again," he says as he lets my dress sail to the floor.

Jax sucks in a breath as if he's in pain. I'm glad that I decided on the barely-there panties. The brazilian briefs are a tease since they're see-through.

Tugging me into him so my naked body presses against his, Jax trails his hands up my thighs, over my waist, and grazes my breast. I can't take this foreplay any longer. When Jax kneads my shoulders, I shift my head slightly and bite on his hand before facing him.

"My turn," I say in a sultry voice that surprises me.

I hungrily kiss Jax while my nails rake down his torso. I use one hand to squeeze his tight ass that I will have my teeth in by the end of the night and use my other hand to tease him. Using just the tips of my fingers, I trace a light path over the hard ridge in his pants, making him growl in the back of his throat.

Pay-back is a bitch.

Smiling wickedly at him, I place small open-mouthed kisses over his heart. When I reach his nipple, I gently bite it before moving to the next one. I take my sweet time with him, enjoying when his muscles contract underneath me. Slowly, making my way down his torso I use the same agonizing pattern Jax used with me; switching from licking, to biting, and wet kisses. Unbuttoning his pants, I drop to my knees in front of him, enjoying the shocked expression on his face.

"Ads," Jax pleads with his bedroom voice.

"Patience," I mock before I slide his zipper open with my teeth, a trick I practiced on him years ago.

Running my greedy hands over his abs, I grab ahold of his briefs and pants and pull them down. I had every intention of making him beg. I really did. I wanted him begging me to touch him. I wanted him to feel just a fraction of how I felt when he was undressing me.

My hands dig into his hips and drag him closer to my mouth. He brushes my hair out of my face and tilts my chin up. He's watching me in awe with pitch black eyes. I blow out the breath I didn't know I was holding, making Jax groan in response. I lick the crease in the middle of the head. Licking up the first drop, I open my mouth to take him but Jax roughly grabs me by the shoulders and throws me onto my bed.

"What—"

Jax's aggressive kiss swallows my protest. Jax is done with me acting like I'm in control. I don't know why, but a man in control in the bedroom is the sexiest thing in the world.

Jax slows down the kiss until his lips barely brush against mine. I arch up to him, trying to get closer. Jax and I stare at each other without speaking, but saying everything without words. Reaching up with one hand, I caress his face. He leans into my hand before sweeping the softest kiss on the inside of my palm.

"I want you, Jax."

"You have me," he says with a grin.

I open my mouth to tell him in detail exactly how I want to have him, but Jax catches my lips with his teeth. I moan into his mouth, wrap my legs around his waist and dig my nails into his shoulders when he grinds into me, making me wetter than I thought was possible. My panties are soaked.

"Oh God," I moan again when I feel him rub against my core.

"You're so wet," he growls right before nipping my neck.

Needing release, I reach in between our sweat-covered bodies and trace the head of his dick with my thumb. I'm rewarded with Jax cursing before he sucks on my earlobe. I shut off my mind and let my body take over.

I lick Jax's chest at the same time that I slide off my panties. Jax sits up on his knees and finishes removing them. Each time his fingers touch my skin, I moan. I need him. I need him like I need air to breathe. When my panties are finally off, Jax brings them to his nose and inhales deeply.

Holy-hotness that was hot. I bite my lip thinking about where else I want him to put his face. Jax licks his way up my body making me a withering, moaning mess. His lips are everywhere. Tenderly he cups my breasts before bending down and tracing my nipples with his tongue. I moan while arching into his mouth. I rake my nails down his back as he moves lower and lower. He dips his tongue in my belly button. Without pause, he moves even lower. It's been too long since I've had him touch me like this.

"Watch me," he says huskily.

I use my elbows to support me as I watch him spread my pussy with his fingers. My breathing becomes nonexistent as he bends his head down to my throbbing clit. He licks the length of my pussy before sucking hard on my clit. I scream in pleasure as my heart kicks into overdrive.

He rolls my clit in his mouth. I pull at the sheets, desperate for my release. His fingers trace the outside of my pussy, spreading the juices, before he penetrates me with two fingers.

"You're so tight." He blows on my clit and I moan my response.

He stretches me with his fingers, preparing me for his impressive size. The pleasure is building fast, I'm almost there. I yank at his hair, stopping him. His eyes meet mine and his lips glisten from my juices. I moan at the sight.

"I need you," I whisper.

He inserts a third finger. I grind into his hand, loving the feeling of him. I hold back my release. I don't want to cum without him.

"Please . . . Jax . . . Now . . . Please."

He licks me one more time, long and thorough, before his tongue is tracing a pattern up my body. I grab his cock and rub him against my clit. His eyes close as he moans.

"Condom," he says as he pulls away.

I nod. I watch his every move as he reaches for his discarded pants on the floor. I tell myself not to think about why he has one in his pocket. I'm glad he's prepared. If he didn't have one, I would think that he's gone bareback with someone else. I don't know why, but I think that would kill me more than knowing he was expecting to sleep with someone else tonight. All thoughts leave as he hovers over me, condom in place.

I close the distance by nibbling his lips with my teeth. He growls, and in the next second, the head of his cock is at my opening. I suck in a breath as he slowly fills me. I can feel every delightful inch of him. I squeeze his biceps, digging my nails into them. He holds still, like he did the first time, allowing me to readjust to his size. I nod, letting him know to move.

"I can't hold back anymore," he says through gritted teeth as he slides almost completely out of me.

I wrap my legs around his waist, deepening the position. "Then don't."

He slides slowly back in, letting me feel every delectable inch of him. He pulls out with the same ease. Staring into my eyes, he bends down and traces my lips with his tongue. I suck it into my mouth. He growls and slams into me.

"OH GOD . . . YES . . . JAX . . ." I scream as he starts to pound in and out of me.

He slides almost all the way out again and slams back in. He does this over and over again. I'm dripping wet. I can feel my juices running down my thighs and onto my blanket.

I lick his ear and suck on the earlobe. "Please," I moan into his ear.

All teasing is gone. He finally fucks me like we both need him to. I run my hands down his chest, digging my nails into his back. He's fucking me so hard my body moves up the bed. He grabs onto my hips to hold me in place. My vision blurs as pleasure takes over.

"Eyes on me." He lifts one of my legs and hooks it over his shoulder.

They snap open, obeying his command. I wasn't even aware they were closed. Everything seems to slow down but speed up at the same time. When I think I can't take anymore, one of his hands shifts to my clit. His thumb moves in circles, giving me the most pleasure I've ever felt. My legs quiver.

Sweat drips off his forehead and onto my chest. I feel it trail down the center of my breast and towards my belly button. My skin is on fire. I'm so close . . . I need more. He's close, too. He's biting his lip in concentration.

He licks my throat. "Cum," he commands in his sexy bedroom voice.

I shake my head. I need more.

He rubs my clit faster. I gasp at the new sensations. I stare into his eyes and see all the love he has for me. He's looking at me as if I'm the most beautiful thing he's ever seen.

"I love you," he says.

I shatter around him. Everything disappears except for the feeling of him inside of me. I'm barely aware of him following me into his own climax. I blink a few times, trying to clear the spots from my vision. His breathing ragged, he lays on top of me. We lay like this for a few minutes until he slowly slides out of me. I wince. Without a word, he walks naked into my in-suite bathroom. I hear the water running. Before I know it, he's returned with a washcloth in hand.

I watch him as he cleans me up. Once he's done, he tosses the washcloth onto the floor and climbs into bed. He pulls my naked body to him. I turn so that my head is on his chest.

"I've missed you," I whisper.

"I've been right here, love, I could never leave you."

"Jax—"

"I know I just . . . I just couldn't watch you with him. I hate when he touches you. It makes me sick just to watch you two hold hands." He says it barely loud enough for me to hear.

I watch his face the entire time. Seeing how truthful his words are hurts me. I hate that I hurt him and led on Kohen at the same time. I don't believe I did anything wrong because I was done with Jax. I gave up on him when he walked away from me the last time. I was moving on, it just sucks that Kohen is going to get hurt because of me.

"It's only ever been you," I murmur into his chest.

CHAPTER TWENTY-FOUR

Feeling something soft and warm on the back of my leg, I move it away quickly, kicking whatever was trying to wake me up.

"FUCK!" Jax shouts at the same time I realize that the something I kicked was a someone and it was a face.

"Crap! I'm sorry," I say while trying not to laugh.

"You think this is funny?"

My laugher dies when I see him covering a part of his face, holding his bleeding nose. I jump out of bed and run toward the bathroom to get him toilet paper, but my sheet has other plans. I fall flat on my face before I even know that I'm falling.

"Ouch," I say into the hardwood floor that I once thought was beautiful, but I now have the urge to cover up with carpet.

Before I can even lift my head, Jax is kneeling next to me, helping me up. Seeing a few drops of blood trickle to the floor, I look up to find Jax's already squeezing his nostrils together. It then dawns on me that it isn't his blood on my floor, it's mine. Awesome. I can't help it, I start laughing. The unladylike laughing too. Snorts and all. Which of course makes it harder for Jax to keep pressure on my nose, too.

"You really find this funny?"

"How can you not find this funny? We both have bloody noses. What are the chances?"

"I learned a long time ago to expect the unexpected when it comes to you. I do have to give it to you, though, I really didn't think you would kick me in the face when I tried waking you up."

I move my hand up to my face and he lets go of my nose. I lead us both to the bathroom for some much needed toilet paper.

"You should have known that you would have gotten hurt trying to wake me up. I'm not known for being the easiest to wake up."

"That's the understatement of the year."

I glare at him as I inspect my nose in the mirror, happy to see that it has already stopped bleeding. I have a nice bruise already forming at the bridge of my nose. If only this was a horrible nightmare. The pain in my face reminds me this is reality. Which of course makes me laugh again. Jax gives me his best stern look, but by the way he's biting the inside of his cheek, I can tell he's trying not to laugh, too.

"Come . . . on . . . this . . . is . . . funny," I eventually wheeze out when I'm able to somewhat control myself.

"I can't believe that you keep hitting my face. That's the only thing I have going for me. How do you expect me to get ladies now?" Jax says with a chuckle.

I narrow my eyes at him. I know he's joking but I can't help feel a little stab of jealousy when he mentions wanting to look good for the ladies. Mentally brushing it off, I turn my shower on.

"Hey, what's wrong?" Jax asks.

"Nothing, I just want to clean up." I notice the blood on my hands and a few drops on my breast, my very naked breast.

It's then that I realize that I'm wearing nothing. Holy shit, I can't believe that I'm prancing around naked, and worse, that I fell flat on my face. The sexiest woman award definitely won't be showing up at my doorstep anytime soon.

"Hey, don't do that."

"Huh?" I ask, confused.

Jax takes a step closer, I take a step back.

"Don't pretend with me. I know you, Ads, you can't fool me."

Another step forward. Another step back. I can't help thinking about Jax being a lion stalking his prey. I love that he's stalking me.

"I don't know what you're talking about." I breathe heavily when Jax has me pushed up against the wall.

He smiles wickedly before raising my arms that I unconsciously crossed to cover myself. He looks at me with such longing that my legs feel like Jell-O. When Jax licks his lower lip, I bite mine to keep from moaning. How embarrassing, he hasn't done anything to me and I'm already fighting the urge to moan. Everything he does is so fucking hot it's hard not to get turned on and lose myself in him.

"Tell me what's wrong."

"Huh?" I repeat like a complete moron.

I have no idea what we are talking about as all I can focus on is that mouth. God, I want to feel his mouth on me again. I arch up to him, silently inviting him to have his way with me. Pinning my hands above my head, he bends and skims his tongue on my throat.

"Are you jealous?" he whispers into my ear.

"Huh?" I ask again.

I really need to find other words. I just can't seem to find a reason to care as Jax's tongue traces my collarbone to my shoulder.

"You got upset about my joke. I'm sorry, love, I shouldn't have said that, but you need to know that you have nothing to be jealous about. You're it for me, Ads. There's nobody else."

"Oh," I say, finally understanding what he means.

"Yeah, oh. Don't pretend that you're fine when you're not. We can only work if we don't shut the other one out. I want us—"

I jump up and wrap my legs around his waist, shutting him up. Jax kneads my ass in both hands and kisses me long and hard. I'm so consumed by the kiss that I haven't even realized that we're in the shower until I feel the hot water prickle my back.

Jax pushes me against the wall and the different temperatures from the hot water beating down on both of us and the cold tile turns me on even more. He presses into me so that his body is holding me up against the wall. I bite my lip when his hand plays with the inside of my thigh. He bites down on my neck at the same time he inserts a finger in my wet pussy.

"OH . . . GOD . . .." I pant breathlessly.

"I can't wait to have you again," Jax says as he slowly takes his finger out of my pussy and brings it to his mouth and sucks hard.

"Please."

"Patience."

I can't believe that he just got me all hot and ready, just to stop. I might actually kill him.

"That word isn't in my vocabulary." I grab ahold of his hard dick.

Jax's clenches his jaw when I run my fingertip over the head of his cock, and lick the pre-cum off my finger.

"You're going to kill me."

"You shouldn't start something that you have no intention of finishing."

He bends to kiss me again, but I quickly duck underneath his arm. As much as I want to finish what he started, I'm sore. Plus my mind is still reeling. I can't believe he's still here. I had a feeling when I woke up, he would be gone. I need a little space, time to clear my mind.

"What the—" Words fail him when he see's what I plan on doing.

I lean out of the shower and point at the bathroom door.

"You're kicking me out?" he asks in disbelief.

I can't believe that I'm kicking him out either.

"I need some time," I admit.

He brings my hand up to his mouth. I watch as he kisses the inside of each palm.

"I'll start breakfast," he says before kissing me deeply.

He trails his finger over my collarbone. Enjoying the fact that my body trembles under his touch. Most likely because I'm denying us both. Just one touch from him and my body is alive.

He's wearing that stupid gorgeous grin of his that I hate and secretly love at the same time. Jax kisses me again and I lick my suddenly dry lips. His pupils dilate, making his green eyes darker. I arch up to him, welcoming his lips.

"I'll have breakfast ready by the time you're out of the shower then." He plants a quick kiss to my cheek, missing my greedy lips.

I try to tear my eyes away from his sexy back. I really do try, just not that hard. His sexy muscles are practically calling my name. They want me to stare and watch them move with each step he takes. His muscles are made to be stared at. My eyes roam down his back to his even sexier ass. What I wouldn't give to sink my teeth in that tight ass, but I need to slow things down. As if reading my mind, Jax stops and turns his head, but keeps his tight ass in my view.

I don't even try to act like I'm not ogling him. There's really no point. I keep my gaze firmly on his ass. I can feel his eyes on me like I know he can feel mine on him. The only difference is that I'm looking at his tight ass in his soaking wet boxer briefs and his eyes are on my face. He's watching me check him out. And enjoying every second of it.

"Seriously, feel free to picture me when you're showering. When you run your soapy hands up and down your body, imagine it's my hands."

Concentrating on breathing is nearly impossible.

"Imagine it's my hands soaping up those perfect tits of yours. It's my hand that will be going in-between your thighs, nobody else."

Breathe in. Breathe out. Breathe in. Breathe out. That is the only thing I can concentrate on. Nothing else matters at the moment. Jax's words consume me, taking everything away, leaving only him and his sexy words.

I'm about to tell him that I don't want to imagine his hands again, I want it to actually be him in that shower with me. All thoughts leave me when he gives me a wink and strips out of his boxers. Who needs to remember to breathe when there's a naked God in their presence? Not me.

He winks before tossing them at me. Quick like a ninja, I catch them before they hit their target.

Without another word, he closes the bathroom door. I can't believe that he's walking around my place naked and I'm standing here in the shower. I want more than anything to follow him, but I desperately need to calm down. I need time to myself to grasp that we're together.

Holy crap, I'm with Jaxon Chandler. My mind can't even begin to process that. What will Logan think? I need to tell Kohen, too. I won't lie to him, I don't see the point. He deserves the truth. I just hope that I don't hurt him too badly.

Rinsing shampoo out of my hair, I try in vain to keep a neutral expression. I fail miserably. I'm finally with the one person that I have always wanted to be with, but never thought I could. It's almost too good to be true. *This will never work.*

No, I will be happy. I will only think of the positives. Nothing can bring me down today, not after last night, not after everything Jax told me. I want to be happy. I want to be happy with him.

With my little pep talk still fresh in my mind, I step out of the shower to quickly get dressed. I can't wait to get back to my man. Hmm. I like the sound of that. I hesitate, wondering what I should wear. I want to look good. The leggings in my hands don't seem like the right choice. I want to be comfy, though. I plan to just stay in all day with Jax, but I don't want to look boring. Should I dress a little sexier, or should I go casual? Ugh, this is stupid! I'm not one of those girls. Jax likes me for me, not for my fantastic fashion sense. I step into my leggings and grab a tank. I leave my hair down and let it dry naturally. There, done.

I use all my willpower to take my time and not sprint to Jax in the kitchen, reminding myself to walk with each step. I'm surprised that I don't smell anything cooking. Guess he's ordering in. Doesn't matter to me what we eat. My kitchen is empty. *Where is he?* He wasn't in the living room and I didn't hear him in the guest room.

"Jax?" I call out.

Nothing.

He left without saying anything. I knew it was too good to be true.

No, he wouldn't do that. He wouldn't just leave me. Calm down. He probably went to get food or for a change of clothes. Yeah, that's it. I tell myself there's a logical explanation over and over again.

Ten minutes later, I'm not any closer to convincing myself than I was the first time. Numbly, I walk over to my couch. I want to be one of those women that you read about, the strong ones who can face anything that gets thrown their way. Sadly I'm not, I'm just weak.

Another half hour goes by and still no sign of Jax. I search my place one more time to make sure that I didn't miss a note or anything that would tell me why he just left. Surprise surprise, I'm empty-handed. I glare at my phone, willing it to light up, telling me that Jax cares enough to text me. Five more minutes. Nothing.

Me: Where are you?

I set my phone down and wait. Then I wait some more. Another five minutes and no response. My temper spirals out of control. I'm pacing as I type the next message.

Me: Seriously, where are you?

Me: FYI, you shouldn't ignore someone you just confessed your love to.

I know I shouldn't worry, but something is wrong. I can feel it. Jax changed his mind. There's no other explanation of why he's not here and ignoring me. Not after last night. As much as I tell myself that he could be stuck in traffic or worse, hurt, I know that's not the case. He's not here because he doesn't want to be here.

He doesn't love me.

It was all words.

I won't be weak anymore, I won't be sad. I will be strong and I will get to the bottom of this. I can't believe he just fucking left without a word. If he wants to end this, then he can be a man and say it to my face. I won't let him walk all over me and ignore me.

The cab ride over to Jax's place is the longest and fastest drive of my life. The longest because I thought I would never arrive and the fastest because when I was getting out it felt like I just sat down. I know when I walk in there, this will be the end. Jax will end this before it even gets started. Again. I don't know how I'm able to make it up to his place, but somehow I do. I'm in the elevator. Once I go in there, he will shatter my heart all over again. Only this time he can't fix it with meaningless words.

Please, please don't be here. Don't open the door. Don't end this. I chant in my head as the doors slide open into his foyer.

When I hear his footsteps, I will myself to stand straight. I won't let him know that he's breaking me. The little sliver of hope that I was hanging onto, the "I'm just paranoid" and Jax just "got busy with work" or something, dies the second I spot him.

This is over.

He doesn't love me.

"Ads," Jax says my name painfully, as if just saying my name hurts him as much as seeing me.

"I just . . . I . . . " *Be strong, don't let him see you break.* "I just wanted you tell me to my face that we're over, that you don't love me."

I'm pretty impressed with myself that my voice doesn't falter, especially at the end. He will never know how much he's killing me. Before Jax has time to say anything else, I push past him and march into his living room. Bad idea. Even the air smells like him. I feel trapped in his place; no matter how far apart I am from Jax, I'm fully aware of him.

"Let me explain," he finally says.

"You're going to explain how you told me 'you love me, that I'm yours and you're mine' and how it was all lies? Or were you going to explain how you fucked me last night and now you're trying to get rid of me? Please explain, Jax, I'm dying to hear it."

Jax doesn't say anything. He won't even look at me. He won't deny anything. So I was right. Being right isn't all it's cracked up to be. More silence. Fine, he wants to play the quiet game. Good. I won't make this easy.

"Come on, Jax. I know you have a speech prepared. You are always thinking ahead so I know you have something planned. Did I fuck up your plan by showing up here and demanding answers? How can you leave without saying anything? After everything, this is how it ends?"

Each time I speak his body tenses; he acts as if my voice pains him.

"Answer me, you fucking asshole! You were the one that came to me! I was letting you go! Why did you even bother coming back?" I scream.

Silence.

I need to try and stay calm. Yelling won't get me anywhere. I glance around, trying to come up with something to say, when my eyes spot a picture on the couch. It's a picture of us taken two years ago at the beach. Logan made me go with them to Miami for a week. Jax forced me out of my lounge chair and into the water with him. I didn't even know somebody took our picture, splashing each other. I study the picture again, and that's when I see it.

"You do love me," I say, my gaze glued to the picture.

"N—"

"Don't lie to me. I know you love me. This isn't one-sided. You felt everything I felt last night!"

More silence.

"Just be honest with me for once in your life!" I stab him in the chest with my finger. "You love me," I repeat.

"Yes."

"But not enough to be with me."

He nods. The pain in his eyes makes me step back. I have no idea what to do. Jax loves me, I know he does. He won't do this, though. Nothing I say or do will convince him to give us a shot. He's given up and I don't know why. It doesn't make the pain any easier.

"Let me in, Jax, don't do this to us. I love you. We can work it out."

"There's nothing to work out, Ads. I love you, but this will never work."

All air leaves my lungs.

"Wh-why?" I stutter.

"Because I love you and want the best for you. I'm not the best. I will bring you down."

"You're not making any sense, Jax! I love you and you're what's best for me. You make me happy."

Jax takes a step away from me. That one step feels like a hundred.

"I wish that was true, but we both know it isn't. I'm not worthy of your love. I'll only bring you down! You were gone, Ads. This entire time you left! And you finally are coming back to us, but it's not because of me. It's because of *him*.

"He makes you happy. He's the one that has brought you back from the dead. I wish it was me, I wish I was enough for you, but I know I will never be enough. You deserve so much more than I can give you."

He utters "him" and "he" as if he can barely manage to speak the words. I wonder what he'll sound like if he actually says Kohen's name. I tell myself not to argue because he's right, he doesn't deserve me, but I can't. I have to try, he's the love of my life. I can't let him go without a fight. I just wish he could do the same thing.

"I want you! I want to be with you. You make me happy, nobody else can make me as happy as you do. I love you. I've always loved you."

Even after saying that, I know I'm speaking to myself. Jax doesn't hear me. He's made up his mind, and nothing will change it. We really are over.

"I'm sorry, Ads, I just can't. I love you, but I have to do what's best for you." Jax speaks as if this it is. This is the end.

"Shouldn't it be my decision? Shouldn't I get a say in 'who's good enough for me?' I'm a big girl, I know what I can handle. Can't you let me make this decision for myself?"

"You'll make the wrong choice. I won't let that happen."

"It's my choice to make!" I yell.

I'm pissed. I'm pissed that I didn't get a choice on who the paramedics rescued first. I don't get a choice now. Jax is making the choice without me. Like the paramedics did all those years ago.

"We're over?" I ask even though I know the answer.

"We never even began. I want you to be happy. I can't bring you down with me."

Screw this distance! I march up to him and embrace him as tight as I can. It takes a few seconds before Jax responds, hugging me back just as fiercely.

"You won't even listen to me, Jax! I love you. I'm living again because of me! I want to be happy again and you make me happy. Why can't you let me decide what I can and can't handle? I won't go back to that dark place, I can't. I won't survive it. I want to be with only you."

"We can't do this anymore, Adalynn." Jax presses a kiss to my head and walks away from me.

"Then why did you come over last night? I was letting you go!"

He studies the floor as if it is the most interesting thing in the world. Everything he's ever said to me is a lie. He may love me, but it isn't enough for him.

"Why did you make me love you all those years ago?"

Silence.

"I love you and you love me, isn't that enough?" I ask.

"It's not enough." Jax says regrettably.

I wait for him to say more, but he doesn't. He doesn't glance up from the ground as I move towards the elevator. When I reach it, I pause. I have to say more, I can't leave like this.

"If you do this, I won't come back. This will be it. I won't keep playing this game with you, Jax. If you let me walk out, I'll be walking out of your life. I can't be in your life knowing that we love each other and you won't do anything about it. I need time to myself to get over you. I need to move on."

His head snaps up and I think he's going to say something, but he doesn't. After a lifetime, he nods. I laugh. A dry lifeless laugh. After everything, this is how it ends? With a nod. Wow. I deserve more than that, I deserve more than Jax can ever give me.

"I was wrong, you don't love me. If you loved me like I love you, you would do everything in you power to keep me, but you're letting me walk out of here. That isn't love, Jax."

I storm out of Jax's place and out of his life without another word. Jax shattered my heart back there and didn't care. He didn't care enough to talk to me, he didn't care enough to stick around. I can't feel anything, I'm numb.

I know I should be huddled in a ball, crying hysterically. Instead I wait in the elevator, perfectly calm. Too calm. I'm not enough for him. How could I be? I'm broken. Broken to the point that I can't even feel anything when Jax turns my world upside down. The sweet little words we said to each other don't mean anything. I gave him all of me, but it wasn't enough. I should have known, this is Jaxon Chandler, of course I wasn't enough for him to take a risk on.

I decide to walk home. I wish I was in workout clothes so I could push myself and run the entire way. Nothing catches my eye, the entire trip home blurs. Everyone is on their way somewhere. To loved ones, I imagine. A city of millions and I'm alone. I did this, I isolated myself from the world.

After another block, I realize it's okay that I'm broken and not perfect. I'm not enough for Jax, but maybe I'll be enough for somebody else. That realization makes me stumble into the street. Luckily I catch myself.

I haven't been the person who envisions the future. I used to be, but six years ago I thought my future was taken from me. I was dead to the world. Now that I've broken through the surface and I'm finally learning how to breathe again, I had a pretty clear image of how my future would be. Jax. He is the only thing I planned on. Even with all the back and forth, I truly hoped we would have a future together.

Imagining my future with anyone else isn't possible. I've been drowning for so long. Jax has always been a constant in my life. I can't even imagine someone else in his place. Not even Kohen. That's what scares me.

I don't want to drown.

I don't want to rely on anyone else to save me.

I'm not enough. I'm not enough for Jax. I've lost him. Even though I repeat those words over and over again, they doesn't stick. It's like I can't really believe it, but at the same time I do.

By the time I reach my apartment complex, I'm dripping in sweat and I need to shower. Still I can't help changing into workout clothes to go run. I should feel something by now, my muscles should protest, but I can't even feel a slight burn. I'm numb.

Making my way to Central Park, I put *Alive* by Zedd on repeat. The fallen leaves crunch under my feet. I lose myself in his music and run. An hour later I'm barely able to stagger into my apartment. I'm still numb. I know my body is on fire from being pushed too hard, I just can't feel it. The worst is knowing I'm empty inside. I'm drowning again and I don't know if I'll ever reach the surface.

CHAPTER TWENTY-FIVE

Three days.

Three days of being numb.

Three days of going through the motions.

Three days is all it takes for me to realize that I need to stop acting. I'm not that person anymore. I've hung out with Harper during lunch, been texting Kohen, and I even had dinner last night with my brother, but it wasn't really me. The last three days I've been a ghost, a shell of a person.

Now I'm feeling everything.

I force myself to keep busy so that I can stop thinking about Jax. Work, excessively baking, and exercising are the only things that make the pain of losing him manageable. If I stop, I hear him telling me he loves me, I feel his hands caressing me, I can taste him. When I remember him, remember us, it takes everything in me to keep breathing, to pretend that everything is normal.

Now I'm choosing to forget him, to forget us.

I'm moving on.

I'm moving on to dinner with Kohen at eight. I glance at the clock to make sure I still have plenty of time. Crap! Five minutes. I'm not even close to ready. Time slips away from me lately.

I race to the bathroom to apply mascara and lipstick. I pin my hair back while I walk to my closet. After slipping into jeans, I opt for the first shirt I see. Black. To match my heart. I snatch a pair of my favorite Betsey Johnson booties when I hear a knock.

"Just a sec," I yell loudly enough for Kohen to hear me.

Clutching my purse, I saunter over to the floor length mirror. I look decent for only having five minutes to get ready. My cheeks are a little red from running around. I'm surprised how put together I appear. When I reach the door, I pause. I'll have to act like everything is fine. I can't let Kohen know I'm dying inside because of another man. I give myself a little pep talk before unlocking the door. I beam at Kohen. He's in a simple pair of jeans and a blue dress shirt.

"Hi!" I say too cheerfully.

"You take my breath away," he says in return.

I chew on my lip. I can't help but compare him to Jax. Which of course is unfair. I can't compare the two. They are two different people, of course they are going to have differences.

"Thanks. You're not hard to look at, either."

"These are for you." He extends a beautiful arrangement of blood red tulips.

Telling him thank you, I set them on the table. I love that he has them in a vase. He's always thinking about me, always wanting to make things easier.

I link my arm through his and follow him to the elevator. As the elevator descends, I realize that I've been going about the Jax situation all wrong. I shouldn't be hiding, I shouldn't be hurt. He didn't do anything that I hadn't expected. I've always known he wasn't the man that I would marry. I hoped he would change that, but deep down I knew it would never happen.

Kohen squeezes my hand. I force my frown to disappear. He's not Jax, he's better. He isn't pushing me away. He wants me. I need to open up to him on our date tonight. He deserves to get to know me.

Conversation flows easily with Kohen. The only thing that I would change about our date would be the place. I hate going to fancy places that serve the smallest portions and it costs five times more. I'm happy with a burger and fries. Finger food and cold beer. Can't get better than that.

Somehow swimming gets thrown into the conversation. I'm surprised when he tells me he used to swim in high school.

"No way! I was a swimmer too!"

"I know." He flashes me his dimples.

We talk back and forth of the pros and cons of competitive swimming. The cons is an awfully short list. Early morning practice. I'm surprised that Kohen is just as passionate about swimming as I am. I love sharing this part of myself with him. Another thing in common.

"You were very talented. Why did you stop?" Kohen asks.

I start to recite the usual speech, but pause. I don't need to give him some fake BS just to make it easier for me. I need to tell him the truth, which will lead to the next series of questions.

The terrifying part is that I'm not even scared to tell him. If I open up to him, I'm giving him the power to break me. The same thing I did years ago with Jax. The warning bells were ringing loud and clear then. Now? It's silent, it's time to let someone else know me. It's time to move on.

"I stopped because it didn't make me happy anymore. Every time I looked at the water I was miserable. I couldn't escape off the pool deck quick enough. One night I attempted to . . ." I shake my head. "I was never able to go back in after I tried to kill myself, until recently."

Silence.

Nervously, I begin digging my fingernails into my palm. This is it. This is when he runs away from me. This is the moment he realizes I'm too damaged. I'm not the person he thinks I am. He surprises me by reaching across the table and taking my hand. I'm relieved he doesn't ask why I thought suicide was my only answer. He knows something terrible happened and he's letting me go at my own pace. That simple act makes it easier to open up to him.

"What made you not . . . never mind, sorry, I don't want to push you to tell me anything."

"It's okay. I want to tell you." I glance around and realize that we're not in our own little world. "Just not here. Do you want to come over for the night?" I ask.

Kohen nods while signaling for the check. I rest my head on his shoulder when we sit in the cab. It's a peaceful silence, neither of us needing to speak.

Kohen gives me a chaste kiss on the lips in the elevator, promising to see me soon. He's going to his place to get something to sleep in. I quickly change into a pair of cotton shorts and snatch an over-sized shirt. It's actually mine and not one of the guys'. I didn't want to chance thinking about Jax because of a stupid old shirt. Which reminds me, I need to toss those out. I can't have them in my place anymore.

I'll do that tomorrow. Tonight it's all about moving forward with Kohen. Every step closer to him pulls me away from Jax. Which is what I need. I just wish my stupid shattered heart would stop holding out hope for Jax. I'm constantly at war with myself; my mind knows Kohen is the perfect guy to move on with, my heart isn't so sure. As much as I try to deny it, I still have hope for Jax. Even though it's just a sliver, it's enough to drive me crazy.

Knock. Knock, I hear at the same time the front door opens.

Weird, I thought I locked that. This whole Jax thing is messing with my mind more than I even realized. I release my lower lip from my teeth. "Hey."

I have no idea why I'm so nervous. This is Kohen. But for some unknown reason, this feels wrong. He shouldn't be here in my space, instead someone with tattoos should.

I need to try that much harder to open up to Kohen. Yeah, that's what it is. I let Jax in, I let him be here for me. I gave him the chance to see me, to break me. He took it. Now, I need to give Kohen a chance to know me. Hopefully I'll be enough for him and he'll still be here after seeing me for me. Only one way to find out.

"Hello," Kohen says, relaxed, in his element at my place.

He moves toward my couch, but I stop him. "How about we hang out on the balcony for a little bit?"

"Sounds perfect."

I walk across the living room toward the balcony. I pause when I get to the doors and notice that Kohen isn't behind me. I'm about to call out to him, but he returns with one of my throw blankets that I keep in a closet.

"Don't want you getting cold."

I manage to smile at his thoughtfulness. It's refreshing to have someone want to take care of you instead of always relying on yourself.

Kohen lays down in a lounge chair and beckons for me to sit in-between his legs. I can't help but compare how my body reacts differently to him than Jax. I force myself to relax into him and ignore that it's not Jax's chest I'm laying against.

Kohen waits for me to gather my thoughts while he rubs my arms. I let the words flow out, not caring if it makes any sense. Just wanting to tell him about myself. Having him behind me, makes it easier for the words to spill out of my mouth.

"I used to be a different person. You wouldn't recognize me six years ago. I was this bubbly person that smiled all the time. My life wasn't perfect, but it was pretty darn close. I had the most amazing parents in the world, not a day went by that I wasn't reminded how much they loved me and how proud they were of me. Our little sister was different from us. She thought dirt under her nails was the worst thing that could ever happen. She was artsy, always dressing up. Even though Logan and I would tease her, she looked up us. I'm pretty sure she thought we could walk on water. We could do no wrong in her eyes."

I remind myself to relax my fist. I know that I will dig my nails into my palms to the point where I draw blood if I don't. Which is not what I need right now. I'm not numb, I don't need to harm myself to feel something. That's not what this is about. I force myself to continue. I can open up to somebody and not have my world crumble. I want that person to be Kohen. I trust him.

"I had goals. Goals that I did everything in my power to achieve. There was nothing more important to me than succeeding. I pushed myself harder each time I got into the water. Swimming consumed my life. My entire world was centered around swimming, until it wasn't."

His hold on me becomes stronger, unbreakable. I love the strength in his arms. Kohen is letting me know he's here without words. I love that he is so patient with me. Not asking the questions that I know he wants answered. He is letting me take my time, share what I'm willing to share. I turn my head slightly so that I can kiss his forearm.

"I wasn't able to get back into the water for six years. I was afraid of not feeling the same. I was afraid of the memories. Mostly, I was afraid of being happy. I didn't think I deserved being happy. Sometimes I have to remind myself that it's okay to be happy." I say the last sentence so quietly I doubt he hears me.

"I promise to help you remember if you ever forget, Adalynn."

I snuggle into him closer. I'm glad that I'm confiding in him. It's not as hard as I thought it would be. I want to be done and just go to sleep in his arms, but I know I need to say one more thing.

"My parents and sister are . . . they're . . ." I struggle for the words.

Even though I know that they're dead and aren't coming back, it's hard to form the words out loud. My throat tightens.

"It's okay, you don't have to tell anything you don't want to. Just know whenever you're ready, I'm here. Nothing can ever keep me away from you."

Those are the words I needed to hear. All doubts of not being enough for him evaporate.

"My parents and sister died six years ago. I was with them when it happened."

I don't elaborate and Kohen doesn't make me. He drags me closer to him as if he's afraid I will run away from him and shut him out. I try to say more, but nothing comes out. I'm not ready to tell him everything yet. Just being able to say this much to him is a huge accomplishment.

We head to my room holding hands. It's surprisingly refreshing to share with someone that doesn't know me or my past. I was afraid opening up to him would push him away. I'm glad that I was wrong. He needs to know me, to really want to be with me. I can't pretend anymore, not with him.

His arms wrap around me as he spoons me from behind. This as as close to content that I've felt since Jax told me I wasn't enough. Whenever I was with Jax, I always had a nagging feeling in the back of my mind that it will never last. I never feel like that with Kohen. He always does everything in his power to show me how much he wants me. He is the exact opposite from Jax.

He's the light and Jax is the darkness.

I'm done with the darkness.

I want to bask in the sun.

I want to be with Kohen.

Even though my mind knows this, it's hard to ignore that my heart aches because I'm in somebody else's arms. I can't help that my shattered heart is comparing them. Like the way that I have to remind myself to relax into Kohen's arms when my body naturally molds into Jax. It's a good thing I don't listen to my heart anymore. Following my heart is the reason why it's demolished into a million pieces without any hope of healing.

I wish that I could just shut it off. Like I used to. It would make this so much easier. My heart wouldn't be aching for Jax. I would be satisfied with Kohen. It would be as easy as flipping a switch for me. Too bad I know exactly how hard it is to flip that switch back on. It's taken me six long years to feel again, to want to live. No matter how easy it would be to go numb again, I couldn't do that to myself or Kohen. He doesn't deserve to be with someone who isn't really there.

As impossible as it seems, I need to move on from Jax. I almost want to laugh at that idea. I've told myself over and over that I need to move on. Telling myself to do something isn't as easy as following through.

When I look where Kohen has taken us for lunch the next afternoon, I'm surprised that I don't have to force a smile. The last time I was at Cedar Hill was with Jax. I haven't been able to come back here since that day. I thought the image of him leaving me would have tainted the love I feel for this place. I was wrong. Nothing could change the way I feel when I'm here. I feel free.

"I'm so glad I'm here with you," Kohen says.

"Why?" I step out of his embrace to lay the blanket on the grass.

"Because it's your favorite place and I wanted to be with you here."

The way Kohen says it's my favorite place makes me drop my smile for a few seconds before I paint on my fake one. I don't remember telling him this was my favorite spot. I pretend fascination with everything going on around us, but I'm replaying our time together, trying to remember when I told him about Cedar Hill.

Nothing.

I know I didn't tell him. I wouldn't have been able to because of how things ended with Jax the last time I was here. *How could he possibly know this is my favorite spot?* I come up with a million different answers that are way out of the possibility of reality. I'm overreacting.

This is Cedar Hill, it's everyone's favorite spot. Yes, that's it. He just assumed this would be mine. I can't even swallow that thought. I know that isn't it even though I want to believe it. Kohen isn't one to assume anything. Logan. Kohen wanted to spend the day together and make it special so he asked my brother. Yes, that's it. That makes the most sense.

With that miniature freak out averted, I grin at him for his thoughtfulness. Pushing past my crazy ideas, I make the best of the day with the wonderful man beside me. Kohen went all out, not that I'm surprised. Kohen doesn't know how to do anything half-assed.

He has lunch from my favorite deli, cupcakes from the bakery, and wine in plastic solo cups. It might be considered simple to some, but to me it's perfect because he took time out of his day to go across town to get my favorite things, just to make me happy. You can't beat that.

After I eat two and a half cupcakes, I split the last one with him. I recline back and enjoy the September sun while Kohen strokes my hair. I wish that I brought my camera, even if I feel like that would be betraying Jax. No matter how many times I tell myself that it doesn't matter what Jax thinks, I still can't convince myself that next time I'm here with Kohen, I'll bring my camera.

The rest of the day passes quickly. Time gets away when you're enjoying yourself. Hand-in-hand, Kohen and I walk to our apartment building. Kohen seems agitated that he has to work in an hour and can't go to dinner with my brother and Connor. Which is why I squeeze his hand and rest my head against his shoulder while we ride the elevator.

I'm glad that Kohen decides to stay with me as long as possible before he has to leave. He follows me to my room and sits on my bed while I change and freshen up in the bathroom. As much as I want to text Connor and make sure that it's just him and my brother taking me to dinner, I know I can't. There isn't a discreet way to ask if Jax is tagging along. Plus, I don't see Jax coming. I hope that my gut feeling is right. There's no way I'll be able to eat dinner with that man yet.

Kohen chats with me while I wash my face and reapply mascara and lip gloss. Next, I French braid my hair to the side. I ignore Kohen's comment again about not wanting to go into work tonight so that he can come with me. Instead I wonder what I'm going to wear and pretend I don't hear him. I've heard him complain all day about it; him complaining is the only downside of our wonderful day together. At first I understood, thinking he was just tired from work, wanted a break, or even something terrible like someone dying on him. Nope, none of those are the reasons. He wants to ditch work and go to dinner with me because he doesn't like that Connor will be there. As in Connor, my brother's best friend, the same Connor I consider as another brother.

I laughed at first when he told me that. I thought he was kidding. I even tried putting myself in his shoes, wondering, but came up blank. Yes, Connor is a huge flirt, and hot, but gross, he's Connor. I could never, and I mean never, look at Connor as anything but an annoying brother. Just thinking about it makes me want to laugh. Too bad I'm still annoyed that Kohen even thinks that. And every time he complains about going to work, it pisses me off all over again.

"How about you have dinner with me at work then come back here and go to bed early since you're tired?" Kohen asks.

"Hospital food?" I ask, while rolling my eyes.

It's amazing that he can tell I'm tired. It must be a super power of his that I wasn't aware he had. Kind of like how I was under the impression that I'm awake and excited to go out to dinner with my brother and Connor. I haven't seen them as much as usual because I'm always with Kohen. I have to remind myself not to quip Connor's that more than capable of keeping me up. Yeah, I don't think he would find that funny.

"It's not that bad," he says.

"I'd rather eat Logan's gym socks!"

Kohen doesn't respond which is a good thing. I'm close to throwing a shoe at him at the moment. I can't believe I want to yell at him and laugh at the same time. Must be another super power of his.

Even though Kohen doesn't know Connor got me the simple white dress in my hands, I can't help my smug smile while I tug it off the hanger. I had planned on changing into jeans and a shirt because of the chill in the night air, but this dress had been calling my name ever since Kohen opened his mouth about going to work with him. Also, I haven't worn the dress yet and I know Connor will be happy that I'm wearing it.

I look at the full length mirror in front of me and smile. The white sundress that Connor bought me on his recent trip to California is beautiful. The halter top shows enough cleavage to look sexy, but not too much where the girls are giving a free show. The dress hugs my slim waist and flows out right above my knee caps. Connor did an excellent job selecting this dress. I select a simple pair of ballet flats before leaving my closet to show Kohen.

"Besides, I want to go out with them. It's our weekly dinner and I'm not —"

"WHAT THE FUCK ARE YOU WEARING?" Kohen screams with disgust in his eyes.

"Excuse me?" I ask, while rubbing my hands down the dress.

He marches to my side, seizes my forearm and practically shoves me back into my closet. "You are NOT wearing that!" Kohen says while rifling through my clothes.

I know I should keep my mouth shut. Kohen is shaking in rage. But I don't. "Last time I checked, you're not my father. You will not tell me what I can and can't wear!"

"You're not going out dressed like that!"

"Like what?"

"A slut!" Kohen hurls a long sleeve top and a pair of jeans at me.

He is so fucking lucky that the clothes landed at me feet and not my face. I would've snapped if they hit me.

"A slut? Because my ass is hanging out, right?" I turn my head to look at my butt. "Oh wait, the dress goes to my knees! Wow, I'm such a slut! I can't believe I'm not on the corner right now."

"It's not the length that's the problem. Now go get some actual fucking clothes on. You're not leaving dressed like that and tomorrow I'm going to go through your clothes for you."

I just laugh. Which of course is opposite of what I should be doing based on his fist closing like he wants to hit something. Kohen stomps over to me.

"YOU. WILL. NOT. DRESS. LIKE. A. FUCKING. SLUT." Lacing each word with disgust, he squeezes my forearms tighter.

Shut up Addie! Now is not the time to talk to him. Wait until he calms down. That little voice begs me to be quiet.

"Let go of me," I say calmly even though I want to shout.

He doesn't let go. He continues to stare at the offensive dress as if he can magically change my outfit with his eyes.

"Now, Kohen!"

Kohen takes a few deep breaths and I can see him the tension leaving his body. He releases me. I don't even need to see the bruises his hands left. I can feel them. I maneuver closer to the door. He probably won't touch me again like that, but I don't want to risk it. He's in control again, but I'd rather be close to an escape just in case.

"You will not dictate what I wear. I am not a slut, nor do I dress like one. I've only slept with one person, for crying out loud."

Kohen's face turns a little green and he's breathing deeper as if trying not to throw up. Hopefully it's because he just realized how he's acting and not because I've slept with someone that isn't him.

"If you ever, and I mean ever try to tell me what I can and can't wear, we will be done. I'm a grown woman and if I want to walk outside naked, I will walk outside fucking naked and you will say nothing about it!"

"Adalynn—"

I cut him off. I do not want to hear how sorry he is right now. He needs to leave so I can have some much needed space. He just ruined a perfect day for no reason. I know he's sorry, I know he wasn't fully aware what he was doing or saying. But it doesn't change the fact that I want him to leave. Now.

"I think you should go," I say quietly before picking up my discarded flats.

Kohen jerks me in for a hug, but I back away.

"Ad—"

"No, you need to leave. I'll talk to you tomorrow. I know you're sorry. It's fine. I don't care. I'm over it. I need to leave. I'm already going to be late."

I don't even wait for a response. I stomp into my closet, angry that I have to throw on a cardigan to hide the bruises on my arm. My front door opens and closes and I sigh in relief. He can apologize all he wants tomorrow. Tonight I need a break from him and his irrational jealousy.

All frustration leaves the second I see my brother at the restaurant.

"Late as always." Logan says while stepping out of the booth to give me a hug.

"Name one time," I demand.

"I can name more than one time for every single day that I've known you," Connor pipes up while embracing me.

"You're annoying. Remind me why you're here again?"

"Because you love me and I know you're going to need your fix before I leave?"

"My fix?" I ask.

"Of seeing my good looks." He turns around and wiggles his butt. "Oh and my ass, I know how much you can't keep your eyes off it."

Logan groans. I pretend to gag.

"Hurry up and sit down before we're forced to leave."

Connor fakes having a heart attack. "How you wound me."

"Shut up," I plead.

"Beautiful dress." Connor says when he finally sits down besides me.

"Thanks, this ugly guy that can never take a hint got it for me." I wink.

Connor raises an eyebrow. "Fine, see if I bring you back anything."

That's the second time Connor has mentioned something about leaving. I look from him to my brother. Both are grinning.

"Good news?" I ask, already knowing it is.

Both nod, not giving anything away. Fine. I'll play along. I grab my glass of water and pretend to pull a Harper on Connor.

"Okay, okay, relax, Addie," Connor says hastily.

Good move on his part. I'm not in the mood to play games tonight.

"We're going to London," Connor says at the same time Logan says, "We got the deal!"

I tell both of them how I'm not surprised. What's the deal for? I have no idea. But what kind of sister would I be to ask questions on something that I should already know? Which of course makes me feel guilty. I've been so occupied in my own drama that I have neglected my brother.

"How long will you guys be gone?" I ask, hoping that they didn't already tell me.

Logan rubs his jaw. Not good. Connor is the one that answers. "Two weeks."

I can't help the panic that is starting to take over. I can barely even remember the last time my brother left the country without me. When he was in college and I still had our family.

"I'm not leaving for two days," Logan says, sensing my unease.

"I'll be fine." I don't know if I say it for my brother's benefit or mine.

An hour later they're dropping me off, promising to call every day. Which of course I tell them not to do. I don't need my brother or Connor worrying about me. I'll be fine.

Two weeks.

Fourteen days.

The thought is both thrilling and nerve-racking.

Whenever Logan leaves, it's always as short as possible and he either has Connor or Jax keeping me occupied. Connor is out since he's going which only means Jax. I feel dizzy until I force myself to suck in oxygen. Logan wouldn't do that to me. He wouldn't make Jax keep tabs on me again. No, he can't. He knows we're not on good terms. *Overprotective doesn't even begin to describe him.*

Fuck!

CHAPTER TWENTY-SIX

"You don't have to tell me anything you don't want to, Addie," Liv says. "I'm here for whatever you need. If you want to talk about the weather for the next hour, I'm all ears. However, you need to open up to someone. Once you do, you'll feel better. Maybe not at first, but eventually."

"Day-by-day right?" I ask, repeating that stupid saying Liv's always says to me.

She nods. "Day-by-day."

"I don't know where to start."

"Start with whatever you want to tell me."

Glancing down, I immediately force my finger to stop drawing random designs on my thigh. I wasn't even aware I was doing that. It's something that I've always done when I'm too stressed out, close to my breaking point. It helps calm me down. *Where did I pick up this habit?*

I think back, trying to remember the first time I started doing this. I was still swimming because I remember drawing random patterns on kick-boards. So it was before the accident if I was still swimming. Hmmm. I remember crying in the dark and feeling someone drawing on me with their finger.

Jax.

I was crying for Jax. I couldn't stop picturing him on the floor bleeding because of Wyatt. He didn't know how to make me stop so he helped me into bed, and drew random things on my back with his finger tips until I fell asleep. He still does it. I get flashes of him doing it whenever I've been nervous, scared, or needed him. While I was in the hospital, underneath the table at a charity event, while he tutored me. The flashes go on and on.

Then, as if I can't help myself, I replay every time he would draw on my naked back with a sharpie. Despite everything, he's still my strength. Remembering our time together helps me open up to Liv about the night that changed my entire life.

"Arguing, I remember arguing with my mom and dad."

Liv doesn't say anything. I know she's giving me time to gather my thoughts and emotions. I've never talked about the accident before. For six long years, I've been quiet. It has been easier to not relive that night. I wish that with time, the memory had blurred, but if anything it has only gotten sharper.

I can remember every little detail: the pain, the smells, the cries, the emptiness from not being able to do anything but listen to them die. I never once believed I would be able to talk about that night. I promised myself I wouldn't. I thought reliving that night would kill me. Hopefully I'm stronger than I realized and I can talk about that dreadful night that changed everything without losing myself again.

"They wanted to know something." I rub my flat stomach. "I can't remember what, though. I was yelling at them to drop it. It was my decision to keep the secret."

I close my eyes trying to recall the details of the fight. Something tears at my brain, begging me to let it in. I shake my head, tossing away the painful memory before I can grasp it. I'm choosing to forget something important.

"I can't remember why I was screaming at them to leave me alone."

"Can't or won't?"

I shrug in answer. I massage my temples and try with everything in me to recall the fight. Jax. No matter how hard I try, I can't stop picturing his face. As much as it's killing me to not ask Liv, I can't. I know I'm not ready for those answers yet. Instead I let myself block out something vitally important. I tell Liv as much as I can recall about the fight. Putting the pieces together as I talk, but still having gaps in the puzzle that's my life.

"I was so mad at them. They told me I had to tell them the truth, or I had to leave. They were going to cut me off until I told them everything. I kept yelling at them because they were being so unfair. They promised they would give me more time. They lied. Hadley squeezed my hand to try to calm me down, but I yanked my hand away and moved from the middle seat to the one next to the window so I wasn't next to her anymore. I wanted to be left alone. Funny, I got what I wished for."

I pick up a glass of water and force it down my too-tight throat. I wish I could forget the harsh words I said to my parents, but those words are forever engraved in my mind.

"We were about a mile away from our house when I saw the lights. Everything seemed to slow down but speed up all at once. Hadley was holding out her earphones to me with the most welcoming smile I've ever seen, our mom looked like she was crying, and my dad was silent and staring at me in the rearview mirror, trying to get me to look at him. I refused to meet his eyes because I was afraid of what I would see, so I looked out the window at the headlights that were coming in the wrong direction."

I'm aware that I am drawing patterns on my hand. I wouldn't be able to stop even if I wanted to . . . I need the calm that Jax brings, like I need oxygen.

"I tried to yell at my dad to stop, but nothing came out. I watched horrified as the lights grew closer and closer. Blinding me. I heard the impact more than felt it. I think I was still in shock and the pain didn't register yet. I can still hear the sound of my dad's head hitting the window and glass shattering."

I hear the sound as clear as I can hear myself breathing. I have the sudden urge to throw up. I swallow the acid rising up my throat. I need to get this out more than anything. The words are spilling out on their own accord without any thought on my part. It's liberating in the most painful way imaginable.

"When our car went airborne, that's when the screaming started. Everyone was screaming except for my dad. I still have nightmares of the silence when the car finally stopped in the ditch. Then the ringing started. I tried to cover my ears to shut the noise off because it was so loud and it was hurting my head, but my hands weren't working. I forgot that we were in a car accident. The smell of rubber confused me because I thought I was asleep somewhere in my house. I knew I wasn't in my bed, but I didn't know where I was.

"I kept trying to open my eyes, but every time I got close to opening them, I was out again, only to be awoken by the ringing again. I don't know how long I was like that until I was finally able to open them. The sight was so horrible that I immediately started to scream. I was in my worst nightmare and I knew no matter how many times I closed and reopened my eyes, the scene in front of me wouldn't change. My family was dying and there was nothing I could do but watch."

Not being able to sit still, I head over to the window. A man walks his dog and across the street a couple hold hands as they wait for a taxi. I would guess teenagers. They don't seem any older than seventeen. Fitting. It feels like a lifetime ago that I was seventeen without a care in the world. Then everything changed. Like everything always does. The worst that could happen had happened and there was nothing I could do but watch. I hated being helpless. I never want to feel powerless again.

That's why I know no matter how I feel after talking with Liv, that I will be okay. I won't be fine, but I'll survive. I'll keep living, breathing, because they can't. I won't just sit back and watch my life unveil before my eyes. I will always be a participant in life. I won't give up. No more watching. Never again.

With newfound calm, I'm able to step away from the window and sit back down on the couch. I hug the pillow to my chest again. It's a small comfort that I need right now. I give Liv a small smile so she knows that I'm okay. She's so patient with me, pushes me when I need it. She understands me. The other therapists didn't. They always tried to fix me. They never let me realize that I had to fix myself. Nobody can fix me; Liv just helps me see the pieces that are ready to be put back together.

"Do you want to talk some more, or save the rest for another day?" Liv asks.

"Continue. I need to get it out. It's strange, I never thought I would be able to talk about it, but now that I am, I know I need to get it all out, or I won't be able to."

Liv nods in understanding.

"When I realized that screaming wasn't going to stop time, I tried to get out of my seat to get help. I could see the blood dripping down my legs and onto the floor. My right hand wasn't working because it was broken and dislocated and my left arm was stuck. It felt like hours until I was finally able to free my left arm. I broke my thumb and three fingers in the process of getting my hand unstuck between my seat and the door. I didn't even feel the pain. I pushed it all aside so I could reach Hadley. She didn't stir once. I could see that my mom was starting to come to, so I called out to her."

The memory is so vivid that I'm reeled back into the past. I don't fight it like I usually do. I need to relive it one more time to be able to move on.

"*Mom!*" *I yell, trying frantically to unbuckle my seatbelt.*

"*Add—*" *she whispers, but stops as if just moving her mouth causes her too much pain.*

"*I can't . . . I can't get out. My seatbelt is stuck! Can you move? Can you see Dad? Hadley isn't moving!*"

"*Ad—*" *She tries again, but stops.*

I wait for her to say something else, but she doesn't. I panic all over again. She's not stirring. If I lean as far forward as the seatbelt will allow, I can barely see the rise and fall of her chest.

I keep struggling to get free. Each and every time I use my left hand, pain shoots through my fingers and up my arm, causing me to scream as if somebody is stabbing me. I've never thought anything could hurt this badly. Tears run down my face, but I don't give up. I can't. I need to reach my sister. She's the only thing that matters. Not the pain. Not the broken bones. Those will heal. My sister needs me.

"*Hadley.*"

Nothing. Absolute silence.

"*Hadley!*" *I yell louder.*

More silence.

My eyelids feel heavy. I know I only have a few more seconds before sleep takes over. I fight it, fearing that if I close my eyes now, I won't be able to open them again. My mom's voice is the strength I need to keep my eyes open and keep fighting.

"*I'll always love you my sweet beautiful girl. I-I—*"

"*Don't talk, Mom. Save your strength. I know you love me. I love you so much. I'm so—*"

"*You have nothing to be sorry for . . . Be the person that I raised . . . I'm so proud of the woman . . . that you're becoming.*"

She starts coughing, the kind of coughing that sounds like she's choking. The sound alone makes my heart stop. It's the red dots flying on the dashboard that have me screaming in terror. Blood. My mom is coughing up blood and the only thing I can do is sit here and watch her suffer.

When she finally stops coughing, she speaks again. I know that this is the last time I will ever hear her voice. With each word, I can tell how much pain she's in and how much effort she expends to say words that most people take for granted. Nobody ever realizes how much they take for granted until it's too late. Even words.

"Hadley will . . . need . . . you. Be strong for her. Tell Logan . . . how much I love him. Never forget . . . how much I love . . . you three."

"Mom!" I cry.

"Shh you'll . . . be . . . fine without . . . me sweetie." She whispers so quietly I barely can hear her.

"Mom, don't. I'm so sorry!"

I start screaming again. I scream for her to say more, but she never does. I stare at her unmoving body. I don't know how much time passes until I finally break. My mom is gone and it's all my fault.

"I blamed myself the instant that my mom died. I watched her die. Slowly and painfully and there wasn't anything I could do. I silently promised that I would take care of Hadley. I failed. I failed all of them."

"You used past tense. You usually use present tense. Do you not blame yourself anymore?" Liv asks.

I'm too shocked to speak. I did use past tense. I meant what I said. I blamed myself. I don't know if I still do or not. It's hard to accept change when I've believed for the past six years that I was responsible for the crash. I always thought I was too weak to save them. If only I was stronger. If only I was able to reach my phone sooner.

"I felt so weak. I still do sometimes. I kept telling myself to stay awake, but I couldn't even do that. Every time before my eyes closed, I didn't know if they would open again. I was glad. I didn't want to be in a world where they didn't exist. Then I would think of Logan and I would feel so guilty. Guilty that I wasn't strong enough, guilty that I was giving up. The list was never-ending."

Liv waits for me to get everything out. My heart hammers so hard that I'm sure it's going to beat out of my chest. I have to finish reliving that night. I don't know why or how, but for some reason, I feel like I will be better once it is all over. With each word I say, I feel lighter.

"I was losing hope. I knew it had been hours since the accident and still nobody came. I kept thinking that the person that hit us was just getting help. I knew she wasn't. I hoped that she was in worse pain than I was. The pain I felt from the accident was nothing compared to listening to my mom die and knowing that my dad had been dead the moment his head hit the window. I couldn't see him to be sure, but I never heard anything from him the entire time I was trapped."

I drink the ice water in front of me. My throat tightens again. Either from talking too much without pause or because of the horrible story that is my life.

"The only small sliver of hope I had was that one of the passing cars would see our car or hear my screams. I had to have hope because of Hadley. I could see her breathing. Even though it looked like each breath was causing her pain, it still gave me hope. Whenever I was lucid enough, I would call out her name. She never responded. I would watch her breathing and match my breaths with hers. If she was going to die, I wanted to die with her."

Just remembering feeling so lost, so alone, sends me back into the car.

Something flashing catches my attention right before sleep takes over again. I blink the fuzziness away and use my broken left hand to wipe blood from my eyes. I don't need to feel the cut on my head to know I'm in bad shape. I'm losing a lot of blood. I see another flash and hope blossoms again in my chest. Help is here.

Finally.

I start to close my eyes when another flash catches my attention. That small feeling of hope vanishes as quickly as it came. Nobody is here. Nobody is going to save us. It's my phone.

Phone!

I try to move towards it, but my feet aren't responding. I can't even feel them. I haven't been able to feel them since the car hit us. I haven't even thought of them because I didn't feel anything.

Panicking all over again, I force myself to concentrate on moving my feet. I have to be able to move. If I can get out of here, I have to be able to walk to the road. I see Hadley stir right before she lets out a whimper that will forever haunt my soul.

Hadley needs me.

I give up on moving my feet. They're not listening to me and it's wasting my time. Time is not on my side right now. I search everywhere around me, trying to think of a way to get out of my seatbelt.

The flash goes off again, alerting me to a new text. It's exactly what I needed. That little flash lit up my surroundings, allowing me to see my swim bag. I know I have nail clippers in there. I always keep one in there for water polo. I'm thankful that I never get around to taking it out when polo season ended and swimming started.

Biting my lip to keep from screaming, I reach over with my left hand to grab it. Pain shoots through both arms and I bite down harder. Blood fills my mouth from biting too hard and I let out another scream.

I wrench the bag onto my lap. Every cell in my body tells me to close my eyes, the pain will go away if I close them. I can't. I need to cut my way out of here.

With agonizing slowness, I cut my seatbelt with my nail clippers. I'm forced to use my right hand since my left can't grip the clippers. My shoulder howls at me to stop. To take a break. Tears gush down my face while I whimper in pain.

A lifetime goes by before I'm almost free. I turn my head towards Hadley again. Her slow breathing keeps pushing me when everything in me is insisting that I give up. I won't give up on her. She needs me.

My blood blinds me as it spills into my eyes and down my face. I blink the blood away, and focus on my seatbelt. I exhale when I realize I'm done. Using my left hand, I tear the last few threads apart.

I'm free.

Moving quickly to my sister, I check her pulse. I need to make sure I'm not crazy and I wasn't imagining her breathing this entire time.

Thump . . . Thump . . . Thump.

It's there. Faint. But there. I'll settle for faint over nothing.

"Hadley, open your eyes. Please. Open your eyes for me. We're gonna be okay," I plead with my unconscious sister.

I search for my phone on the ground. The rain has stopped and it's gotten lighter outside so I can make out shapes on the floorboards.

"We were out there all night. Nobody noticed. My entire world was falling apart and everyone kept going about their lives. All it would have taken was one person! One person to see us and things could have been different."

"You're angry at the world because it kept spinning while your world stopped."

Liv doesn't say it like a question. She knows that's how I feel. I've said it before during therapy, countless times. I answer her anyways.

"Yes."

I now know how impossible it was for someone to see us that night. Our car veered off the hill and it was pouring. You had to have known that the accident happened to have seen us. The driver who hit us, Emily Hayes, could have gotten help, but she didn't. Instead she drove home and died from internal bleeding. Her reckless driving killed my family. I hope she suffered unimaginable pain.

Finally, at sunrise, somebody, somehow, noticed our car and called the cops. He didn't even stop long enough to see if anyone was inside. He drove away thinking he did a good deed.

I wish I could say that I'm thankful for that unknown man, but I can't. Yes, he called the cops and that's why they came to the scene. But I've always wondered "what if?" What if he got out and searched our car? Would things be different? Would Hadley still be alive?

"I'm gonna get us out of here. I promise," I vow to my unconscious sister.

Spotting my cell phone on the floor, I reach down to grab it. Relief comes and just as quickly as it disappears. Dead!

I laugh at the absurdity. Everyone always reminds me to charge my phone in case of an emergency. I never do. I always forget to charge it until it's dead. Now I need my phone because of an emergency and it's dead. I can't stop laughing even though it causes pain in my chest. I'm losing it.

The phone slips from my grasp when I hear Hadley sob.

"Had?" I ask timidly, afraid I'm losing my mind and I'm hearing things.

"Ads?"

Despite everything going on, that one word makes me smile.

"It's gonna be okay. I'm gonna get us out of here."

She barely manages to nod. She is unrecognizable with blood and bruises covering her skin. She looks so tiny and afraid. I need to do something. I need to get us out of the car. I don't know how I'm going to get us out since I still can't feel one of my legs. My right leg has started throbbing, which is good. If I can feel it, then that means I should be able to move it soon.

I calculate ways to get us out of the car and to the road. I come up with nothing. I know from countless CPR classes that I shouldn't move her in her condition without proper equipment. I will crawl to the road if I have to. Drawing a deep breath, I try to wiggle my right foot. I scream in pain when it cooperates. I lean over and kiss Hadley on the forehead.

"I love you. Be strong. I'm going to go get help."

She doesn't respond, not that I thought she would. She hasn't made any other sound since she whimpered my name. The only way I know she is still alive is from her shallow breaths. I don't have much time.

With all my strength, I crawl over the center console, dragging my left foot. I bite down on my tongue, trying not to yell. My voice is already raspy. I need to save it for when I reach the road.

Turning my head, I see my dad. I wish that I closed my eyes so that I wouldn't have the image of glass shards through his face forever imprinted in my mind. Needing to make sure that this is real, my dad is really gone, I touch the side of his neck.

This is real.

This is my life.

My dad is dead.

My mom is dead.

Hadley and I will die too if I don't get us help.

As much as it kills me that I have to shimmy over my dead mom, I have no choice. It's the only way out. I close my eyes as I do it. Every cell in my body begs me to stop. I can barely breathe through the pain, but I don't give up. I can't.

My hand grazes the door handle and I shout in relief when I tumble to the ground. I drag my body through the mud on my hands and knees. I let out the scream I've been holding in. It hurts. The pain is unbearable. I shut my eyes for a second when nausea hits. I try to take deep breaths through my nostrils, but I can't suck in any oxygen. My chest is on fire.

I panic. This is it. I'm going to die on the wet ground before I have a chance to get help for Hadley. Each tiny breath feels like I have a truck on top of my chest, constricting my airway.

I can't breathe.

I can't open my eyes.

The pain is starting to drift away . . . like me.

I'm panting, I need air. I try to stand, but my legs won't obey. I rock myself back and forth on the couch and struggle to suck in oxygen. I'm going to suffocate. Dizzy, I'm vaguely aware that Liv has crunched down in front of me. I breathe in time to her. It works. After a few more deep breaths mimicking Liv, I'm finally able to breathe on my own.

I'm walking towards the window before I realize that my legs are moving. I look out but I don't see anything. My mind is elsewhere. All I see is rain and blinding lights. Something I shouldn't be seeing since the sun is shining.

"I'm sorry," I say.

"Why do you feel like you have to apologize?"

I know she is hinting at more. She knows that I'm not apologizing for my freak out even though I feel like I should be. I'm saying sorry for so much more.

"For everything."

"It wasn't your fault," she says.

"Of course it was! I'm the one responsible! If I wasn't fighting with them, my dad would have been paying attention! I said things that I can never take back! I ruined everything. I killed them. I killed them. I killed them."

"You weren't the one who fled an accident. You weren't the one who decided not to call the police to inform them what happened."

"I know!"

"Then why do you blame yourself? You didn't force that woman to drive away."

"Emily." I snap. "The drivers name was Emily Hayes."

Silence descends. Liv waits until I unclench my fist before she continues.

"You're not Mother-Nature. You didn't ask for the rain that night. You were mad and expressed yourself. You said things you didn't mean. They knew how you really felt, they knew you loved them. You aren't the cause of the accident. You didn't kill them."

"I know," I admit, surprising us both.

I test that word over and over again in my head, looking for doubt. There isn't any. *I didn't kill them. I didn't kill my parents. I didn't kill my little sister.* I chant those words over in my head till they blend together. I feel lighter. I can breathe easily without the guilt of killing my family hanging over my head.

Liv has a huge smile on her face as if she can read my mind. The pain is still there, but it's a different pain from what's been there for the last six years. The pain I felt for blaming myself was all-consuming. I couldn't deal, so I shut everyone and everything out.

I don't feel like that anymore. The pain of knowing that they are never coming back is there, but I am able to breathe. I don't want to be that girl anymore, that isn't really here because she lost her family; I want to be that girl who makes her parents proud.

I've been wanting happiness for awhile now. I've been trying. I've been convincing myself that I was happy, but I don't think I truly was until now with the weight of the guilt finally off my shoulders. I'm not carrying that burden anymore. I can't fight the smile that plays on my lips.

"Acceptance."

"What?" I ask, confused.

"Acceptance. You've reached acceptance, Addie. That's what you're feeling right now."

I test the word out for myself, "Acceptance."

After gathering my purse, I turn and give Liv a hug. I don't say anything. She has helped me so much. I don't know where I would be without her. Yes I do, I would still be pretending, most likely. Living without actually breathing.

I walk out without another word. I spot my brother in his usual seat waiting for me. He stands as I approach him. I wrap my arms around him. My rock.

"Thank you for always being here for me even when I try to push you away. I'm sorry that I shut down and lost myself. You didn't deserve that. You lost them too and had to deal with losing me even though I was still here. I love you Logan," I say into his chest.

Logan is speechless. I can see that he is trying to rein in his emotions.

"I know how much you want to be here for me. But right now I need to be alone. I just have to get my head on straight. I promise I will see you before you leave tomorrow. Just . . . I . . ."

"You got it, baby girl." He kisses me on top of my head. "I'll see you tomorrow."

I smile at him before I leave. I walk around for what feels like hours, but I have no sense of time. I wander the streets of New York without a destination. I keep replaying the word "acceptance" in my head. Is it really this easy? Am I just pretending or am I really better? I know I can't be that girl I was before the accident. I'm still me, though. Just a different version of myself.

I'm going to continue getting better for the four lives that were lost that night; my dad, my mom, my little sister, and me. I died that night. They were able to bring me back, but I lost something that I can never regain. That piece of my soul, that has forever changed the person that I am, died that night.

A laugh that I will know anywhere snaps me back to reality. Please, please be wrong. I know without a doubt that I'm not. I see a man's back against a brick wall while a leggy blonde sucks on his neck. I can't see the man's face, but I don't need to see it. I can tell from his unruly hair, the muscles showing through his custom suit, who he is. It's Jax.

Glancing around, I realize where I am. I'm standing a block away from Jax's apartment building. Of course I am. Where else would my legs carry me?

I stand still, unable to move or look away. I hear him tell me how much he loves me in my mind while some blonde whispers in his ear, causing him to laugh and shake his head. I want to scream at her to get her slutty hands off him, but I don't. I freeze, mouth open, while the man that I love lets some tramp have her way with him in the middle of the sidewalk.

I thought the pain of Jax's rejection was the worst thing that he could do to me. Now I'm not so sure. Seeing him with her floods the pain of losing him back to the surface again. Instead of the heart-shattering pain from before, I'm fucking furious. Especially when I see who the slutty blonde is.

She's the troll from the bathroom who was considering dyeing her hair based on Jax's preferences. As if they can feel my staring at them, they both turn their heads my way. The troll looks amused while Jax pales. Good.

Not needing to witness what happens next, I turn around and run away. Jax shouts my name so I run faster. I'm thankful that I wore flats instead of the wedges I pulled out of my closet. The would have made my escape impossible.

I'm about to reach the corner when I'm jerked to a stop. All my anger from not being enough from Jax rises to the surface, and seeing him with the blonde troll pushes me one step closer to losing it. All the pent up anger from not being able to change what happened six years ago makes me lose it. I take all of it out on Jax in the form of a slap.

He releases his tight hold on my wrist as he stumbles back. I'm barely able to keep myself from falling into him. My right hand burns from the force of the blow. I've hit him before, but that was child's play compared to the slap he just received.

There's an entire imprint of my hand on his left cheek. Good.

"Don't you EVER fucking touch me again!" I shout.

"Wait, Ads!" he yells after me.

I jump into a cab and scream out my address at the poor driver. I apologize and pretend like I'm not the crazy person he just saw smack some guy on the street. I sigh in relief when the driver veers away right when Jax tries to open the door. I don't look back even though every part of me begs me to turn around and ask the driver to stop.

CHAPTER TWENTY-SEVEN

I unlock my front door, hurl my purse on the ground, and slam the door. I continue visualizing the scene over and over again with the stupid melody of him telling me I'm not enough. A sick torture that I can't escape. I need help. I need a friend right now. Without any thought, I drop to the floor and dig through my purse for my phone. I ignore all the missed messages and call the only person I can. She answers on the first ring.

"Hello love!" Harper sings into the phone.

Throat tight, I weakly choke out, "Hi."

"I'm on my way. Keep the door unlocked," Harper says before hanging up.

She doesn't ask if I want company. She knows I need her. I had a tiny second of doubt that I shouldn't have called her, that I should be strong enough on my own, but I made the right choice. Needing someone else every once in a while isn't a bad thing. It doesn't make me weak.

I desperately want to change into something comfortable, but I can't find the strength to move. Today had been one hell of a day. I feel as if someone took a metal bat to my head then realized that wasn't doing enough damage so they grabbed the biggest knife they could find and stabbed me repeatedly in the chest.

Somehow I manage to stumble my way to my balcony. I gulp in the cool night air. I should run back inside for a sweater or a blanket, but I can't. Instead I collapse in one of my lounge chairs and wait for Harper.

It's not long when I hear her calling my name. I'm too tired to raise my voice. Even though I'm emotionally drained to the point I feel like my head will explode any second, my mind won't shut off.

I see the blonde troll making Jax laugh while he tells me I'm not enough. I relive the way his eyes sparkled as he confessed his love for me. Then as if that's not enough, I see Hadley extending her headphones while the sound of my dad's head smashing into the window as I soundtrack that plays over and over again. The images blur together until I can't decipher what I'm seeing.

"What happened, Adalynn? Can you hear me?" Harper talks too fast, panicked.

All I can do is nod. Well, I think I nod. My whole body quakes. Is it from the cold outside or from the coldness inside of me? I'm vaguely aware that Harper keeps talking, asking me more questions that I can't answer. All I hear is Hadley painfully saying my name one last time. Her last word was my name.

She was the only one besides Jax to call me Ads. I've never let anyone else call me that, even before she died. She thought it was Jax picking on me when we were younger, that's why she started calling me Ads. To her horror, it was only a nickname, a nickname that only Jax could use, as he patiently told her. Too bad Hadley has always gotten her way even with Jax. He couldn't get her to stop calling me Ads. It became their name for me.

When I heard Jax call me Ads the first time in the hospital, I couldn't breathe through the pain. I would never hear my little sister call me that again, it would only be Jax. As much as it hurt in the beginning, I couldn't tell him to stop. I think on some level he knew how much I needed it even though I dreaded it. I needed a daily reminder of her that wasn't tainted from that night.

He gave me that.

I'm aware that Harper has wrapped me in a blanket and is speaking on the phone. I can tell that she's frantic and all I can do is watch while my mind goes round and round. Troll . . . Jax . . . car accident . . . Hadley. A constant replay.

"She's here, but not. Her eyes are lifeless and she keeps saying Hadley over and over again."

Harper pauses to listen. Normally I would care who's on the other line, I think. I can't find the energy to care. Not tonight. Tonight I just want to sleep even though it's pointless. Sleep won't be coming anytime soon.

"No, I didn't want to worry him. Besides, something tells me she needs you right now."

Another pause.

"Because . . . she keeps saying your name too," Harper says quietly as if she doesn't want to admit this.

Her voice drowns out again as I relive the last words I ever said to my dad in my head.

I was hurt that he didn't trust my judgment. He kept asking questions I couldn't answer. I promised . . . someone . . . it would be our secret . . . nobody would know that it was . . . I groan as that thought floats away, leaving me with more questions I don't have the answers to.

I was mad that my Dad was pushing me. Mad that my parents ambushed my last swim meet by inviting Jax. I wanted to hurt my Dad. I wanted him to feel how I felt. I said the most untruthful words I've ever spoken out loud. Words that I can never take back. Those will forever be the last words he's ever heard from me. At least with my mom, I was able to say sorry and tell her how much I loved her. I will never get that chance with my dad.

Startling Harper, I jump off the lounge chair and fall to the floor in front of the iron railing. I rock back and forth. I would expect anyone to start freaking out right about now, but nope, not my best friend. She sits right down besides me, throws an arm around my shoulder and hugs me while she helps sway me back and forth. She doesn't say anything, neither do I.

Harper's arm drops from my shoulder and she's gone. I want to cry out to her. To tell her I won't always be this broken, that I need her, that I can't be alone right now. I even manage to open my mouth to beg her to stay, but nothing comes out. I just continue to rock into the railing.

"Please . . . Please . . . Help . . . Sister . . . Hurt," I choke out to the paramedic who is trying to put something over my mouth.

"Shh. I need you to stay calm for me. Okay? Let us do our job. We got her now." He says it reassuringly, I'm sure to help me relax.

I don't feel relaxed. I need to see her. Where is she? Why aren't they working on her? I'm fine. Just a few broken bones. I attempt to tell him again that I'm fine, but nothing comes out. Panic breaks through the surface and I struggle against them, desperate to see Hadley. Where is she? The morning sun blinds me, making it impossible to see without squinting.

Gathering all the strength that I have left, I push the paramedic out of my face, force myself to sit up and scream as loudly as I can, "Hads! Help, Hadley!"

The paramedic gently but firmly pushes me back down onto the gurney. I don't struggle against him anymore. I'm dying. My breaths are coming slower; this time I don't fight it. I couldn't even if I wanted to.

"We're losing her!" someone shouts in the distance.

I'm surprised he sounds so far away. The guy is hovering over me. Why does he sound so far away? Everything starts to float away. I feel lighter.

Before my eyes close for the final time, I see her. They have my sister. She has a mask over her face. A woman runs out of the ambulance with the defibrillator. The man doing compressions doesn't pause while the pads are placed on her chest. Everything clicks into place. I gather enough strength to keep my eyes open just a little longer. With everything inside of me, which isn't a lot, I stay awake. This may be the last time I ever see her alive again. I won't think of what it's going to be like to not have her in my life.

Time stops.

One . . . Two . . . Three . . . Four . . . Five . . .

Breathe.

I need you!

"We have a pulse!" the woman announces.

As the blackness takes over, I only have one thought.

She's alive.

The ground disappears beneath me. I breathe in the scent that reminds me of home. It's so strong that it lures me out of my self-inflicted torture. Wrapping my arms around his neck, I cuddle into his chest fully aware that I should resist him but I can't. Not tonight. Tonight I want to be in his arms. Tomorrow I'll be strong. Tonight I'll be weak in Jax's strong arms. Jax's lays me in my bed and starts to pull away.

"Stay," I manage to squeak out.

"I'm not going anywhere, Ads. I'm just going to talk to Harper then get you in some pjs. Then we will cuddle like old times. Okay?"

He kisses my nose and waits for me to nod against his lips before walking away. At the door he gives me a warm smile then disappears to talk to Harper. I wait for a minute or two but when I don't hear the front door opening and closing, I get restless. My mind has finally cleared enough that I am fully aware of what's going on again. I don't want to hide away in my room. I need to face Harper so that she knows I'm not mental.

I tiptoe around in the hallway and pause as they speak in the living room. I'm spying. I mold my body close to the wall so I can't be seen while I listen.

"I knew something was wrong immediately. She sounded like she was crying," Harper informs Jax.

"She doesn't cry."

"I know! That's why I came here without another word. I was prepared to see her bawling her eyes out or something . . ." Her voice trails off.

"But that's not what you found?"

"She was here, but wasn't. She was just gone. She was outside when I came in. From a distance I thought she was asleep, but when I got close I heard her mumbling and saw that the light had left her eyes."

Nobody says anything for a while. I can hear Jax pacing back and forth. Even after everything that has happened between us, I know he wants to be here for me. He can't help it even if he knows he shouldn't. Just like I should force him to leave, be strong enough without him, but I can't. Not tonight. Tonight I need Jaxon Chandler as much as I need to breathe.

I also know that when the sun breaks through my plum curtains, that it will be over. We will go back to our separate lives, my heart broken all over again, and this time I'm willingly allowing it to happen.

"Hadley's her sister right?" Harper asks quietly, as if she's afraid to ask.

"Hadley was her little sister."

"I won't ask anymore questions. If Addie is ever ready to tell me, I'm here for her. I'm not very forthcoming with information, either, so I understand."

My entire body relaxes. I thought she would have pushed for answers and I'm glad that I was wrong. She isn't pissed at me for keeping something like this from her. Which of course makes me wonder what she's hiding. I know she's hiding something, but I won't press. When she's ready to open up, I'll be here for her. Just like she is for me.

"Thanks," Jax says, breaking the silence.

"For what?"

"Calling me."

"Don't make me regret it. I already had Logan's name on my screen, ready to press the call."

"What stopped you?" Jax asks for both of us.

"You. She called out your name. I was here for almost an hour before I called you. She was either silent or saying Hadley. Then she said your name. After that, I knew I had to call you."

I would give anything to see his face. I want to see if he's freaking out or not. I move away from the wall to go in there, but Harper's voice stops me.

"I'm gonna go. Something tells me that you can do more for her than I can."

Not wanting to be found, I slip back inside my room. Right before I shut my door, I hear Harper threaten Jax.

"I don't care that you've been in her life forever, I will murder you," Harper says darkly. "If you make her worse than she is now, you will regret ever breathing. I promise you."

Whoa. She's a badass. If I was on the receiving end of that, I'm pretty sure I would have pissed my pants. I've never heard her talk like that before. Each word was laced with such promise that I have no doubt that she will follow through.

Footsteps come down the hallway so I'm forced to run across my room and jump on my bed. I should pretend to be asleep. I don't. I just wait. Straining to listen, I hear the door shut and then heavy footsteps. I perch on the end of my bed and hold my breath. I count to twelve in my head before I hear Jax sigh loudly. *Don't leave. Please don't leave me again.*

Jax opens my door. He doesn't say anything and neither do I. Silently, I watch him walk over to my dresser and pull out pjs.

"I'm gonna help you into this."

It's the only one of his shirts I kept. I couldn't part with it, it's the very first shirt I stole from him. It's faded, has a large hole on the hem, but otherwise in decent condition.

"If you don't want me to, I'll turn around, but I'm not leaving."

All I hear is he isn't leaving. He's going to stay. I try to give him a small smile to let him know that I'm okay, but I fail.

"Hands up."

Raising my hands, I study his face. He doesn't take his gaze off mine while he removes my shirt. He slides his old shirt over my head, but before sliding it all the way off, he reaches behind me and unclasps my bra. He slips each strap off my shoulders and tugs my bra out of the sleeve, all without taking his eyes off mine.

"Up."

I stand and rest my head on his hard chest, exhausted. He unbuttons my pants and slides them past my butt.

"Sit," he orders quietly when he's pushed them down as far as he can.

Jax finishes pulling off my pants with practiced ease. Even though the pain from seeing him is so painful that I have to rub my chest, I'm happy he's here. It's as if I'm losing him all over again. Which is stupid. He wasn't even mine. Can't lose something I've never had.

". . . everything or just the end?" Jax asks

"What?"

Jax regards me with a small grin. He knows why I wasn't paying attention. I love that he isn't treating me differently, like I'm made of glass. I love that he's still being the Jax that I know and love. Love. No. I don't *love him love him*. I love him like a dear friend. Yeah, I can't even swallow that down without an eye roll. Hopefully if I say it enough times, I will start to believe it. If only it was that simple.

"I asked if you heard everything or just the end."

I shrug in answer. I have no idea how he knows that I was listening to him and Harper, but then again it's Jax.

"Thought so," he says as he gets up.

I can't help the panic that overtakes me. When he strides past my door and to the bathroom, I'm finally able to breathe normally. *He's not leaving.*

Jax holds up my hair brush like it's a gold medal. His face falls when he sees my panic. In a few long strides, Jax is bending down so that we're on the same level.

"I'm. Not. Leaving," he says slowly.

Resting my head against his forehead I give him my first real smile tonight. It's small but it's real. Just being in his presence comforts me. It reminds me of our childhood, simpler times. After another minute or two that goes by too quickly, I finally pull away from him. I have to remind myself that he's only here for the night. He isn't staying. I only have this one night with him before reality returns.

If I only have tonight with Jax, I'm going to make the best of it. I'm going to say good-bye to him for good. After tonight, I will move on. It will hurt, most days will be worse than the day before, but I'll survive. The worst has already happened to me. I can handle losing the man I love. I don't want to, but I'll move on to someone else. It might be Kohen. It might not. I know whoever I fall in love with, I will never be able to feel the same way I do about Jax. Jax is my great love. My soul yearns for him.

"I don't remember hair brushes being part of our sleepover requirements when we were younger," I say over my shoulder when he starts to brush my hair.

"Well, since you don't need a first aid kit for me, I thought we could change tonight up a bit." He shrugs like it's not a big deal.

I try to act nonchalant even though I feel anything but nonchalance remembering the countless times I patched up his dad's handiwork.

"So you're going to brush my hair?" I ask again.

"Yes and you're going to talk to me."

I don't say anything. What do you say when an unbelievably hot man tells you he's going to brush your hair while you pour out your feelings? Nothing. So instead I relax into him.

"Where were you going tonight? Shouldn't you have been at dinner with Logan?" Jax asks me after about ten minutes.

The soft strokes of the brush almost hypnotize me into sleep, but remembering where I saw him and what he was doing jolts me awake. Gritting my teeth, I count to five slowly, attempting to calm down.

"I was going for a walk," I say once I'm sure I won't lash out at him.

He nods as if this makes perfect sense. After another minute he sets the brush down on the nightstand. Then he drags me to him so I'm resting against his chest while he leans against the headboard. I melt into him thinking that the interrogation ended.

"How was therapy?"

I should have known better. Jax isn't known for letting things go.

"Fine."

"Obviously you got worked up. That's why you went on a walk. That's why I found you like I did." He says the last part quietly.

I don't even attempt to count and calm down. I can't. Not about this. I'm out of bed glaring at him.

"Who do you think you are? You don't know me! You don't care! You weren't here! You didn't find me! Harper called you! You left! You fucking left me like always!"

I'm crackling in anger. My entire body trembles from the physical need to hit something or someone, but I refuse to give into the urge. In the next second, Jax wraps me in his arms. I thrash, squirming to get away from him. It's pointless, I know it, but I can't stop fighting him. I don't need him. I want to hurt him. Not because he's Jax, but because he's here. I don't want to be the only one dying inside.

"I-I . . ." I can't even say I hate him. I don't, and no matter what, the words won't come out.

Out of nowhere a memory of Jax leaving me standing in the middle of LAX airport bombards my thoughts. I'm begging him to stay with me in California, not to go back to NYU. He didn't even look at me as he broke my heart and walked away, without a promise to return. As I concentrate on when this was, everything surrounding it, the vague memory drifts away, leaving more questions.

"You left me," I murmur again and again.

I repeatedly pound my fist into his chest. He doesn't say anything or try to stop me. I'm not hitting him hard enough to hurt him, but even if I was, I doubt that he would stop me.

"It's okay," Jax says once I drop my hands to my side.

I gaze into his green eyes. His sincerity is why words tumble out of my mouth without any conscious thought.

"They left me. I listened to them die, Jax. I wasn't able to do anything but watch as my mom died right before my eyes! I'm so mad at them. All of the time. Why did they die and I survived?"

My legs give out, but before I can fall to to the floor, Jax catches me. Instead of carrying me the short distance to my bed like I expect, he sinks to the ground and leans against my bed frame with me in his lap. I rest my head against his shoulder and lay my hand over his beating heart. Jax stops rubbing my arm, laces his fingers through mine. Warmth radiates off his hand. He makes me feel safe.

"How could they leave me? I can't . . . I miss them every day. There's days I wake up and I forget about the accident and I'm happy. I'm blissfully happy. Then reality comes back with a vengeance and I lose them all over again. There's times when I even go as far to call out for my dad. I hate that! I hate not knowing when I'm going to wake up and think that they're alive. I fucking hate that I live for those mornings, just to be truly happy, only to be crushed all over again."

Jax wipes his thumb over my cheek and it's then that I realize I'm bawling. Reaching up, I touch my face. The wetness I feel is foreign. I don't cry. Ever. I haven't cried in six years.

"I'm so angry! All of the time! I'm so angry at them! They left me!" I cry into his shirt.

I don't know how long we stay like this, me sobbing into his shirt while he holds me. He never tries to tell me it will be okay or some other bullshit advice. He kisses the top of my head while drawing patterns on my arms. It feels like I'm going to run out of tears, but just keep pouring down my cheeks. I can't stop mourning what I lost, what was stolen from me.

I cry for the death of my parents.

I cry for the death of Hadley.

I cry for the death of me.

Feeling like it's been hours since I started weeping I try to calm down. Which of course just makes me cry harder. Why can't I stop sobbing? I clutch onto Jax, afraid that he's going to get up and leave me like this.

"Don't . . . I—"

"I know, just let it out. I'm not going anywhere," Jax whispers into my hair.

Just hearing that he isn't leaving me is enough to help me breathe again. I gave up wiping my face a long time ago since it's pointless. I snuggle into Jax's chest and breathe him in, willing the tears to stop. After what feels like another hour, the tears finally dry up. I wipe my face and nose with the end of Jax's dress shirt.

"Sorry," I mumble, not feeling sorry at all.

Jax brushes the hair out of my face and kisses my nose. "Don't be."

When I'm finally calmed down again, Jax picks me up as if I weigh nothing and strolls to the bathroom with me in his strong arms. He cleans off my face with a warm towel while I sit and watch him take care of me. Once he's satisfied, he carries me back to my bed. After covering me in my blanket, he turns off the light. My side lamp is on so I can still see clearly, but I'm not blinded by the light anymore. He kicks off his shoes. After stripping out of his shirt and carelessly throwing it on the floor, he unbuttons his pants.

"We're gonna cuddle like old times and if you want to talk more, I'm going to listen. If you just want me to hold you, then you'll be in my arms all night."

I study his face while he strips out of his pants. As much as I want to stare at other places on his body, I can't. Nothing has changed between us and I need my friend right now.

Jax peels back the duvet and slides in next to me. He lifts his arm in the air, an invitation for me to cuddle. I don't need to be told twice. I eagerly lay my head on his chest, and wrap my leg over him, while he holds onto me tightly. I melt into him, expecting to sleep but to my surprise, I open up more.

"I told Liv about the crash . . . It was like I was there all over again. Reliving it all. I could see it all as clear as I can see you. I was so scared. I didn't know what to do. I couldn't save them. I couldn't—"

"Stop. You did everything that you could. You need to stop blaming yourself. It wasn't your fault. I miss them too, but I'm not sorry that you're here, Ads. I need you to be here. I can't imagine losing you." His voice cracks.

Gazing into his eyes, I know he's telling the truth. Which makes it impossible for my heart not to break a little more. He loves me. I know he does. Everything he does proves it over and over again, but he's not willing to do anything about it for whatever reason. Hearing the sincerity in his voice shatters me.

"I don't know how to live without them," I admit.

"One day at a time," he says, repeating what Liv has told me countless times.

"I know, it's just hard." Stalling, I nuzzle closer to him. "I felt like I was betraying them somehow. I wouldn't allow myself to be happy because they weren't here. Anytime I started to live again, I could hear my dad's head hit the window. I'd hear my mom's last words and, mostly I would see Hadley's lifeless body while the paramedics tried to save her."

"They wouldn't—"

"I know. That's why I started trying. I realized that if things were different and she was here instead of me, I wouldn't want her weighed down by guilt. I would want her to live to the fullest because I couldn't. I would want her to live for me. That's what I'm doing. I'm living for all of them, especially Hadley. She was so young, she didn't get to experience life. I feel like I tainted their memories somehow because I haven't been experiencing life for so long."

I close my eyes and picture my parents and my little sister. Instead of seeing their lifeless bodies, I see them alive and happy. I see my dad hugging my mom while they dance in our kitchen, and I see Hadley twirling around the house in a tutu when she was eight. I'm surprised that the images don't make me fall apart. Instead they make me smile, a sad smile, but it's still more than I've been able to do in the last six years. Anytime I remember them, I've always felt guilty. It's strange not having that guilt anymore.

"That's why I won't go back to the way I was. I can't. I know if I do, I won't be able to pull myself out of it again. And I couldn't do that to them.

My mom told me to be strong and I need to start being the strong person she believed I was."

Jax doesn't say anything and I'm glad. He kisses the top of my head. Seconds turn into minutes with neither of us speaking, just basking in each other's warmth. Eventually Jax ends the silence.

"I'm proud of you. You're the strongest person I have ever known. You had your entire world turned upside down, everything was taken from you, but you didn't give up. You—"

"I did give up."

Jax turns my head so that I'm forced to look at him.

"No. You. Did. Not. Give. Up." He says each word slowly. I manage to give a little nod because I don't trust my voice.

"I've watched you for the past six years. You continued to fight even if you weren't aware of it."

I start to interrupt him, but he places a finger over my lips, silencing me.

"Every day you got up and went to school. You graduated top of the class and now you're pursuing a career we both know you don't really want. You've been through more than anyone should at such a young age, but you never gave up. I don't want you feeling guilty because you think you haven't been living. You have, just in your own way. You had to overcome everything going on in your head to fully come back to us . . . to me."

I desperately want to kiss him, but I can't. I know he believes every word he just said, and for some unknown reason, I believe it, too. I kept fighting . . . It just took me six years to realize what I was fighting for . . . I was fighting for me, for life.

"I don't remember our sleepovers being so depressing," I say, trying to lighten the mood.

He forces out a laugh. "Yeah, because sneaking into your room against my best friend's back was sunshine and daisies."

"You know what I mean."

"I know," he says with a sad smile before reaching over me to turn off my side lamp.

"You know, if you ever want to talk about that, I'm here," I say into the darkness.

Jax's body tenses. I immediately regret bringing up his past. If he wanted to talk about it, he would. I mentally curse myself.

"I don't even know what to say." Jax breaks though my internal rant.

"Whatever comes to you," I say, repeating what Liv has told me several times.

I count to thirty. I'm positive that Jax is just going to change the subject or go to bed. This is untouched territory for us. We've never really spoken about all those nights long ago. It's kind of like an unspoken promise to not mention it, even back when I was patching him up. I'm about to open my mouth to relieve the tension in the room when Jax finally speaks.

"Okay."

CHAPTER TWENTY-EIGHT

Okay.

I will myself to stay perfectly still. He's never once ever talked about what happened in his house. I don't want to move or talk. Heck, I don't even want to breathe in fear that Jax will snap out of it and shut down on me. That I'm used to. Jax is always shutting people out, especially me. *Please, please open up.*

Jax has stopped drawing patterns on my back, and instead squeezes me so tightly that I'm positive that I'll have bruises by my ribs. I don't care. If a few bruises is all it takes for Jax to open up to me, I'll gladly show them off. Jaxon Chandler is about to confide in me.

I've counted to one hundred . . . twice. Still nothing. It's time for me to push him like he has pushed me to do things I reluctant to do.

"Have you ever talked to Wyatt about it? Has he ever said sorry or anything?"

Even though I asked, I already know the answer. There's no chance in hell that Wyatt has ever apologized. He isn't sorry. I doubt that pathetic excuse of a man is sorry for anything.

"You already know the answer."

"Enlighten me anyways."

Jax doesn't say anything at first. He squeezes me a little tighter to him, if that's even possible. I suck in a breath to keep from wincing. *It's just a little pain.* I remind myself that the pain is worth it.

Almost like he can read my mind, Jax releases his death grip. He still clings to me, but now I'm able to breathe normally without my ribs feeling like they're going to burst into my lungs.

"Wyatt isn't the kind of person to apologize." Jax rakes his hand through his hair, a gesture I know all too well. "Besides, what would I ask him? Oh hey, Dad, remember when you used to beat the shit out of me? Do you ever regret it? Did you ever feel bad? Did you ever want to kill me, or did you just settle for beating the shit out of me until I begged for death so the pain would stop?"

Tears sting my eyes from hearing the truth in his words. I knew it was awful, I saw it. Heck, I even had to Google how to sew because he refused to go to the doctors for stitches. I just never imagined it was that bad. Which, of course, is stupid. I guess I didn't want to believe it was that bad. I can't comprehend how someone could torture their own kid. The only thing I'm sure of is that Wyatt Chandler shouldn't be able to breathe. He shouldn't be allowed to practice medicine, when he's the reason why Jax would sneak into my bedroom at night. Wyatt is the perfect actor, pretending to have been the best role model for his soon. When you're a renowned cardiovascular surgeon, nobody questions you.

"I hate him!" I finally manage to spit out.

"I wish I could say that . . . There was so many times that I've said that, I even believed it, but I realize that I can never hate him."

"Even after everything he's done to you?" My voice cracks.

"Even after everything, I can't hate him." He pauses to collect himself. "On some level, I understand why he did it."

"What?" I roar, wishing that the light was on so I can see his face. The tears that I've been fighting to hold in silently roll down my face.

Jax not hating his father is one thing. I was okay with that. People have their own feelings. I mean, I hate the man enough for both of us so it's fine. But to understand why Wyatt used Jax for his personal punching bag is not something I'm okay with . . . I'm not equipped to handle this.

Yeah, cause somebody deserves to get a glass vase thrown at him because there was water on the bathroom floor after his shower. Several pieces were embedded into his back since he was only wearing a towel when Wyatt came storming into his room that morning. Jax went the whole day with pieces of glass in his back because he couldn't reach them himself.

One of the millions of memories that haunt me about Jax's past comes rushing forward.

"Have you seen Jax?" Logan immediately asks me before I can shut the front door.

I drop my swim bag onto the floor, dread sinking in. Instantly I paste a fake smile on my face to hide my fear. "No. Wasn't he at practice with you and Connor?"

"No, he didn't show up for practice. Chris said that he left early, sometime during fifth period. Just got up and walked out of class."

My earlier dread is nothing compared to what I'm feeling now. I saw him this morning when he came over to take us to school, but that was it. He didn't even look up at me when I said good morning. I knew something was wrong then. I just didn't know how to ask him if he was okay with everyone in the kitchen. So instead of talking to him, I watched while he ate my last yogurt. He barely joked about it too. I should have cornered him then and sought out answers.

My heart pounds loudly, my hands tremble, I need to tell my parents about Jax's secret. If I do, I know Jax will find some way to deny everything. He won't risk being taken away from his dad, from me. I've tried over and over again to make him see reason. I know our parents will take him in, but he won't let me confide in them. Every day I live with the fear of his Dad going too far.

Cursing myself for not pushing the subject this morning, I fidget with the straps of my practice suit. I can't stay still. I'm itching to fumble into my bag for my phone and text Jax, but I don't want to in front of my brother.

"How did you get home?" I ask instead, pretending that I'm not scared shitless.

Jax didn't sneak into my room last night. Every night I make sure the house alarm is off and that my window is unlocked, just in case he needs to sleep over here. When he's here, I can take care of him and know that he's okay. When he's not, I always think the worst. I always imagine him bloody, broken on the floor, unable to move. I usually don't get any sleep, and if I do, I have nightmares.

"Connor." Logan focuses on his phone again.

"Hmm, well I haven't seen him since this morning when he stole my last yogurt." I try to act like I'm not worried so that I can get to my room as quickly as possible. "I didn't see him at school at all, but I hardly do unless

I eat lunch with you guys. I just thought you guys went off campus for lunch. Have you called him?"

"Huh?"

"See that shiny thing in your hand? It's called a phone. Use it. Call Jax," I snap at him.

Logan doesn't know things about his best friend that I do, but still, he should realize something is wrong if Jax wasn't at practice. Jax never misses practice.

"I did. No worries though, Addie, he'll text me when he's feeling better."

"Feeling better?" I squeak out.

Logan rubs my wet hair. "Don't worry, you won't get sick before your meet this weekend."

Forcing myself to laugh, I just nod. Jax getting me sick was the last thing on my mind.

"Okay, well, tell him I hope he feels better." I move towards the stairs. "I'm gonna jump in the shower. I didn't have time after practice since Mom had to go pick up Hads from ballet."

He nods. "Connor is gonna bring over something to eat since the parentals have that charity thing. Want to watch a movie with us?" he asks while he texts away on his phone.

"No. I'm just gonna eat in my room then go to bed. I'm pretty sure Coach is trying to kill us with all the in-n-outs we had to do today." I don't even wait for a response before dashing up the stairs to my room.

I'm tearing into my bag as I reach the top of the stairs. As I near my door I'm already calling Jax. It goes straight to voicemail.

"Call me when you get this . . . I'm worried," I say as I open my door.

I lock my door before turning on the light. I scream when I see a pale Jax sitting on my bed, head in his hands. He lifts his head and gives me a weak smile.

"Hi," he whispers.

"Ja—"

I hear Logan running up the stairs.

"What's wrong Addie?" Logan asks on the other side of my locked door.

Jax winces as he tries to get up. I hold up my hand to tell him to stay put. He doesn't move again, but he doesn't take his eyes off my door, either.

"Sorry, I thought I saw a spider," I call with a false laugh.

"Thought you saw a spider?" Logan asks.

"Yeah, but it was just lint. I'm gonna jump in the shower then I'll be down to grab some food."

"You're lucky the guys weren't here. I don't think Connor and Jax would ever let you live that down. I thought somebody was in there trying to kill you."

I force myself to chuckle again. Logan's steps drift away and when I can't hear him anymore, I sigh.

"That was close," Jax says.

Putting my hands over my face, I force myself to take deep calming breaths. "We need to tell someone," I manage to say when I finally lower my hands.

"I have five more months left and I'm free."

"Jax, I can't keep lying. You could die!" I plead with him.

He attempts to stand but he's too weak. "If you do, I'll lose everything." I know he's talking about college. A new life for himself, out of his father's shadow. "I can't risk going into the system. The beatings aren't as bad anymore."

I hate that I agree with him. On some messed-up level, Wyatt has lightened up since Jax has gotten older. He's not the easily beaten child anymore. Wyatt saves his punishments for when he can unexpectedly lash out at him. Usually with some sort of weapon to make the beating that much more severe. Jax used to suffer from the lick of Wyatt's belt, now it's from anything that Wyatt can find.

My anger disappears when I realize the extent of his pain. I shuffle towards him and decide not to push the subject.

"Ever heard of a cell phone?" I ask.

"Yeah, sorry I didn't mean to scare you," Jax says quietly.

"You didn't."

Jax raises an eyebrow.

"Okay. Fine. But in my defense, I wasn't expecting to walk in here with you in my bed." Jax gaze sinks to the rug. "Which brings us back to the the whole cell phone thing. Where's your phone, Jax?"

"Left it at home. I didn't have time to grab it this morning. I barely had time to grab my car keys."

Forcing myself to remain calm, I ask the question I'm dreading to have answered. "What happened?"

Wincing, Jax turns around and carefully lifts his shirt. At first I think Jax's back is covered in sparkles. Then I see the blood. Not sparkles. Glass.

"How long?" I ask, already flying towards the first aid kit I keep safely hidden at the bottom of my closet.

After the first night I found Jax, I realized that I needed to get my own first aid kit that had more to offer than a range of Band-Aids. Plus, I'm pretty sure my parents would've noticed if our medical supplies kept disappearing. Walking back to Jax, I attempt the one-eyebrow thing that he does so well. By Jax's smirk, I don't think I pulled it off.

Gripping the tweezers, threatening, I say, "I can either be really nice or I can be really rough."

"I can just have someone else do it," Jax bluffs.

I call his bluff. Waving my hand towards the door I say, "Go right ahead, I'll even lend you my first aid kit."

I know he won't go to anyone else which will mean that he will just suffer. I'm about to say never mind when Jax lets out a big huff of air.

"Fine. This morning."

I busy myself with the tweezers. This morning. Okay, that's better than what I was thinking. I was thought something happened last night and that's why he didn't come over, because he couldn't. At least he was safe last night. I hope. Jax sucks in a breath when I get closer to him.

"Relax, you big baby. I haven't even touched you yet," I say.

Different colors of bruises cover his back. The yellow ones are old, from last Monday's punishment. Jax left his soccer ball out and Wyatt almost tripped on it. By almost, I mean he saw it out of Jax's room and therefore he could have tripped on it in the middle of the night so he punched Jax in the back two times. There are new bruises, though. It's Friday. I haven't seen him since Monday night so these could be from any of the other nights.

"And these?" I ask, lightly brushing my lips to the darkest bruise on his back.

"He had to wake me up on Wednesday. Apparently, I made him late to work so when I came home from school and he was waiting for me."

I'm afraid to ask what he used because I know it wasn't his fist. No, Wyatt only settles for his own hands if he can't reach anything. He wouldn't want to damage his life-saving instruments.

"Okay, I'm gonna start pulling the glass out," I tell Jax once I'm positive that I've cleaned the tweezers enough.

His whole body tenses. Not for the first time, I wish I could take his pain away. I always have to stop myself from telling my parents. The only reason

I don't is because Jax swears he will run away and give up college. He's a senior, but he's only sixteen since he skipped a grade before he moved to California. He has five more months until college and he's free of Wyatt. He's gotten full academic scholarships from the best Ivy leagues.

Connor and Logan are going to New York, Jax is still undecided. I know moving 3000 miles away from his father will be good for him, it will give him a fresh start. I can't help my heart breaking when I think about it, though. Every time his scholarships are brought up, I have to mold into a carefree smile even though I'm dying. Five more months and Jax, the boy that I love, might be on the other side of the country. Five more months and I won't have to picture a broken, lifeless Jax on the floor, bleeding out from the hands of his father. We can survive five more months.

It has to be enough, I can't lose him. We've come so far.

I turn his face towards me so he can see how serious I am. "Every night, come here. It's the only way I'll know you're safe. I can't keep wondering if he's—"

He lands a whisper of a kiss on my more than willing lips. "If that's what you need, then I promise every night I'll be here."

I refuse to smile, not until I'm sure that he knows I'm not going to bend on this anymore. My hands shake as I prepare myself to ask something from him that I know I shouldn't. It's risky, any night his father could suddenly care enough to check if Jax is home, and if he does, he'll be at my house. I shudder as I think of Wyatt finding out. I don't care about my parents, I'll be relieved if that happens.

"Every night Jax. I don't care, if you're not here, I'll tell my parents. I won't risk your life. I'd rather you run away."

He squeezes my hand. "I promise."

I kiss his shoulder blade, before getting to work. After pulling out the fifth piece of glass I murmur, "Why did you wait until now to have me take these out?"

"I think asking to go to your room so you can pull out glass might have raised some questions from everyone. Don't you think?"

"Okay, but you could have just snuck in here," *I point out.*

"Everybody was already up. Besides I thought I could patch myself up for once." *He grins. I don't return it.* "Once the adrenaline left, I knew that I needed your help, but it was too late to ask."

"When did you calm down?" *I ask quietly, too afraid if I speak too loudly he'll stop talking.*

"When I opened your fridge."

"How—"

"I saw you only had one more yogurt and I pictured your face watching me eat the last one. So I grabbed it and waited for you to come down the stairs." He winks at me. "Ow!"

"Whoops." I repeat him from this morning when he took the first bite of my last yogurt.

"I'm in pain here."

"So was my stomach all morning," I complain, but pluck the last piece of glass more gently.

"You'll forgive me soon enough," Jax says with a laugh then winces immediately.

There isn't anything to forgive, but I'm not gonna tell him that. Grabbing my phone, I look at the time. Connor will be here any second and I told my brother that I was jumping into the shower. I know I'm being paranoid, but I can't help it. Logan finding out that Jax stays the night is the least helpful thing that can happen. He won't be pleased.

Feeling me tense behind him, Jax turns around. "What's wrong?"

"I need to take a shower," I say.

"And?"

I ignore him and inspect the cuts in his back. Luckily none of them need stitches. I hate when Jax makes me stitch him up. I shudder, remembering the first time two years ago. We had to be as sterile as possible so he didn't get an infection. When Jax passed out from the pain, I snuck into his house and stole supplies from Wyatt's medical bag. I was so nervous that I kept shaking so it took longer and hurt worse. Now I think I'm almost as good as the doctors and that's pretty good in my opinion since I'm only fifteen.

After re-cleaning the wounds on his back and applying antibiotic ointment, I put one small Band-Aid on the only cut that needs it. They're not as bad as I first imagined when I saw the tiny shards of glass sticking out of his back. I can't help but tremble thinking about Jax going through the motions of high school with pieces of glass in his back. This kid is something else.

"I don't know," I finally say.

Always able to read my mind, Jax turns around and hugs me.

"I'm okay," he says into my hair. "It's just a few scratches."

"I hate him!"

"I know."

I hate that Jax can forgive his father. He should despise him for everything that Wyatt puts him through. This is why Jax is better than anyone I know, he isn't capable of hating anyone. I, on the other hand, hate Wyatt Chandler with a burning passion. If he was on fire, I would roast a marshmallow on the flames coming off his body.

"Hurry up with the shower so we can get to bed," Jax says as he releases me.

I take the quickest shower known to man and that's saying something since I'm a swimmer. Speed racer status, I jump into my pjs and run a comb through my tangled hair. Once I'm decent, I return to my room to see Jax sitting on my bed doing his homework. Following his lead, I grab the one page of geometry I have left. I finished most of it before practice.

"I had more!" I say when I see him eyeing my homework.

"Before or after practice?"

Sometime he knows me too well. It should be annoying, but it's not. "Before." I'm about to say something more, but my stomach growls loudly, making both of us laugh.

"Go down and eat." Jax holds my homework hostage. "This will be here when you get back."

"Fine."

I race down the stairs. The front door opens at the same time that I reach the last step.

"Come on in," I say jokingly to Connor.

"Ah . . . Ah . . . Ah," Connor wiggles a finger in front of my face. "Be nice or I won't share any of my pizza and I even got your favorite."

"Have I told you how much I love you lately?" I steal the small box of pizza that I know is mine and lead him to our massive kitchen.

"She's gonna be trouble when she's older," Connor informs Logan.

"Don't remind me," Logan says as he pulls down three glasses.

"Three? Aren't you missing a glass?" Connor says, making my heart beat rapidly. He can't possibly know that Jax is here.

"Hads is at her friends for the night." Logan pours soda in all three glasses.

Opening the fridge, I ignore the rest of their conversation as I stare at the yogurt filling the middle shelf. It's practically overflowing with Greek yogurt.

"Did Mom go shopping?" I ask even though I know she didn't.

"I don't think so, why?"

"Just wondering," I say with a smile as I snag a Powerade and close the fridge.

Connor takes their box of pizza and follows Logan to the living room. I wait a few seconds until I hear the T.V. before I open the fridge again and steal two yogurts and a bottle of water. After loading the yogurts, spoon, water, and Powerade in a bag, I grab a Cliffbar out of the pantry. I don't know when's the last time Jax ate, but I'm betting he's starving like usual.

My steps are slow as I balance everything while climbing the stairs. Jax locks my door and accepts the orange soda from my hands. He takes a sip before setting it on the nightstand. I spread all the food on the floor, sit down and wait for Jax to join me. Once he's settled, I reach into the bag and hand him a Powerade and grab a slice of pizza for me. Jax helps himself to pizza with a smile on his face.

"Thanks," I say, pointing my pizza at the yogurt on the floor.

Lightly bumping his shoulder with mine he asks, "Am I forgiven?"

I nod and lean against him while I finish eating. After three slices, I yawn loudly, exhausted, ready for bed. I wasn't kidding when I told Logan my coach worked us hard today. I shove the homework that I will have to rush to finish tomorrow into my backpack before crawling into bed.

Jax throws all the trash into a pile next to my door and then comes back over to my bed. I scoot over and raise the blanket for him. Without waiting, Jax lays next to me and touches his lips softly against mine. I smile as his fingers find mine. I fall asleep listening to him breathing while he clasps my hand.

"He blames me." Jax says, pulling me out of the past. "So he took it out on me whenever he could."

"What?" I ask calmly. Jax isn't making sense.

"My mom. She left him and he never got over that. I think he blames me. That's why I always tried to be the perfect kid. That's why I was able to skip a grade when I was younger. I pushed myself to be the best. I thought if I was good enough, she would come home and we would be this happy family again.

"I never gave up hope that she would come home. I just needed to be better. And whenever I made him mad at me, I thought he was punishing me to teach me a lesson. If I learned my lessons and I wasn't bad anymore, she would come home." He snuggles closer to me and breathes me in. "She never came home. She didn't want us, didn't want me."

I feel Jax's pain as if it's my own. I can't even imagine being a child and thinking that. He was so young when his mom left. I don't need to ask if the beatings started when she left. Everything in me screams "yes." I see Jax as a bruised child and I have the sudden urge to vomit. I swallow it down and take deep calming breaths. I will stay strong. Jax doesn't need to be taking care of me.

"I still don't understand," I say quietly into the dark.

"He loved her. He loved her more than anything, more than me. I know he never wanted a child. He despises children, but he gave her one because he wanted to make her happy, but I didn't make her happy, I made matters worse. He would have given her the world. I know what it's like to love someone and not be able to have them. It breaks you." His voice trails off.

I turn my head, looking at his face even though I can't see anything because we're surrounded in darkness. I know he's doing the same.

"He was stuck with a kid that he didn't want. I remind him of her. I look just like her. I will never forgive him and what he did isn't right, but on some level I understand."

A lone tear trails down my face onto his chest. For some godawful reason, I see where Jax is coming from. I understand what Jax is getting at, but that's as far as it will ever go. I will never comprehend why Wyatt did what he did, and I won't pretend to understand. Some things in life are never meant to be solved. I learned that the hard way.

"You're. Not. Him," I say loud and clear.

When Jax stays silent, I try another approach.

"You don't have to be broken, Jax. You're not him. You will never be him. You don't have it in you. You can't even hate him!"

I feel like if I can get it through his head that he's not his father, we can be together. I know this is our make-it-or-break-it point. If Jax doesn't believe me and believe in himself, he will shatter us. We will never have a chance if he thinks that he's his father. He will never be with me if he thinks he will hurt me.

"I am him! Don't you see, Ads? I might not beat little kids, but I'm still fucked up in the head. Look at what I do to you!"

"What?" I ask, wishing that I didn't once the word leaves my mouth.

"I play with you. Over and over again, I lead you on. I let you get close, just to pull away. I can't love you the way you want me to. I can't be loved by you. I'm dark. I can't bring you down in the darkness with me. I won't."

"Jax, I want to be there with you. Where do you think I've been since high school? Taking a vacation? I've been where you are. Shutting the world out. Thinking I don't deserve happiness. I know what that feels like. Heck, I'm there most days! If you're surrounded by darkness, than that's where I want to be. Let me be your light. We'll fight it together. We're better together. Don't you see that?"

"I am not surrounded by darkness, I *am* the darkness, Adalynn." I shiver at his tone. When he speaks again, he's calmer. "It can't be like that. You deserve more. You deserve someone better. You deserve him."

"Kohen?"

"Yes, Kohen. The doctor. You don't see it, but I do. He's a new beginning, I'm the one who reminds you of your past. He won't remind you of what you lost like I do. He makes you smile. He's given you a reason to live again."

"You're wrong!" I whisper.

Neither of us yells. We're barely talking above a whisper, but I can hear each word as if it was announced through a loudspeaker.

"I'm not. You just don't see the change in yourself that I do."

"I gave myself a reason to live again. Not you. Not Kohen. Me! The only people in this world that can take credit for helping me live again are gone! They were taken from me. And you're just going to walk away from me."

"I'm here. I'll always be here for you, Ads. As a friend. That's all we can be. We can't be more." Jax says it so sadly that it breaks my heart even more if that's possible.

We remain silent. I don't pull away from Jax, if anything I mold my body closer to his. Wishing that I can melt into him so that I never have to be apart from him. He holds me as tight as he can without hurting me, as if wishing for the same thing.

A lifetime passes in minutes before I ask, "This is it? There's nothing I can do to change your mind?" I'm desperate for a sign that we can be more.

"Be with Kohen," Jax whispers.

I can't even manage to nod. Tears run down my face and I make no move to stop them. I let them fall. I feel them slide from my cheeks onto

Jax's chest. Jax shifts and gently lifts my chin with his thumb and presses his mouth to mine.

I know this is it. This is our last kiss. This is goodbye. After this, we will be over. No more pretending that I'm moving on from him while secretly hoping that we will work it out in the near future. No, none of that. This is it. After tonight, I'll be moving on. Eventually I'll be happy. Eventually I will be able to be his friend again.

Slowly I kiss him back. Memorizing every second. The way his tongue feels gliding over mine. The small moan that escapes my lips that he breathes in. It's a slow kiss that will forever be etched into my soul.

Jax rolls on top of me. He stares into my eyes as he brushes hair out of my face. I watch him memorize my face, knowing he is saying goodbye too, and that he wants to remember everything about right now just as desperately as I do.

I need to see him. "Wait." I break away from our kiss to turn on my lamp.

"Much better." Jax drags me back to him and lays over me again.

I smile up at him with tears in my eyes. I would give anything to be with him. To be enough for him. To be the one that will make him truly see what a wonderful person he is, inside and out.

Jax bends and follows the trail of each tear with the whisper of a kiss. He barely presses his warm lips to my skin, and I feel each and every kiss all the way to my toes.

I want to confess my love for him. I want to tell him that I don't want to love anyone else, that I can't love anyone else. I want to hear him tell me everything is going to be okay as long as we have each other. I want the big gesture. A piece of me shatters knowing that will never happen. Eventually Kohen will give me the big gesture and someday maybe I'll love him back.

Another piece of me breaks away.

Forcing all thoughts of tomorrow away, I focus on the man I love hovering over me with love in his eyes. This is how I want to remember us. Together, in love. Nothing else matters. All of the petty fights that led us to this moment don't exist. Nothing but Jax exists in this moment.

I trace every line of his face with my fingertips, never taking my eyes off his. Jax does the same and bends every few seconds to peppers my face with soft kisses. Intertwining our hands, Jax leans down for the last time and presses his warm lips to mine. He traces my lips with his tongue. Ever so slowly, he really kisses me. The second his tongue touches mine the tears are back again.

I'll never experience this again. Nobody kisses me like he does. Nobody can make my body feel alive and cherished at the same time like him. There is only one Jax. There is only one true love for everyone and he is mine. Jax squeezes my hand and I squeeze his back. He doesn't speed up the kiss and neither do I. He kisses me slowly, tenderly.

A little piece of me shatters even more.

No matter how much time passes, I know I will never stop loving Jaxon Chandler. He's my first love. My one great love. The kind of love they write stories about. And I never had a chance.

I wish that I could keep kissing him for forever. Wishes don't come true. Time moves too fast. The kiss is over before I want it to be. It was a perfect kiss. A perfect kiss to end our shattered love.

Nine years ago, I kissed the love of my life on my fourteenth birthday. Tonight, we're ending a long, broken love story with the same perfect kiss. This is the end of us.

CHAPTER TWENTY-NINE

Yawning, I snuggle closer into the warm chest behind me. I moan contently when Jax's strong arms tighten around me and he kisses the back of my neck. I turn into him so that my face is pressed against his chest, head resting on his arm. As I press my lips to his chest, I wish that time would stop. I want to be forever held in this man's arm. Just like this, in love. Too bad that time doesn't stand still and that our reality can't let us be together.

Closing my eyes, I breathe him in, loving the way my face breaks into a huge smile just by being near him. He reminds me of home, of hope. I'll miss his touch. I'll miss everything about him.

Wiping a tear from my cheek he whispers, "None of that."

I nod, but the tears keep flowing.

"What's wrong?" he asks into my hair.

I swallow the lump in my throat. "I don't know how to say goodbye." I start to weep silently.

He has a sad smile as he caresses my face. "This isn't goodbye, Adalynn. I'll aways be here. I'll never leave you. Whenever you need, me I'm here." He places his hand over my heart.

I cover his hand and mumble, "I know . . . it doesn't make this any easier." He sucks in a ragged breath. "I know this is what we both need . . . so you have to understand that I'm going to need distance. Jax . . . I can't be around you for awhile. I need space . . . Or I won't—"

"I know," he says, regret clear in his voice.

The urge to kiss him is so strong that I force myself away from the warmth of his body and out of my bed. My body hates the distance that I'm putting between us. *It's for the best.* Knowing that doesn't make this any easier.

"Breakfast?" I ask, needing to do something, anything instead of being in the arms of the man I love, knowing that I can never have him.

After Jax nods, I flee to my bathroom to brush my teeth, but mainly needing a minute alone. Not a second after I flush the toilet, Jax walks in.

My face turns beet red. "Ever heard of a thing called privacy?"

Jax ignores me and grabs his toothbrush that I haven't gotten around to throwing away. Once his toothbrush is in his mouth, he snags mine, squirts toothpaste on it, and hands it to me.

"Thanks."

"Relax. You've thrown up on me. I've seen you pee before. At least this time you were sober." Toothpaste drips down his chin. Without thinking I reach up and wipe it away with my thumb.

"You've never seen me pee and you didn't now. I was already pulling my panties up," I say once I'm finished brushing my teeth.

"Freshman year."

My eyes are trained to his toothbrush. It doesn't belong next to mine. It never did. Forcing the tears away, I snatch it and toss it into the trash. Jax nods as if he knows that it doesn't belong here either.

It's maddening that until yesterday, I haven't cried in six years and now throwing out a pointless toothbrush makes the tears threaten to spill over. *Because in some way you're throwing out Jax.* That little voice in my head reminds me bitterly as if I had a choice in the matter.

When I'm not on the verge of crying any longer, I murmur, "I'm confused."

"I know."

Following him out of my bathroom to my kitchen, I think back to freshman year of high school. That feels like a lifetime ago, which it is. So much has happened since then. I'm still coming up with a blank, though. I wasn't the type of girl to party in high school. Even if I wanted to, nobody gave me alcohol because they were afraid of Logan or Jax beating them up. Those two were beyond annoyingly protective in high school. I can only remember two times in high school when I got drunk. Once freshman year and the other was the day before junior year.

"You're such a liar. I only got drunk—"

"Twice," Jax says while opening the fridge.

"How do you—"

"I was there for the first one. Heard about the second."

"What are you talking about?" I ask after I set a pan on the stove and turn on the flame.

Jax backs our from the fridge, grabbing everything we will need to make breakfast, with a smile on his face. When he sees that I honestly have no idea what he's talking about, his grin turns smug. "Oh, so you don't remember I take it?"

"Cut the crap, Chandler."

"Say please and I might tell you, Maxwell."

I roll my eyes as I mumble, "Please."

He lays pieces of bacon onto the hot pan. "Who was the tiny person with the brown hair on your team? Super loud, super—"

"Lexi," I say, all traces of humor gone.

"That's the one! Remember that 'little' sleepover you went to at her house and it turned into a party?"

Remembering it all too well, I bite out, "Yes."

"Well, you may not have noticed, but Connor and I actually turned up at the party that night."

"I know. I remember."

"Huh? Oh well, I didn't think you noticed since you were pretty hammered by the time we showed up. I let you finish—"

"You let me?" I ask, enraged.

"As I was saying . . ." He points the spatula at me with a grin that drops the second his eyes land on my not-so-amused face. "What's wrong?" he asks, full of concern.

"Nothing," I mumble underneath my breath.

God, I'm being ridiculous. This was high school. I have no idea why I'm letting something that happened over nine years ago still affect me.

"Ads."

"I'm being stupid. Tell me the rest of the story since most of the night is a blur."

Too bad I already had a play-by-play from my "dearest" friend Lexi the next day.

"Okay . . . Well since you were already smashed, I let you finish the drink you were working on, then Connor and I took turns switching your red solo cups with cups of water," he says with a grin. "You never noticed."

Bitterly I ask, "When does the peeing part come in?" I'm ready for this conversation to be over.

"I'll tell you if you tell me what's gotten your panties in a twist." Jax holds his pinky finger up to me.

Knowing that he won't stop until he gets his way, I pinky promise him. He returns to cooking breakfast.

"Excellent." He smiles in victory. "Where was I?"

"You were just explaining that you and Connor liked to ruin my fun even back then."

"Ah, that's right. So eventually you tried to leave the party. So of course I followed you. You got to the mailbox before you fell on your face. You 'tripped,' your words not mine." He turns his head towards me to give me a wink. "After helping you sit up, you grabbed your stomach and said you had to pee. By the looks of it, I knew you wouldn't make it back to the house so I started to help you walk over to the bushes on the side of her yard . . ."

No! I thought that was a terrible nightmare, especially when Lexi told me what her and Jax did all night long.

"So you helped me pee in her bush?" I ask, mortified that I forgot. Apparently my mind knew how traumatizing that was so I repressed it.

"Not exactly . . ." Jax says with a chuckle, making me nervous.

"Jax!" I warn.

"After a few steps I knew we would never reach the bushes with you falling over yourself so I picked you up. I thought we would get there faster. I thought you could hold it. I was wrong . . ."

Jax laughs loudly it's hard to process what he's saying. Staring at him, I try to piece the puzzle back together. I don't remember much after the mailbox. I remember a bush and my dress being held up by strong hands . . . Jax's hands.

"Oh God! You held my dress up while I peed!"

"After . . .yes, though I didn't think it mattered at that point."

"What are you—"

Oh fuck. Please no!

"We didn't make it to the bushes. You peed on me about three steps away from it. You managed to hold the rest in so I could help you pull your panties down and lift your dress up while you finished."

"OH . . . MY . . . GOD . . ." I say through my hands. I refuse to lower my hands and look at him.

"Yup. So you can imagine why seeing you pee on a toilet doesn't bother me . . . So I've had you pee on me and puke on me . . . Let's not go for round . . ." his voice trails off.

There won't be a round two, or three. After today we won't hang out like we used to. After he leaves, the spell will be broken and reality will hit. We won't have any more secret kisses, any inside jokes, he will be Logan's friend. Once he leaves, I lose the love of my life.

Trying to lighten the suddenly dark mood, he nudges me with his shoulder. I force the morbid thoughts away and concentrate on that night nine years ago. Sitting on my stool, hands covering my face, I try to picture the scene Jax describes, but I come up with a blank.

"It doesn't make sense," I say quietly.

"What doesn't?" Jax asks as he sets a plate down in front of me.

Still talking through my hands I ask, "Why were you with me? You were with Lexi all night."

Before I know whats happening, he's pulling my unwilling hands off my face. "What are you talking about?"

Forgetting my humiliation, I admit to him that I know he slept with her. "Lexi . . .That brunette who is super loud, the chick you fucked that night."

This time his laughter isn't forced. Awesome. All of anger I felt all those years ago, when Lexi woke me up bragging that she slept with Jax, bubbles to the surface. I knew then what I know now, Jax wasn't mine and will never be mine.

"It's not funny!" I snap.

"So that's why you refused to talk to me for two weeks . . ." Jax chuckles as he tries to fight the smile on his lips. "Even when I came over at night you just handed me the first aid kit and went to bed. All because of that?"

All traces of humor are gone. I wish I was able to block out those two weeks, but I can't. Those were the worst two weeks of my life, being pissed at Jax and then being pissed at myself for being mad at him. He could sleep with whoever he wanted, I had to remind my fourteen-year-old self. I want to lie to him, but he'll see through me. I nod.

"I was with you all night," he says with hands on my thighs.

All I see is honesty in his eyes. Which doesn't make sense.

"Lexi said you had sex with her."

"Lexi said a lot of things."

Yeah, that's the understatement of the year. I used to think she was so "cool" because she was a junior and wanted to hang out with me all the time. That was before I realized she was only hanging out with me to get closer to Jax. Our friendship ended pretty much the next morning when she confirmed that she slept with him.

"I didn't sleep with her."

I roll my eyes at him. He grips my chin so I can't turn away.

"Not that night. Not any night. I've never slept with her."

"But she said—"

"She said a lot of things, Ads. You know better than anyone that she would lie to anyone willing to listen."

I nod, knowing the truth. "But she was hanging all over you that night."

"Yeah, for about five seconds."

"No."

"Yes. For a whole five seconds, I decided to see if I could get a reaction from you. Then I stopped because I realized it was pointless."

He's lost me. "What?"

"I was a kid. Even back then, I was in love with you. I was trying to make you jealous. I didn't know . . . I mean, I thought you liked me, but I wasn't sure at the time. Those two weeks of silence confirmed my suspicion, though."

I rub my temples. "I'm confused."

Running his hand through his unruly hair again, Jax sighs loudly. "I thought if I could make you jealous then I would know if you cared about me the way I cared about you . . . I never slept with Lexi or anyone in high school."

I hate that I don't want to hear the answer, but I ask anyways. "And college?"

He reaches for my hand, but I jerk away. If he touches me I'll crumble.

"If you're asking if I was a virgin when we slept together, the answer is yes." He caresses my face with his hands. "I didn't lie to you."

I suck in a ragged breath. All this time I thought he was lying to me. I never regretted losing my virginity to him even though I thought he was experienced. I'm glad that I was wrong. It doesn't escape my notice that he uses past tense. I want to ask what he's lied to me about since then, but I don't think I'll want to hear the answer to that, either.

"Do you know who slept with her?" I ask, getting us back on track. I don't want us to focus on losing our virginity to each other.

"No idea," he says with a snicker.

"What's funny?" I ask.

"You refused to talk to me for two weeks. Two long weeks. All because Lexi got laid that night and I took care of you." He has a smirk on his face that I ignore while digging into my yogurt.

We eat in a comfortable silence. By comfortable, I mean Jax holds my hand while my mind races over and over again. I have no idea when he's planning on leaving, and as much as I want to keep him here forever—I would even settle for handcuffing him to my bed—I just want him to leave already. Its *beyond* confusing. The more he stays here with me, touching me, being so sweet, the more I want to convince him to give us a chance. Which of course is beyond idiotic. We've been down that road way too many times. At this point, I've lost count. I have to keep reminding myself that I'm free.

I'm free of my past.

I'm free of Jax.

If only my heart could get on the same page, I would be golden. Barely managing to finish my yogurt, I push my full plate away from me and stands up. Surprisingly, Jax doesn't comment. He probably can sense my nerves, making it impossible to eat.

"So . . ." I cringe at how awkward I'm making this.

"So . . ." Jax repeats, all traces of happiness gone.

Unable to face him, I step on the pedal of the trashcan to lift the lid. I clear my plate while I talk. "I should start getting ready . . . I'm supposed to hang out with Logan and Connor before their flight tonight."

Jax moves behind me to clear his plate, but I sidestep out of his way so we don't accidentally touch. Lovey-dovey time is over. Reality has come too soon, but now that it's here, I can't ignore it. Jax knows how I feel and I know how he feels. Nothing is going to change. Something that I need to remind myself repeatedly so that I don't throw myself at Jax and beg him to never leave me.

I shouldn't have to beg someone to be with me. He either wants me, or he doesn't. He's made it clear that he doesn't. *Time to move on.* A stupid tear slides down my cheek; hastily I wipe it away. After a few deep breaths, I get myself under control.

"Right."

"Are you gonna be there?" I ask, hoping that he can't tell how desperately I want him to say yes at the same time I want him to say no.

Jax shakes his head. "We celebrated the other night. No need to be girls about it, they're only going to be gone for two weeks."

"Right." I shuffle my feet, feeling awkward standing in the kitchen in my raggedy pjs with Jax in his shirt from last night and black briefs. It should be illegal to look that good after waking up. I didn't even get a chance a check my hair in the mirror earlier. I can feel the bird-nests.

"Well . . . I'm just gonna go get changed . . ." Yup, not awkward at all. Points to me.

"Yeah, me too," Jax says as he follows me out of my kitchen. I have to force myself not to run and lock myself in my bathroom.

As awkwardly as humanly possible, I linger in the doorway and watch Jax dress. It's a sight that I can never tire of. His abs flex while he bends to retrieve his clothes from the floor. As he slips his legs into his pants, I bite my lip. This would be so much easier if he wasn't the most beautiful man in the history of the world, inside and out.

"I need you to stop," Jax says in that deep bedroom voice I love.

"Huh?" I ask, puzzled.

He zips his pants, "It's taking everything in me to stay over here . . . I'm not strong enough to do nothing when you keep looking at me like that . . . I'm only human."

Face reddening, I simply manage to squeak out, "Oh."

All that's left is his shoes and then he will be gone. *He's leaving.* I know eventually we will be friends again, but it won't be the same. It can never be the same. I was naive to think that we could ever be friends like before. Everything changed the first time he kissed me on my birthday all those years ago. Everything changed forever when he told me he loves me.

It hits me like crashing into a brick wall. I can't have him leave. I want a forever with him. I don't want to be with anyone else. I don't know how. There's no substitute for him. He will forever be my first choice, the only choice I want.

"Stay," I whisper so quietly, I doubt that he can hear me. He freezes. He heard me.

"Ads—"

"I know. I know for whatever reason, you think you're not good enough. You think that you'll pull me down with you. You're wrong. God, you're so wrong. I love you."

I close the distance between us and stand in front of the man I love, trying for the last time to make him see what I see.

"You brighten my world. You're the air I need to breathe. I need you. I love you! I just want you. Please, Jax. I know you love me. We can make this work. Jump with me. All you have to do is love me, Jaxon."

Tears stream heavily down my face with the truth of my words. His eyes shine.

Gently, as if I'm made of glass, he caresses my face. "I can't, Ads. I'm sorry. You have no idea how sorry I am. I would have given anything in the world to hear you tell me you love me once upon a time, but it doesn't matter anymore, too much has happened. I can't. I'm sorry, but I can't do this."

"What do you mean? What's happened? All that matters is that we love each other."

"I can't tell you, not yet. When you're ready, you'll see I'm doing us a favor."

My voice raises. "Tell me! I want to know why you're giving up on us!"

He remains silent, refusing to tell me the truth once and for all. I push him away from me. Something that I can't focus on flashes through my eyes. For some reason that tiny flash of black and white brings tears to my eyes. Jax is keeping something important from me. Whatever it is, it's the reason why he's ruining us. It's not just his dysfunctional past and his fear of commitment. There's something else, something worse.

"You're keeping something from me! Tell me, I deserve to know what's driving us apart."

He remains silent.

"Please," I beg.

"I can't force you to remember. One day, you'll be ready to hear the truth. When that day happens, I'll be here if you need me, but you won't. When that day comes, you'll hate me forever."

My stomach clenches. Something tears at my mind, but no matter how much I concentrate, I can't reach it. I rub my temples and will the memory to come forth. It doesn't. I watch as he leaves my room. It takes a second for me to follow him to my front door. When he opens it, I slam it closed.

"Tell me!"

Without facing me, he asks in a strangled voice, "What were we fighting about six years ago, the day of the accident?"

I want to scream in frustration. He isn't making sense. He turns to face me, his cheek wet with tears. Whatever I'm repressing is bad.

"What do you remember from that day?" he asks.

"We weren't fighting. My parents flew you three out for my birthday. You guys met us at my swim meet, surprising me. We had dinner together after." And then the accident happened.

He shakes his head.

"Tell me what I'm missing."

"Do you remember what was happening between us before that day?"

My silence is answer enough. For some reason it's fuzzy and it shouldn't be. I thought I was only blocking out the accident and the memories of my family. Until now, I had no clue that I was forgetting something major between us. I study him, begging him silently to explain. If he doesn't, if he chooses to let me live in the void, I will never be able to forgive him.

"We weren't talking, Ads. We didn't talk for the three months leading up to the accident. You refused to take my calls."

I put my hands in my face and weep. "I can't remember!"

"And I can't help you."

My hands fall to their sides. "Why?"

He wipes his face with the back of his hand. "Because you're not ready." He reaches behind him and opens the door again. "When you are, you'll remember."

"If you leave without telling me the truth, I'll never speak to you again. You and I will be done." I step closer so he can see how serious I am. "I will erase you from my memory. Every laugh, every kiss, every touch, will be gone. I will forget everything about us, Jaxon. You'll be just my brother's friend. If you leave without telling me why I stopped talking to you, you will be dead to me."

The tears flow down both our faces. He caresses my cheek. I don't pull away, I allow myself one last touch from him. His hand falls back to his side.

"You'll hate me when you remember. Either way I lose you, Ads."

"If you tell me the truth right now, I promise I won't hate you," I vow, desperate for answers.

"You can't promise that. Just know that no matter how much you despise me when you find out, I've hated myself for these last six years, and I'll never forgive myself for what happened."

"I'll remember."

"I know," he says before walking out the door.

I sob as I watch him leave. I hate that my mind has betrayed me. I hate that he's hiding something important from me. My legs give out as I bawl for something that I lost, but can't remember. I rub my face as I replay every encounter I've ever had with him. I promise myself I'll do this only once; after that I'll throw away everything of his, anything that reminds me of him. The memories blur. I can't remember a single thing about Jax in the few months before my seventeenth birthday. It's as if during that time, Jax didn't exist, which is a lie. I know it, I can feel it.

What am I forgetting? I couldn't block out the accident, the images of that night have been burned into my soul, forever haunting me, but I've successfully erased an entire chapter out of my life.

What was so traumatizing that I forced myself to forget?

CHAPTER THIRTY

My mind is elsewhere while I hang out with Connor and Logan. The questions are on an endless cycle in my mind. I can't stop thinking which memories are fake, and which are real. Several times I've attempted to ask Logan, but the words wouldn't come. I have a nagging feeling he wouldn't tell me anyways if I asked. I feel like they're all in this together.

"Why so glum? You don't need to worry." Connor sits down next to me on Logan's sofa.

"Huh?"

Without missing a beat, Connor says with a smirk, "I'll send you a picture of this sexy face every day." He even goes as far as to point to said face. "So you can cheer up. You won't go a day without seeing me."

He's attempting to lift my mood, but for the first time, it's not working. I know he's in on it, too. All these years, they have kept something vital from me. I just wish I knew what. I don't even know if I have the right to be upset with them. *They might have a good reason.* No, I push that thought away. I deserve the truth.

When Logan comes up behind us with bags of Thai food, I open my mouth to ask him the question that's been on my mind since I got here, but nothing comes out. I've been here since twelve. It's now eight. I lost count of how many times I've attempted to voice my thoughts.

I force myself to stay calm. I don't need to get into a fight with them right before they take off. They'll be back in two weeks. I've waited six years to find out the truth to something I don't even have the questions to, I can wait fourteen more days.

Standing up quicker than I thought was possible, I snatch the bags from my brother and sit back down. I didn't even get a plate. I ignore Connor's jab and dig into my food. After shoveling half of my Pad-see-ew into my mouth, I glance up to see my brother and Connor watching me.

"When's the last time you ate?" Logan asks, voice full of concern.

"Eh . . . This morning?" I hate that it comes out a question. And hate even more that I feel like I can't trust them. I know they won't tell me, I need to remember on my own. Their eyes narrow.

"Relax. I was busy. I'm eating now." I don't mention that I was busy forcing myself to remember something that I've chosen to forget. I went for a swim, hoping the water would relax my mind enough for me to latch onto my memories. No luck.

Lowering his food, Logan studies me. "Are you sure you're okay? You can always meet us out there."

"Yes! I'll book your flight now." Connor plucks his phone off the table.

"No!" I force myself to relax.

If I react, they'll continue in this pointless charade until I agree to go. Which I can't afford to do at the moment. I won't be able to keep my thoughts to myself. I'll lash out at them, and possibly ruin their meeting because they'll be concentrating on me.

"Ada—" Logan starts, but I cut him off.

"No. I'm fine really."

This isn't their fault. They weren't the ones that chose to forget, I did. Heck, they might not even know. There's a lot they don't know about Jax and me. As much as I want to believe that, I can't. It's a gut feeling that I can't ignore.

"I have bad days more than good days, but I can honestly say I'm going to be okay. I haven't been able to say that since the accident and actually mean it. I'm okay, Logan."

Logan doesn't respond for so long I panic. I can see how much of a struggle this is for him. He's used to telling me what to do and I go with it, always wanting to make his life easier and not really caring what I do.

I care now. I'm taking charge of my life.

"Okay," Logan says with a wary smile.

"Okay," I repeat.

The rest of the evening passes in a blur. My phone beeps with a new text message, I ignore it. I want to spend the evening with them, without interruptions. Which is hard since I have to keep reminding myself to focus on them instead of my missing memory. No matter how much I try, I can't get Jax out of my head. Ironic, the one thing I want to remember involves the one person I want to forget.

Pushing back the thoughts about Jax, I listen to their conversation.

"Yeah. I have everything taken care of. Relax, Logan. Not my first time," Connor tells my brother.

"Sorry man. This is just—"

"I know," Connor says with a grin.

I tune them out again as they talk about business. The two of them can get lost in their own conversation for ages. Forcing my thoughts away from Jax, I think of Kohen instead.

I can understand to a point why he gets mad, but I'm not going to make excuses for him anymore. He might not be fully aware of what he's doing when he's upset, but he needs help. I can't be with him if he keeps lashing out at me. I'm finally living again and I won't live under his shadow.

I don't want to give up on him . . . not yet. Even though he has his issues, he's a good person. He's the only one not keeping secrets from me. He's the only one I can fully trust. I have to offer him the benefit of the doubt, and give him room to change. He and I will work. For a few seconds, I wonder if I'm trying to convince myself or if I actually believe it.

I believe it.

"You seem different," Logan says, bringing me out of my head.

"Uh . . . Thanks?"

"It's a compliment," Connor chimes in.

"Okay . . ." I say slowly.

"You're okay," Logan says.

"Yes," I say, answering him, even though it wasn't a question.

"I'm glad, baby girl."

I want to tell him everything about the affair with Jax, but I don't. I promise myself that I'll tell him truth when he comes back. That's when I'll seek answers to my missing memory.

Logan yawns loudly. Holy hell. I'm tired just looking at him. "When's the last time you slept?" I ask.

He waves me off.

"I'm serious, Logan. You need to sleep more. You need to take better care of yourself." The fear of losing him overwhelms me and I force the tears away. Which is a new thing for me. I never have to fight this hard not to cry. It's inconvenient, to say the least.

"Relax. I've just been putting in more hours to make sure everything is ready for our meeting. Once the deal is finalized, I promise I'll sleep for a week straight."

"Not good enough," I say while I stand up to leave.

"Ad—"

"No." I gesture at Connor. "We're leaving." I point at my brother. "And you're going to bed."

Connor seems like he's about to protest, but I glare at him, making his words die on his lips. Logan gets up and hands my purse and jacket to me.

"Thanks." I tap my foot at Connor, who nurses his beer on the couch.

"Fine." He sets down the Corona. "You win. Let's go."

He gives my brother that one-arm-hug thing guys do. "Meet you at the airport."

"Don't be late," Logan says sternly which makes him laugh. Connor is never late.

"I'll miss you," I tell my brother as we embrace.

"I'm only going to be gone for two weeks."

I nod, words escaping me. I don't want him to leave. I know it's two weeks, but it feels like a lifetime until I'll see him again. *Two weeks and hopefully I'll find out the truth.* After giving Logan one more hug, I leave his penthouse with Connor. The second the elevator door closes, Connor interrogates me.

"Any plans with the hot doc while we're gone?"

"Nope," I say, which isn't a lie.

We don't have plans. Well, anything set. I have plans to ambush him at his apartment tonight, but that's not a set plan. So technically I'm not lying.

Connor nods. Then with a tight smile he asks, "And plans with the best friend?"

"Harper?" I ask, needing to make sure. I sense we're not talking about my best friend, we're talking about his.

"Not your best friend. But when you see that little fire cracker, tell her I said hi."

I stare at the closed elevators door. I can't tell him what's going on with Jax. If I do, he'll tell Logan, and Logan won't leave. He needs to leave. I need to figure this out on my own.

The elevator reaches the parking level and we walk to his car. Opening the passenger door for me, Connor remains silent. I'm hoping that the subject is dropped. Even thinking about it makes me cringe.

Connor waits until we're on the road, heading the short distance to my place. "Jax . . . any plans with him?"

"Nope," I say, not wanting to go into details.

"Have you guys talked lately?"

"Yup."

Connor doesn't give up, he keeps pushing. "About . . ."

Keeping my eyes on the road, I decide to confide in him. He isn't a stranger. This is Connor. If I can't talk to him, then I don't know who I can talk to. Besides, he might have unexpected insight on Jax.

I look at him then turn away. "How much do you know?" I ask, squinting to spot the stars in the night sky. I can't see any because of the city lights.

"A little of this . . . A little of that."

I force my hand to stay in my lap even though I really, really want to smack him across the head. Just once. "Connor," I warn.

I can feel Connor's eyes on me, but I don't face him. I can't. If I do, I'll lose my resolve, and ask him about my blank past. I need to ease into that.

"I know pretty much everything that's been going on lately. Even before Jax said anything, I knew there was something go on."

"What did he say?"

When Connor doesn't answer right away, I scrutinize him. His features are serious, all traces of humor gone. I know instantly that I made the right choice to talk to him about this. I should have done it sooner. *Maybe things could have been different.* I squash that idea. No matter what he says, it won't change anything. Jax is keeping something from me. I can't forgive him.

"Let's get a beer," he says, opening his door. It's then that I notice we're stopped.

When Connor comes around to open my door, I start to tell him that it's fine, we can talk about this when he returns from his trip, but he interrupts me.

"We're both going to need a beer to handle this conversation."

I nod, knowing he's right, but I still make an attempt to stay in the car. "You do realize you have a flight to catch tomorrow?"

Connor pulls me out of the car. "You do realize that I'm going to be sleeping the entire flight, right?"

"Fine," I say as I follow him into a little pub.

We're at one of my favorite pubs in New York. It's about a block away from my place so I've always been able to walk a short distance to grab a beer. The boys love it here, too. I need to bring Harper here. I make a mental note to call her tomorrow so that we can come here and talk about everything that happened last night.

This pub is the perfect place for something like that. It's crowded to the point where you won't be overheard, but quiet enough where you don't have to yell. Other than a few lamps attached to the walls near the tables, the only real lighting in the place is the bar. Three huge lighting fixtures hang from the ceiling above it. The glass wall behind the bar gives the illusion that you're the only one in the place when you're sitting at a table against the wall. Which is exactly why I choose a table near the back while Connor goes to order our beers.

Connor returns with two beers and two glasses of clear liquid in shot glasses, and shoots me a smile when I glare at the shot glasses. He knows I'm not a shot drinker, I'm barely a drinker at all.

"No." I say at the same time Connor says, "Yes."

"No." I say when he places my beer and the offending shot in front of me.

Ignoring me, Connor downs his shot and waits for me to do the same. I don't. Which just makes him smile even wider. "One shot for one secret," he prompts and wiggles his eyebrows at me.

"Shots for secrets?"

He nods and pushes the shot closer to me.

"Do I get to ask the questions?"

He shrugs. "If you want to, but I don't think you'll ask the right question."

I eye him while coming up with a plan. I have to tread lightly. "Fine, first shot you tell me something you *think* I want to know, and the next one I ask the question I want to know."

"How many secrets do you want the answers to?"

"I only need one."

He leaves without a word. A few minutes later, he rejoins me with two more shots. He lifts the first glass and clinks it to mine. I gulp the vodka down, my insides feeling like they're on fire the entire time. I can feel the burn all the way down to my stomach.

I gulp down half my beer. "Start . . . talking," I wheeze when I can finally find my voice again. I hate vodka.

"Where would you like me start?"

"How about with the secret I just earned from that shot." Any amount of patience that I have has disappeared.

"Jax has started seeing—"

"What!" I roar.

"Let me finish," Connor says, not caring in the slightest that my world is falling apart again.

As much as I remind myself it doesn't matter what that liar does, I can't help the sickening sensation that overwhelms me and it has nothing to do with the taste of vodka in my mouth.

"He's seeing Olivia. For about a month now."

I think I might pass out. What happened to the troll? Jax is dating my therapist. I think that's illegal. Patient confidentiality and all that. Where does he get off? Where does Liv get off? She's married and twice his age. I've told her things about us that nobody knows. Oh God.

"As a patient . . ." Connor says, breaking through my horrid thoughts.

Spitting out my beer, I choke out. "What?"

Connor squeezes my hand. "He's been getting help."

My mind spins and it has nothing to do with the small amount of alcohol that I've consumed. Jax is seeing my therapist. He's getting help.

"Why her?"

Surely there has to be a million therapists in New York. Okay maybe not a million, but pretty freaking close. Why her? I can't believe she didn't tell me. Then again she can't. Connor studies his beer bottle. Suddenly his label fascinates him. I know whatever he's going to say, I'm not going to like it.

Still examining his bottle he says so quietly I have to strain to hear, "Don't kill the messenger, but it's because of you."

"Me?" I'm *this* close to banging his head against the wall to get answers.

The words tumble out of Connor's mouth as if he can't hold it in anymore. "She's helped you. We've all seen it, Addie. You weren't here. Then you started working with Olivia and all of a sudden, you started coming back. We all thought we'd lost you."

Connor looks up at me, expecting me to disagree or jump down his throat, I'm assuming. I give him a weak smile, which encourages him to continue.

"I think on some level Jax needed to see her. I don't think he would have been able to get help from anyone else. He saw the change in you. He kept telling Logan and me that you were going to be okay. He believed that you were coming back to us before Logan or I saw it. If he's going to get help, it has to be from Olivia."

"Why didn't he tell me?"

Connor just raises an eyebrow. "Is that your question?"

I shake my head and force away all thoughts of Jax. I don't care if he's seeing Liv. I can't care, not anymore. Not after him refusing to reveal my own memories to me. Connor point to the only remaining shot glass on the table. Hastily, I bring it to my lips. It doesn't taste any better going down a second time.

"What really happened six years ago between Jax and me?" I ask before I set the glass down.

"I don't know what you're talking about."

"Cut the crap. You said a shot for a question. I took the shot, now answer me! I deserve to know what happened, what I can't remember!" My voices raises, my earlier frustration gushing back with a vengeance.

When he meets my eyes, regret fills his brown ones. "I'm sorry, but I can't."

I slam down my hands. "Why?"

"Ask me anything else and I'll tell you."

Everyone in my life is lying to me. I thought I could always count on my guys, but I was wrong. Without a word, I get up.

"Addie, wait," Connor says as he reaches for me.

I step to the side so he doesn't touch me. "Jax refuses to tell me what happened. Now you, too. What is so bad that I don't deserve to know?"

He runs a shaky hand through his long blonde hair. "It isn't my secret to share."

"Whose is it?"

"Yours and Jax's."

I need to hit something. "I don't remember and Jax isn't telling me anything! If it's my secret then tell me, I want to know!"

He sighs. "I can't, I'm sorry."

"Why?"

"Because we were told that we needed to wait until you remembered to talk about it. If we brought it up before you were ready, you would . . ." His voice trails off.

"I would what, Connor?"

He gulps loudly. "You might attempt suicide again if you found out before you're truly ready to remember."

He makes no sense. "What are you talking about?"

"Why did you try to kill yourself five years ago, Addie?"

I hate that I have to answer him. "Because I felt guilty about the car accident and them dying."

"Who?"

Is he stupid? Does he really need me to spell it out for him? He raises his eyebrow. Apparently so.

"My parents and Hadley. I felt guilty that I survived. I didn't think I could live without them, so five years ago I swallowed enough pills to kill me. If it wasn't for Jax finding me, I would have succeeded."

"No."

"What do you mean, no? That's why I tried to kill myself."

"That wasn't the only reason."

I will seriously hurt him if he doesn't stop speaking in riddles. "Then what was?"

He stays silent. I want to bang my head against the table. I'm no closer to assembling the pieces then I was this morning.

"You're not going to tell me?"

"I'm sorry, but I can't. You need to be the one to remember."

I glare at him, hating that another person I thought I could trust is keeping something from me. "Have a safe flight."

He reaches for me but I yank my arm away.

"No, Connor! If you're not going to tell me, fine. I'll find out eventually. From this point forward, we're no longer friends. Friends don't keep things from each other."

"Adalynn!" he shouts as I flee.

I rush back to my apartment building, to the only man in my life that isn't lying to me. When the elevator doors close, I press Kohen's floor instead of mine, figuring I should just get this over with before I lose my nerve. I need to talk to him and tell him things need to change if he wants to be in my life.

I lift my hand twice to knock, but each time I pull away at the last second. I don't know why I'm so nervous. I have nothing to fear from him. On my fourth try, I'm finally able to knock.

CHAPTER THIRTY-ONE

Hesitantly, I knock again. The first time could barely be considered a knock since you couldn't hear it. I should just call him. I grab my phone to do just that, but when I hit the home button, nothing happens. I forgot to charge it . . . again. *I really need to start remembering to charge this sucker.* Sighing, I rest my forehead on his door, I wanted to talk to him tonight before I chicken out. Suddenly the door gives away and I'm falling.

"Ouch," I say when I face-plant into Kohen's hard chest.

Once I'm able to recover and stand on my own, Kohen asks, "Are you okay? Did something happen?"

I bite my lip, my nervousness flooding back again. I have no idea what I want to tell him now that I'm in front of him. Okay, that's a lie, I know what I want to say, I just don't know where to start.

Nodding, I give him a weak smile that doesn't reach my eyes. This may be it for us. He might leave me, too. Panic comes so quickly that my step falters. *I'm going to be alone.* Kohen mistakes my panic for something else. He takes several steps back with his hands in the air. Surrendering.

"I won't hurt you. God, Adalynn, I could never hurt you. You mean too much to me. Please don't be scared of me . . . don't leave me." His voice cracks and his eyes glisten with unshed tears. He thinks I'm leaving him and it terrifies him.

"I'm not . . . I'm not leaving." He still doesn't put his hands down or make a move to come closer. "I'm not afraid of you . . . I'm here to talk." Deciding that I'll have to be the one to make all the moves tonight, I slowly approach him. "Let's go sit down so we can talk."

Silently Kohen leads me over to his couch. He motions for me to sit so I do. Surprising me, he walks over to the wall across from me and leans against it. We stare at each other, neither of us speaking. My mind races. He needs to stop trying to dictate what I wear and lashing out in jealous rampages.

"I'm so—" he starts at the same time I say, "This needs—"

"You go," we both say at the same time.

"I'm so sorry, Ad—"

"No, Kohen. I don't want to hear how 'sorry' you are. This needs to stop."

His face pales. The thought of me leaving him makes him sick. He's so different from Jax. It would be refreshing if it wasn't so painful.

"You can't! You can't leave me. I love you!" Kohen pushes off the wall and runs the few steps over to the couch to haul me into his arms. "I can't lose you. I won't!"

This might be harder than I originally thought. I didn't realize he cared about me so much. Sure, he's said he loves me, but I've always brushed that off. Even though he doesn't know everything about me, he loves me. He wants me.

I pull out of his embrace. "I can't be with you if you don't change. I won't."

"I'll do whatever you want, just promise you won't leave me. We belong together." He says this so seriously that I have no doubt that he truly believes this.

Maybe we do. I don't know. I've never really given him a chance because of Jax. Maybe the right guy has been in front of me this entire time, I just chose to be blind. I'm not ignoring it anymore. I'm moving on.

I glance around his apartment. I feel like I'm really seeing it for the first time even though I've been here before. It's so neat, almost OCD neat. There's a picture of me on the end table that I've never noticed. It must be new. I don't even remember taking it. I'm laughing in the picture, the wind blows my hair so that it's wrapping around my face. He must have taken it when I wasn't paying attention.

Immediately I feel guilty. He's been nothing but here for me and all I've done is push him away. Out of sight, out of mind. All because I was hung up on Jax, on something that was never going to happen. I've been so wrong. I've been chasing after the wrong guy while I have the perfect guy right in front of me . . . well, almost perfect. But I think he can change; I hope that he will change for me. I hope someone will change for me.

"You need help," I say at last.

"I know, I—"

I put up my hand to stop him, cutting him off again. I need to get this out before I lose my nerve.

"You've hurt me." Kohen face falls, full of shame. "You keep saying you didn't know what you were doing, but on some level you had to know. You've left bruises, you've called me names, you're jealous of Connor for no reason, and Jax." Guilt washes over me again because he had every right to be jealous. "You don't trust me and you take it out on me. If you want me to give you another chance, then you need to get help."

"I—"

"No, let me finish. You have to get help. I've seen you take your anger out on co-workers, too. It's not healthy. One day you're going to seriously hurt someone. I know you don't mean to, that you don't want to. I'm willing to give us a shot and see where this goes if you get help. I won't let you hurt me again. Verbally or physically. If you ever talk to me like you did the other night or lay a hand on me again, I will walk out and you'll never see me again." I'm surprised at the sternness in my voice.

Kohen gently grasps my hand. "You are so precious to me, Adalynn. I will do anything you want as long as you're mine. I won't lose you." Slowly, he lifts my hand to his warm lips and lightly kisses the back of it.

"You'll go get help?" I whisper.

His dimples are prominent as he speaks. "I already am."

"What?" I ask, even though I heard him clearly.

"The next morning after . . . the . . ."

"Jealous rampage?" I offer.

"Yeah, that works . . . I went and got help. I'm seeing a therapist once a week and I'm taking a class two times a week with other people like me. I want a chance with you. I knew that you wouldn't give me another chance unless I proved to you that I'm going to change. I'm not that man anymore. I'm going to be better, I'm going be better for you."

I don't know what to say. I can't believe that he's trying to change, to change for me. Somewhere in the back of my mind I know that he hasn't had time to make progress yet, but I drown out that thought.

"Okay," I say at last.

"Okay?"

I interlock our fingers. "Let's take this slow. I want to try with you." *I haven't tried with you because I'm in love with someone else,* I finish in my head. *Loved.*

"I can go as slow as you want," Kohen says with a twinkle in his eyes.

That annoying voice in my head is telling me to take this slow, that I just ended things with Jax this morning. I think that's why I smash my lips against his. He hesitates at first, but once I slip my tongue into his mouth, he kisses me back, fiercely. I lace my fingers through his blonde hair, but I imagine his hair is darker.

Kohen presses wet kisses down my jawline. I tilt my head so that he can reach my neck. I picture Jax's tongue licking down my neck. I moan which drives Kohen mad. He bites down on my neck. I whisper Jax's name . . . Out loud.

It's like someone just dumped an ice bucket on me. My entire body stills. Kohen, too distracted, didn't hear me. He keeps licking and biting my neck, oblivious. *Thank God!* That would not have gone over well. When Kohen finally realizes that I'm not into it anymore, he pauses, his eyes dark, confusion etched on his face.

"Did I do something wrong?"

Wow. I'm the worst human being on the planet. I have this gorgeous man in front of me, wanting to worship my body, and I'm thinking of someone else. I moaned out someone else's name. Kohen deserves better than me.

"No. I'm sorry . . . I can't do this." I get a whole half a step away from him before he's clutching me, forcibly so that I can't move, but gentle enough where he doesn't hurt me.

"No. I'm sorry. We'll go slow. I'm sorry. Don't leave. You can't leave me, Adalynn. I won't let you." He tugs me into him, my back to his chest.

I will my body to relax into his. It's a lot harder than usual. My body refuses to melt into him because he's not the person I yearn for. I force my unwilling body to mold into him anyways.

He kisses me right below my ear. "Stay," he whispers. "Don't leave."

I nod and he squeezes me tighter.

Spinning me around so that I'm facing him, he cups both hands on my face. "Stay the night with me?"

I open my mouth to tell him that I can't, but I stop when I picture Jax and the troll, him lying to me before leaving me. Connor lied. Logan is lying to me. I only have Kohen.

"Please, Adalynn. I need you. Nothing will happen, I know you're not ready for that yet. I just need to hold you in my arms. I thought I was going to lose you."

I don't feel like smiling, but I make myself anyways. Those are the words I want to hear, just from the wrong guy. "Okay," I say because I need to move on. I need Kohen to help me move on from Jax.

Kohen briefly brushes his lips over mine and clasps my hand. Silently, he leads me to his bedroom. I stop when I see the door to the spare room cracked open. I've never been inside this room before as it's always closed. I don't know why, but I'm curious.

"What's in here?" I ask, pushing the door open a little further.

He reaches around me and slams the door. "Nothing. Just junk," Kohen says with a tight smile which only piques my interest.

"Um, okay?" I ask skeptical. "If it was just junk then why can't I go in there?"

"That . . . that room is full of my mother's stuff. I only go in there when I'm feeling alone. I usually lock it. I'm sorry, but I don't want you in there. You can go through anything else you want, but that room is off-limits." He says it sweetly, but it's laced with panic.

Immediately I understand. "Don't worry about it, Kohen. I won't go in there if you don't want me to. I was just curious. I'm sorry if I upset you."

He doesn't say anything as he digs into his pocket and locks the door with a key.

"Wow, that's not insulting," I mumble.

"What was that, babe?" Kohen asks over his shoulder.

"Do you not trust me? I'm not going to go in there once you fall asleep. I understand why you don't want me in there. You can trust me."

"I trust you, Adalynn. Never doubt that. It's just a habit." He shrugs like it's not a big deal, but his eyes are tense.

It doesn't escape me that he still keeps the door locked. I let it go, for now. I have secrets of my own that I keep locked up inside me. The only difference is that my secrets are a part of me and not in a room inside my apartment.

Taking charge, I grip Kohen's hand again and lead him to his bedroom. I've been here a few times so I know exactly where I'm going. When we enter his room, my take-charge attitude floats away.

I'm stuck staring at a blown-up picture of my face. It's the picture from his living room. He's mounted it to the wall in front of his bed. I turn away from it and glance around. For some reason the bed seems larger, more intimating. I'm being crazy. I'm just in a weird mental state, that's all. It's the same bed that he's always had, fitted with the same expensive blood red sheets. His furniture is black, opposite of what I would've pictured when I imagined his room. It seems out of character for him to have dark furniture, it doesn't match his light personality.

I tense more when I realize it might fit him more than I thought. He isn't all light. If he was then we wouldn't be facing a gigantic hurdle right now. He's changing, changing for me. Nobody else has attempted to do that for me, ever.

"Want a shirt to sleep in? I have scrubs you can wear too, but they're going to be huge on you."

"Sure," I squeak out.

Kohen hands me a pair of navy scrub pants. I open my mouth to ask for a shirt, but stop, when he removes his. I can only manage to stare. Kohen works out . . . a lot. No matter how many times I've seen him without his shirt, I can't help my hormones spiking.

"Thanks," I choke out when he passes it to me.

Kohen chuckles while he turns to give me privacy. I would rather change in his bathroom, but this is good enough. Quickly I strip out of my tank and jeans. I toss them on the chair in the corner and slip his shirt over my head. It's still warm and smells like his sexy cologne. My stomach tightens for some unknown reason. Since the shirt covers everything, I toss the pants at his back and jump into his bed.

He leaves the pants on the floor and strides over to me. It's the only thing out of place in his room and it makes me laugh. My laughter dies when he climbs into bed with me. He reaches over and switches off the lamp on his nightstand, surrounding us in darkness.

"Relax," he says when he hauls me closer to him. "Come away with me," he whispers into the darkness.

Suddenly I'm glad that he's holding me and that I'm not laying on his chest. I don't want him to see how broken I am from his words. It really has nothing to do with him, everything he's doing is perfect. I just wish he was somebody else.

"When?" I ask, knowing that I'm going to go anywhere he wants because it's the right thing to do.

"Tomorrow. I have a house in the Hamptons. I've been wanting to take you there for a while now." He drags me closer to him so that my back is fully pressed against his chest.

"Why?" I'm stalling.

"Because I know how much you love the water and I want to enjoy the ocean with you. I think a weekend away is exactly what we need. We can leave first thing in the morning and be back Sunday night so that you won't miss work."

"Okay."

I want to ask him how he knows that I'm not working tomorrow, but I don't. I probably told him sometime last week that I took off today and tomorrow because I needed an extra day to relax. I can feel Kohen's grin against the back of my head.

"I love you," he whispers.

I tense because I can't say the words back. I don't love him and I won't be that girl who says it back just because a guy tells me he loves me. Instead I snuggle as close to him as I can.

"Good night," I murmur.

"Good night, my love," Kohen replies with a little edge to his voice.

"All set?" Kohen asks when I enter his apartment the next afternoon.

"Yup," I say as I drop my bag next to his on the floor.

Kohen woke me up with kisses this morning and breakfast in bed. And when I say this morning, I mean before the sun even came out. He was cheery, excited to leave the city for a few days. I just grumbled and wished for sleep. I didn't get much last night because I kept tossing and turning. My brain wouldn't shut off. When it finally did, I dreamed of Jax . . . well, I had a nightmare is more like it.

But now that I've showered and I'm fully awake, the nervousness has taken hold. I'm restless because this is the first time I'm going away with a guy that isn't Jax. *Going away will be good for us.* I need a distraction and a few days away at the beach with a hot guy is exactly what the doctor ordered.

Kohen collects our bags. He holds out his free hand. For some reason I hesitate; this is it. If I take it, I will be sealing my fate with him. *No more*

Jax. He's out of your life. I take it and squeeze his hand while he leads me out of his apartment. He doesn't let go until we reach his car.

"Thank you," Kohen says once he's done lining up our bags in the back of his Lexus.

"For what?" I try to think of anything special I did for him today. I come up blank

"Thanks for letting me steal you. I know that you're a little on edge because your brother left so I wanted to take your mind off it."

God, if he's any sweeter I might get a cavity. "Trust me. I should be thanking you. I needed to get out of the city for a few days. I'm glad that I'm gonna be with you." I say the last part quietly, but I mean every word of it because I have no one else, no one left to trust in my life.

Kohen gives me that breathtaking smile of his before starting the car. Immediately I plug in my phone and select one of my favorite playlists for long drives. It's catchy music that you can sing to, but quiet enough where you can still have a conversation. It's perfect. Basically, I rock at making playlists.

I hum along to the first few songs and watch New York City fly in a blur. Kohen is quiet, which I appreciate. I have a lot on my mind. I can't stop thinking about my relationship with Jax. All lies. I see his face when he told me loves me for the first time, I feel his lips on mine, I hear his laughter. More lies. I want to push things further with Kohen because of Jax. I want Kohen to make me forget him.

"Wake up, babe," Kohen says softly into my ear.

I mumble back something and turn my head. It's only then, when I feel the kink in my neck, that I realize the car has stopped. I manage to open one eye to see Kohen standing beside me. I open the other and gasp when I spot the beautiful ocean in front of us.

"Wow!" I say, sitting up to take in the view.

"Want to take a walk on the beach?" Kohen helps me out of the car.

"Yes," I say immediately.

Kohen laughs at my enthusiasm. "Don't we need to stop and get groceries?" I ask when we pass the house.

"I took care of it. Fridge is full and our bags are put away upstairs already. Oh and I texted Harper and your brother to let them know where you were."

I tilt my head to see him grinning down at me. I smile back. "You did?"

"Of course. I knew you would want them to know where you were and since you fell asleep I did it for you . . .You don't mind, do you?"

"Of course not," I tell him while I give myself a mental high-five.

I'm so glad that I deleted my text thread with Jax. I know that it would have been torture to re-read every text that he's ever sent me.

"Great. Now let's take that walk."

Once we take off our shoes, hand-in-hand, we head to the edge of the water. I dip my feet in. The ocean is chiller than I expected, but I warm up to it after a while. Kohen doesn't. He keeps jumping when the waves crash and the water pools around our feet, making me laugh each and every time.

"It's freezing!" he shouts as I try to steer him further.

"Don't be such a baby." I smirk when he finally lets me drag him in deeper, but not deep enough to get his shorts wet.

"You do know that we're going to freeze to death, right?"

"And I'll love every second of it. Now come on." I dive into the ocean still wearing my sundress that I chose because it's a warm autumn day. When I surface a couple feet away from Kohen, he's standing where I left him.

"Come on!" I shout. He just shakes his head, an amused expression on his face as he watches me.

I roll my eyes and sink back underneath the water. This is my favorite place. Underneath the water, where all you can hear is the ocean crashing above you. I wish I had gills so that I never had to surface, that I could just stay here forever, in the silence. I turn over on my back and lay on the ocean's floor. I submerge my hands into the soft sand and watch as it slides between my fingers. My body sways back and forth, moving naturally with the waves. Suddenly I'm pulled out of my oasis.

"What the hell?" I yell. I'm a little mad that he yanked me up so hard. Especially since I was at peace.

Kohen's eyes darken at my outburst and I immediately regret snapping at him. He's breathing heavily, as if just that small act angers him. Not good.

"I thought you were drowning," Kohen says softly when he see that I'm okay. He visibly relaxes.

He's changing. He wouldn't have been able to calm down if he isn't changing. With the old Kohen, I would have ended up bruised. Progress.

"I'm sorry. I was just . . . ." The words die on my lips. I don't know what to say. I don't know how to explain to him what I was doing.

"Finding yourself again," Kohen says with a knowing smile.

"Yeah, something like that." I wrap my arms around him. I can feel him shaking underneath me. I don't even feel the cold, I love the water that much. "Let's go warm up."

Kohen gives me a quick kiss on the lips and nods. Our clothes cling to our bodies as we make our way out of the water and walk back to Kohen's house.

His home is beautiful, everything I imagined when I pictured it this morning. Flowerbeds line the driveway up to a two-story house made of different shades of grey stone. There's a wraparound porch, complete with a swing facing the ocean. I can't wait to have my morning smoothie tomorrow and watch the sunrise. The front door is massive, domineering in a blood red that resembles his sheets back home. I spin around and take it all in.

"Do you have any neighbors?" I ask when I notice that I can't see any other houses.

"Of course, they're just a short drive down the road. I bought this place because it's so far away from everyone else. It feels like we're the only two people here, doesn't it?"

My stomach clenches. "Yeah."

I didn't realize it was so isolated out here. I wish I stayed awake in the car so I could have been paying attention. It dawns on me that I can't escape to my apartment if I freak out. I'm here with just him.

"I'm hoping that we'll make this a monthly thing."

This is Kohen, not some serial killer. "That sounds nice."

Once we're inside, Kohen leads me upstairs to the master bedroom. "I'll use the shower downstairs and then I'll make us lunch. Everything you need is in the bathroom." He grabs a change of clothes and leaves the bedroom.

Instantly I'm relieved that he isn't pushing us. He's letting us take things slow and giving me the space I need. I walk into the bathroom and I'm immediately in love. The huge jacuzzi tub can easily fit five people. I sit on the edge and finger one of the bubble bath bottles on the side. My smile widens when I recognize that it's my favorite scent. I look at the rest and find all my favorite stuff. Forgetting the shower idea, I turn the nozzle for the tub and pour a generous amount of lavender bath salts followed by the bubbles.

While the tub fills, I inspect the bathroom. I'm not surprised that all of my things are in here. All of my face wash and soaps are in the shower already, along with a loofah. I open the top drawer and I discover that he even bought me a new razor, and my favorite brand of tampons. What I wouldn't give to see Kohen buy these. He wasn't joking when he said he wants to make this a monthly thing. I open the last drawer and I spot a new hair dryer, straightener, and a curling iron. If he keeps this up, I won't even need to pack next time.

Once my hands are shriveled up like a prune, I force myself to climb out. Not gonna lie, it takes a good amount of effort on my part. I'm pretty sure I could live in this tub. After drying off, I step out of the bathroom to search for my bag and stop in the doorway. Kohen laid out clothes for me on the bed. For some reason I don't find this sweet. Even though they're the clothes I packed, I feel like it's his way of trying to tell me what I can wear. Which is stupid since I was going to select that exact pair of leggings and sweater. I'm being irrational.

I force myself to let it go. Kohen is just being thoughtful like he was when he bought me all the bath stuff. I quickly get dressed. I ignore the irritation bubbling inside me when I realize that he touched my underwear. Once I'm decent, I brush my hair. As I'm leaving the bedroom, my phone chimes with a new text message.

I curse at myself when I pick it up. It's practically dead. I should have let it charge this morning while I was getting ready. Whatever, I'm not going to need my phone anyways. Pressing the unlock button, I read Harper's text.

Tinkerbell: Hey I went by your place today to see how you're doing, but you're not there. Let me know when you come home and I'll bring over ice-cream and wine :)

I start texting her back so I can tell her that I won't be back till Sunday, but of course I can't because my phone dies. I search all over the room for the bag with the charger, but I can't locate it. Opening the closet, I discover my bag on the floor. I unzip it to find that it's empty. Kohen's unpacked everything. Maybe he plugged in my charger for me. I search every outlet. No charger.

As I'm coming down the stairs I remember that Kohen mentioned texting Harper and my brother, informing them we went away for the weekend. So then why did she ask where I was? His messages might not have went through, the service out here might be spotty. A little part of me doesn't believe that, though.

"Hey, do you know where my charger is?" I ask Kohen when I reach the kitchen. He's dressed in low-hung jeans and nothing else. I'm not ashamed that it takes me awhile to raise my gaze from his abs to his face.

"No, sorry, babe. I didn't see it. That's why I unpacked everything for you, I saw that your phone was dying so I was looking for your charger." He shrugs then continues chopping on the cutting board.

"So you didn't see my charger?" I ask again because I know I packed it. It was the last thing I put in my bag before I zipped it. I remember because the cord got in my way.

Kohen turns around with a smile. "Nope, that's usually what I mean when I say I didn't see it." He walks over to the cupboard for plates.

"Okay . . . where's your charger?" I ask.

"I forgot it," he says with a shrug.

"You didn't bring your charger?" I ask, dumbfounded.

Kohen is always the responsible one. Why wouldn't he pack his charger? But I don't understand why he would lie to me, either. Something isn't right.

"I just said I didn't," he snaps.

I decide to drop the charger thing. It's not that big a deal. It's definitely not worth arguing about and setting him off before our weekend even starts. I'm so over fighting. Fighting with Jax, and the war with myself wondering if I should be here or not, is exhausting.

"Did the text go through to Logan and Harper, though?" I ask with forced lightness in my voice.

"It should have. Why?"

"Just wondering. I got a text from her before my phone died, asking where I was." It's my turn to shrug.

Kohen turns around with the same smile on his face, but it seems forced. Weird. "You can use my phone if you want to check that they got it."

I'm tempted to take him up on the offer, but I feel like it's a trap. To see if I trust him enough. I decide to let it go. I can always use his phone tomorrow to call Logan and ask how his flight was. Yeah, I'll do that. It's not like I can call him now since he's on a plane and I can't call Harper since I don't have her number memorized. Something that I'm going to have to do in the future in case this happens again.

I wave off his suggestion. "No, it's fine. I'll check in with Logan tomorrow."

Kohen nods and carries our plates outside. I grab the glasses of wine that he's already filled. I take a sip while I follow him. Walking up to him, I kiss him on his cheek for his thoughtfulness. He managed to pick up my favorite wine and prepare one of my favorite meals. Pesto pasta with roasted tomatoes. Yum.

"It's perfect," I tell him as I sit down.

"You're perfect." He captures my hand and kisses my palm.

I don't even bother to correct him as it will just cause a fight between us. Like it usually does whenever he calls me perfect. I'm so far from perfect, it's laughable.

CHAPTER THIRTY-TWO

I curl up closer into the warm arms around me. They squeeze me tighter. I'm afraid that I'm dreaming so I keep my eyes firmly shut. I'm in Jax's arms again. I don't care about the repercussions of being here with him. If I'm dreaming, I never want to wake up. I want to forget about the secrets and be happy in the arms of the man I love. Eyes still tightly closed, I turn around so that I can snuggle into his chest. Inhaling deeply I feel like I'm home.

"Are you really here?"

"Where else would I be, babe?" a voice that doesn't belong to Jax whispers back.

Immediately my entire body tenses. It wasn't real. I'm not with Jax. It was just a dream. When I open my eyes, Kohen's dark blue ones stare back at me. If I wasn't in Kohen's arms right now, I would smack myself. I can't believe that my dream of Jax was so vivid that I carried it with me when I woke up . . . actually I can. Jax isn't the type of guy easily forgotten, dream or otherwise. I take a couple deep breaths and count to five. I can do this. I can move on. Kohen is changing, he wants to be better for me, for us.

Remembering that I never answered him I say, "I thought you would be up by now."

"I've been up for an hour or so. I just couldn't get out of bed. I finally have you and I'm never going to let you go." He squeezes me closer to prove his point. I know that I should find his statement endearing, but I don't. The way he said "never" isn't settling well with me.

"Do you want to go on the boat today?" Kohen sits up and yanks me with him so that I'm still using his chest as a pillow.

"I would love to," I say with more enthusiasm than I'm feeling.

"Great. Then we should start getting ready. There's a storm coming so we need to be back before it hits." Kohen climbs out of bed.

"No more sleep?" I complain.

Kohen stops in his tracks on the way to the bathroom. "You've slept enough, Adalynn. It's time to get up now. You might be able to take a nap later when we get back since you'll be awake all night this time." He shoots me a warning look before continuing to the bathroom.

Well, I guess someone isn't in the mood to be playful this morning. Rolling my eyes, I wonder if the tampons in the bathroom are for me or for him. With his moods swings this morning, it's a tough call. Hesitantly I walk over to the bathroom.

"Do we have any special plans tonight?" I reach for my toothbrush.

Kohen doesn't answer me at first. He continues to brush his teeth without looking at me. Its obvious that he's mad, I just have no idea why. He was fine a few minutes ago. If he's seriously mad about my joke, he needs to get over it. I enjoy my sleep more than anyone I know and that's not something that's going to change.

"Everything is special if you're involved," Kohen says once he's done brushing his teeth.

I can't help the nervousness sinking into my voice when I ask, "Well, is there anything special for tonight since you just said you want me awake?"

If he's hinting that he wants to take our relationship further, I'm out of here. That is not going slow and it's not what I want. Even though taking our relationship to the next level might help me wash away my feelings for Jax, I can't. I'm not ready and it wouldn't be fair to Kohen since there's a good chance I'll be picturing Jax which is so not how I've imagined our first time.

Kohen marches over to turn on the shower. He takes deep breaths, trying to calm himself, I think. Again, I have no idea what's going on. All I asked was a simple question.

"I would just prefer that you don't pass out on me again." He strips out of his gym shorts, steps into the shower and closes the door.

Feeling guilty that I'm ruining our morning and the only day we're going to be here, I contemplate joining him in the shower. I know it's not my fault for how he's acting this morning. If I'm enough for him, I should be able to snap him out of it and make him happy.

Chewing my lip, I lift my shirt, but stop before it even grazes my belly button. I don't want Kohen to see me naked for the first time pissed at me.

Deciding to let him calm down, I change into a bikini and a pair of shorts, despite the chill in the air. I'll make us breakfast and call my brother while waiting for everything to cook. *Perfect game plan.* I steal Kohen's phone and head down the stairs.

In the kitchen, I press the home screen on Kohen's phone. I frown. It's password-protected. He's never had one before. I know the easiest thing would be to ask for the password, or to at least wait for him to come down here. I do neither. The easiest way is always the most boring. Hmm . . . My finger hovers over the screen. I can't think of anything to guess. I doubt it's his birthday . . . which I don't even know. I try mine instead. I'm not surprised when it vibrates in my hand, informing me that I didn't crack the code.

I set his phone on the counter and start making pancakes. There's a lot that I don't know about Kohen. That isn't soothing since I'm trapped here with him until tomorrow when we go back to the city. I need to make a point of getting to know him before we return. This is our make-it-or-break-it vacation.

I'm not tip-toeing around someone I'm in a relationship with, I've done enough of that with Jax. If I continue to have this sick feeling in the bottom of my stomach, I have to end it. Kohen isn't the type of guy to use as a rebound. He's the plan-your-future-with, marrying type of man. I can't even say who I see in my future. Before I always saw Jax, but now it's just me. Alone.

I jump a good three feet in the air when Kohen startles me. "Why is my phone down here?"

"Breakfast is almost ready." I ignore his question.

His sandy brown hair is still wet from the shower. A few drops drizzle down his wet hair and onto on his white pull-over. I start to feel hot. My reaction to the sight of him takes me by surprise. My mouth waters, imagining what he'll taste like if I lick up the water. I swallow loudly.

Kohen walks towards me and grabs plates from the cupboard. "Why is my phone down here?" he asks again while he hands me the plates.

And just like that, I'm back to being nervous around him, and not because I'm attracted to him. "Thanks," I say timidly. I put pancakes on both of our plates, add syrup, and fruit on the side. "Can you grab us orange juice?"

Kohen is already pouring juice in two glasses. I carry our plates to the patio table outside to enjoy the nice weather before the storm comes in. It's still sunny, but dark clouds roll in and the waves crash violently into each other. I love storms.

"Are you going to answer my question?" Kohen snaps my attention back to him.

I sit beside him in the beige fabric-covered patio chair. "Sorry. I didn't think it was a big deal. I was going to call my brother to see how his flight was."

Kohen doesn't touch his food. I can hear his teeth grinding. He takes a deep breath to calm himself. A move that I'm familiar with.

"Next time can you just ask? I don't like my things out of place."

"Yeah, sorry."

Wow. I had no idea he would make such a big deal out of this. He's acting like I destroyed his house while he was in the shower, not grabbing his phone from the charger and bringing it to the kitchen. Besides he's one to talk. I don't recall asking him to unpack my stuff.

"It's fine. Next time just ask."

I don't see us lasting past this weekend. As much as I want to end things with him, it's better to wait until we return home. I'm trapped here. No phone, no car. Besides, I'm hoping that we can turn this morning around. *He's having a rough morning,* I need to stop reading into something that's not there. Everything will be fine once I get him out of his funk.

"I didn't even call him. You have a password now so I couldn't get into your phone."

Kohen nods but doesn't explain. I'm not surprised that he doesn't want to share why he has a password on his phone. However, I did think he would unlock his phone for me and hand it over so I could call Logan. Whatever, I'll call him before we leave. We both eat our food in silence. It's not a comfortable silence either; tension swims in the air.

Once we're both done eating and have packed lunch for the boat, we're ready to go.

"Can I use your phone please?" I ask to Kohen's back.

"For what?" he asks.

Deep breaths. It shouldn't matter, I want to shout at him, but I find the calm that I'm not feeling and say as nicely as possible, "I want to check on my brother."

My earlier pep talk is flying off towards the horizon. I have to end things with him. I open my mouth to demand that he take me home, but nothing comes out. I need to break up with him in a crowd, not when I have no escape if he loses control over his rage.

Kohen doesn't answer me. So I'm forced to wait . . . and wait. Finally, he turns around to face me. "How about you call him when we get back? We need to get going or we won't be able to enjoy our day because of the storm."

Forcing myself not to groan, I smile at him and pick up our towels. "Sure. Let's go." I don't wait for him to respond. I stomp out of the house and walk over to the dock, and to the waiting sailboat.

Our day has yet to begin and I'm already wishing that I never got out of bed . . . or came. Kohen is acting strange. He isn't being mean or anything, but something's off. I can't explain it. I don't know why, but I'm nervous. Not nervous in a scared way, but in a way that I fear that I'm about to lose him. I can't find it in me to care. I wonder if it's because everything that happened with Jax is fresh in my mind, or if deep down I know I don't belong with Kohen. I've been trying to push myself towards him while I'm still in love with Jax. Even though Jax and I are through, I need time to myself before jumping into anything.

Two long, dreadfully painful hours later, I jump off the white sailboat and march toward the house. I'm fuming. I don't think I've ever been so upset in my life. And I can't even get out of here because he *stole* my charger! I don't care what he says, I know I packed it. It didn't just disappear. For some reason, Kohen thought having me all to himself meant that I couldn't communicate with the outside world. He needs to take a class on how to be a boyfriend, because nobody wants a controlling man in their lives, overstepping at every turn.

"Calm down, Adalynn," Kohen says, racing behind me.

I ignore him and pick up my pace. Our "romantic" boat ride was anything but pleasant. It started off fine. I left everything that happened on the beach and tried to enjoy the rest of the day with him. Wishful thinking on my part.

Kohen freaked out when a group of guys on another boat were watching me. I can feel a headache coming on just thinking about it. He pulled me into the cabin and practically forced me into one of my dresses that he packed in our bags. Apparently I look like a slut in just a bikini top, shorts, and a cardigan. Yeah, cause the girls on the other boats were dressed ready to go to church. They didn't care that it's cold out. Most didn't bother with a top and their bottoms were swallowed up by their asses, leaving everything on full display. But I'm the slut. Yeah.

I just laugh as I stomp up the stairs to the house. Kohen reaches me before I'm inside. My hands shake at my sides. I want to smack him, that's how upset I am. That was so embarrassing! He treated me like an errant child. I force my arms to stay at my sides, even though I'm itching to take the control Kohen has stolen from me.

"I'm sorry. I need to think before I say anything. I'm working on it, Adalynn. I'm not perfect!"

Flashes of the bruises, the hateful words Kohen has spoken to me, and Jax's secrets rush forward. Making the anger I keep bottled up, erupt.

I turn on him, each word laced with the rage crackling inside of me. "I never asked you to be perfect! All I've asked is for your respect, but you can't give me that! I already had a dad, I don't need another one. YOU. WILL. NOT. TELL. ME. WHAT. TO WEAR."

Kohen raises his hand and hits me across the face. The force of the blow makes me stumble closer to the steps of the house. The exact steps I should be running up to flee. Instead, I square my shoulders. I will not run scared.

Tenderly I touch the side of my face. I wince as soon as I feel my cheek. It's burning hot. I force the tears not to fall. I will not cry in front of him, I won't give him the satisfaction. HOLY SHIT! I've never in my life been slapped and I never want to be experience this again, especially from him.

I grit my teeth and match his stare. He smirks at me. Actually fucking smirks. I think I missed that day in high school when they taught boys like him to smack girls around and then smile.

I find my voice. "DON'T YOU EVER FUC—"

Slap! That first smack was a whisper of a caress compared to this one. The asshole didn't even bother to hit my other cheek. No, that would have been too nice. Kohen gets right in front of my face. It takes every ounce of willpower to stand my guard as he strokes my injured cheek.

"You will not talk to me like that again. You will learn your place by my side."

I laugh, which I know is the last thing I should do in the situation. I can't help it. He must be high. Does he honestly think I'm going to stay with him after this? I open my mouth to tell him just that, but then close it. Panic takes over . . . I need to escape. Now. I turn around in an attempt to flee, but Kohen has other plans for me.

"Where do you think you're going?" he says into my ear as he painfully jerks me to him.

"I'm leaving," I whisper but it's loud and clear.

My teeth chatter as I tremble against him. Kohen laughs, enjoying the fear he's causing. He presses his lips to my ear. I try to squirm away, but he's gripping me too tightly that I can't breathe and I'm forced to let him lick my neck. I swallow down my lunch.

"Just let me leave. I won't say anything."

Kohen chuckles again and trails one hand down to my chest. Roughly he grabs ahold of my breast and grinds his thick erection into my ass. I close my eyes, willing myself to find that empty void I used to live in. If I can find that place, I can get past this. I can get past Kohen and his disgusting hands.

"I told you that I'm not letting you go, Em. You're mine."

Who the fuck is Em? I want to ask but I remain silent. He's stolen my ability to speak. I'm that terrified.

Releasing the death grip on my breast, he licks my neck again. "And I plan on taking what's mine tonight." He shoves me away from him and spanks my ass before striding into the house.

I don't even think about it. I run.

Before my feet even reach the sand, I'm yanked back. I cry out in pain, frustration, and angery. Of course it wouldn't have been that easy. Kohen isn't going to let me go. Okay, I need to be smart. I can't go for the obvious moves or he'll stop me.

I'm crying while Kohen drags me back into the house. None of my tears are for the pain I'm feeling. No, they're all for my stupidity. I should have seen this coming. God, how could I be so stupid? He's shown me his true colors before, I just chose to ignore everything. I wanted him to be better, I wanted to move on from Jax. I desperately wanted to be loved by someone.

Because of that, I'm stuck in a house that could be in the middle of nowhere. Kohen said we were going to the Hamptons, but we could be anywhere. I slept the entire way here. That false security I was feeling seconds ago has vanished. If he does have neighbors, I doubt I'll be able to reach them before Kohen finds me. He knows the area, I don't.

It dawns on me that this was his plan the entire time. That's why the fridge and pantry are stocked, and not just for the weekend, but a few weeks. I thought him buying all my favorite things was a sweet gesture; it was anything but sweet.

"You never texted Harper or my brother." I don't ask him. I know the answer. I've known the answer the entire time. I just ignored it. I hoped for the best.

"No, but you knew that. That's why you've been wanting to call Logan, isn't it?"

I spit in his face. He backhands me again. At least this time he hit my other cheek. Generous. I grin as I watch him wipe my spit off of him. The searing pain in my cheek was worth it.

Seizing my forearm, Kohen ushers me along with him. I try in vain to grab anything within reach as he forces me from the kitchen and into the hallway. I can't take anything without him seeing. *Be smart.* I can get through this, I've survived worse. I'll survive whatever Kohen has in store for me.

"Where are we going?" I ask.

"*We're* not going anywhere." Kohen opens a door to the right of the hallway, the door directly across from the living room. It's the same room I didn't bother to look at last night. I skipped the "tour" saying that I was tired and wanted to go to bed.

Throwing me into the dark room, Kohen gives me a sad smile. "I didn't want to do this, but you gave me no choice, Em."

"My name is Adalynn!" I shout.

He doesn't say anything as he turns to leave. Oh my God. He's going to lock me in here. "You don't have to do this Kohen. You can still walk away." You psycho.

Kohen ignores me. "If you'd just let me love you, we wouldn't be here. You forced me to do this, Ads. But you'll see I'm right. You'll thank me. We belong together."

"Don't call me that." For some reason I don't care that he's going to lock me in here anymore. I never want to hear him use Hadley's and Jax's nickname for me. I can handle anything he throws my way, but not that.

"Oh, right. Only your precious Jax can call you that. Don't worry, you'll realize he doesn't love you like I do."

"You're right," I say, surprising him. "Jax loves me. You're incapable of loving anyone . . . especially me."

His dark expression returns. "We'll see." Kohen closes the door and locks it.

There's no light. Putting my hands out in front of me, I stumble around, trying to find a way out even though I know it's pointless. I take three steps before I hit a wall. I trace every inch of the wall I can reach, but nothing. I do the same thing to the other two before slamming my hands against the door. There's no hope. The only escape is through the locked door. Leaning my ear against the door, I strain to listen, but that's pointless too. I can't hear anything. The tears finally come.

I'm locked in a room smaller than my closet, in pitch darkness. My only way out is the door. A door that can only be opened from the outside. Ignoring the pain in my hands, I punch the wood over and over again, begging for help at the top of my lungs. In the back of my mind I know that Kohen's probably soundproofed this room, but I don't give up. I scream for Logan, for Connor, and lastly for Jax. I scream for them to rescue me.

Nobody hears my cries. Nobody is coming to save me.

I'm still screaming as I remember my dad telling me bedtime stories when I was younger. The princess always found her way out. She would realize that she was strong, strong enough to take on anything that came her way. After that, I always hated fairytales that ended with the prince saving the day. I almost forgot that I don't need anyone to save me. I'll save myself, just like the princesses in the stories.

I sit down across from the door. I wipe my tears. I'm not going to cry. I'm going to be the princess my Dad believed I was. I won't let Kohen break me. Eventually he'll open this door and let me out. I know that. I need a plan. Because the first chance I get I'm running and I won't look back. I'll either get away, or I'll die trying.

The light stings my eyes. I squeeze them and cover my face to block the sudden blinding light. They snap open when his hands brush my cheeks. He cradles my face so gently that if I wasn't locked into a dark hole, I would think he feels guilty. I'm not falling for that again.

"I'm so sorry, Em. You just made me mental. I'm so sorry. Forgive me please. You just have to listen and I'll never hurt you again." Kohen kisses my sore cheek.

Reaching up, I cup his face. "I know. I shouldn't have talked to you like that. You were right." I'm positive that I'm about to throw up that I cover my mouth. I pass it off as a sob and lean my head against his forehead.

Play nice. You need to escape. Fake it.

"I can't believe I hit you. You make me so mad. Promise me you won't anger me anymore. It kills me to hurt you, Em."

There's that name again. I don't bother asking who she is. I've seen the movies. She's a girl that I resemble. A girl that he's killed. How many Ems have there been before me?

"I promise . . . Can . . . I . . ." I pretend to stumble over my words.

Caressing my face, Kohen places a chaste kiss on my lips. Somehow, I'm able to stop from grimacing.

"What? All you have to do is ask, Adalynn."

So now I'm Adalynn again. I shake my head.

"I'll give you whatever you need."

"No, I don't deserve it. I shouldn't have said anything," I whisper.

Another kiss. "Please talk to me, baby. I'll do whatever you want."

"I wanted to ask if I can come out . . . to spend the night with you . . ." I force myself to draw a calming breath before I say the biggest lie in the world. "I can't sleep without your ams around me."

Kohen stills. I scoot closer until our lips touch.

"I just want you to love me," I say against his lips.

Do not throw up.

"I love you so much," Kohen says against my lips.

Not being able to say the words back, I kiss him. I drown everything out. I drown out that I'm stuck in a hole with a lunatic, that I'm probably going to die soon like the other Ems, and focus on the only thing that makes me able to hold on. I think of Jax. I picture his face, his lips. My imagination is running wild that I can actually smell him. I pretend that Kohen is Jax and kiss him like I would be kissing Jax right now.

When Kohen pulls away, we're both breathless, but for different reasons. He enjoyed the kiss, I tried not to throw up in his mouth.

"It's late. Let's have dinner before we go to *bed*."

The way he says bed makes my chest tighten. I feel like I can't breathe. He has no plans of sleeping tonight. The tears prickle but I force them back. I wipe my eyes before we leave my prison.

I wrap my arm around his waist and rest my head against his side. "What do you want me to make you for dinner?"

Kohen laughs, a laugh that I used to think I could love one day. I was so terribly wrong. "You're too cute. I'm going to make us dinner. I want to cook for you for the rest of our lives. I'll always take care of you."

I step away from him but clasp his hand and kiss his fingertips. This is easier if I pretend that he's Jax. I can almost stomach it.

"I know."

He snatches my hands and tugs me back to his side. I remind myself to stay calm, but I'm still trembling. He knows I'm lying. He's going to hurt me again. *Distract him.* As soon as that idea blossoms, it dawns on me why he's angry again. My knuckles are bleeding from punching the door.

It isn't until he strokes underneath the bleeding flesh that I feel the pain. "What did you do?"

I cast my eyes down, hoping that he thinks I feel guilty. "I just wanted to be with you."

He tilts up my chin with his now blood-covered finger. "You did this to yourself to be near me?"

Instead of kicking him in the balls, I lean into him. "All I've ever wanted was to be close to you."

His blue eyes shine with happiness. I match my smile to his. Inside I'm screaming, *YOU'RE FUCKING CRAZY!* He leads me the rest of the way to the kitchen and pulls out a chair for me.

"Don't move, I'm going to get my first-aid kit." He says it sweetly, but I know he's threatening me.

Once he leaves, I move to the patio doors. They won't open. I turn the locks, but they it still won't budge. Glancing up, I notice another lock at the top right hand corner. There's no way this will be my escape unless I have a key. I haunt everywhere for some kind of weapon. Bingo! The knife rack. I tiptoe towards it then fling myself back into my seat when his loud footsteps near. I calm my breathing so that he doesn't notice anything is wrong.

He sets the first-aid kit on the table and then takes the seat next to me. "I wish this afternoon never happened. You'll never know how sorry I am," he says as he inspects my knuckles.

"Stop that. If you didn't, we wouldn't be here. You didn't mean to hurt me. And now that I understand how much you love me, it won't happen again. I will never act like that again. I can't stand it when you're angry with me."

Yeah . . . because you like to smack me around.

I force my attention back to Kohen instead of the shiny object that will help me escape. I can't let him realize my plan. If I have any hope of leaving him, he needs to buy into my lies. I keep my smile firmly in place as he rambles about our future. I ignore every word and replay Jax telling me he loved me for the first time nine years ago.

All too soon, Kohen carries the first-aid kit into the bathroom. Before returning to my side, he snags an icepack from the freezer. "Here. This will help the swelling."

"Thanks."

Setting the ice pack on my face, I watch him with love shining through my eyes. I've mastered wearing a mask for so long that it slips easily into place. Every smile and every kiss I blow his way, he believes. He doesn't detect the pure hatred I feel for him. He doesn't see that I'm planning my escape. I imagine sinking a knife into his chest where his heart should be.

Half-way through dinner, I squirm in my seat. I wait for Kohen to notice. It takes a lot longer than I expect. When he acknowledges me I ask, "May I be excused to use the restroom?"

Kohen nods his approval. "You know you don't have to ask."

I rest my hand on top of his. "I know. . . It's just that I didn't want you to think I was leaving . . . I can't believe that you thought I could leave you. You know I don't think that's possible, right?" I don't even have to lie. I know that there's little hope for my escape.

His smile is anything but charming as he says, "Cause you know I'll find you again?"

Leaning over, I nip his ear with my teeth. He moans and I imagine stabbing him in the throat with his fork.

"No, because I could never leave you. You love me," I whisper before walking away.

I force myself to calmly head to the bathroom. I see the front door, but I don't make my move. Not yet. I need to prepare. I don't even bother with the lock as I shut the door. I don't want to give him any reason to hit me, or worse, lock me back into my prison.

As quickly as possible, I open the drawers. I smile triumphantly when I spot the small white first-aid kit. Grabbing what I need, I secure it in the side of my bra so he doesn't notice. I flush the toilet and wash my hands. I make sure that everything is tucked away before I join him back in the dining room.

When I'm almost done with dinner, I yawn then wince.

"Are you okay, babe?"

I nod and wipe away an imaginary tear. Kohen springs out of his seat and squats in front of me before I can blink. He's fast. I need to remember that.

"What's wrong?"

"I'm just sore." I look away and wait for him to pull my face towards his.

Bingo.

"I want to be with you. I just wish that it could be . . ."

I smile in my head when he asks, "What? How do you want it to be?"

"Since it's our first time, I just wanted everything to be perfect. I want it to be perfect for you . . . I'm not perfect right now."

Kohen's eyes gleam with regret. "I'm so sorry ba—"

I cut him off. If I hear him call me baby one more time, I might lose it.

"Don't be, it's my fault. I just wish that we could wait." I place my lips close to his again. "But don't worry. It doesn't have to be perfect. I'm just over-thinking it."

Kohen yanks me out of my chair. He crashes his mouth against mine and kisses me roughly. Keeping up the act, I kiss him back. I even go as far as moaning into his mouth and clinging to him like I'm desperate for him.

Kohen breaks away first only because I force myself to keep kissing him. I have to make this believable. Tonight is the only night I have. I won't let him have me. I won't be his prisoner. I will either escape or I'll die. Either way, I'll be free.

As Kohen turns around to lead the way to the stairs, I make my move. Slowly I slip the scalpel out of the side of my dress. I keep my eyes on Kohen's back. He continues walking, oblivious. I jerk my arm out of his and aim for my target. His neck. He turns at the same time I slam the scalpel into him.

I miss.

Instead of his neck, I sink it into the top of his shoulder. I don't know who screams louder, him, or me when I crash into the foyer table from the force of his blow. Glass scatters everywhere. I push myself to my feet, ignoring the glass embedded into my hands, and run the short distance to the door. My legs are kicked out from underneath me.

I grit my teeth as glass rips through my too-thin dress and slides into my back. Blindly, I reach for a large shard that I can use to stab him. His hands wrap around my neck.

I stare into his black eyes as he strangles me. I need to find . . . something to hurt him . . . with. My vision blurs as the remaining oxygen begins to leave my body.

There!

Clutching the shard in my hand, I stab him in the thigh. The second it sinks into him, he releases my throat. He yanks it out and blood gushes out of him. He tries to control the bleeding with his hands as I crawl away from him.

Kohen screams at me as I crawl to the door. Ignoring him, I fumble with the locks. He's staggering to his feet by the time I open it. He yells again, but it's swallowed up by the screeching alarm I was unaware he set.

Running out of that disastrous house as fast as I can, I stumble down the porch and onto the grass. It takes a second too long to gather my bearings. Once I'm able to breathe in the fresh air, I flee. Rain has moistened the sand, making it that much harder to gain distance.

Every few feet, my legs carry me from the biggest mistake of my life. I look behind me to make sure Kohen isn't following. As the rain falls harder, I push myself faster, forcing my feet to carry me through the thick sand.

Along the edge of the small cliff, I duck behind the bushes and pant. I brush the branches and leaves out of my way so I can peer through them. Slowly I sit up to look over the bush. The heavy rain screens the house from view. Not hearing signs of Kohen, I lunch forward into a run.

Thunder rumbles off every thirty seconds, a welcoming distraction from the constant ringing in my ears. The sky is dark, the angry ocean crashes into the side of the cliff. Rain pours down so hard it's impossible to see more than a few feet in front of me and even then I have to squint to make out objects. The lightning is the worst; it's mocking me by illuminating the entire area. The thunderous bang of the angry sky matches the heavy beating of my heart.

Just keep moving forward. Kohen will kill me if he finds me. These thoughts spin on a wheel, not allowing anything else in to distract me. Each step takes me away from the one man I thought I could trust. Kohen made it easy for me to believe his lies. I never thought he was capable of truly hurting me, I thought he loved me. I wanted to believe that he loved me, that I was capable of being loved.

I was wrong on so many levels, it's almost laughable.

The rustling in the bushes to my right catches my gaze. I keep my focus on the bush as I run. I don't see him. *It's just the storm,* I tell myself, but I feel Kohen watching me, waiting for me to mess up, so he can capture me. I can't let that happen. I force my exhausted legs to push harder, to carry me faster. I squint and spot a thick evergreen in the distance. That's my target. If I can get there, I can hide again for a breather.

Finding energy that wasn't there before, I sprint forward, towards the tree. From the continuous downpour, it's harder to move around in the sand. My left foot gets stuck in the mud and I tumble hard onto the ground.

"Fuck!" I yell as my hip connects with a jagged rock.

Luckily, thunder decides to strike at the same time I yell, drowning out all noise. Placing one hand on my hip, I use the other to help me scramble to my feet. I plant my hand on my hip as I continue to run. Pain shoots through my hip with each step, but I can't stop. If Kohen finds me, it will be worse than any injury I've suffered tonight.

Managing to make it to the tree, I quickly step behind it. Gasping for air, I lean my head against the trunk and rest for a second. I lift the bottom of my mud-splattered shirt to evaluate the damage. *Just a scratch,* I tell myself even though I know I need stitches. Thick mud covers my clothes in clumps, leaves and twigs are tangled into my hair.

My entire body tenses when I hear a noise. I can't tell if it's him or wind from the storm. I wait for what feels like minutes but is mere seconds, unmoving, locked into place. *It's just the wind. Not him. I left him. Keep moving!*

I look around the tree to see if I can glimpse what I heard. Nothing. I press my hand back to my hip before I run from the protection of the tree, into the darkness, and farther away from Kohen.

I pause long enough to glance around to try and figure out which direction I should be running towards. Its impossible to tell where I am with the rain beating down from the angry night's sky. I see lights in the distance that appear to belong to a car. I sprint in that direction. As I get closer, I spot the beam of lights again and I know they're headlights. *Keep moving. I'm a survivor. Get to the road.* If I make it to the road in time to stop that car, I'll be safe.

With my escape less than a mile away, I push myself with newfound energy. I finally reach the last bend of the private property. The waves slam into the cliff's side below me, spraying ocean water onto my path. I trip on a root that has surfaced and fall into a large puddle, cutting my hand on a sharp edge.

Ignoring the pain in my hand, I jump to my feet. I sprint again towards my only escape. Pain registers soon after and I stop. I look down and realize that I must have cut my thigh, too. I push past the agonizing pain. I bite my lip to keep from screaming, and force myself to run through the pain.

I finally reach the last few steps before the clearing on top of the cliff. The road is right there. My escape, my freedom, is only a few steps away. I wipe the rain and filth from my soaked face to clear the blurriness from my eyes.

Lightning strikes, illuminating the night sky. The roaring thunder muffles my scream. My heart sinks into my stomach. There he is. Kohen's glaring right at me. His hair is dripping wet with rain and mud, his clothes are soaked and torn. Out of the corner of my eye, I see the car making the last turn, but I know I will never make it.

I failed.

I should have known that he would be here waiting. Kohen wouldn't let me go that easily. He can't let me go. He's going to catch me and he's going to kill me. I see it in his dark, murderous eyes, before he makes his move. I sprint towards my freedom at the exact moment he barrels towards me.

My life is finally over.

Jax. I summon strength from him even though he's nowhere near me and run with all my might. Kohen follows, but slips on the mud and grazes my elbow with his fingers. Not enough to catch me.

I run out in the middle of the road and wave my hand towards the oncoming car. I close my eyes from the blinding headlights and hope that he stops. I'm not moving. The driver will either stop or he will kill me. Either way I've found my escape from Kohen.

The rain makes it harder for the car to stop and it's still heading towards me as the driver slams on his brakes. The screech of the tires drowns out the storm.

The car is coming right at me, but I stand my ground. I'd rather it hit me than drive off and leave me here with Kohen. I refuse to let that outcome happen. No, the car will either stop or it will hit me.

One or the other.

Fitting, a car will either save me or kill me. Oh, the irony.

The lights come closer . . . closer. The car isn't stopping. I close my eyes and brace for the impact. Screaming finally pierces my ears, my screaming.

CHAPTER THIRTY-THREE

My body bends from something slamming into my side. Hands fasten on me. I open my eyes right before my face smashes into the cement. My arms reach forward, trying to crawl away from Kohen, but it's pointless with him on top of me. He flips me over and licks the blood running down my cheek.

The car crashing, can't dilute the noise of Kohen's malicious laughter in my ear. I manage to kick him in the balls. He leans back as he howls in pain, cupping himself. I jump to my feet and start to run. I fall to the ground . . . hard. Screaming from the internal pain, I grasp for my ankle. Before I can check the damage, Kohen stands me up.

He slaps me. "You're going to be sorry."

I spit in his face. "Fuck you!"

He smiles as he wipes off the spit. I swallow my fear. *I lost. Kohen is going to kill me.* As if reading my mind, Kohen punches me in the face. My head connects with the pavement as I fall. He makes me feel helpless as he climbs on top of me. I told myself I would never feel helpless again. He stole yet another thing from me.

Clasping my head with his large hands, he forces a kiss on my unwilling lips. Then he bashes my head back onto the concrete. I try to make my mouth work, but it doesn't cooperate. I can't even scream. I'm dazed . . . I start blinking rapidly, fighting with everything in me to keep my eyes open. If I lose consciousness there's no telling what he will do to me. He slams my head into the ground again and my eyelids close. Darkness takes over . . .

I don't know how long it is until my eyes flutter open again. I blink the rain out of my eyes. I test my legs. They work. My hands obey when I ask them to move. That's good. I groan in pain and I know my voice is back. My little nap has given me enough strength to fight him. Small blessings.

"Get off me!" I scream as I attempt to wiggle out from underneath him.

It's then that I realize my clothes are off me. Swallowing the bile in my throat, I touch my hip. I nearly cry in relief when I feel my rain soaked panties. He hasn't raped me. Yet.

Kohen laughs at me. His weight holds down my body. One hand presses against my throat making breathing difficult, while his other makes a rough grab for any part of my body that he can touch. His intentions become all too clear when his hand roams below my belly button. I start bucking like crazy, trying to toss him off me. Kohen leans down so he can lick my cheek, the same one he punched moments ago.

Something in me snaps. With his face still close to mine, I turn my head towards his and bite the first thing that my mouth comes into contact with, which happens to be his ear. Perfect. I bite down as hard as I can. Kohen's agonizing screams gives me a sickening pleasure. *I won't go easy. If he wants me, he can come and get me.* Kohen slams my head back down on the concrete, causing me to release his ear. I spit blood in his face when he comes back into view and smile at him.

"You're going to pay for that, Adalynn."

I smirk at him. "Wort—"

All words die when he bangs my head down again. The world goes black.

My head is spinning, it feels like I got hit by a bus and then a soccer team decided to use my head as a ball. Not good. I try to wipe the rain from my eyes but I can't. Kohen . . . Oh God! Lightning lights up the sky and I scream but no noise comes out. Kohen has his hands wrapped around my neck. His hands dig into my throat. I can see it in his eyes, he's going to murder me.

I start thrashing around, but nothing happens. All it does is make Kohen grasp my neck tighter. Kohen smiles down at me, showing the most haunting grin I've ever seen in my life. I can't let him kill me. My knee connects with his tailbone. He winces, but doesn't release his hold on my neck.

I claw at his hands. The evil smirk on his face lets me know that he's enjoying this. He loves that I'm helpless, underneath him and he's in control. He has all the power. It's up to him if I live.

I don't stop fighting him as I picture everyone I love. I close my eyes so their faces are the last thing I see, not Kohen's. I picture Jax's face last. The memory of him is so vivid I can almost hear him shouting my name.

Out of nowhere Kohen is shoved off me. Gasping air, I hold my neck. It's more than tender to the touch. Someone gently presses fingers to the pulse point on my neck. I keep gasping in air. I have no idea how Kohen is off me, but I know the danger isn't over. I need to get away from him fast, before he recovers and finishes me off.

Instinctively my head turns to the right to follow the sounds of pounding and grunting. I spot two men fighting. One limps, not fighting back as the other man pounds into his face. It's too dark to make out who's who, but I pray that the person on the ground is Kohen. As lightning strikes again, my eyes widen and the tears finally start to come.

Jax.

Jax stands over Kohen, beating the shit out of him. After wiping the rain and tears from my eyes, I attempt to stand, but my legs collapse underneath me. I desperately need to be near Jax, like I need oxygen to breathe. I crawl my way toward the biggest mistake of my life and the love of my life.

When I finally manage to crawl to them, I notice that Kohen is out cold. He's unrecognizable. All I see is blood. Everywhere. Blood covers Jax's hands and streams down Kohen's face. I try to call out to Jax, for him to stop, but nothing comes out. Not a sound. My voice won't work.

I don't give up. I can't. As much as I want Jax to kill Kohen, he can't. Jax will end up in jail if he kills him. Kohen isn't worth it. I try again to stand, but my leg isn't working. Whenever I put pressure on my ankle, I fall over. I know it's broken. When Jax drops an unconscious Kohen onto the ground I think the attack is over. It's not. Jax grips Kohen's head in both hands. Seeing his intentions, I will my voice to work this time.

"Jax," I choke out.

It's barely audible to my own ears. I have no hope that Jax hears me, especially with the roaring noise of the storm over us. By some miracle, at the last second, Jax whips his head in my direction. Kohen forgotten, Jax lets go of his lifeless body and rushes to me.

"Ads," Jax says quietly as he crouches beside me.

He lifts a red hand to my face. I cringe from instinct, from memory. My body remembers being hit, again and again. Jax mistakes me shuddering away from the blood and drops his hand. I grab his hand that is pulling away from my face and press it to my swollen cheek. Even with the rain soaking his hair, dripping in his face, washing the blood away, he is still the most breathtaking man I've ever seen.

As my mind realizes that I'm not in immediate danger, the adrenaline pumping through my veins recedes, and in it's place is pain. All the pain I was pushing down, ignoring so that I could escape from Kohen, rushes forward. Tears sting my eyes, but I refuse to let them fall.

Silently I scream. No noise comes out thanks to Kohen crushing my windpipe.

I'm safe. Jax is here. I can rest.

"Don't close your eyes!" Jax yells above the storm.

Blinking, I try to focus on him but I can't. With a will of their own, my eyes flutter shut. Vaguely I'm aware of the ground moving underneath me, making my head spin and intensifying the nausea I've been feeling all night. My gag reflex has had a workout tonight so when another wave of nausea hits, I can't swallow it down as I've been forced to do all night. Nope, instead I turn my head and throw up all over the warmth that is surrounding me.

In the back of my mind, I'm aware that the warmth that I'm throwing up on is Jax, my savior. Time slips away from me after all of the bile is out. One minute Jax is squatting down on the ground with me in his lap while he holds my hair out of my face, and the next I'm sitting in his car with the lights on, his phone flashlight in his hand, as he regards me with pure hatred.

I shrink back. I've never seen him look at me like this, or anyone before, even Wyatt. On closer inspection, I notice that he isn't glaring at me, not really. He's glaring at my neck, I can only imagine what it looks like. Jax holds his hands up, silently letting me know that he won't hurt me. I know that. Jax could never hurt me. Yeah, like Kohen could never hurt me. Gah! I'm so stupid!

"I would never hurt you, Adalynn," Jax says, reading my mind.

Closing my eyes, I nod. I know this. I hate how much he is suffering, how angry he is. I know it's not directed at me, but it's my fault. If I wasn't so consumed with having someone love me, truly love me, I wouldn't be here. I wouldn't be bleeding, in pain, and unable to talk because the man who's been telling me he loves me had his hands around my neck.

"Open your eyes, Adalynn," Jax pleads.

I comply, hating that he didn't use his nickname for me. My eyes water again, but I force them not to spill. *I will not cry. I'm a survivor. I won't cry because of Kohen.* Turning off the flashlight on his phone, Jax stares at me, all signs of hatred gone.

"Keep those beautiful eyes on me. Don't close your eyes, Adalynn."

He waits and I nod even though he didn't ask a question. He maintains his focus on me while calling 911. As he tells the dispatcher where we are and what's going on, his eyes never leave me. They roam my face, pausing over my swollen cheeks and again at my throat. He pales as he hangs up the phone.

For some reason, I try to cover myself. I know it's stupid. There really isn't hiding anything from Jax at this point. I'm wearing rain-soaked bra and panties.

"FUCK!" Jax curses while squeezing his hands into fists. I can't help tensing, as the waves of anger rolling off him, even though I know he will never hurt me.

"FUCK!" Jax curses again while throwing the phone in the back. I jump at the sudden movement and wince.

Angrier than I have ever seen him, he rips off his bloody shirt and uses the only clean portion to apply pressure to my still bleeding hip. I swallow, moistening my dry throat so that I can talk.

Jax doesn't say anything with words, but says everything with his gentle touch. I open my mouth to say something, anything, but nothing comes out. Not because I can't, but because I have no idea what to say. What do I say him? He just came to my rescue. That's who I was running to, the headlights, it was him. On some level, I knew it was him, that's why I never gave up. He was the strength I kept finding when I didn't have any left. I knew he was near, I knew he would find me.

Tentatively, I extend my good hand and caress Jax's face, needing to feel him again, needing the reassurance that Kohen didn't kill me and that I'm here with Jax.

"You found me," I whisper.

"I'll always find you," Jax promises right before his lips crash into mine.

I welcome the sweet taste of Jax's lips. The pain I was feeling seconds ago vanishes and all that remains is his lips on mine. The kiss isn't anything like our "goodbye" kiss, it's something more, much more. This is the kind of kiss that makes promises that I'm afraid to acknowledge.

"Ads," Jax whispers against my lips before diving back into my mouth.

Arching up so that I'm closer to his mouth, I'm suddenly blindly aware of my ribs. I suck in a painful breath. After placing one last chaste kiss on my lips, Jax pulls away.

"What hurts?"

Everything. "My ribs."

He opens his mouth, but pauses when we see red and blue flashing lights. Jax curses under his breath so I know whatever he's looking at is bad. I don't glance down. I can feel it just fine so there is no reason to look. The wailing of the police cars and ambulance coming closer are the last things I hear before everything goes black.

Immediately I panic when I open my eyes to bright blinding lights.

"Jax!"

"I'm right here," he says into my ear.

I nod, regretting the decision to wake up as soon as I realize I'm in an ambulance. Which is stupid, I know that's how it works. You get hurt, nearly choked to death, you get to ride in an ambulance. It just never occurred to me when Jax was dialing 911 that *I* was going to have to be in an ambulance. My past rushes forward.

"I can't . . . I can't be here," I attempt to sit up and try to pull the oxygen mask off of my face, but my hands are restrained. "Let me go! I can't be here! Please!"

I start sobbing, hating that I'm in the back of an ambulance against my will. Aren't there patient rights about these kind of things?

Jax leans as close as possible to my face without disrupting my mask. "Look at me."

"I need to—"

"I know. Just look at me. Focus only on me, Ads." Jax strokes my hair. "Let everything else fade away, the ambulance, the past, and only focus on me." He kisses my nose. "Can you do that?"

"Yes." I choke out.

"Good. It's just you and me from now on."

It isn't lost on me what he said. He's talking as if we have a future. That thought makes me want to laugh. I know his game. He's distracting me with pretty words. I'll take it. Anything to get my mind off the last time I was in an ambulance. I feel a pinch in my arm, a tell tale sign of an IV being inserted.

"Why am I strapped down?" I squeak out when the paramedic comes into view.

"We were told you might be . . . overwhelmed in here so we had to strap you down since he refused for us to sedate you. So as long as you stay calm, I won't have to put you to sleep."

As she continues to talk, she begins inspecting my injuries. I gaze at Jax with a questioning expression. Jax sighs heavily.

"I know you hate to be drugged more than strapped down so I went with the lesser evil."

I nod and struggle not to scream when the paramedic that I'm going to nickname the Angel of Pain inspects my ankle.

"It's broken. I know it. Let's not touch it," I gasp through gritted teeth.

Jax glances at my leg, then back at the Angel of Pain, and leans back over me so that he's all I see. He smiles down at me and I smile back. Subtly he nods, and before I can scream, his lips are on mine.

Jax doesn't play fair.

The kiss before was urgent as if he needed to kiss me as much as I needed him. He kissed me like he needed oxygen, like he couldn't help it. Now he's kissing me as if it's the most natural thing in the world.

He continues to press feather light kisses to my lip. I know I only have a few more kisses left before he stops and we're back to "just friends who don't kiss" so I'm going to take full advantage of Jax. I slip my tongue in his mouth and I'm only vaguely aware of the Angel of Pain tending to my ankle. All I can focus on is the taste of Jax.

All too soon, he slows the kiss down and pulls away. I think I let out a small whimper. Hopefully the Angel of Pain passes it off as a whimper of pain instead of what it was. Jax gazes at me. God, he's beautiful.

"So are you," he says with a grin.

Wonderful. I said that out loud. I open my mouth to speak again, but someone beats me to it.

"Mr. Chandler, I'm going to need you to come with me," someone says after opening the back doors of the ambulance.

I lean up while Jax turns around to face a police officer. Jax nods before turning to me again.

"No! You can't go. He didn't do anything! He was protecting me! You should be arresting Kohen!" My voice cracks, it's barely audible but the officer hears me.

Jax's body tenses at the use of Kohen's name. I ignore him and focus on the officer.

"I'm not here to arrest him."

"Oh." I sigh in relief.

"I'm here to tell Mr. Chandler that there's still no sign of him."

"Him?" I ask even though I know who he means. I just need confirmation.

"Kohen Daniels."

He's missing. Somehow, he was able to escape without being seen. And I know that he will find me again. I won't be safe as long as he's out there. He won't let me go. Jax squeezes my hand, letting me know he's here for me. Kohen might not be able to let me go, but neither can Jax. For just a second, I forget about the secrets he's keeping from me and bask in his warmth. With Jax, I'm safe.

The End.

Stay tuned for the second
installment of the beautifully series.
Beautifully Mended.

ABOUT THE AUTHOR

Courtney Kristel graduated from The Fashion Institute of Design and Merchandising, but she couldn't shake her true passion for writing. She's currently working on the second novel of the Beautifully Series, Beautifully Mended. When she isn't creating stories to share with the world, Courtney usually has a book in her hands or is searching for new music to add to her writing playlist.

49048711R10248

Made in the USA
Charleston, SC
18 November 2015